The Wind in the Embers

A Story of the Fall of Rome

Book 1 of the Amulet Series

Malcolm David Logan

Book Cover by Rebekah Haskell and Nicholas Paredes

Maps by Nicholas Paredes

Second Edition 2024
ISBN-10:
ISBN-13:

To Marianne

Chapter One

437 AD

I tell you I am not who you think I am. It may occur to you, as I lay everything out to you, that someone put me up to it. We both know there are those who could benefit from warping your perception of me. Aetius[1] perhaps. Sebastianus certainly. Nevertheless, as disagreeable as my words may be to hear, I promise you it is only I, telling you the truth.

For the sake of your reign.

For the sake of the Empire.

I do not want to open a rift between us but to bring us closer. The time has come to reveal myself. I am not the woman you have supposed. I am not so simple. I am not so guileless, although it has served me well to have people think it so.

The soldier came to me in the night. He stood below my window and called up to me. It was a brazen thing for any solider to do, even a Goth. But those were brazen times. The city had fallen; the barbarians were rampaging through the streets. He stood below my window and called up to me by name.

I leaned out of the window and told him to go away, to leave while he still had the chance. He was worried for my safety and wanted to spirit me away to a place where I could not be harmed. He was sincere; I could see it in his eyes. It was then, I suppose, it first occurred to me he could be of use to me. But I didn't go with him, at least not then. I was certain Priscus Attalus[2] would send a guard to escort me to the Lateran Basilica, where it was said high Roman dignitaries and members of the aristocracy were being granted sanctuary.

I could see the disappointment on his face. He was such a sweet young man and so obviously taken with me. I was still young enough to be flattered by the attention of men, just twenty-one. I could feel the power I had over him and it was exhilarating. We are such fools when we are young.

We had met only once briefly. His name was Emilius. He was a survivor from Radagaisus's[3] army, drafted into the Roman service after the capture and execution of that headstrong brigand. He had served under Alaric[4] in Greece and was one of a party of men brought in to advise the Senate on how to respond to Gothic demands that the gates be opened, and the city surrendered.

I attended that meeting, sitting at Priscus Attalus's right hand as an affirmation of his imperial authority. The Senators were all in a dither. They bickered among themselves and tried without success to focus on what the soldiers were telling them. One by one, the soldiers came up to give their view of things, which were all of a piece, namely that Alaric, whose motives were primarily political, could be counted on to be merciful if the city were handed over as he demanded. Emilus, who was waiting for his chance to speak, kept stealing glances at me, licking his lips, and shifting his feet. He had the most stunning blue eyes. They were offset by pale white skin and hair as black as ebony. When at last it was his turn to speak, he spoke directly to Priscus Attalus, repeating what the others had said and adding that Alaric might even find it in his heart to forgive the Emperor his disobedience.

Well, I can tell you, the air went out of the room when he said that, and I could see Priscus Attalus was ready to erupt. I stepped in to prevent an ugly scene and addressed myself to Emilus, asking him what he meant by suggesting the

---

1. Pronounced: ee-tee-us

2. Pronounced: pris-cus uh-tal-us

Emperor lacked the sovereignty to act as he saw fit.

To his credit Emilus didn't miss a beat. He declared what everyone in the room already knew, even if they lacked the temerity to say it. Priscus Attalus had been proclaimed emperor and sent to Rome by King Alaric after the previous year's siege for the express purpose of doing the King's will. His failure to do as expected was the reason Alaric had come back at the head of an army, determined to cashier his unruly puppet and take authority for himself. It was not news. Everyone knew it. But only Emilius had the audacity to say it. And for that I admired him.

He went on. The only question, he said, was how to manage the inevitable. The Goths were going to enter the city, of that there could be no doubt, but it didn't have to be a calamity. Alaric was a Christian. He was inclined to be merciful. All the Emperor had to do was avoid antagonizing him any further by resisting his demands.

I gave Emilus a reassuring smile and turned to Priscus Attalus. I urged him to send a messenger to King Alaric expressing his willingness to cooperate. Priscus slumped back in his chair and grumbled something under his breath. I turned back to Emilus and thanked him for his advice. He touched his fist to his breast and bowed in deference, but as he backed away he looked up me with a strange little smirk as if we were conspirators in some devious plot.

I gave him no satisfaction. Yet neither did I rebuke him. I saw no disadvantage in continuing to remain inscrutable.

On the other hand, Priscus Attalus was in no position to be vague. He should

---

3. Pronounced: rad-uh-gay-sus's

4. Pronounced: al-uh-rik

have communicated his willingness to cooperate quickly and clearly to the Gothic king. Instead, he dawdled. As a result, the next day, the Goths broke down the Salarian Gates and entered the city to the shrieks of the affrighted citizenry. It was almost impossible to believe. This could not be happening. This was Rome. It had stood inviolate for eight centuries—and now this!

So Emilus came to my window and urged me to come away with him. I told him I was waiting for an escort to the Lateran Basilica, which was when he told me Priscus Attalus had been arrested and hauled away in chains. I realized then no imperial escort would be coming to get me, and my best chance to get away lay with him. Still, I hesitated.

Even at that hour, with the city in flames, I held out hope my beloved would appear and save me. I had waited through two long years and three sieges. To wait a little longer didn't seem unreasonable. But I was fooling myself. I was drifting along in my girlish infatuation, thinking only of what my heart longed for. For this vain fancy I had risked the fury of the Goths. For this delusion I had spurned my brother's demands to return to Ravenna, to safety.

Which is what I was trying to explain to you when we quarreled so bitterly the other night. I was the same way when I was young. I was convinced we were fated to be together, and no one could change my mind. As a result, I put myself in danger.

Even worse, I put the Empire at risk.

Honorius was right. I should have been in Ravenna, not Rome, for had I died at the hands of the Goths, the succession would have been in imperiled. But I wasn't thinking straight. My judgment was clouded. I was blind to the political realities, and it nearly cost me.

I wish you would take advantage of my experience and listen. We must always think of our duty first. We do not have the luxury of loving whoever we want.

We are Augustus and Augusta, you and I.

Oh, Placidius, I wish you would listen to me. I am your mother.

Flavius Placidius Valentinianus, soon to be Emperor Valentinian III, sole Augustus of the Western Roman Empire, lowered his mother's letter into his lap, reclined on his pillow, and gazed out at the countryside. He was passing through the northern part of the province of Dalmatia accompanied by a retinue of more than three hundred soldiers, servants, and attendants. It was a rugged country of eroded limestone ridges, formed here and there into craggy towers and pocked with numerous caves and hollows, the perfect place for Hun brigands to hide. He was glad his soldiers were well armed and practiced in the art of war.

He weighed the letter in his hands. It had some heft. It was a stack of parchment leaves bound along one edge and formed into a codex of more than two hundred pages. It must have cost a great deal to produce, but it was not the finances that gave him pause. Rather, it seemed strange the letter had come into his hands at all, for it was presumed to have been lost, or stolen perhaps, but in any case, it had vanished from his mother's possession some months back only to turn up now.

His mother had been composing it for months with the explicit intent of presenting it to him when he assumed his rightful role as sole Augustus of the West. She had not kept it a secret; she had told him about it as she was writing it, but she refused to let him see it, trying to arouse his interest with an air of suspense. It didn't work.

Flavius Placidius Valentinianus, known familiarly as Placidius[5], had his own ideas about how to rule the Empire and didn't want his mother's advice. When the letter was lost, he figured that was the end of it, but his mother was nothing if not tenacious and couldn't be put off so easily. She resorted to trying to communicate its contents to him verbally. He pretended interest as long as he could and then his face betrayed him. She asked him sharply if she was boring him, and when he tried to hedge, she grew indignant and insisted on the importance of what she was telling him. They bickered back and forth, and then she broached the subject of his relationship with Candida. He had had enough. He stormed out, and the matter was not revisited again until a week before his departure.

The second time had gone no better than the first. Again they quarreled. This time he threatened not to go at all if she would not stop pestering him about Candida, and as for marrying his cousin Licinia[6], he had not yet made up his mind. This really pushed her over the edge, and she lashed out at him in a way she had never done before.

Justa[7] happened to be in the room at the time, sitting beneath the window sewing when their mother lost her temper. She smiled at him in that smug, condescending way of hers, then turned to Mother and asked if she should fetch Aetius "to put a lid on things."

Mother ordered her out.

Nothing more was said after that, and Placidius figured he was through the worst of it, when the letter suddenly turned up. It was a strange co-

---

5. Pronounced pluh-sid-ee-us

6. Pronounced: li-sin-ee-uh

7. Pronounced: juh-stuh

incidence. No one had said a word about it before setting out, but now here they were, well on their way to Constantinople, and his mother was badgering him again, this time in the form of a ponderous letter.

He looked out at the countryside, at the muscular backs of his Nubian bearers, and then down at the letter again. At least this time her carping was couched in a story he found entertaining. His mother had never told him about the young soldier named Emilius. For that matter she had never spoken of her experience in Rome during the Gothic Sack. This was a side of her he had never seen before, and he had to admit he found it interesting. It was like she was a completely different person.

He returned to the letter.

Chapter Two

Emilus would not take no for an answer. He persisted until I gave in and agreed to go with him, but on one condition. He had to go to the Goths and ask after the whereabouts of the man I loved, my absent savior. He readily assented, so I went down and met him in the street.

He led me to a block of dilapidated insulae[1] and to a cellar room where he thought I would be safe. He distrusted the sanctuary of the churches when it came to safeguarding someone of my prominence. Deceit and treachery were everywhere, he said. I should trust no one.

After making me comfortable, he went out into the streets to make some inquiries. Being a Goth himself, it was easy to pass himself off as one of the plundering army. When he returned, he had bad news.

The man I was looking for was not in the city. He had gotten it confirmed by several sources. It was common knowledge, for my beloved had been a favorite of Alaric, the Gothic king. It had been with great regret that Alaric had parted with him, but he had done so at the Emperor's request, as a condition of their agreement after the lifting of the previous year's siege. After having been a hostage with the Goths for nearly ten years, at my brother's orders, my beloved had been sent on to act as a hostage with the Huns.

Oh, this hostage business. I tell you it is a tricky and delicate thing. It is, of course, the function of a hostage to keep one's enemies at bay, and at all times the hostage is the representative of a hostile power. But the intimacy that develops between a hostage and his captors can approach filial love over time, and if the hostage is a woman, well.

I was devastated at the news that he was not among them. At first, I refused to believe it. I told Emilus to go back and check again, but he assured me his information was sound. I wept. He would not be rescuing me. It was too much to bear, especially after that horrible thing I had been compelled to do to Serena. It had all been for nothing.

Emilius urged me to take heart. I had to put away my grief and consider my predicament. If we remained where we were, we were at risk of being discovered. We could try to flee the city, but the implications of getting caught were too dire. The streets were crawling with crazed, vicious brutes. He thought I should consider surrendering to Alaric and throw myself on his mercy, for Alaric was a shrewd leader and would see the value of having me as a hostage. As long as he could use me to extract valuable concessions from my brother, he would not let me be harmed.

"But what if my brother refuses him?" I said.

Emilus thought there was little possibility of that. Surely, my brother would be willing to offer something to secure my release. Besides, the Gothic king was not asking for much. He only wanted what the Goths had always wanted for thirty years, what they had briefly won and then lost — a piece of land on which to settle, a grant of territory within our borders on which to put down roots, and in exchange they would act as federates and contribute to the defense of the Empire. Emilus thought my brother would grant these concessions when he learned I was being held, and I would be returned to Ravenna unharmed. But he did not know my brother; he did not know Honorius.

I refused to do it. Knowing that my beloved would not be coming to rescue me, I was disheartened and in no mood to entertain political gamesmanship. I only

---

1. Roman apartment buildings

wanted to go home. When Emilius tried to reason with me, I dug in. Priscus Attalus had been taken away in chains. They were probably torturing him as we spoke. I would not allow my person to be so violated. I demanded that he help me escape. Reluctantly, he agreed.

The plan he came up with was simple. We would bribe the guards. The problem was we had nothing to bribe them with. I had left the Domus Augustana in a great hurry with nothing but the clothes on my back. A return to the palace now was out of the question. So, Emilus proposed to go out into the streets and see what he could find. In other words, he proposed to join in the general looting.

My initial reaction was revulsion. I was the princess of Rome and could not be a party to the pillaging. But Emilus patiently explained that things had changed; the old order had fallen; a new wilder, ungovernable power had been unleashed. We could not pretend otherwise. We had to face facts. If I hoped to retain my position, I needed to survive. And to survive, I was going to have to do things that another princess at another time would have found objectionable.

Those words resonated with me. They were similar to advice given to me by Stilicho[2] years earlier, advice that had formed a part of my motivation in dealing with Serena as I did. You see, even then I was not a stranger to expediency. So, I gave in, and Emilius went out plundering on my behalf.

When he returned, he had a large cache of goods. We sat at a rough oaken table in a dim cellar room and sorted through the loot. He had some elegant glass vessels, some Oriental fabrics, and a few gold coins. But the most interesting thing he had was a curious amulet cast in lead, circular in shape and showing a scene of Christ entering Jerusalem. It bore a three-line inscription that read, "God be with you." It was clearly an artifact from an earlier era. I lifted it by the horsehair strands in the candlelight and inspected it. It did not glitter or shine, but there was something special about it, something deep and powerful that stirred me. I asked him where he had gotten it.

At first, he was reluctant to tell me, but, presently, at my insistence, he revealed he had taken it off the neck of a suicide, an old man they had found hanging from the balcony of an insula. They had cut him down; he was lying in a heap in the gutter. They had gathered around him to see if he was carrying anything of value when they became distracted by a sudden commotion behind them.

A woman had rushed into the street, screaming. She was trying to escape the clutches of her attacker, and she was all but naked. Her clothes were ripped and hung in tatters. Her arms and shoulders were covered in scratches. She stumbled and fell, her pendulous breasts swinging, her buttocks lifted grotesquely like an animal in rut. Her attacker appeared in the doorway behind her. Seeing her sprawled on the ground, he loosened his trousers. Laughing drunkenly, he stumbled forward, but his feet became entangled in his trousers, and he fell. Frantic with terror, the woman ran. The other looters, foreseeing great sport, ran after her. They all disappeared down an alley, leaving Emilus alone with the body.

The dead man was a strange-looking creature. He had deep facial scars and a deformed mouth. Given the nature of his scars, he might have been a Hun, but his eyes lacked the Oriental slant of those people, and he was larger in stature than the typical Hun. In any case, his strange appearance made Emilius uneasy. He was about to abandon the body altogether when he noticed something of value: the amulet. He lifted it from the neck of the dead man and slipped it into his purse.

I tilted it in the light and read the inscription again. I told him I wanted it.

He put his hand on my wrist and looked at me with the solicitude of a lover. "Are you sure?" There was a strange glint in his eye, a peculiar eagerness I

---

2. Pronounced: still-ick-oh

found unnerving.

"Yes," I said, and he smiled.

I dropped it into my purse.

Suddenly there was a pounding at the door.

We swung around in alarm. Emilius drew his sword and listened. Then he motioned for me to follow him and together we slipped out the back and made our way down a narrow passageway into the darkness of the night.

We traveled along a series of streets to the Clivus Pullius. We were headed for the Esquiline Gate. Halfway there, we came across a group of ruffians looting a wine shop. They were drinking straight from the amphorae[3] *and stumbling around in a drunken state. They blocked our path.*

There were eight of them. Their leader was a large ugly thug with a swollen eye and broken teeth. He looked me over lasciviously and demanded Emilius hand me over to him.

Emilius remained calm. He explained that I was the princess Galla Placidia. He told him that he was bringing me to King Alaric on the King's orders. The man didn't believe him. He said if I were the princess of Rome, the sister of Emperor Honorius, I would be in Ravenna. Emilius told him he was mistaken,

---

3. Tall terracotta jars with two handles and a narrow neck

that I had been residing in Rome for some time, consulting with the usurper Priscus Attalus, trying to persuade him to surrender the crown, only a portion of which was true. The man didn't believe him. If that were so, he said, the princess would be at the Lateran Basilica seeking sanctuary, not out on the streets with some lowly mercenary. At this, the others closed in. One of them reached out and put his hand on my shoulder. I shrank back.

Emilius didn't react. He spoke firmly. He told them I had fled the palace after it had been set on fire and had gotten lost trying to find the basilica and by this course of events had come into his custody. He had sent a message to the King, knowing full well the value of his prize, and had been instructed to bring me to him with all speed.

"You don't want to interfere with the King's order," he told the man.

This gave the man pause, but another of their number spoke up and pointed out the absence of my retinue. "Where are her servants?" he asked. "Where are her slaves?"

The truth was I had left them behind to avoid being identified as a person of prominence, to avoid just such a situation as this. Oh, the irony. I shot a worried glance at Emilius, but he only smiled back at me.

Again, the big thug demanded I be handed over. Another made a filthy comment about the ripeness of my maidenhead. At this, the others grew restive and pressed in. One of them grabbed my palla[4] and tore it away. Others laid hold of my arms. Ugly, brutish hands grabbed my breasts. One of them stumbled forward, clutching the fabric of my stola[5], and fell to the ground, tearing it down its length, exposing my leg to the hip. The sight of it roused them to unbridled lust and I would have been raped had not Emilius pulled his dagger and stabbed one of them through the heart.

The sudden appearance of bloodshed in their midst stunned them. Before they could make sense of what had happened, a new voice was heard. It was a member of the Gothic guards. Three of them had appeared out of nowhere dressed in scale armor and carrying spears. They ordered the ruffians to back off and demanded to know what was going on.

Emilius told them I was Galla Placidia and repeated his fiction about taking me to the Gothic King on his orders. The earnest conviction with which he repeated this lie persuaded the guards. For some reason, they needed no further convincing, and that's how I came to be standing before King Alaric flanked by Emilius and the ruffians.

I know there are those who claim Alaric was a crude and uncivilized beast with no hint of grace or refinement, but they didn't know him. He was a stern man, that much is true, cold and distant when he was not roused to anger, and ruthlessly violent when he was. But he was not without penetration. He was not without intelligence. Any consideration of the way he bargained with my brother, your uncle, over all those years should tell you as much.

When we were first brought before him he was sitting at the head of a long table in a dimly lit pavilion in the Gardens of Sallust, reached by a path through the smoking ruins. He sat bent over, kneading his brow, his bearded face half bathed in shadows. When he looked up, his eyes fastened on Emilus.

"Do we know you?" he asked.

Emilus started to speak but Alaric waved him off and shifted his eyes to me.

---

4. An elegant mantle worn by Roman women over the shoulders and fastened by a brooch

5. A long sleeveless robe worn by Roman women under their pallas

"You," he said. "We know you. You are Galla Placidia, the ripest fruit in the imperial orchard." He let his eyes drift down the length of my body to where my stola had been torn and the contour of my leg was revealed. His eyes lingered for a moment, taking it in. Then he found my eyes. "Don't bother answering," he said. "We have it on the best authority." He gestured to the shadows, and a man stepped forward whose carriage and deportment were known to me. "Priscus Attalus tells us you've been supportive of our suit with your brother. He tells us you were helpful in persuading the Senate to pay the ransom two years ago when we came calling."

"I don't like people to starve," I said.

"Nor do I," he said. "But some people are not so solicitous of the feelings of others. Some people think only of themselves." He turned his gaze to Priscus Attalus who lowered his head in shame.

"I deplore selfishness," the king said. "A man should realize who he is—should know where he stands in the order of things and not challenge those above him. It's not Christian." He shifted his eyes to the ruffians. "You," he said, pointing to the big ugly thug. "Who's your master?"

The man bowed his head and went down on one knee. "You are my King."

"I've been generous with you, have I not?" Alaric asked. "I allowed you to sack and pillage all you liked."

"You did, my King."

"And yet when you were told to let this lady pass, that it was my will you do so, you refused."

"I thought he was lying," he said. He swung his gaze to Emilius. "She had no retinue. She was alone with him. It was highly irregular."

"But this man outranks you. His attire should have told you that."

The man's face fell. "I thought he swiped his clothes off a dead soldier. I thought he was an imposter, working for the Romans."

"Oh, you did, did you? You decided that for yourself." The King got to his feet and came around the table. "You must think yourself pretty sharp. Am I right? Tell me, I'm right."

The thug muttered an apology under his breath. His hands were shaking.

"Men like you cannot be trusted," Alaric said. "Men like you will bury a dagger in their sovereign's back as soon as they get the chance."

The man's eyes filled with tears.

"Do you know what your problem is?" the king said. "You are of little value to me, and you think too much of yourself, without reason." He drew his sword.

The man began to weep. He prostrated himself at the king's feet and begged for mercy.

The king gave a snort of contempt and sheathed his sword. "Take him away," he said. "Strip him of his weapons and enslave him. Then he will learn where he stands in the scheme of things."

He dismissed the other ruffians without a word, and then he turned his attention to Emilius. "I'm sorry. Tell me again where were you going with the princess? If you were bringing her here, you were headed in the wrong direction."

"I was trying to evade the marauders. I was trying to protect her."

"It seems you failed in that."

Emilus admitted it was so.

"I wonder," the King said—he pinched his lower lip— "if I really know you. I wonder if I have taken the proper measure of you. Yes, you are a Goth, but that by no means makes you trustworthy. Let us review. First, you were fighting on behalf of Radagaisus. Then you were drafted into the Roman army and sent against us at the second siege. Correct?"

Emilus nodded.

"Once the siege was lifted and Priscus Attalus was elevated to Emperor, you were, in effect, on our side. But then, alas, Priscus proved unreliable" — a weighty look in Priscus Attalus's direction — "which necessitated yet another siege, putting you in opposition to us again. Finally, once we had Priscus in our custody and restored to obedience, you were enlisted by him, with our blessing, to bring us the princess." He paused a moment to reflect on this. "It dazzles the mind, doesn't it? One cannot tell who is a friend and who is a foe." He shook his head. "I ask you again, who are you?"

"I am a good soldier who is fulfilling my duty."

"What duty?" the King said. "To whom?"

Emilius seemed about the answer, but then thought better of it and began to smile.

It was strange behavior to say the least and might have gotten him killed, except that Alaric was looking elsewhere and didn't notice. The King lifted his chin and stroked the column of his throat before he gathered his hands behind his back and began to pace. "I have often remarked the clarity with which some men perceive the truth when they know they are no longer in control. It is not ideal, but, in a way, it is admirable, certainly better than those who refuse to face the facts even as the evidence mounts against them."

He looked in my direction. "Your brother the Emperor is of the latter type. He steadfastly refuses to negotiate in good faith even though he lacks the resources to claim the advantage. Even now, when he has lost Rome, the jewel of the Empire, he remains in Ravenna, refusing to come out, spitting defiance in my face so that I must find another way to bring him around. He is a selfish, arrogant fool, your brother. On the other hand, Priscus Attalus may let his pride get the better of him, but he knows his place. He sees the big picture, especially after he has been reacquainted with reality. He is correctable, and, fortunately for him, he has something else going for him. He is of use to me."

There was a long pause for effect, completely terrifying. He continued. "You are of use to me as well, young lady. I would not like to see you harmed. Whole and untainted, you are a prize. But I am not above returning bruised fruit to the vendor if it displeases me."

Again, he let his eyes wander down the length of my leg. "I wonder about you," he said. "I wonder if you are similar to your brother, selfish and arrogant, willing to see your citizenry starved and your cities plundered in order to maintain a false sense of pride, or if you are of a more practical bent, like Priscus Attalus here."

I started to speak, but he cut me off.

"Be careful and gauge your answer carefully. I put great stock in first impressions and do not brook deceitfulness. Your brother, arrogant fool though he is, has one virtue. He is consistent. From the day your father passed away and Honorius was elevated to the throne, he has never been anything but predictable. He said from the start that he hated the Goths, and everything he has done has only reinforced his sick prejudice. Your brother wears his heart

on his sleeve. But what about you? If I ask you a question, can I count on you to answer it truthfully?"

I said that he could.

"All right," he said. "Then tell me this. Was this young soldier here trying to help you escape?"

Emilius glanced at me with a curious expression, a look more of anticipation than dread, as if he were hoping for a different answer than the one I was likely to give.

I answered without hesitation. "Yes," I said. "He was." And with those words I condemned him to death.

But there was no disappointment in his eyes, no outrage, no dejection. Instead, there was a strange look of gratification. His eyes moved to my purse and a smile played around the corners of his lips. It was the most extraordinary thing. I have never been able to account for it.

They took him away and executed him. It all happened incredibly fast. Do I have any regrets? Well, of course I do. He tried to rescue me. He did everything I asked of him. He was brave and dedicated. Which is really just another way of saying he was everything we want a good subject to be, and the loss of a good subject is always tragic. But I too have a role to play, and I cannot perform it if I carelessly cede my prerogatives. There is a time and place to relinquish the upper hand, Placidius, and that is when you have considered all the consequences and made a rational choice — not when you are being coerced into it by the softness of your feelings.

I tell you I am not the woman you think I am. I am different.

Flavius Placidius Valentinianus put the letter down and gazed out at the countryside. Then he picked it up again. He paged through it.

This cannot be right, he thought. *My mother could not have written this.* He lifted his eyes again.

No one had mentioned it, not a single person. You would have thought someone would have mentioned it, the recovery of something so critical. But no one had. The letter had been lost, and then it had been recovered, and no one had said a word. Something wasn't right.

Still, his mother had offered an explanation, not in anything she had said, but in the pages of the letter. Where was it?

He thumbed back through it, page after page, looking for the place where she had talked about it, somewhere near the beginning. When he couldn't locate it, he began to read the letter again from the start.

16th day of Iulius in the year of our most honorable consuls Aetius and Sigisvultus

Galla Placidia sends many greetings to Flavius Placidius Valentinianus. I pray you well. I am writing today to on the occasion of your impending departure to the East to accept your birthright as Emperor of the West. As well, I am writing to offer you my sincerest congratulations on your upcoming nuptials to Licinia Eudocia and the auspicious event that your union portends, the knitting together of the two halves of the empire, East and West, which has not been a reality since your grandfather, Flavius Theodosius Augustus, achieved it some forty years ago.

I am writing to you because I have much to say that cannot be properly expressed aloud, not only because of the danger of prying ears but also due to the great length of what I have to tell you. It is better read at your leisure over the long journey ahead rather than in a face to face talk.

This correspondence prefaces a narrative, which is the story of my life. I had been preparing it for some time with the hope of giving it to you before you departed for Constantinople, but it was misplaced. Fortunately, it was found again with the help of Aetius, whose persuasive abilities you know well. I am sending it to you by swift courier so you can have it early in your trek. Keep it close to you. Trust no one. Suffice it to say there are those who would like to prevent you from having the benefit of my advice and experience.

There is so much to tell you, so much of vital importance to the future of the Empire, yet the interaction between us has been strained of late; it seems we cannot converse without quarreling. Writing is really the best way to communicate with you unhindered. By this method I can continue the flow of my thoughts uninterrupted by your frequent objections and rebuttals, and you can come to appreciate the cumulative logic of what I have to tell you. Furthermore, I am of the firm opinion that you cannot fully grasp the value of my counsel until you truly know who I am.

Yes, I am your mother, but I am much more as well. Until now, the few glimpses you have been allowed into my character have been carefully calibrated to maintain your deference to me and ensure your obedience. Of late, however, as you have grown into manhood, you have begun to perceive my many flaws and to resent me for them. While that may suffice for other families, it cannot suffice for us. You are about to take on a role that is difficult in the extreme. To be emperor demands great discernment, dauntless courage, and deft political acumen. For those who fail, there is everlasting shame, a diminished Empire, and, quite possibly, death. But for those who succeed there is everlasting glory, as there was for your grandfather, Theodosius.

During my twelve years as your regent, I had the benefit of your grandfather's example, as well as the cautionary examples of your two uncles. But you, Placidius, have had little to guide you. For this reason, I long ago made it my purpose to lay out before you the whole history of my life, as the daughter of an emperor, as the sister of two emperors, as the wife of both an emperor and a king, and as a ruler in my own right, as your regent. Few fledgling emperors have had access to a person of such long and varied experience. I hope you will accept what I have to tell you in the right frame of mind.

I began this project nearly ten ago, preparing it against the day when you would assume your full authority as Augustus. I read it through again recently upon its recovery, adding a few small comments and addendums to bring it up to date, including this preface.

There is much here I have never told you before and perspectives on events you have never heard me express. There will be a few things I say now that may contradict what I have said before. Therefore, you will be best served to keep an open mind.

I want to begin by telling you about a young soldier I encountered years ago during the Gothic sack. I want you to know what I did to him. This is not the man I refer to herein as "my beloved," a person whose identity I will reveal to you in due course. No, this is a man I knew for just a short time, a good man, a decent man, to which I did something cruel yet necessary, as is often our sad lot in life. It is not easy to be in charge, as you will discover. It's how you meet those challenges that will determine your success or failure as Rome's new emperor, Valentinian III.

Placidius stopped reading. He was unconvinced. Being told to keep an open mind didn't sit well with him.

He gazed straight ahead, past the four tall figures of the Nubian litter bearers to his full entourage, a long train of attendants and courtiers. Farther up were the serried ranks of the Army in the Presence of the Emperor, marching eight abreast with their flags and standards. On the road behind him, stretching out for more than a mile was a long snaking column of soldiers, nobles, courtiers and slaves, flanked by the rumbling convoy of the baggage train. Placidius ordered his bearers to stop. The entire caravan ground to a halt. He ordered his litter lowered.

When his litter was within a foot of the ground, he stepped out and called for his adiutor[6].

"Cyrus," he said as the sandy haired fellow strode up. "I've been reading the letter you delivered to me from my mother, the quite lengthy one. I wonder, where did you say you got it?"

Cyrus paused a moment in exaggerated contemplation. He bit his lip. His looked upward and to the right as if following a butterfly in flight. He put his finger to his brow. "I think it was the cura epistolarum[7], Liberius." He lifted his finger. "That's it! I've unraveled the mystery!" He grinned, coaxing nervous laughter from the onlookers. "In any case, that would make sense. He *is* the curator of your correspondence, isn't he?"

"Well, yes, of course. But then why didn't he deliver it himself, along with the rest of my correspondence? Why did he give it to you?"

Cyrus shrugged. "I'm at a loss to explain," he said. As Claudian wrote of Eutropius, 'Who knows why people do the things they do. People are inscrutable. Or just block-headed.'"

---

6. Chief general assistant, adjutant

7. Keeper of the emperor's correspondence

Everyone laughed. Placidius laughed too. He liked Cyrus, whose droll antics never failed to amuse him. What's more, he and Cyrus were the same age and shared common interests. Both of them were great admirers of the poet Claudian, who had written panegyrics in praise of the Emperor Honorius, Eutropius having been one of the latter. Cyrus turned his horse around.

"Wait," Placidius said. "You have not been dismissed."

Cyrus stopped and turned back. "Yes-s-s-s," he said. He lifted his brows and drew out the word in a comic manner. "Can I be of service, my liege?"

Placidius smiled despite himself. Cyrus was funny and charming. It wouldn't do to rebuke him while the others were watching. With a weary shake of his head, Placidius waved him away. He would speak to him about his impertinence later. But speak to him he would. For things had changed.

Placidius was no longer merely the son of the Augusta now, the fledgling Caesar[8], the Most Favored Boy. He was the right and proper Augustus, and his marriage to his cousin would seal his status, making him sole emperor of the West. To be spoken to so casually by his inferiors was no longer acceptable. Cyrus was going to have to learn to be more respectful.

In fact, a lot of people were going to have to start treating him differently, military men and court officials, men who had always deferred to his mother and treated him like a spoiled brat, and most especially Aetius, the arrogant master of soldiers[9]. If Aetius thought he could treat him the way he had treated his mother all these years, he was in for a shock.

---

8. The title of the heir apparent who would become Augustus on accession to the throne

9. Supreme military commander

Placidius got back into his litter and ordered his slaves to raise him up. They lifted the two poles that bore the ornate box onto their shoulders and waited for his command to carry it forward. Once Placidius was comfortably situated on his pillows he gave the order. He heard the creak of leather and tromp of boots. The dust rose and hung in a thin pall all around him. He drew the curtains to keep from sneezing.

He picked up the letter again. In spite of his misgivings, he was engrossed. What if it were true? What if he was seeing a side of his mother he had never seen before? He had never really thought of her as a young woman, a person his own age, and she had never spoken about her years as a hostage with the Goths. If nothing else, this promised to be entertaining.

He read on.

Chapter Three

It's a hard thing to be emperor, Placidius. You must make hard decisions. You must make sacrifices.

I've watched you bristle at the notion of breaking off your relationship with Candida and I can't say I blame you. When I was your age, I too loved the company of my peers and was convinced that a certain someone would save me from the obligations of my rank. But I was sorely disappointed. Our duty is bigger than ourselves, and we must learn to manage the expectations that come with it. We must not seek to evade them.

I'm proud that you've agreed to accept your responsibilities and travel to Constantinople to wed Licinia. I'm sure she'll make you a devoted wife. If you're fortunate, you may find her desirable as well, perhaps even as desirable as you have found Candida. But if you do not, you must not think of it as a letdown, for by producing an heir with Licinia, you will be doing the one thing that is necessary to unify the Empire and strengthen it against its enemies. You will be doing your duty. But that doesn't mean you have to be miserable.

To be an effective emperor, you must be strong and confident and have the courage of your convictions. You must know that when you choose a course, even one you may find regrettable, you are doing it for the right reasons. You will be criticized and questioned. You will be challenged and opposed. And if you are not strong in your convictions, you will be deceived and manipulated.

You may find it the hardest thing of all. I certainly did. For me, as a woman, it was more difficult still. For we women are counseled to defer to the better judgment of men. What's more, should we ever question our role as subordi-

nates, we are taught to think of it as a flaw in our natures. Everything we are told circles back to self-doubt, which keeps us timid and pliable. But I did not have the luxury of self-doubt. I had to make decisions affecting the future of the Empire, decisions that fell to me, in many cases, because my brother could not be counted on to act wisely.

Thank God I was not without counsel. Having been brought up under the guardianship of Stilicho, I had the greatest counselor of all. He taught me many things about leadership I have never forgotten, one of which was the difference between duty and allegiance. Without a grasp of that subtle distinction, I would never have survived. And somehow Stilicho was able to communicate it to me. But I'm afraid I have failed dismally in trying to communicate it to you.

Duty and allegiance are not the same thing, Placidius. Lesser men will think they are, but as emperor, you must know the difference, because someday you may have to sacrifice your allegiance to accomplish your duty, as I did.

Alaric took me captive. We remained in Rome for a few days during which time I was treated humanely and accorded all the dignity and privilege of my rank. Then one day Alaric came to me, along with his brother-in-law Ataulf[1], and two or three counselors and retainers. He was in a sour mood. He had made the decision to pull out. His attempt to force my brother's hand by sacking the Eternal City, the symbol of the Empire's strength and stability, had yielded only more obstinacy from Honorius.

Alaric's intention in sacking Rome had been to coerce Honorius into a fight. Failing that, everything else he had done, invading Italia, besieging the city, elevating a puppet emperor, burning and looting, had failed. Having stripped Rome of its riches, he had gotten everything he could from it. Although its symbolic value was great, it was of little strategic value to the Goths. They could have remained there a decade and never elicited a battle with Honorius.

Alaric was frustrated by his failure. He roared at me as if I were to blame. "Your brother is a stubborn fool! Does he think this is the end of it? Does he think I'm finished?"

I bowed my head. "I don't know what he thinks."

He glared at me. "What's the matter with him? You're his sister. You grew up with him. Tell me. Is he dimwitted?"

"He doesn't like to be embarrassed," I said.

He opened his mouth to hurl something back at me, but my response made him stop.

"Embarrassed?" he said.

"Also, it is incorrect to say I grew up with him," I went on. "It's true we were brought up under the same roof, but my brother and I were raised in different households. Honorius had his own from the time he was declared Emperor at the age of ten. Mine remained under the guardianship of Stilicho until I was eighteen."

At the mention of Stilicho's name, Alaric's face darkened. This was no surprise. I had anticipated it would have that effect. Alaric's relationship with Stilicho had been fraught, to say the least.

---

1. Pronounced ay-taulf

They had started out as bitter enemies. Stilicho had repulsed Alaric's invasion of Thrace when Alaric was still a young Goth, just one of many tribal leaders trying to take advantage of Rome's porous borders in the years following the Battle of Adrianopolis. Stilicho was impressed, however, with Alaric's skills as a commander. And so, when the usurper Eugenius tried to overthrow my father and seize the throne, Stilicho, ever loyal to the house of Theodosius, bolstered the legions by recruiting Alaric and his men into the Roman army. Together they defeated Eugenius at the Battle of Frigidus and won a great victory that reunited the Empire and burnished both their reputations.

But Alaric wanted more. In his view the Goths had sacrificed greatly on Rome's behalf and deserved to be rewarded with a grant of land on which to settle. For eighteen years the Goths had wandered from place to place seeking a place to put down roots. Yet wherever they stopped, the Romans chased them off. Now, having demonstrated their loyalty, they expected to be rewarded with a homeland. But Stilicho had other ideas. He spurned Alaric's demand, and in response Alaric invaded Greece.

As you know, Greece is in the Prefecture of Illyricum[2] and therefore falls under the jurisdiction of the Eastern Roman Empire. Its defense is properly in the ambit of Constantinople, but the Eastern armies were away fighting the Persians and lacked the manpower to repel the Goths, so Stilicho, thinking he would do the East a favor, stepped in. He pursued Alaric south into the Peloponnese where the Goths escaped by sea to Macedonia. Stilicho went after them, and after a long, difficult fight, the Goths slipped away again, this time to northern Italia where they laid siege to Mediolanum.[3]

Stilicho didn't want an ongoing war with the Goths. He had other pressing

---

2. An administrative division of the Late Roman Empire roughly equivalent to the modern day Balkans

matters to attend to, including a revolt in Africa[4] and a tribal uprising in Britannia. If he could have appeased the Goths by granting them land, he would have done it. But Honorius wouldn't hear of it.

By then Honorius had been emperor for six years, but he was no more competent in dealing with the Goths than his predecessor had been. His first response was one of self-preservation. He moved the seat of government from landlocked Mediolanum to Ravenna where the marshes around the city provided a natural defense against invasion. Then he sat and waited for Stilicho to drive the Goths out of Italia.

It proved more difficult than he thought. After a long fight, the Goths were finally chased from Mediolanum only to fall on Verona. Fed up, Stilicho counseled a truce to discuss Alaric's demands, but Honorius considered it a betrayal to give in to the Goths. He accused Stilicho of being a traitor.

I had never heard anything so absurd in my life, and I told my brother so. As Emperor he was a poor judge of character and had been entertaining the counsel of fools. I demanded an audience. I was emotional and overplayed my hand. My brother belittled me and dismissed my objections as the ravings of a silly girl. I was only seventeen at the time. It was then I recognized the importance of holding my emotions in check. Nothing is ever achieved by letting our emotions get ahead of our good sense.

Despite his disdain for my opinion, Honorius did eventually agree to a truce, if only temporarily—and it's a good thing he did, for it held Alaric in check while the Roman field army dealt with an entirely different invasion, one that

---

3. Modern day Milan

4. A Roman province on the northern coast of Africa comprising modern day Algeria and Tunisia

would have brought the Empire to its knees had Stilicho had to fight Alaric at the same time.

Radagaisus was an independent Gothic king, unaffiliated with Alaric. He had been encamped with his people north of Noricum[5] on the plains west of the Carpathian Mountains. They had been driven there by the Huns after being expelled from their homeland in Sarmatia[6] . Coming under Hunnic pressure once more, Radagaisus and his people migrated south, encountering Roman resistance, to which they responded by assembling an army of twenty thousand and marching across the border into Italia, burning Flavia Solva and devastating Aguntum on the way.

Stilicho confronted them with an army of fifteen thousand at Florentia[7] and defeated them. Radgaisus was put to death and his followers were sold into slavery. Only the higher-status soldiers were spared. They were drafted into the Roman military to replenish the ranks. Among them was Emilus, the young soldier I betrayed. For Stilicho it was a brief moment of triumph, then everything fell apart.

With negotiations underway to secure the Goths a homeland, Alaric grew impatient and marched his army southeast to Epirus[8] . As part of Illyricum, Epirus was under the jurisdiction of the East. One can only assume Alaric was honoring the spirit of the truce by withdrawing from Italia and heading east, but Honorius didn't see it that way. He ordered Alaric pursued and eradicated.

The timing couldn't have been worse, for at that exact moment a huge force

---

5. Modern day Austria

6. Modern day Ukraine

7. Modern day Florence

of Vandals, Suebi, and Alans were crossing the Rhine and invading Gaul[9]. Stilicho was caught flat footed. Suddenly, he needed every available man to defend Gaul. Without waiting for Honorius's permission, he sent a message to Alaric asking him to refrain from attacking Epirus and holding out the promise of a major concession if he would desist.

When Honorius got wind of it, he was livid and ordered Stilicho arrested. Stilicho was not so naïve as to believe Honorius's assurances he would not be harmed, but he was frustrated and exhausted by my brother's gross misman-agement and was ready to quit, so he turned himself in, was taken in chains to Ravenna, and put to death.

I was devastated. Stilicho had been a friend and mentor to me. After the death of my father, he had stepped in to raise me. I honored and respected him. At some level I even loved him. To lose him to such a petty, vindictive act on the part of my brother was deplorable. But the monumental stupidity of my brother didn't end there.

To "teach Alaric a lesson", he ordered the massacre of the wives and children of the tens of thousands of Gothic mercenaries serving in the Roman army. The predictable result was the alienation of those once loyal soldiers who now deserted our army and flocked to Alaric's banner. Overnight, the Roman army was bled dry while Alaric's numbers were bolstered. Far from dissuading the Goths in their ambitions, my brother had given them the means and justification to go on the offensive.

Feeling revitalized and reinvigorated, Alaric announced a change of plans.

---

8. Modern day northwest Greece and Albania

9. An administrative division of the Late Roman Empire roughly equivalent to modern day France

Far-off Epirus no longer interested him. Now he was hunting for bigger game. With Stilicho out of the way who could stop him. The Goths would strike at the very heart of the Empire, he announced. The Goths would strike at Rome.

Within a fortnight he landed his forces at Tarentum and marched up the peninsula meeting little resistance from Rome's leaderless and diminished forces. Soon he was standing outside the gates of Rome where he put the city under siege. He had several demands. First, he wanted a ransom of five thousand pounds of gold, thirty thousand pounds of silver, and forty thousand freed Gothic slaves. Next, he wanted a large swath of territory within the Empire on which to establish a homeland. Finally, he wanted to be given the status of master of soldiers, the highest rank in the Roman military, an audacious request, for it would effectively make him Stilicho's successor.

Honorius rejected the terms. From his well-defended palace at Ravenna two hundred miles away, he urged the people of Rome to resist. I was in Rome then, awaiting my beloved, and I can tell you the mood was grim. The initial hope of rescue by Ravenna quickly foundered.

Trapped inside the city with no hope of escape, the Senate capitulated. They agreed to pay Alaric his ransom and gave him the title of master of soldiers. But when the Senate balked on the question of granting him a homeland, Alaric proclaimed a new emperor to replace Honorius, someone who would do his bidding. The man he chose was the urban prefect of Rome Priscus Attalus.

The Senate had no choice but to go along with the proclaiming of a new emperor. Resisting Alaric was pointless. He held more sway over of the inhabitants of the city than Honorius did. Getting on his good side by whatever means necessary was the first step in ending our terrible ordeal. I told the Senate I endorsed their decision. It was a matter of choosing their duty to Rome over their allegiance to Honorius. As the daughter of Theodosius and the sister of the Emperor, my affirmation helped subdue their reservations, at least those among them who favored the idea.

And so Priscus Attalus was made emperor by proclamation of the Senate, but no one was under any illusions about who held the real power in Rome, no one except maybe Priscus himself. Unfortunately, he was not nearly as tractable as Alaric would have liked. He hedged when Alaric ordered him to arrest the dissenters and resisted when the Gothic king told him to raise a body of troops and invade Africa. Furious at his impudence, Alaric, who had withdrawn his troops from Rome with an eye to deploying them elsewhere, sent them back to Rome to teach Priscus a lesson.

Panicked, Priscus shut the gates. Alaric demanded they be opened. When Priscus vacillated, the Goths broke them down, and Alaric unleashed his soldiers to sack the city at will. In the end, Priscus Attalus was taken prisoner, and so was I, after attempting to flee with Emilius.

A few days later, I stood before Alaric and invoked Stilicho's name, knowing it would cause the Gothic king to see me in a new light.

"Your brother ordered him executed," Alaric reflected. "That was unwise. He was the one person who could have saved him."

I acknowledged the truth of this. "Honorius doesn't like to be told what to do. When our father died, Honorius was only ten years old, too young to rule in his own right, so Stilicho was assigned to be his regent, and later on his chief of staff. In my brother's mind, Stilicho had been telling him what to do for far too long. It was inevitable, I suppose."

Alaric shook his head. "Pathetic," he said.

"Inexcusable," I said.

He glanced up at me. "What are you thinking?"

"To manipulate the obstinate all you have to do is demand the opposite," I said.

Alaric quirked an eyebrow. "What are you suggesting, that we should tell your brother that we don't really want a homeland, that we shall be content to wander the Empire endlessly like nomads?"

"Maybe."

He smirked. "I think you'd better stick to weaving and reciting verse and leave the politics to me."

I bowed my head and begged his pardon.

He told me, rather stiffly, that I would be treated with dignity and respect during my captivity but only if I didn't get cute and start causing trouble. In other words, I was to behave myself and I would be pampered and indulged, as if that were all a pretty young princess could ask for.

He and his retainers were heading out the door when I made bold to speak.

"You're going to cut off his life's blood," I said.

One of them stopped and turned back. "What?"

"You're going to go to Africa and embargo our grain supply," I said. "You're going to cut off his life's blood."

The others had passed out the door, but this one remained behind. It was Ataulf, Alaric's brother-in-law, the brother of his wife. "Who told you that?" he said.

"I know what Priscus was ordered to do," I replied. "I advised him to obey. But even if I had not known, I could have figured it out. If I were in your shoes, I

would do the same."

Ataulf smiled, amused by my boldness. "Oh, you would, would you?"

"I would."

He regarded me for a long moment. Then he chuckled and withdrew.

When he was gone, I looked down at the amulet Emilius had given me. It had given me the power to speak so boldly to my captors. I was sure of it. What's more, I felt sure that by doing so I had gained an advantage I would not otherwise have had.

I held it in the palm of my hand. It was no mere ornament. There was something different about it. Something special.

Fear is the devil, Placidius. You must respect it, you must be wary of it, but you must not let it control you. As a captive of the Goths, I was afraid, but fear is not what drove me. Even the most courageous heroes, brave men like Aetius and Stilicho, will admit to being afraid. But they never let fear be their masters. Nor should you.

There will be those who try to intimidate you. You can count on it. Do not surrender to your impulses. Try to keep your head. Your ability to maintain self-control under pressure will give you the advantage.

Listen. There are those who counsel against fraternizing with the enemy. To them, compromise and understanding are signs of weakness. Vilify the enemy, they say. Keep them on the defensive. Honorius and his ilk were of this opinion. Their reflexive insistence on revenge brought the Empire to the brink of destruction. But behind their policy was little more than fear.

I was of a different opinion. I could see no advantage in resisting my captors, but there was much to be learned by winning their confidence. This was the path I chose.

Obviously, there was a measure of self-preservation in what I did. But I didn't act to avoid discomfort. I acted to stay alive and bide my time, to permit myself the opportunity to work into a more favorable position. I had to be patient and give my captors no reason to distrust me. I sought their interest. I sought their companionship, for if I could win their faith, I could have some influence over them.

This was not an opinion I had reached out of the blue. I had been counseled to think this way by Stilicho who always espoused the value of getting close to one's enemies. At the very least one could become acquainted with their vulnerabilities, which could be exploited if necessary. But in the best of all worlds one could develop a genuine affection for them, which might help to relieve the enmity and build a mutually beneficial accord. He was not merely theorizing. He had lived it.

As the son of a Vandal cavalry officer, Stilicho was half-barbarian by birth. As such, he was little regarded by the military hierarchy. Yet there was no denying his skills as a soldier and a diplomat, and rather than begrudge those who disdained him, he sought to befriend them. As a result he rapidly moved up the ranks despite the handicap of his birth.

He came to the attention of my father after successfully negotiating a treaty with the Persians. The two of them hit it off and my father promoted him to the rank of comes sacri stabuli.[10] Shortly thereafter he was made comes domesticorum.[11] And after his ringing victory at the Battle of Frigidus, my father made Stilicho the master of soldiers, the supreme commander. He had achieved all this not by fighting his enemies but by befriending them.

In fact, so enamored was my father of Stilicho he arranged to make him a part of the family. He married him to his niece Serena, the daughter of his brother. As it happened, Serena and I were close in age but far apart in temperament and might have remained little more than cousins had not fate intervened. Shortly after the marriage, my father became ill and seeing he was not long for this world, he charged Stilicho with being my guardian, which effectively made Serena a sort of mother to me, a role for which she was not well suited.

Yet as hopeless as Serena was as a mother, Stilicho was as good a father as a girl could ask for. You have to understand. My father died when I was just three years old. I barely remember him. Consequently, Stilicho is the first one who comes to mind when I think of a father figure.

As much as Honorius despised him, I loved him. He took me into his confidence and let me see the framework of his thinking. He challenged me with problems of a political nature to see how I might handle them, encouraged me when I did well, and corrected me when I did wrong. I'm sure he wished Honorius would've given him the same consideration, but he never did. It's a pity. My brother could've learned a great deal from him.

When I was eighteen, Stilicho came to me with an unreadable expression on his face and asked me to join him in the peristyle[12] of our villa. We sat down in that lovely colonnaded garden open to the sky and surrounded by vine-covered

---

10. The Count of the Stable, responsible for the horses and pack animals of the army

11. The Count of the Imperial Household, a high military official in direct contact with the emperor

arcades. He took my hand in his and imparted the sad news that my eldest brother Arcadius[13] had died.

I felt little on hearing this. I had not seen my brother since I was eleven. Even before that, we were not close as he was ten years older than me and born of a different mother. Yet as little as his death meant to me, it meant a great deal to the Eastern Roman Empire where Arcadius had been Emperor.

Before my father Theodosius passed away, he had divided the Empire between his two sons, making Arcadius Emperor of the East and Honorius Emperor of the West. He wanted no rivalry between them and by this measure sought to appease them. He appointed Stilicho as a sort of referee to make sure they remained friends and colleagues.

This worked well enough until now, but with Arcadius's passing things were thrown into uncertainty, for although Arcadius had left an heir, the child was only seven years old, too young to rule in his own right, and since his mother was already dead, the government would have to be run by a regent, someone outside the family, until the boy came of age. This duty had fallen to the praetorian prefect Anthemius[14].

Stilicho knew Anthemius and didn't trust him. He feared we faced a dangerous situation in the East. He informed me he intended to travel to Constantinople to attend Arcadius's funeral and see to the succession, and he wanted me to come along with him.

I was briefly taken aback. He had never asked me to play such an important role in the affairs of state before. Of my father's three children, I was the least

---

12. A garden courtyard surrounded by a porch formed by a row of columns

13. Pronounced ar-kay-dee-us

consequential by far. From the start, Honorius and Arcadius were slated to become emperors, but I had never been considered for anything more than a convenient political marriage to some wayward figure my brothers wanted to keep in their good graces. Now I was being asked to play a different role, and I immediately saw what it was. "You want me for my legitimacy."

Now it was Stilicho's turn to be surprised. His head snapped back like a cat that had sniffed something funny. "Why, yes," he said.

I continued my thought. "Of course, it would be better if Honorius went, but Honorius is uncooperative, so you want me there to demonstrate that the House of Theodosius is behind you."

Stilicho lit up. "That's right, Galla!"

"I'll go," I said.

Stilicho raised a hand. "Not so fast. Think it through. What if your brother orders you to remain at home?"

"I'll go anyway," I said. "My first duty is to the Empire."

Stilicho smiled and patted my hand. "You are brave, Galla. Your father would have liked that about you."

We sat looking out at the garden, at the amaranth and gladioli, the narcissi and oleander. At length, he said, "Honorius doesn't trust Anthemius either, you know. We are of one mind when it comes to that. The only issue on which we differ is who should replace him."

---

14. Pronounced an-them-ee-us

I was flattered he had chosen to confide in me. Important men rarely accord young women such consideration. In reality, Stilicho himself was not known to be very generous when it came to women. He often treated his own daughters with indifference. As for his wife, Serena, he treated her with a chilliness bordering on contempt.

Theirs was an arranged marriage, one made of political necessity, but it didn't have to be loveless. Not all arranged marriages are, as you will come to realize. Stilicho had it in him to be kind and generous, but Serena made it hard. She was not quarrelsome or shrewish, quite the opposite. She was timid and mousy and given to tears. Being married to her must have been exhausting, and Stilicho was an important man with many crucial demands on him. Taken altogether, I could hardly blame him for the way he treated her.

But now he was displaying a different side of himself.

"Naturally, Honorius wants to assume power at Constantinople and reunite the Empire. But if we are to be honest, we must acknowledge that he cannot even rule the West. Take the Prefecture of Illyricum, for instance. It has been retained unlawfully by the East ever since it was lent to them to assist them in their war against the Goths. In traveling to Constantinople, I intend to settle the dispute once and for all. Illyricum will be ours again. But it will require a strong army to hold it, one your brother doesn't presently have."

I turned to him. "You're thinking of settling the Goths there, aren't you? You're thinking of giving them a homeland in Illyricum."

Stilicho grinned. He was impressed.

"Getting Honorius to go along with it won't be easy," I said. "He hates the Goths. They've frightened and embarrassed him. He wants them defeated and disgraced. He'll never agree to allow them to settle on Roman soil, even if you succeed in clawing Illyricum back from the East."

"Stubbornness will be your brother's undoing," he sighed.

We sat in silence for a moment. A butterfly flitted past. I watched its graceful flight as it lighted on a hyssop leaf. It had wings of iridescent blue. It raised and lowered them slowly. Presently Stilicho said, "I suppose you know, because women talk about such things, that his marriage to Maria was unconsummated? Not just without issue, mind you, but unconsummated. The public blamed my poor daughter, of course. They accused her of being too devout, but Maria confided in me. She told me Honorius refused to sleep with her. And not because he was celibate, God knows. He had plenty of concubines. Perhaps too many if you believe some reports. No, Honorius refused to consummate the marriage out of spite, because he resented being forced to marry my daughter." Stilicho rubbed his temples. "As his regent, I had to arrange a politically advantageous marriage for him. As his master of soldiers and head of the army, it made sense for our two families to come together. It's what your father would have wanted. Ahead of the nuptials, Honorius made no objection, preferring not to oppose me to my face. Yet he was simmering with resentment, and once they were wed, he refused to grant me what I wished for. He refused to let my blood be mingled with his in the form of a child."

"And then Maria died," I said.

"Yes, she died," he said. "But that was not the end of it, as you know."

"Thermantia," I said.

"Yes, Thermantia. But having rejected one of my daughters, your brother is unlikely to embrace the other. I'm only going along with it because Serena wants it."

"Serena?"

"She fears what might happen if our ties to the House of Theodosius are cut. Ever since Maria died, she has been on edge. She jumps at the slightest sound, worried that Honorius's soldiers are coming to arrest us. She bites her nails. She paces the floor. She has trouble sleeping. To calm her, I agreed to approach your brother to offer Thermantia in marriage. I expected him to laugh it off, but he agreed. I have no confidence he will consummate the marriage. He only agreed so he could thwart me in the only way he dares, by refusing to produce an heir with the blood of my family in its veins."

"But he must produce an heir for the line to go on."

"True, but this is Honorius we're talking about. Resentment and spite rule him." He shook his head. "Despite my best efforts, he still thinks I'm plotting to overthrow him. It makes no sense. If I had wanted to overthrow him, I could have done it when I was his regent. It would've been easier then."

"He knows you would make a better emperor than him. It gets under his skin."

"He's only hurting himself. His inability to trust me makes him incapable of relying on the one person who wants most to protect him. He should go to Constantinople himself and leave me here to deal with the rebellion in Gaul, but he can't, because he fears I'll join the rebels and seize the throne while he's away."

The rebellion he was speaking of was the Rebellion of Constantine III started by a Roman soldier in Britannia who took that lofty name for himself as a way of making himself look grand. By exploiting the disaffection of the underpaid and overworked legions in Britannia, he got himself hailed as emperor, then crossed the channel and won the allegiance of the equally disgruntled legions in Gaul. Before long, a powerful rebel army was moving south toward Italia with the object of overthrowing Honorius. The armies sent by Stilicho to defeat it had so far been unsuccessful and with each passing day the danger became greater.

"In any case," he said, "someone must attend to matters in Constantinople. Anthemius can't be permitted to seize power. We must take control of the East, recover Illyricum, and reunite the Empire—which is where you come in Galla."

"Me?"

"Yes, to secure the reunification of the Empire I need you to make a sacrifice. I need you to marry my son, Galla. I want you to marry Eucherius."

My jaw dropped. Eucherius! It was unthinkable. We had been brought up together. We had been childhood friends. We had wrestled and played together. As infants, we had bathed together. Eucherius was in all respects a brother to me. I didn't want to marry him. I had given my heart to another.

Stilicho immediately grasped the problem. "It's that boy who visited us last summer, isn't it? You fell in love with him." He gave me a pitying smile. "Oh, Galla, the passions of youth are intoxicating, but you must accept the fact that he is gone and won't be coming back. It was a courageous thing he did, agreeing to become a hostage, but he has gone to fulfill his duty, and now we must fulfill ours. I need you to marry Eucherius. For the good of the Empire."

Much as I hated to admit it, he was right. Among people like us, marriage is a valuable bargaining chip. We must use it wisely to achieve an edge. Stilicho had made a similar sacrifice in marrying Serena, a fragile, hysterical woman who had been my father's adopted niece and who Stilicho had married at my father's request. It could not have been easy for a proud man like Stilicho to marry such a weak person, but he did it for my father, and for the good of the Empire, and now I was being asked to do the same. How could I refuse?

"A marriage between you and Eucherius will augur the birth of a child," he said, "and that child, in the absence of issue from Honorius and Thermantia, will become heir to the throne. Naturally, Honorius will perceive it as a threat.

He will try to stop the marriage, but if we wait to make the announcement until we are well away from Ravenna and bound for Constantinople, he will be forced to accept it."

"A marriage between you and Eucherius will augur the birth of a child," he said, "and that child, in the absence of issue from Honorius and Thermantia, will become heir to the throne. Naturally, Honorius will perceive it as a threat. He will try to stop the marriage, but if we wait to make the announcement until we are well away from Ravenna and bound for Constantinople, he will be forced to accept it."

"Why? How?"

"If we are in Constantinople when the marriage takes place, the threat will be perceived to be to young Theodosius II and his regent, Anthemius, not to Honorius. Honorius would rather have you residing in Constantinople with the next generation of the House of Theodosius than here with him. When he learns of your engagement to Eucherius, he will abandon any attempt to recall us to Ravenna. He will gladly let us go."

"And when we get to Constantinople, we will depose Anthemius and assume the regency for ourselves?"

"That's right."

"And if Honorius feels threatened by my child, he will have to produce his own offspring, which means he will have to consummate his marriage with Thermantia."

"Precisely."

"And either way the heir to the throne will have your blood running through his veins."

Stilicho's expression hardened. "I'm trying ensure the survival of the House of Theodosius, Galla. It's what your father would've wanted."

"I know," I said. "I support you."

He gave me a guarded look.

I smiled.

His expression softened. "I'm not asking you to do this for my sake," he said, "but for the sake of Rome. If Honorius refuses to produce an heir, the house of Theodosius in the West will come to an end, and your father's dynastic ambitions will be thwarted. The only way to prevent that from happening is for you to accompany me to Constantinople and marry Eucherius[15]. Will you do that for me? Will you do that for Rome?"

"Without a moment's hesitation," I said.

He wrapped his arm around me and kissed the crown of my head, something quite out of character for him as he was not a man given to overt displays of affection. I was touched. I felt closer to him at that moment than I ever had before. Sadly, we would never be that close again because three months later he was executed by Honorius. Eucherius was eliminated too. My brother's insecurities had finally gotten the better of him. He cut off his left hand to spite his right. Naturally, I was devastated.

It was an awful time, not just because of the murders of those I held dear, but because my brother's recklessness nearly brought the Empire to ruin. Without a strong general to protect him, Honorius had little choice but to recognize

---

15. Pronounced yew-cair-ee-us

the sovereignty of the usurper in Gaul. Constantine III was legitimized as his co-ruler. The Empire, already divided between East and West, was further divided, making it vulnerable to the Goths. And none of it had to happen. Honorius's obstinacy was what brought it about. Repairing it would take time.

I must tell you, Placidius, I worry that you have something of your uncle in you, the way you dig in and reject good advice just because you don't like the person offering it to you. Closed-mindedness is never a good quality in a ruler. We must rise above such petty behavior. These as precarious times, Placidius. We must be equal to the challenge, if we expect the Empire to survive.

Now you can see. The sacrifice I'm asking you to make is no different from the one I was willing to make at your age. I would have married Eucherius without a second thought, although the idea repelled me. I would have done it because Stilicho asked it of me, and I trusted him. My own feelings barely entered into it.

One more thing. During my meeting with Stilicho in the garden we heard screams coming from elsewhere in the villa. We recognized them as the voice of Serena. We rushed from the peristyle to a storage room off the kitchen where we discovered two slaves holding up the body of a young woman who had attempted to hang herself. She was clawing at the rope, coughing and sputtering as a pair of men struggled to hold her up. Serena stood to one side, fists pressed to her mouth, screaming hysterically.

Stilicho rushed in, righted a stool, and slid it under the woman. Then he loosened the noose and helped the men lower her to the floor. Taking the woman in his arms, he knelt beside her and stroked her hair. He spoke gently to her with a tenderness I'd never seen him display with any woman before.

All this time Serena went on screaming until Stilicho shot me an exasperated look and cocked his head sharply at her. I went over and shook her and told her to get hold of herself.

Quaking and sobbing, her voice hitching in her throat, Serena's hysteria subsided, but, as it did, she looked at me in dread like a rodent looks at a snake and ran from the room.

Perhaps she had a premonition. Serena was haunted by premonitions. As a youth she had suffered an incident she believed caused her to be cursed. On a walk through the forum, she had idly taken a necklace from a statue of Rhea Silvia, the mother of Romulus and Rhemus, and placed it around her neck. No sooner had she done so than an old woman appeared and cursed her for her impiety. As it turned out, the old crone was the last of the Vestal Virgins, guardians of the temple, so her curse carried some weight, or at least Serena believed it did. At the time Serena was an indifferent Christian and still fearful of the old pagan gods. From then on, she was plagued by premonitions of her own demise, and in recent weeks she had begun suffering nightmares involving me.

After Serena fled, I turned my attention to the poor creature in Stilicho's arms. Her face was familiar. She had come to us six years earlier, a slave taken in one of Stilicho's many battles, but apparently someone of more than normal consequence, for Stilicho had always treated her with a deference he did not accord the others. Only later did I realize who she was, and I understood why he had always been so kind to her and what a great tragedy it was that she had taken her own life, for she had not survived. She had not been cut down in time.

As for Serena, she was right to be afraid of me. Although she had been like a mother to me, bringing me up from a child and teaching me womanly pursuits like spinning and weaving, she had always been shy and distant and exemplified a pitiable feminine fragility that I vowed never to emulate. Before long, fate would set us on a trajectory where her weakness would become a threat to me, and I would have to do something about it.

Poor, weak, misguided Serena. In time her delusions would become a self-fulfilling prophecy.

49

Poor, weak, misguided Serena. In time her delusions would become a self-fulfilling prophecy.

Chapter Four

Placidius lowered the letter and sat looking across the campfire at his attendants and aides. They were eating their supper, laughing and talking. No one was paying him any mind.

He picked the letter up and examined it again. Here was more evidence that its authorship was dubious, this business about Stilicho. It just didn't ring right. During all his years growing up, his mother had almost never mentioned Stilicho to him. Sure, he knew she had been raised by him, but she had not talked about him other than to say he was a kind and decent man who treated her well.

This new version of events, with Stilicho as her mentor and confidant, seemed suspect, especially the part where Stilicho asked her to marry his son, Eucherius. The proposed union was not implausible as a political matter, but his mother had never mentioned it before, not even during their quarrel over his betrothal to Licinia Eudocia. Peculiar. If she had gone through something similar, wouldn't she have brought it up?

Placidius called across the fire to his adjutant and asked him to summon his curator of correspondence, Liberius[1]. Cyrus had claimed to have obtained the letter from Liberius. Placidius was curious about who had delivered it.

At some length Liberius appeared. He was a slight, slump-shouldered man with a nervous habit of brushing his hair off his forehead. Placidius

---

1. Pronounced lie-beer-ee-us

asked if something were the matter, and he answered in a timid, submissive manner, saying there was not. Placidius asked him about the letter.

Liberius claimed ignorance.

"See here now," Placidius said, annoyed at the man's timidity. "Is it not the duty of the curator of correspondence to inspect all my letters before they are delivered to me?

Liberius lowered his head.

"Then why not this one?"

A one-word reply. "Arsenius."[2]

Arsenius was Placidius's chief of staff, a gruff, impatient man with a bluff, imperious manner. In discussion, he was often curt to the point of insolence and seemed to regard Placidius as little more than a spoiled child with little knowledge of bureaucracy or politics. Placidius had made it a point to sack him as soon as they reached Constantinople.

"Do you mean to tell me Arsenius intercepted this letter and prevented my curator of correspondence from inspecting it before delivering it to me?"

"Oh no, I didn't say that." Liberius kneaded his hands and brushed the hair out of his face. "I know nothing of that letter in particular. It's just – well, sometimes Arsenius likes to appraise the correspondence before it reaches me, the better to evaluate it."

"Evaluate it for what?"

Liberius shrugged.

"But that's not his job!"

"I agree," Liberius said. "And I have endeavored to speak to him about it, but he is quite adamant."

---

2. Pronounced Ahr-see-nee-us

Placidius was peeved. He dismissed Liberius and made it a point to admonish Arsenius at the earliest opportunity. But now it had grown late, and the others were all going off to bed. He looked around for his personal bodyguard and, finding them curiously absent, made his way to his tent unguarded.

Inside, the tent was dark, a punishment-worthy dereliction on the part of his servants whose duty it was to prepare his bedchamber for nightfall, or so it seemed to him until he heard a stirring in the bedclothes. His heart picked up a beat, and a delicious exhilaration took hold of him. He moved over to the bedside and whispered.

"Candida?"

A small female grunt greeted him.

Placidius flung off his clothes and slid in next to her. She was nude and her back was turned to him. He snuggled up against her and pressed himself against the soft round curve of her buttocks. She squirmed in annoyance and swatted him away.

"Oh, come on," he said. "Don't be like that."

"I'm tired," she said. "Leave me alone."

She seemed serious, but she had taken off her clothes and gotten into his bed. Certainly, she had done so with carnal intentions, even if she had dozed off while waiting and was now half lost in sleep. He felt sure he could rouse her with a few well-placed caresses. He let his fingertips run down the curve of her hip into the narrow gully of her pelvis. He kissed her, nuzzling the nape of her neck. When she didn't object, he ran his hand down the flat of her belly and between her thighs where his fingers probed her, seeking her wetness. She spread her legs and turned to him, opening her mouth to receive him. He dove in hungrily. It was then he noticed the bitter taste of wine on her breath. He drew back. "You've been drinking."

"What of it?" she muttered, knitting her fingers behind his neck and pulling his mouth to hers.

He resisted. "Who have you been drinking with?"

"Nobody," she said. She raised her head and pecked his mouth with kisses.

He pulled back from her. "Was it Stephanus?"

She heaved a sigh and turned away. "Not this again," she said irritably.

For a moment he regretted spoiling the mood, and it occurred to him that he might've been acting unreasonably, but earlier that day he had seen her chatting with the handsome young man who was her groom, and it had struck him as a little too flirtatious.

"I don't like it when you talk with the servants. They're beneath you."

"Beneath me?"

"Yes."

"Oh, don't be ridiculous. I'm going to Constantinople to become the mistress of the Emperor. Why would I want to trifle with a lowly horse wrangler like Stephanus?"

She was being sarcastic, trying to communicate her distaste for the new arrangement she would soon be living under. Earlier she had told him she understood the necessity of his marrying his cousin Licinia. She had assured him she was content to carry on as his mistress and would make no objections. But now she was acting as if she was offended. To tell him one thing and show him another was classic Candida. She was as evasive as a specter, which only made him want her more.

"Are you angry with me?" he asked.

"Be quiet and kiss me."

But his erection had grown flaccid. To divert her attention, he returned to the question of her drinking. "You've had too much wine."

She dropped her head onto her pillow with a grunt. When he tried to kiss her, she pushed him back.

"Come on," he said. "Don't be angry."

She turned her back on him.

He snuggled against her, cupped a hand under one breast, and rubbed himself against the crease of her buttocks.

"Stop it," she grumbled and elbowed him away. She got out of bed.

He could hear her getting dressed.

"Where are you going?" he asked.

"Away from you."

"Come back to bed. I'm sorry."

"You know what's wrong with you, Placidius? You can't appreciate a good thing when you have it." A moment later she was gone.

Placidius lay on his back in the dark with his penis slumped against his thigh. He could order her back, but that would only make her pissier – and then he would be unable to perform. It was a problem, this random flaccidity of his. Other men were goaded to greater potency by a woman's defiance, but not him. Not usually. Not unless she truly challenged him. Then it was different. He wondered if God was punishing him for some sin he was only dimly aware of.

He recalled a story, commonly told among the guard, about how Aetius had demonstrated his sexual prowess in the face of feminine resistance. After he had defeated and killed Bonifacius[3], Aetius had ordered his enemy's widow, the beautiful Pelagia[4], brought to him in his bedchamber. He

---

3. Pronounced bon-uh-fah-see-us

4. Pronounced puh-lay-gee-uh

informed her, so the story went, that he intended to marry her. As soon as they were married, he went on, she would owe him the duties of a wife. But, he told her, he was an impatient man and could not wait. It was a flaw of his. He apologized, but he intended to assert his privileges at once.

She screamed and tried to get away from him, but he caught her from behind and dragged her into bed. She resisted him with the ferocity of a lion, which roused him. He ravished her repeatedly and with such passion that in the morning she lay woozy, her eyes swimming in her head, having climaxed several times with great intensity. The next day Aetius married her. As they stood before the priest, she wore a lopsided grin and cast moony glances at her insatiable paramour.

The part about the cockeyed grin and the unfocused looks always brought gales of laughter when the story was told among the guards. Aetius was a hero in their eyes, even though some of them had fought against him in earlier conflicts. It seemed he could do no wrong, even though nothing could be further from the truth. Aetius was guilty of numerous crimes and would have to answer for them in the future. Placidius would see to that.

He got up and went outside. His personal bodyguard was nowhere to be found. He made a mental note to reproach them in the morning. He took a tinder from the fire and went back inside to light the brazier. While he was doing so his eyes fell on a scroll apparently left behind by Candida, something she had been reading while she waited. He picked it up and unrolled it.

It was a curious document, the transcript of a sermon by Nestorius. The name rang a bell, but Placidius couldn't quite place it. He read a portion of it, something about the rejection of the title "Mother of God" for the Virgin Mary. Religious matters gave him a headache. He tossed it aside.

Then he picked up his mother's letter. Despite its dubious authorship, it promised to be more interesting than a dry, rambling sermon by some desiccated old clergyman. He sat down on the edge of the bed in the dim light of the brazier and continued reading.

Six weeks after leaving Rome, we were camped on the Calabrian coast, preparing to cross over to Africa. There was tension in the air. The Goths had seized a number of ships to make their escape, but they didn't know how to sail them, and the sailors had all run off. On Alaric's orders, a number of them had been tracked down and dragged back, but they were sullen and uncooperative, so the Gothic King ordered a few of them tortured as an example to the others.

It was a nasty, brutish business and portended evil, for you cannot force a sailor to sail, as anyone who has experience with such things can tell you. The Goths were not a seafaring people and had no idea of the cooperation and common purpose required to sail a ship, much less a fleet of ships trying to cross a tempestuous sea like the Mediterranean. I tried to give Alaric my counsel, but he rebuffed me.

It wasn't just that he regarded me as a privileged and vacuous woman lacking the mental faculties of men. It was also that I made him uncomfortable, for I reminded him of someone he didn't want to think about. I reminded him of his long lost wife.

About a week after we departed Rome, Alaric informed me of a messenger he had sent to my brother wherein he announced his intentions. He knew Honorius didn't have an army large enough to stop us, and so he was heading to Africa to seize our grain supply. He knew, as our enemies have known throughout history, and as the vile Vandals know today, that severing Rome from its grain supply does more damage to us than sacking and looting. He said as much in his message to Honorius, lamenting that, as the sack of our ancient capital and the stripping of its wealth had not been enough to bring him to his senses, he would now unleash the ultimate depredation – he would starve the people of Rome, which would turn them against their emperor.

Alaric was confident Honorius would now be forced to grant the concessions he demanded, and as a result I would be returned to Rome. I told him I didn't share his optimism. He was astonished by my candor and seemed to consider it a case of girlish fecklessness on my part, as if in telling him this I had unwittingly opened myself up to be taken and enslaved, not realizing that if my brother refused to cooperate, my value to the Goths was next to nothing. I did realize it, of course, and saw no advantage in refusing to acknowledge it. But Alaric could not see me as anything other than a silly young woman, and he read my attempts at candor as naiveté.

He put a hand on my thigh and issued a warning. If Honorius did not give him the answer he wanted, he would come and see me. I told him he was a man who could have any woman he wanted but would find he got more than he bargained for if he tried to force himself on me. I reminded him that I had been brought up in the house of Stilicho, the significance of which failed to register with him. He put his hand between my thighs and leaned in, coming within inches of my face. I could feel his hot breath and see the hunger in his gaze. He told me he would have me. I told him I knew his wife.

He snatched his hand away and stood up. He started to leave the room but then swung around and looked at me like I was something curious and potentially dangerous. The question he wanted to ask was written all over his face.

"I was brought up in the house of Stilicho," I explained. "She was our slave."

He didn't want to believe me at first, but he knew it made perfect sense. Stilicho had taken Alaric's wife prisoner after the battle of Pollentia, along with hundreds of other high-level Goths. Her capture and enslavement undoubtedly saved her life during Honorius's purge of the Gothic federates. That Stilicho would have taken her into his household to keep her safe was not only a recognition of her value to him as a hostage but also a measure of his respect for his rival.

"We always treated her with decency and respect," I said. "We treated her the way we would've wanted to be treated in the same circumstances." My meaning was not lost on him.

"You speak of her in the past tense," he noted with undisguised apprehension.

I nodded slowly, sadly. "It was an accident," I said. "She was out riding during a thunderstorm and was thrown from her horse."

"She was permitted to ride?"

"Like I said, we treated her the way we would've wanted to be treated."

He took a moment to absorb this.

"Stilicho respected you," I explained. "He always considered you a worthy adversary. He treated your wife like a hostage, not like a conquest. He was good to her." I didn't tell him she had grown so despondent in her captivity that she had taken her own life.

He looked me over as if trying to decipher me. The sadness in his eyes was unmistakable.

Later, when I went to speak to him about the sailors, he refused to see me. My familiarity with the plight of his wife had brought up a pain he didn't want to revisit. Consequently, the Goths kept blundering along in their treatment *of the sailors, and as a result, their plans were put at risk.*

You might think I was sanguine about this, but I was not. If the Goth's failed to cross the Mediterranean, nothing could be brought to a head, which meant nothing lay ahead for us but months of wandering the Italian countryside, burning and pillaging, just more waste and misery.

Sometimes, Placidius, you must consider the unthinkable. Yes, losing access to the grain supply would have been a terrible hardship — as we have come to find out — but Alaric was not Genseric[5] and the Goths were not the Vandals. Alaric was not looking to establish a separate kingdom of his own on Roman soil. All he ever wanted was to live peaceably within the confines of our borders, undisturbed by threats of expulsion, and to serve in our defense. Had he gone to Africa, he would have used the situation to force Honorius's hand. Once he had gotten what he wanted, the grain shipments to Rome would have resumed.

But the Goths were never going to make it across the Mediterranean unless they could enlist willing sailors, and they were going about it all wrong.

Alaric might have been out of reach to me, but Ataulf, the brother of his wife, was within reach. Ever since our first encounter in Rome he had been sneaking looks at me. He thought he was being crafty, but I knew he had feelings for me, and it gave me an idea.

One day when I was down by the river, I caught sight of him watching me from behind some bushes. I took off my clothes and waded into the water. I stood waist deep, turning this way and that, stretching up to wash my hair and bending over to rub my ankles. I gave him quite a show. That night I sent him a message requesting to see him. He wasted no time in granting it.

---

5. Pronounced gehn-sir-ick

We met alone in his tent. He was sitting on a bench, whittling a branch into the shape of a wolf. He could carve figures into wood or chisel rocks into the most exquisite shapes. His talent was remarkable. He kept the flap of the tent closed, even though it was sweltering inside. He told me to sit down. Although it was meant as a command, it came out as a request. There was always something timid and deferential about Ataulf. Even when he intended to be authoritative, he came across as obliging. I suppose it was a weakness in him, but I always found it endearing.

I told him they could not keep mistreating the sailors if they expected to get to Africa. I explained the complexities of sailing. I told him they would have to establish a kindred feeling among the sailors if they expected to get their cooperation, and they would have to pay them.

To his credit, Ataulf didn't reject my advice out of hand but listened attentively. At first, I thought he was trying to flatter me, but I soon realized he was genuinely interested in my opinion. He had been impressed by my candor in endorsing their plan to cross to Africa, even though Alaric had dismissed it as a ploy to win better treatment. And he had interpreted my betrayal of Emilius not as a weak-willed attempt to save my own skin but as a tactical measure as impressive in its efficiency as it was coldblooded. He had read me accurately. But there was something he wanted to know. He set aside the figure he was carving, but he kept the knife in his lap.

"Is it true that you knew Alaric's wife?"

I told him it was.

"You said she was well treated."

"As far as I know."

His brows lifted. "As far as you know?"

"I didn't know her intimately. We were not confidantes. She was a slave. I am a princess."

He said, "If I were captured and hauled before Honorius, and he were to ask about your well-being, I could say, 'I was a general and she was a hostage. I didn't know her intimately.'"

"Which would be true."

"Whether you were mistreated or not."

I gave him a friendly smile. "I have been treated quite well, as you know."

"Do I?" he asked.

"You do now, as I just told you."

He smirked. "My brother-in-law doesn't trust you," he said. "You're the sister of his enemy."

"And what about you? How do you feel about me?"

"I find you interesting," he said. "But I suppose you already knew that."

"Yes."

"You realize, of course, that if it were purely a physical attraction, I could take you right now."

"You could," I said. "But then what would you say to Honorius about how you treated me?"

"I'm not worried about that."

"Maybe you should be."

"I'm not going to hurt you," he said. "You're my insurance."

"I'm your hostage."

"And potentially more."

This surprised me. "I don't understand."

"You know things. You're not stupid. And you're right about the sailors. I can see that."

"But you're worried about my motives."

"Maybe. A little. But there's a bigger problem." He leaned forward, setting the knife on the table between us. "We can't pay the sailors because we have no money. We're bankrupt."

Ataulf was always full of surprises. From the very first, he kept me guessing. It was one of the things I loved most about him. But he caught me flat-footed with this one. How could the Goths be bankrupt? They had just finished stripping Rome of its treasures, not to mention extorting a huge cache of gold and silver from the Senate. They should have been rich beyond imagining, but Ataulf claimed they were broke. How could this be?

Ataulf explained: Among the Goths it is customary for soldiers to keep what they loot. To try to extract it from them without their permission would be viewed as theft and provoke insurrection. As for the gold and silver the Senate had provided as a ransom, the Goths no longer had it. Alaric had sent it back to Honorius as a precondition for reopening negotiations. Alaric was awaiting his answer.

I thought it was foolish for Alaric to have done so and said as much. Ataulf agreed and admitted he wouldn't have done it, but Alaric felt he had more than enough leverage with the Emperor's sister as a hostage and with the threat to the grain supply they posed. The thing was, Alaric desperately wanted to restart the negotiations and felt he was within striking distance of winning the concessions he demanded.

"And yet there is no answer from Honorius," I said.

"Not yet."

"Not ever."

Ataulf's brow creased. "But we are threatening your grain supply and holding you hostage."

"Honorius has spies. He knows your situation. He has no confidence in your ability to cross the Mediterranean. He'll wait to see if you can do it before he concedes anything."

"And what about you? Has he no concern for the safety of his sister?"

I looked him straight in the eyes. He really had the most extraordinary green eyes. "Tell me something," I said. "You admitted you would not have done as Alaric did. Why not?"

"Because I am not as confident of the leverage we have."

"And why is that?"

Here Ataulf faltered, so I helped him. "It's because my brother never asked for my return as a precondition for reopening negotiations, and you found that curious."

"That's right," Ataulf said.

"You are right to lack confidence in my value to my brother. I am nothing to him, a mere ornament, at best, which means my value to you as a hostage is negligible. As for your threat to the grain supply, that depends entirely on your ability to get to Africa. Failing that, you've got nothing. But I have a plan for getting the sailors to work for you. Would you like to hear it?"

Ataulf picked the knife up off the table and slid it into its sheath. "Go ahead."

From that moment forward we were partners.

As you look at it now, you may consider my actions treasonous. You would not be the first one to accuse me of betraying the Empire. But to this day few have really appreciated my purposes, neither my accusers nor my defenders. The standard explanation offered by those who defend me is that I was a hostage and was forced to do it — not entirely true. To some degree, I acted out of self-preservation, but my primary motivation was to rescue the Empire from the reckless obstinacy of Honorius and the fools who advised him.

At this point the Goths had been laying waste to the Empire for thirty years. Fighting them had been a drain on our economy and a dangerous distraction. It had kept us from responding decisively to uprisings and incursions across the realm. My brother's refusal to give them what they wanted had made us weak and vulnerable. If the Sack of Rome were not enough to drive the point home, the threat to the grain supply should have brought Honorius to the bargaining table, but instead he took the money he demanded as a prerequisite to begin negotiations and stonewalled again. At that point, my duty to Rome became unmoored from my allegiance to the Emperor.

Certainly, Honorius was not alone in his selfish disregard for the people he ruled. There were those who encouraged him in his conviction that Rome and the Emperor were one and that as long as he remained safe, the Empire would prevail. Among those sycophants was Olympius, the court minister who was instrumental in persuading Honorius to eliminate Stilicho and undertake the massacre of the wives and children of the Gothic federates. A stronger man would have rejected such idiocy, but Honorius's stubbornness, combined with his insecurities, made him an easy mark for those who sought to control him.

If you take anything from this, Placidius, take this. Do not become a tool in the hands of others. Keep your most ardent supporters at a distance. Let them think they know your intentions while keeping your purposes secret. Never be fooled by flattery. Know the difference between those with agendas meant to advance you and those seeking to subvert you. Know your enemies better than you know your friends. Never shun them. To do so is arrogance. If an opportunity arises to know them intimately, take it. For the man who knows his enemies is the most powerful man in the Empire and should be.

With Ataulf's support I went to the sailors and urged them to cooperate. I assured them there would be no more punishments and vowed they would be rewarded once we got to Africa. This last part I won as a concession from Ataulf who was at some pains to extract it from Alaric. They both knew that if they reached Africa they would once again be in a position to demand a ransom. The sailors, obedient to the will of their princess and trusting in my assurances, complied. They went out and rounded up their fellows, and within a fortnight we had a fleet of ships manned and ready to sail.

But the whole episode had taken too long. By the time we got to sea it was early autumn and a storm had rolled in. The sailors were all for turning back, but Alaric insisted we keep going. Impatience was his greatest weakness. Time and again, what Alaric could have won with a measure of forbearance he squandered by impetuosity. This time, however, there was something else driving him. He had fallen ill and feared he would not live long enough to see the accomplishment of his ambitions.

The sailors sailed into the teeth of a mounting tempest. The seas tossed the ships. Three were sunk. Hundreds of soldiers and sailors drowned. In the course of the storm, I was swept overboard and would have gone under were it not for Ataulf's valiant effort to save me. He cinched a rope around his waist, tied the other end to the mast, and dove in. The waves rose up around him and sent him crashing into the troughs. He kept pin-wheeling his arms in a furious rotation, digging for all he was worth, going under for long periods of time, until I thought I had lost him, only to pop up again, still swimming.

At length he reached me and took me around the waist. I wrapped my arms around him. Then he grabbed hold of the rope and began to haul us hand over hand back toward the ship. It was an amazing demonstration of his strength and a clear indication of how much he cared for me. I was touched, and when he smiled at me, I smiled back at him warmly, letting him know the depth of my gratitude.

When at last the storm abated, the fleet was in ruins. The remaining ships limped back to Calabria where we remained for several weeks while Alaric's condition worsened. Despite the best efforts of his physicians, the disease could not be vanquished and by the end of the month Alaric died, having fallen short of his ambitions.

Ambitions, Placidius. To perish before we achieve them is a great tragedy. For a man like Alaric, whose ambitions were so far-reaching and who had advanced so far in achieving them only to fall short in the end, it was doubly tragic. For those left behind whose own ambitions paled by comparison, it seemed only appropriate to subordinate their own wills to those of their fallen king and carry his mission forward. Their selflessness moved me.

Among the Gothic people, it is a pagan custom to bury their king in a riverbed, and although Alaric had been an avowed Christian for most of his life, this custom was undertaken.

Let me tell you, it is no mean feat to bury a man in the bed of a river. First, the river must be diverted, which means digging a diversionary channel deep and wide enough to carry the flow. The burial itself requires a grave sufficiently deep to keep the river from disinterring the body. Lastly, the river must be returned to its original channel after the burial. For weeks, the surviving soldiers poured themselves into this grueling task. I was so impressed by their perseverance I lent a hand.

I was sunk to the calves in the bed of the river, digging with a long-handled shovel, sweat coursing down my brow, my palla streaked with dirt and mud, when I chanced to look up and see Ataulf regarding me from a distance. He smiled a smile of such openhearted gratitude I couldn't help but smile back. Later he came to me and presented me with a gift: a pair of men's trousers. He told me he was aware that such attire was looked down upon by well-to-do Romans, and in particular was never worn by women, but that if I was going to get down in the dirt with the common laborers, I might as well dress the part. We had a good laugh. I did wear the trousers, and I was glad to do it.

While I am on the subject of dress, I should say I still had the amulet given to me by Emilius in Rome. It stayed near my heart always. Even when I was swept overboard and nearly drowned, the amulet stayed with me. As I said before, there was something magical about it, and I often prayed over it, lifting my heart to God, seeking His guidance as I held it in my hands. It became one of my most cherished possessions.

After Alaric's death, the Goths gathered to elect a new king. This they did by a vote of all the men of the tribe. It was a foregone conclusion Ataulf would be nominated, but he was not without his challengers. To improve his chances, a group of his supporters came to me and asked for my endorsement. The esteem in which the Gothic people held me might seem curious given my status as a hostage, but it underscores the fact that they were never really our enemies. All they ever really wanted was a seat at the table. They could have been good friends and allies, for they admired us and sought to emulate us.

I made my endorsement, and Ataulf was elected. Later, he came to me and asked me why I had done it. "Is it only your contempt for your brother that drives you, or is there something else?"

I could see what he was getting at, but I wasn't yet ready to make my feelings known to him. I carefully considered how to respond. I could have told him it was because he had saved me from the tempest, or I could have said it was because he had trusted me enough to take my advice about the sailors, but I told him neither of those things.

Instead, I simply said, "I have come to recognize the value of a good man, even if he was not born a Roman."

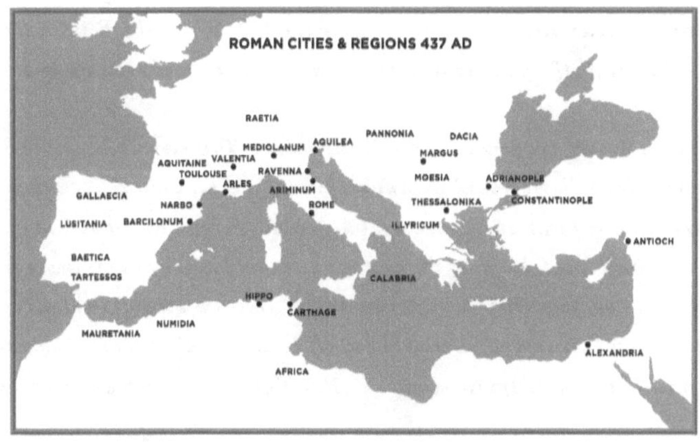

Chapter Five

Tragically, the Goths' inability to reach Africa threw them back upon the land. They pillaged the southern Italian peninsula for weeks. They plundered what they needed to survive, an expedient that filled me with sadness as this was my country and I should have been looking to its defense.

But I was in no position to stop them, and the Goths needed to do something to feed their people. Ravenna had fallen silent on the question of negotiations. No doubt those in power had heard of the Goth's failure to reach Africa, and of Alaric's demise. They were almost certainly assembling an army to march on us and trap us in the southern peninsula while we were weak and desperate.

What could be done?

Making another attempt on Africa was out of the question. The fleet had been battered to pieces. Repairing and refitting would take months. Besides, the sailors had run off again. To survive, we were going to have to escape by land.

I met with Ataulf, the new king, to offer my advice. To his credit, he didn't view me cynically as Alaric would have done, but trusted my counsel, even though by any measure I was still his enemy. I urged him to head for Gaul – to travel north with all speed, hugging the western coast, and staying as far away from Ravenna as possible. Distance was imperative. Once we were off the Italian peninsula and into Gaul, we could head off in any number of directions and frustrate Rome's attempt to pursue us. Ataulf agreed, and we moved at once.

But Honorius didn't send troops to pursue us, and for good reason. Gaul was in turmoil again and he had been forced to dispatch the bulk of his army north and west to deal with it. Thus, our flight up the coast went unimpeded. However, without knowing it, we were running straight into trouble.

You may recall how I told you earlier about Constantine III, that upstart Roman soldier who got himself proclaimed emperor in Britannia, then crossed the channel into Gaul and marched south, peeling off support from Honorius along the way until he had an army large enough to compel your uncle to recognize him as co-emperor. Well, as astonishing was his ascent, so was his downfall.

The problem with being a usurper is that your success demonstrates the ease with which the thing can be done and encourages others to try it too. Hence, no sooner was Constantine III granted the status of co-emperor by Honorius than he was forced to deal with an uprising among his commanders. The uprising was put down, but the commander sent to suppress it made an alliance with the Franks against his emperor, and, before he knew it, Constantine III was facing a rebellion. Fearing that the bulk of his forces had gone over to his rival, Constantine III decided it would be easier to topple Honorius than face his challenger, so he marched on Ravenna but was repulsed and fell back on Arelate[1] where he was caught between Honorius's army on the one hand, and the army of his former commander on the other. He was defeated, captured, and executed.

It was this diversion of military resources that permitted us to move up the Italian coast unimpeded. But by the time we crossed over into Gaul the disorder had entered a new phase. Yet another uprising was taking place, this one from a body of troops formerly loyal to Constantine III and led by a Gallic nobleman named Jovinus. Jovinus blamed the chaos afflicting the Empire on the ineptitude of Honorius and was determined to overthrow him. He made common cause with the rebel commander who had ousted Constantine III and together they engaged the Roman troops sent to Gaul by Honorius.

Of course, all this time Honorius was safely ensconced in his palace at Ravenna, some 500 miles away from the fighting, but we were close by. Having crossed the border, we found ourselves less than 150 miles from the battlefront. News of our arrival there was carried to Jovinus who wasted no time in dispatching an emissary to enlist us. At the time we numbered more than 5,000, many of us women and children, but there were more than 2,000 battle hardened soldiers among us, a force large enough to tip the scales in the rebels' favor.

Ataulf was inclined to accept their offer, reasoning that, if the rebels prevailed, they would install a new emperor on the throne of the West, someone more amenable to the Goth's demands. But there were no guarantees, and the situation was so volatile it was just as likely the coalition would split apart and the component parts would turn against each other. If that happened, I could end up the hostage of some other army – one less inclined to treat me kindly.

---

1. Modern day Arles in France

I went to Ataulf with an idea. I told him Honorius had never been willing to negotiate even-handedly with the Goths because Alaric had never been willing to demonstrate his loyalty to Rome. I suggested a potential opening existed with Emperor Honorius if Ataulf, as the newly elected Gothic king, would demonstrate his loyalty by an act of allegiance.

"An act of allegiance?"

"Yes, for example, if you were to kill Jovinus."

Ataulf studied me carefully. "If I didn't know any better, I would say you were trying to save your own skin. After all we've been through together, do you still doubt my determination to keep you from harm?"

The declaration of love hidden behind his words was not lost on me, but I also recognized the harsh reality we were facing. If he died and I was taken prisoner, what difference would it make how much he cared for me? We needed a plan. We could not sit around and wait for events to overtake us.

I was not at all confident of what I was telling him. Nothing Honorius had ever done suggested that killing Jovinus would earn the Goths anything but more of the same , but it seemed worth a chance. I pressed Ataulf to give it a try.

He was unconvinced. "Why not just join the rebels and take our share of the spoils when Honorius goes down?"

"Two reasons," I said. "First, Jovinus cannot be trusted. He's already proven that by changing sides twice. Can there be any doubt he would do it again if it suited him? And second, I am a daughter of the House of Theodosius, and I don't want to see the dynasty my father established destroyed by my brother. If we act in good faith and help him defeat the rebels, I believe we can win his gratitude."

Ataulf scratched his chin and thought it over. "And what if we do all this and your brother the emperor still refuses to negotiate?"

"Send him Jovinus's head as a gesture of goodwill. If you do this and he still refuses you, I'll make an appeal on your behalf. Together we can persuade him. I'm sure of it."

At first, he seemed doubtful, but then his eyes fell on the amulet, and when he lifted them again, he was of a different frame of mind. He smiled and said, "You are my little fox, Galla Placidia, nimble and quick. I will do as you advise."

He had put his faith in me, but I had betrayed him, for I had no confidence that killing Jovinus would achieve anything worthwhile.

To implement his plan Ataulf pretended to go along with the rebels' request for an alliance, and together they took the battle to Rome, but at the last moment, when the rebels were back on their heels and at their most vulnerable, Ataulf withdrew. The rebels were routed and put to flight, whereupon he pursued them all the way to Valentia[2] where he trapped them in the town and put them under siege. Three weeks later, beaten down and half starved, they sought terms. Ataulf demanded they hand over Jovinus as a condition of surrender. They did, and Ataulf cut off his head.

A week later Jovinus's severed head turned up at the port of Narbo at the headquarters of the urban prefect with a note from the Gothic King saying he had performed this service on the Emperor's behalf. Then Ataulf waited for Honorius's response.

Weeks went by. Let me tell you, no one was more anxious during those weeks than I. If Honorius disappointed the Goths again, I would lose all credibility with Ataulf and might even be seen as a traitor by that good and decent man who had put so much faith in me.

At long last, the answer came, but it was not what I expected. Honorius acknowledged the service done for him by the Gothic King and was prepared to reward him by welcoming his best fighters into the Roman army as federates, with Ataulf as their commanding officer. It was a slap in the face.

I went to Ataulf with a heavy heart. I told him I was prepared to follow through on the promise I'd made. I would make an appeal to the Emperor on his behalf.

Ataulf shook his head. He wouldn't hear of it. To endorse the Gothic cause would mark me as a traitor among my own people. I would never be able to return to Rome with my chin up. We argued about it, and, as we did, Ataulf's chief lieutenant Wallia burst in full of bluster and demanded we answer the Emperor's insult by laying siege to the port at Narbo. Ataulf rejected this out of hand and Wallia stormed out. The situation was growing more tense by the moment. Even so, Ataulf would not allow me to risk my reputation. "Instead," he said, "I will make another gesture of good will toward your brother, one that will prove to him how sincere I am in my devotion. I will release you."

I was stunned. My sudden liberation, without a corresponding demand, would send a ringing message of acquiescence to Honorius that could hardly be mistaken for anything other than complete submission. But would my brother accept it?

Ataulf was taking a huge risk. By giving me up, he was surrendering the best bargaining chip he had. Should it yield him nothing, it would call into question his leadership and invite rebellion. I would not let him put his reign at risk. Besides, I didn't want to leave him. I could see his offer of liberation was more than a strategic consideration. He was in love with me and he wanted to give me the one thing he thought I wanted more than anything. But I surprised him.

"I'm not going back," I said. "Even if you release me, I won't leave you. I'm

staying here with you so we can finish the job we started."

His face lit up, for he had read my words as they were intended, as a reciprocation of the affection he had shown me. He approached me in the soft glow of the brazier and took me in his arms.

"Little fox," he said. "You never cease to amaze me. Every time I think I know you, you show me still greater depths. You have conquered my heart." Then he kissed me.

Oh, Placidius, I know what you have been told about my marriage to Ataulf, that I was forced into it against my will, that I resisted him with every fiber of my being but was overcome by violence. But nothing could be farther from the truth. In all my life, I have only ever loved one person as much as I loved Ataulf, and no man was ever as kind to me as he.

As I look back, I am reminded of how close I came to marrying a man I didn't love, back when Stilicho wanted me to marry Eucherius. Had I done so I would have missed the experience of knowing true love and been left wondering what it was. But Stilicho asked me to marry Eucherius for a reason, a reason that had nothing to do with endearment. At the time, Honorius had been stubbornly refusing to produce an heir. By marrying Eucherius, the succession would've been ensured, and the House of Theodosius would have carried on, no matter what Honorius did.

You see, since then nothing much had changed. Honorius had divorced Thermantia the moment Stilicho was dead and from then on he had contented himself with whores and concubines and made no attempt to marry again. Thus, I was still the Western Empire's best chance of producing an heir, but my marriage to Ataulf introduced a whole new dynamic, something I waited until my wedding night to reveal to him.

I patiently explained to him that under the Roman rules of succession if the

Emperor failed to produce an heir the offspring of his sibling would be the next in line for the throne. Ataulf was astounded.

"Are you saying what I think you're saying?"

"If you give me a son, the Emperor will have no choice but to negotiate with you, because your child will be his successor."

Ataulf lowered his head into his hands.

"It's true," I told him.

When he looked up, he was grinning.

"But what about the Roman people? Won't they object? Won't they see the birth of our child as something akin to a foreign invasion?"

"Some will," I said. "But others will see it as a way to avoid the ongoing civil strife Honorius threatens them with. No one wants another civil war. The birth of a son between us establishes a clear line of succession and promises an end to the conflict between the Goths and the Romans. It offers security and stability, which means most Romans will welcome it."

"Really?" he asked.

"Yes, " I said.

He made a whoop of laughter and caught me up in his arms.

When the news spread through the camp, there was cheering and rejoicing. Not only would the Goths finally get the recognition they deserved, but within a generation they would be co-equals with the Romans. My act of selfless generosity, born out of love for their king, had liberated them, and I had become an object of reverence. Even dour Wallia bowed down before me and pledged his devotion.

But all was not sunshine and rainbows. There were among the Goths a dynastic clan who hated Ataulf and resented his leadership. These were the Amali, a rival house to the house of Balti from which Ataulf was descended. The Amali believed they were the legitimate rulers of the Goths and that the Balti had usurped their birthright. Following the death of Alaric, they campaigned to have their chief elected to the kingship, a man named Sigeric[3] , but my endorsement tipped the scales in Ataulf's favor, and from that day forward Sigeric was my enemy.

I don't know how he learned about it — quite possibly Priscus Attalus shared it with him at some point before his execution — but Sigeric knew what I had done to Serena, and he was prepared to use it against me when the time was right. He revealed it to me in the midst of the marriage celebrations and warned me not to get too comfortable, for I would not be Queen of the Goths for long.

Ah, Serena, even in death she haunted me. I could not forget what I had done to her.

I have thus far withheld this regrettable episode from you, Placidius, lest you think me cruel, but I will relate it to you now, for you cannot really know me until you know what I did to her. It is something that makes me heartsick to this day. But I had to do it...for the good of the Empire.

---

3. Pronounced si-je-rick

Back then, back in the days before the Gothic sack, when the idea that I might one day be taken hostage by the Goths would have seemed ludicrous, I was forced to contend with a crisis of a different sort. We were residing at Stilicho's villa outside Rome, Serena, the servants, and me, about thirty of us altogether, when we got news of Stilicho's execution. It was overwhelming.

Serena immediately went into hysterics. She was certain the Emperor would be sending soldiers to murder us. The notion was absurd. My brother was shallow and resentful, but he was not so petty as to concern himself with two women he considered beneath his consideration, not when he was busy teaching the Goths a lesson by ruthlessly massacring their wives and children.

Honorius had always regarded me as little more than an afterthought, more of an adornment to his imperial presence than a real sister. It was a good thing I was considered attractive, or I would have been banished to some distant place and forgotten. As it was, I was summoned to court once or twice a year to stand by his side for the opening of some festival or function. He barely even spoke to me on those occasions.

We were not full-blooded siblings. He and Arcadius were born of my father's first wife. I was born of his second. My mother, Galla, was the daughter of Emperor Valentinian I. My mother's half-brother was Emperor Gratian. I had a stronger imperial lineage than either of my brothers, but it hardly mattered. I was a girl, and they were boys, and so I was relegated to the role of a bauble, an ornament to be passed around and admired.

Even when we were children, we were not close, this in spite of the fact that were brought up under the same roof for a brief period of time. On the death of my father, Stilicho was awarded the guardianship of all three of us as per my father's wish, but Arcadius was already eighteen and was immediately sent to Constantinople to assume his role as Emperor of the East. Honorius was ten and took up residence with us at Stilicho's villa where he lived in separate quarters adjacent to our own. Mostly he kept to himself, a sullen, peevish boy, chafing under the parental authority of our appointed guardian.

I have only dim memories of our time together as a family there. Once, when Honorius was twelve, Stilicho threw a lavish birthday party for him. I remember it because there were jugglers and acrobats and musicians and clowns and many sweet things to eat. A great many dignitaries came to pay homage, but Honorius only made a brief appearance, frowning and morose, as if the whole thing were a tiresome imposition.

Being impressionable, I formed the idea that all young men of aristocratic upbringing behaved in this way. Eucherius, who was a friendly, open-hearted boy, didn't really count in my mind because we were the same age and neither of us had yet learned to act properly. It wasn't until some years later when a young aristocrat of great promise, a boy of fourteen, came to stay with us, that I saw how courteous and sociable a young man could be. Perhaps that's the reason I became so infatuated with the new arrival, and he became the idealization of young manhood in my mind, the one I dreamed of and longed for.

In any case, Honorius and I were never close, and when I learned that he had ordered the death of Stilicho, I grew to despise him. My hostility only deepened when I learned he had orchestrated the massacre of the wives and children of the

Gothic federates. Even an eighteen-year-old girl with no practical knowledge of the politics could see that such a thing could only make things worse, as indeed it did. It goaded Alaric on to his second invasion of Italia, which put us under direct threat at the villa and drove Serena into fits of hysterics. We had to escape, or risk being taken prisoner by the Goths.

I rounded up our collective household, the servants and slaves, and informed them that we were heading to Rome to seek refuge with the Senate. Rumors swirled: Araminum had been sacked, the Goths were heading south in great numbers, straight toward us. Serena was panicked at the idea of being exposed on the open road where she feared we might be waylaid and molested by bandits. I told her that remaining at the villa was much more dangerous. She wept and plowed her fingers through her hair. I ignored her and prepared for our departure.

We left the villa and arrived in Rome in late autumn. The city was frantically preparing its defenses. Honorius had done nothing to confront the Goths or impede their progress. They were approaching rapidly and were reckoned to be less than a week away. I asked for an audience with the Senate, and it was granted.

The men of the Senate were uncertain how to respond. They didn't have the military resources in Rome to repel the Goths, and, short of an army sent from Ravenna, they were defenseless. Some favored laying down their arms and asking for terms, but most considered it inconceivable Rome could be sacked. After all, it hadn't happened in 800 years. Surely, the Emperor would send troops to protect us.

I was not so optimistic and said so. Naturally, there were those among the senators who resented my candor. There are always those who would rather cling to some outmoded idea of their exceptionalism than face the facts. Rome had always been invincible. It would continue to be so. They were sure of it. Ironically, the one thing they needed in that moment to save them was a measure of humility, something to give them a clear-eyed view of the situation, but humility was not in their skill set.

Yet, although they were not willing to face facts, they were willing to indulge in fantasies. A certain group of senators, those most insistent on Rome's infallibility, were pagans. Sure, they wore all the outward trappings of being Christians and went to mass and donated to the Church, but when the Goths gathered outside the walls and put the city under siege, they reverted to their old pagan ways. They insisted this terrible thing had happened because the gods who had protected our ancestors for centuries – Jupiter Juno, Apollo and the like – were offended and must be appeased.

At first, Pope Innocent was appalled by their request, but as the Goths settled into the siege and no sign of help was forthcoming from Ravenna, he yielded. I thought the whole idea was absurd, and I told them so. They grew even more annoyed with me and asked me why I had not returned to Ravenna when my brother had summoned me.

How they knew about the summons was obvious. Serena had told them. In her anxiety, she had let it slip. I began to realize she was a liability, and I was going to have to deal with her if I was going to survive this.

The real reason I remained in Rome in defiance of my brother's summons was the prospect of being rescued by my beloved. The young man who had come to stay with us at the villa when I was a girl — the boy I had fallen in love with — had been a hostage of the Goths since the hostage exchange orchestrated by Stilicho after the Battle of Pollentia. There was every reason to believe he was still among them. If we could open negotiations with the Goths, I could speak directly to him, and we could work out a solution. I was sure of it. But first I was going to have to work around the intransigence of those ridiculous pagans in the Senate.

The weeks dragged on, and the Goths tightened their grip. They took control of the Tiber River and cut off the food supply to the city. The people began to starve. I met with Priscus Attalus and we came up with a proposal. I met with a small group of senators and told them I knew a young Roman who was being held as a hostage by the Goths. If I could contact him, we could reach an accommodation with the enemy. I urged them to send an envoy.

The senators agreed we would ultimately have to offer terms, but they worried that if we acted in haste, the conservative coalition, which was still hoping for the intervention of the gods, could paint us as disloyal. They wanted to wait for further justification.

I failed to see how being slowly starved to death was not justification enough, but they would not hear of it – not yet. Worse yet, there were some among them who could not keep their mouths shut. Word of our meeting leaked out. Soon it was being bruited about that a small group of senators led by the princess Galla Placidia were seeking accommodation with the Goths. This was very dangerous, for if we were to be liberated by Ravenna and this came to light, we could be accused of high treason.

I met privately with Priscus Attalus to discuss it, and he agreed we would have to find some way to deflect suspicion from ourselves.

Later, Serena came to my room. She was distraught. She had heard the rumors. She was worried that if we remained in Rome the Goths would overrun the city and slaughter us.

"Oh, this is it, Galla!" she cried. "I had a premonition some horrible fate would befall us. This is the fulfillment of the curse put upon me by the Vestal Virgin. If we remain here, Rome will be destroyed, and we will be murdered."

She fell to the ground at my feet and begged me not to seal her fate. She was shaking and blubbering and clawing at my stola. I shoved her away.

"Get up!" I snapped. "Stop being so weak. The Goths will not hurt us if we compensate them for their clemency."

"Compensate them for their clemency! Oh, please don't talk of buying them off. They are beasts. They will take our money and kill us. Can't you see that?"

At that moment I'd had enough. She was irrational and wild. She would certainly report my words to the Senate, and if we got out of this alive, she would undoubtedly inform Honorius as well, not because she wished me ill, mind you, but because she was being slowly driven mad by her own imagination.

The next day I went to Priscus Attalus and laid out my plans for dealing with her. He was astonished at my coldheartedness, but he didn't try to dissuade me.

We went to the Senate and reported what we had heard. We told them Serena, whose instability was well known, was hysterical and had reached out to the Goths and begged them to have mercy on her. Using the influence of her station, she had promised to open the gates to them if they would not kill her. It was a complete fabrication, but entirely believable. We accused Serena of treason, a crime punishable by death.

Here, in accordance with a script worked out in advance, Priscus Attalus made a plea for mercy in consideration of Serena's disturbed mental state. As the Senate talked it over, I stood up and called for the sentence to be carried out, arguing that our precarious position made us vulnerable to betrayal from every side, and if the Senate were to take pity on Serena, others would see it as permission to ignore the authority of the state and reach out to the Goths. Much as it broke my heart, an example would have to be made with her. Then I turned aside and wept.

My tears were not false. Serena had been the closest thing to a mother I had ever had, and she had always been the kindest and gentlest of souls, but she had become a liability and had to be dealt with.

Despite the tragedy of the situation, my plea to the Senate had a beneficial effect. All suspicions against me vanished. No one could square the rumors of my disloyalty with the image of me standing before the Senate calling for the execution of the woman who had raised me. Overnight I went from being the most untrustworthy person in Rome to the most respected. Under the circumstances, everyone had to make sacrifices, but I had made the greatest of all.

When the executioner was dispatched to carry out his duty, I insisted on going with him. It is too easy to execute people when you are in a position of power. And if you don't feel any revulsion toward it, it makes it easier still. Divorcing yourself from the act keeps you from experiencing the repugnance you should feel. If you must execute someone it, Placidius, face it. Get as close to it as you can. Intimacy will prevent it from becoming a habit with you.

When we entered the room, Serena instantly recognized what was about to happen. Her face went white. She pressed her hands to her mouth and wailed. The executioner carried no weapon; he intended to strangle her. When he stepped forward to grab her, she dodged around him and ran for the door. I hindered her long enough to let him catch her. She was still fumbling at the latch, weeping hysterically, when he took her around the waist and hauled her back. She kicked and thrashed wildly. She bit him, smearing her teeth with blood like some feral beast. He struck her with his fist and knocked her to the floor. He tried to climb on top of her, but she wriggled free. She staggered to her feet and flung herself at me, eyes wild with terror. I pushed her away. I will never forget the pain and horror in that expression.

He caught her up again and threw her down. This time her head struck the floor, and she was stunned. He crawled on top of her and put his hands around her throat. She bucked and writhed. His grip tightened. She began to gag. He bore down on her, teeth clenched. Her eyes bulged. She fought frantically. The last thing she saw in this world was the girl she had raised, the closest thing she had ever had to a daughter, standing over her with tears of regret in her eyes.

By degrees her thrashing subsided. She quivered once through her whole body and lay still.

It was awful. I would not wish the experience on anybody, but I did what I had to do. We can't let the weak take us down, Placidius. Sometimes we must be heartless and cruel, but never without a good reason. Serena had to be removed so the Empire could survive.

Now you know who I am. Now you know what I'm capable of.

Chapter Six

Placidius lowered the letter and gazed off into the distance. Then he picked it up again and scrutinized the characters. He knew nothing of his mother's hand. She routinely dictated her communications, so the size and shape of the characters told him nothing. If he had ever seen her handwriting, he could not remember it.

This could have been written by anyone, he thought. His skepticism about the author's identity had grown with every paragraph. The person depicted in it pages bore only the faintest resemblance to the woman he knew. Yes, Galla was shrewd, opportunistic, resilient, but she was not devious and unprincipled. On the contrary, she was a devout Christian who had devoted much of her life to the Church. The woman in the letter, by comparison, was a coldblooded killer.

And he wasn't buying the story of her joining forces with the Goths against her brother the Emperor. Family was important to her. She valued her lineage and viewed her gens[1] as noble. The Goths, on the other hand, were little more than animals, uncouth and ungovernable. They were not calm, reasonable people in search of redress for legitimate grievances. And he *knew* his mother had not willingly married Ataulf. She had been coerced into it, kidnapped, raped, and held against her will. She was the victim in this, not the Goths. Unbelievable!

---

1. A clan descended from the same ancestor

He craned around in his sedan chair and called for Cyrus. A few minutes later the young, sandy-haired fellow appeared astride a white horse. As always, he was grinning. The horse was a surprise.

"Where did you get it?" Placidius asked.

Cyrus leaned down and stroked the stallion's neck. "Remarkable, isn't it? It came to me in an inheritance."

"Really?"

"A distant uncle died, a retired military veteran who keeled over while tending his cabbages. What the Vandals couldn't kill, horticulture put under." His eyes twinkled, and he laughed with gleeful abandon. His laughter was contagious. The retainers and servants joined in. Even the Nubians who were bearing the sedan chair chortled.

Cyrus continued. "Unfortunately, he was an indifferent farmer," he said. "You might say he was reckless in policy, cultivating his enemies, planting the seeds of his own destruction."

Another whoop of laughter followed by an outburst of hilarity from the others.

Placidius looked for an opportunity to interrupt, but Cyrus kept going. "Still, he died with his dignity intact, my poor uncle. Yes, he succumbed to a superior foe. Nevertheless, the field was strewn with *the heads* of his enemies."

Shouts of laughter... knee slaps... guffaws.

Placidius grew impatient, but he didn't want to spoil the mood. He wanted the others to consider him a fellow traveler, not a stern, forbidding figure like Arsenius, whose surly attitude made his subordinates want to avoid him. He waited for the laughter to trail off, and then he tried asking his question again.

"This," he said, holding up the codex. "Where did it come from?"

Cyrus looked at it with a touch of suspicion.

"You told me Liberius gave it to you, but he claims never to have seen it. He claims it was intercepted by Arsenius before it ever got to him."

"Really? That seems peculiar."

"I thought so too. Did Liberius give it to you or not?"

"Well, earlier I could have sworn he did, but come to think of it, maybe it *was* Arsenius. I can't remember. There was a lot going on that day – you know, that was the day the scouts returned."

"So," Placidius said, "you're saying Arsenius probably gave you the letter?"

Cyrus shrugged. "It's possible."

"But you're not sure?"

"I'm only sure of one thing, and that's that I am not sure of anything." His eyes twinkled and he began to laugh.

This time, Placidius was not amused. "I'm beginning to think this letter is not what it appears to be. And now I can't get a straight answer about where it came from. Maybe there's been a lapse in my security. Maybe I should hold somebody accountable."

Cyrus's smile melted away. "Please, Imperator, I hope you will not blame poor Liberius when Arsenius was the one who prevented him from carrying out his duties?"

"Liberius should have reported any irregularities."

"But he could only have reported them to Arsenius."

"Or to you."

Cyrus hastened to absolve himself of any responsibility. "Liberius never came to me. The first time I heard about the letter was when it was already in your hands. I believe the problem lies with Arsenius, whose intimidating manner discourages open, honest communication. It's a problem, Imperator, and should be addressed."

He waited for Placidius's reaction.

Placidius stabbed at the letter with his finger. "My mother didn't write this, and I want to know who did. I'm beginning to think someone is trying to mislead me."

Something flickered behind Cyrus's eyes, wariness, or petulance, or maybe even culpability.

"Who would attempt anything so outrageous?"

"I don't know, but I intend to get to the bottom of it."

Cyrus sighed. "I'm sorry. All right. Maybe Arsenius gave it to me. I must have gotten confused; so many documents pass through my hands every day. You know how it is. But now that I think about it, yes. Arsenius gave it to me."

Placidius eyeballed him. "You seem to be getting confused, Cyrus. Maybe you ought to think less about cutting up and more about doing your duty."

Cyrus hung his head. "You're probably right, Imperator. I do tend to get carried away."

"Yes, you do."

"I'm sorry. I don't know what else to say. May I take my leave now?"

"You may go."

Cyrus reined his horse around. The mood had soured; a chilly awkwardness hung in the air. When Placidius looked around, the others ducked their heads or grew very interested in their belts. It was much better when everyone was laughing and joking, and he was sorry he had spoiled the mood, but some things could not be taken lightly.

He leaned back in his sedan chair and ordered his bearers to carry him forward. He settled the codex in his lap and resumed his reading. The next line seemed to speak directly to his present situation, almost as if whoever had ever written it was observing him and watching his reaction.

Your friends are rarely who you think they are, nor are your enemies as obvious as they seem. Truth be told, many spouses are enemies long before they are willing to acknowledge it, and on closer analysis, those who seem to be your enemies are often revealed to be striving for a state of affairs that, if it were achieved, would benefit you both. It is a matter of perspective. The leader of the Empire must know which is which, for the knife that is drawn for you will as likely strike you in the heart as in the back.

For my part, I've always measured the fidelity of others by their love for the Empire, not by their affection for me personally, nor by their dedication to our house, nor to the ideal of Roman virtues, nor to our laws or culture. None of rest of that matters if Rome is gone – and do not for a moment think it cannot happen.

Today we face a greater threat to our survival than we have ever known. In addition, we must deal with the incompetence of our brethren in Constantinople. It all adds up to a pivotal moment for us. Failure to distinguish our friends from our enemies could spell the end for Rome.

Grudges do not serve us. They only distract us from the needs of the moment. What's more, they keep us from recognizing opportunities. Honorius never understood that. He hated the Goths, not only because they had embarrassed him, but because they had caused so much trouble for our father when he was alive. He resented them for their invasion of Thrace nearly four decades before. He resented them for forcing him to recruit other barbarians to oppose them, which ultimately resulted in the elevation of the half-Vandal Stilicho to a position of such power it challenged his own. To Honorius, the Goths were the source of all our woes, and he wanted them destroyed.

But his grudge prevented him from seeing how they could help us. The Goths were steady and tenacious fighters, shrewd and perceptive. In addition, they were fiercely loyal. Had he enlisted them as allies, they would have bolstered our forces and strengthened our defenses. Together we could have built a bulwark against the myriad other barbarian tribes threatening to overwhelm us. Instead, he chose to hunt them to destruction. Even when the prospect of a half-Goth heir to the throne materialized, he would not give in.

I sent him word of my marriage to Ataulf and along with it a request for territory on which to settle. It was not too much to ask. As the newly wed princess of Rome, I was entitled to a dowry, and had I married a Roman, my request for land would have been granted at once. I asked for Narbo, not only because we were camped outside it, but because the Roman garrison there was weak and undermanned. By investing it with the Goths, we could have strengthened it. We could have turned it into a mighty port, a conduit to bring Roman men and arms into southern Gaul. I suggested as much in my letter, but my brother did not deign to respond.

It made me angry. After all we had done for him, eliminating Jovinus, ending the uprising, and offering to invest the port at Narbo, Honorius still refused to make a concession on the issue of a Gothic homeland. I met with Ataulf and Wallia and suggested we take Narbo and make it an accomplished fact. But they demurred, knowing it would be seen as an act of aggression and used as an excuse to attack us. They wanted to adhere to the original plan, which was for me to become pregnant and have a son. Only then, they believed, would we be safe from any misrepresentation of our intentions.

I disagreed. For the Goths to be accepted by Rome, they would have to offer their services as a client state, collecting taxes and providing recruits for the army. They could not do so without a settled kingdom. They must have a grant of land. Under Roman law I was entitled to it. Of course, I still intended to have a child, but the acquisition of land had to come first. After some debate, they gave in.

My son, I have often regretted not telling you the truth about my role in these events. I let you believe the popular story of my captivity including the part about my bearing an unwanted child. I kept it from you to protect you. There were those who would have accused me of treason and condemned me to death. If that happened, I could not have become your regent. Someone else would have been chosen to rule on your behalf until you came of age – someone perhaps, who would not have had your best interests at heart. By maintaining the fiction of my victimhood, I kept us both out of danger. I hope you will forgive me for that.

I sent another message to Honorius, telling him we were going to invest Narbo and run it as a vassal state. We would begin collecting taxes at once, which would be sent along to Ravenna without delay. In addition, a large body of troops would be made available for the imperial army as soon as we received sanction for our actions. I was careful to stress that our actions were not in any way hostile. Quite the contrary, as soon as we were settled in, we would undertake a large-scale project to deepen the port in order to bring Roman men and arms into southern Gaul to discourage future invasions.

To my great relief, I received a reply from him approving our plan, but it was couched in language giving him license to reinterpret our position whenever he saw fit. Wallia didn't like it. He advised against making a move on Narbo until we got better proof of Honorius's sincerity. But I considered the letter with its imperial seal the best way to persuade the Roman authorities within the city to surrender it without a fight. If we waited, Honorius might have second thoughts and rescind the sanction. So, we presented the letter to the governor of Narbo, and the city was handed over to us.

With this, my reputation among the Goths soared to new heights. If I had been a heroine to them before, I was practically exalted now. After nearly forty years of roving the Empire seeking a settled state, the Goths believed they finally had a homeland. As far as they were concerned, taking me hostage was the best thing that had ever happened to them. Wallia made a speech lauding my courage. Ataulf declared his allegiance to Rome. Everyone was relieved and happy. Everyone, that is, except Sigeric and the disgruntled members of his clan.

We moved into Narbo and immediately began collecting taxes and forwarding them to Ravenna. We commenced the port project, and when Honorius requested a conscription of one thousand men, we sent them to Rome, even though their loss weakened our defenses. Months passed, and it seemed we had at last reached a sustainable accord. It looked like our troubles were over. But we were mistaken.

Honorius was always a soft touch for anyone who spoke ill of the Goths, and he had fallen under the sway of a certain recently promoted general who counseled him that our actions in Narbo should be viewed as a provocation. Moreover, this meddlesome general insisted my marriage to Ataulf was a grievous insult to the House of Theodosius and ought to be answered with blood. Not surprisingly, this general had his own agenda; he had long admired me from afar and wanted me for himself.

This general had several notable successes to his credit. Most notably, he was responsible for the siege of Arelate that had brought down the usurpers in Gaul. Honorius thought him brave and clever and considered him a worthy successor to Stilicho, with one distinct advantage: he was a purebred Roman and did not carry the taint of barbarian blood in his veins. Honorius made him master of soldiers and adopted his thinking as regarded the Goths. He initiated a blockade of Narbo, and overnight we went from being allies to being enemies again.

Ataulf was understandably upset and wanted to strike back, but I counseled against it. I could only hope Honorius would temper his aggression once I became pregnant. I persuaded Ataulf to wait. We needed to buy time. So, we remained entrenched in Narbo, neither venturing out to break the blockade nor continuing our efforts to appease Ravenna.

Weeks went by. We began to feel the pinch in food and trade. The bitter disappointment of the Gothic people, to find themselves once again betrayed by the Romans, stirred up discontent. Sigeric and his followers took advantage. They began to agitate against us. Ataulf's position weakened. Then, after six weeks, I became pregnant.

I sent a letter to Honorius apprising him of the situation and reminding him that, should I bear a son, my child would be the heir to the Western throne. To my great disappointment, he didn't respond.

As my belly swelled, I kept praying Honorius would come to his senses and lift the blockade, but nothing happened. Ataulf was beside himself. Sigeric was eating away at his support. To prove to his people that he was not a lapdog for the Romans, he declared Honorius redundant, proclaimed himself emperor of the Western Roman Empire, and named Narbo as the new capital of Rome.

If this was calculated to provoke a response from Ravenna, it failed. The block-ade was tightened, and we began to starve. Finally, when it became clear that the lack of nourishment might endanger our unborn child, Ataulf capitulated and issued the order to withdraw. We left Narbo in shame and humiliation.

We migrated along the Mediterranean coast to the city of Barcilonum[2] in northeastern Hispania, a journey of some 125 miles. There our child was born. We christened him Theodosius in honor of my father. He was a fine, handsome little chap with wisps of honey-blond hair like Ataulf. We were both convinced he would make a fine emperor.

---

2. Modern day Barcelona

For a woman, there is little to compare with the birth of her first child. The restive little life contained within you suddenly emerges into the world as a separate being, in many ways still a part of you, and yet a unique individual, an everyday miracle brought to life. You are imbued with such profound measures of love for which you are not prepared, it leaves you giddy and elated.

We announced the birth of little Theodosius to a cheering throng. To see so much joy, you would have thought not a man among them wished us ill, but you would have been wrong, for there were a great many who resented how quickly we had surrendered and wanted to see us overthrown. But I was oblivious to all that. All I could see was my newborn infant. I was blind to everything else.

Little Theodosius and I were inseparable, which I suppose is not uncommon as the infant is so needy and the mother is the wellspring of all it requires. However, in my case I felt an attachment to little Theodosius that went beyond the usual bond. Perhaps it was the insecurity I felt, being the only Roman among so many Goths, an insecurity compounded by the instability of our situation.

In due course, word came that Honorius had lifted the blockade at Narbo after finding we had withdrawn and had sent his favorite general under sail to chase us down and destroy us. Wallia and some of his top lieutenants, including a capable general known as Theodoric, were for building a fleet and confronting the Romans at sea, but I advised against it. The Goths knew nothing about naval warfare and would have been obliterated. I thought it better to reach out to the Alans and the Suebi in an effort to build an alliance to oppose the Romans after they made landfall in Gaul, but Ataulf was worried such a move would make us look weak and give our enemies ammunition against us. He insisted we could not keep running away from our oppressors. At some point we would have to stand and fight them, and it would be better to do it on our own, without allies.

Seeing there was nothing more I could add, I withdrew to my quarters and contented myself with little Theodosius, cuddling and kissing him, clinging to him as if he were the symbolic embodiment of my survival, exhilarating and wonderful and full of promise, and yet at the same time fragile and vulnerable and under constant threat, liable to be swept away at any moment. Then he fell ill.

Out of nowhere he developed a cough and a fever. His condition rapidly deteriorated. Ataulf and I prayed fervently in the chapel every day, but to no avail. Little Theodosius died within a fortnight of first showing symptoms. We were stunned at the suddenness with which we lost him.

It occurred to me that God might be punishing me for my sins, but I dismissed the idea from my mind. You cannot go around excoriating yourself with guilt, Placidius. It saps your strength. Regret is a different matter. It is constructive to be regretful, to examine your errors in order to avoid them in the future. But guilt holds you back. It makes you hesitant and indecisive. To be an effective leader you must avoid guilt, and you must perceive the work of the devil in those who try to foist it on you.

The death of little Theodosius caused great anxiety among the Goths. Overnight their hopes were dashed, and they were rudely dragged back into their subservient roles as the pariahs and outcasts of the Roman world. This gave Sigeric and his Amali the chance they had been waiting for. They loudly proclaimed their opposition to Ataulf and called for his ouster.

Wallia urged Ataulf to execute a few of them as a warning to the others but Ataulf worried that a heavy hand would divide the populace and provoke a civil war. His refusal to act was his death sentence.

Unbeknownst to us, Ataulf had accepted into his service a close crony of Sigeric's named Erulf. Erulf had been spying on us and feeding the information to Sigeric to build a case against us, but when the public mood swung against us, Erulf decided to take matters into his own hands. He crept up behind Ataulf as he was reclining in his bath and stabbed him in the back. Ataulf slumped over, dead.

In the course of a few weeks all that I loved and lived for was snatched from my hands. I was overcome with grief and in no condition to head off what happened next.

The Amali faction moved swiftly to organize the opposition, and before Wallia could act, the House of Balti was swept from power and Sigeric was proclaimed king.

Given the way Sigeric had treated me during Ataulf's reign, there was little doubt about what was in store for me under his leadership. Wallia tried to help me escape, but it was too late. We were both taken into custody and sentenced to death.

But as fate would have it, the Romans weren't finished with us yet.

After landing at Narbo and retaking the town, they marched west, determined to overtake us and wipe us out for good. When Sigeric heard the news, he was faced with a daunting dilemma. Either he must exhort his people to stand and fight the Romans in the field, in which case they faced the prospect of total annihilation, or he must urge them to cut and run, in which case he would be condemned for being no different than Ataulf, who he had accused of being a coward.

There was one other possibility. A long shot. But worth a chance. And Sigeric perceived it.

He sent an emissary to the Romans with an offer. If the Romans would call off their attack, he would release the Princess Galla and withdraw to the Atlantic coast, far from the Mediterranean, never to trouble Rome again.

Then he waited.

In the interim, I was released from confinement and kept under guard. Sigeric took the opportunity to parade me before the people like a disgraced whore. He struck me and spit on me and tore my clothes until I was bruised and scraped and half-naked. He made me get down on my knees and kiss his feet. He flung me headlong to the ground and howled with laughter.

This treatment was regarded with disapproval by many of the spectators. Some of them may have considered Ataulf's policies a failure, and they may have agreed the time had come to replace him, but they didn't blame me for their troubles, nor did they want to see me disgraced and humiliated. Sigeric's obnoxious performance soured many of them on their new king and gave them a foretaste of the cruelty that lay ahead under his rule.

Then, to make matters worse, word arrived of the enemy's advance. The Roman army was less than a day out and closing in fast. Sigeric's proposal had been brushed off. His gambit had failed. Now Sigeric was up against it. He had to decide, would the Goths stand and fight or would they turn and run?

Sigeric lost his nerve.

He called for the people to run. With little time to organize a proper retreat, the people fled in a panic leaving many of their belongings behind. It was a humiliating rout, particularly as the Romans stopped short of attacking us and remained where they were, watching us run away, with smiles on their faces.

For Sigeric it was the beginning of the end.

One night while the others slept he tried to slip away undetected but was caught and placed under arrest. The person behind this was none other than Wallia, who had been saved from execution by members of Sigeric's inner circle who anticipated Sigeric's downfall and understood the need to replace him. Sigeric did not live out the night.

Listen to me, Placidius. Once you have identified your enemy and detained him, there's nothing to be gained by keeping him alive. A dagger to the heart was Sigeric's fate. His body was dragged into the woods and left to the wolves. Wallia went about it as a wise leader should. Making a spectacle of political assassination is rarely to a ruler's advantage. Better to get it over with quickly and not allow your enemy's suffering to become a rallying point for the opposition.

With Sigeric gone and Wallia elevated, there remained the question of the Romans. Why had they stopped short of attacking us? What did they want?

The answer wasn't long in coming.

For the past six years, the tribe known as the Alans had occupied the province of Lusitania[3] in Hispania. They were a restless and aggressive people. Having originated far away in the steppe country of Scythia, they had migrated across the Empire, impelled westward by the encroachment of the Huns, settling first in Germania and then in Gaul before moving south into Lusitania. Now they were on the move again, heading for Baetica[4] , which would put them

---

3. Modern day Portugal

4. Modern day Andalusia, Spain

uncomfortably close to the Pillars of Hercules[5] where they might cross over into Africa and threaten our grain supply.

Honorius wanted them stopped, but the forces he had sent to face them were not enough. His first thought was to redeploy the army he had sent after us, but on further thought it was decided even that would fall short of the number needed. That's when the enthusiastic general who had pursued us from Narbo got an idea. He would accept Sigeric's terms and allow the Goths to move on to the Atlantic coast unimpeded, on two conditions. First, they would have to hand over the Princess Galla Placidia, and, second, they would have to agree to a resumption of their status as Roman federates.

This was difficult thing for the Goths to swallow. The foederati system had been in place for 300 years. To be a federate meant that the subject people must agree to fight on Rome's behalf or face annihilation. In the early days, the status had been conferred on tribes outside the Empire who were bound by treaty to come to Rome's defense, but when the Goths crossed over into the Empire in great numbers to escape the Huns, Emperor Valens decided it would be better to accept their presence on Roman soil and enlist them as federates rather than try to expel them. Thus, for the first time a foreign power residing on Roman soil was called upon to sacrifice themselves for Rome's defense but without the assurance that they would be permitted to remain permanently in the country they were called upon to die for. Naturally, the Goths balked. The Romans saw their refusal as a threat and attacked them, but failed to wipe them out. The Goths struck back and war ensued. Finally, Emperor Valens, comprehending the seriousness of the situation, committed enough troops to defeat them decisively.

---

5. Modern day Gibraltar

They met at a place called Adrianople. By all measures the Romans held the advantage. So confident were the Romans that they would prevail, the Emperor came along to lead the troops in battle. But the Romans were mistaken. They had underestimated the Goths' commitment to remaining within the borders of the Empire, determined never to be forced back across the Danube where they might become prey to the Huns. The Goths were fighting an existential battle, while the Romans were conducting a police action. Seen in that light, what happened was not surprising.

Emperor Valens was killed and the Roman army was overrun. The Goths broke free and ran amok through the countryside. The next six years were spent trying to weed them out. Finally, Emperor Valen's successor, my father Theodosius, struck a deal permitting the Goths to remain within the Empire if they would serve in the Roman army as federates, essentially the same deal Valens had given them earlier, with the added assurance that they would be given a homeland in consideration of their service.

But by then Rome's problems were multitudinous. Barbarian incursions from the Huns, the Vandals, and the Suebi, among a host of others, kept the Roman's and their Gothic helpmates continuously occupied, and the promise of a homeland kept getting put off. The Goths began to chafe under their obligation to Rome, and, just as before, the Roman's began to resent what they saw as Gothic ingratitude. The tensions boiled over, and in a fit of anger, the Goths lynched a Roman general who was abusing them. In retaliation the Romans massacred several hundred Gothic federates who were watching a chariot race in the Hippodrome. The final straw came when the Romans employed Gothic federates in the vanguard of their operation to overthrow the usurper Eugenius. Thousands of Goths died that day while the bulk of the Roman army remained safely in the rear. In the aftermath, an outraged

King Alaric demanded a homeland for his people without further delay. The Romans spurned him. The result was Alaric's rebellion, which culminated in the Gothic sack of Rome and my capture.

Now the Goths were being offered essentially the same deal for a third time. If they agreed to resume their status as federates, the Romans would allow them to migrate west to the coast of Gaul, a place called Aquitaine, where they would be permitted to put down roots and establish a homeland. The Goths had every reason to be dubious, and no one had any illusions about what it would mean in practice. Once again the Romans would place the Goths in the vanguard of the army heading south to expel the Alans from Baetica. In the ensuing fight the Goths would be the first to die, and in the end there was no guarantee the Romans would make good on their end of the deal.

Naturally, there were those among them who urged Wallia to reject the terms, but he had little choice. Should he refuse, the Romans would go on the attack. Weak from years of fighting and fleeing, the Goths stood little chance of holding them off, and if the Romans overran them, a wholesale slaughter of everyone, including women and children, was likely. With a heavy heart Wallia accepted the terms.

I shall always be grateful to him for taking the time to discuss it with me before making his decision. He wanted to make sure my return to Ravenna would not put me in danger. I assured him I would be all right, although I was not at all certain. In any case, I wasn't about to do anything to jeopardize the Goths' survival. I told him to go ahead and make the deal.

On the day of my departure a great many people turned out to say farewell to me. For many of them I was still their beloved queen, and they were sad to see me go.

Waiting for me on the other end of the line was the fanatical general who had engineered my liberation. He was smug and disdainful. He looked me up and down like he was inspecting a prostitute preparatory to purchasing her services. I loathed him from the moment I saw him.

By now you have figured out who he was. He was the man whose blood runs in your veins. He was your father, Constantius.[6]

---

6. Pronounced kon-stan-ch-ee-us

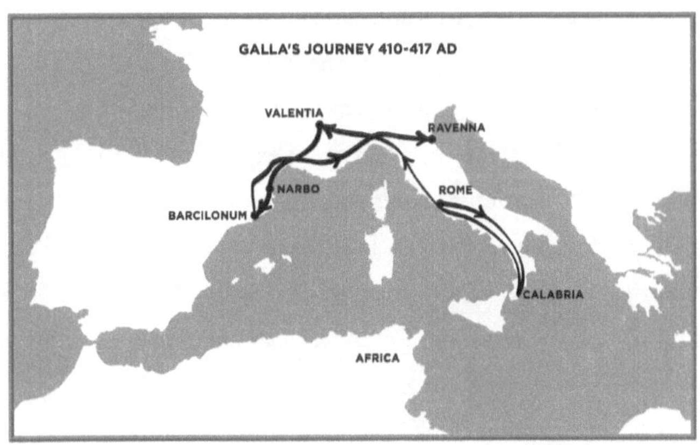

Chapter Seven

Placidius waited an inordinately long time for his meeting with Arsenius. It was hot and he could feel the perspiration trickling down the back of his neck. He wiped at it and grumbled.

A slave came to the door and said the chief of staff would see him. Inside the administrative tent with its white canvas and imperial bunting, the busy official was engaged with two of his aides. He addressed them in a terse manner and pointed to a document in his hand. Then he dismissed them and turned to Placidius.

"Imperator," he said with a slight bow. "To what do I owe the pleasure of your visit?"

His gaze drifted up to a point above and beyond Placidius's head before dropping to the documents he was holding.

Placidius drew up to his full height. "You should not have kept me waiting. I am your sovereign, not your handmaiden."

Anger flashed across Arsenius's face. He turned away for a moment. When he turned back he was wearing an expression of humility. "I'm sorry," he said. "There must've been some mistake. I instructed my servants to admit you as soon you arrived. I'm grateful, of course, that you agreed to meet with me at my headquarters when custom dictates I should have come to you. As you can see, I'm quite busy, and I thank you for your indulgence."

A fly hovered around Placidius's head. He swatted it away. The place smelled of rotting vegetables and curdled milk. The odor made him nauseous. No one offered him a seat.

"In any case, I'm glad you've come," Arsenius said. "There's something I want to discuss with you."

"And there's something I want to discuss with *you*," Placidius shot back. "This letter from my mother." He raised the codex. "I'm told it passed through your hands."

Arsenius looked surprised. "A letter from Galla Placidia? When did that arrive?"

"Cyrus delivered it to me a few days ago. He claims he got it from you."

Arsenius scowled. "That's a lie. I've never seen it before."

Placidius hadn't expected such a flat denial. He stammered a response.

Arsenius jumped on the opportunity to press ahead. "Imperator, this is very important. There has been a secret synod of the Eastern bishops at Constantinople. They've declared jurisdiction over the Prefecture of Illyricum. As you know, the Pope has authority in Illyricum. For them to declare jurisdiction over it amounts to insurrection. They're testing us. We can't let them get away with it."

Placidius was only vaguely aware of the ecumenical rivalries between East and West. Religion didn't interest him. In any case, he didn't come here to discuss religion. He tried again to broach the subject of his mother's letter, but Arsenius cut him off and kept going.

"Your mother's going to be quite upset when she hears about this. It confirms all our worst suspicions. She thought they would try something like this. Apparently, the Eastern court's unlawful retention of the prefecture for so many years has not been enough; they also want to extend ecclesiastical authority over it. This has the fingerprints of Pulcheria[1] on it. We must act."

Pulcheria was his mother's niece, the daughter of her late brother Arcadius, and Placidius's first cousin, a key figure in the imperial court in Constantinople, renowned for her piousness and generosity. More importantly, she was the sister of Emperor Theodosius II and the aunt of Licinia Eudocia, the young woman he was traveling to Constantinople to wed.

It was all very confusing to Placidius, the complex relationships between the various members of the House of Theodosius and their rivalries. He only knew that his mother distrusted Pulcheria, although he had forgotten exactly why. Something to do with her influence over the Eastern bishops. He was sketchy on the details.

Arsenius went on. "You know how strongly your mother feels about papal jurisdiction. She will not see it compromised. As for Illyricum, both she and Aetius are of one mind in declaring the East has no right to it,

---

1. Pronounced pul-kare-ee-uh

ecumenical or otherwise. Illyricum is properly within the dominion of the West. It lies just across the Adriatic from Ravenna. It is ours."

Illyricum had long been a bone of contention between the two halves of the Roman Empire. They'd been bickering over it for years. The conflict had even crept into Placidius's wedding plans. Originally, the wedding was to have taken place in Thessalonika, the capital city of Illyricum, but had been moved to Constantinople to avoid a quarrel over which bishop should preside over the ceremony, an Eastern or Western one. By moving it to Constantinople the question had been settled in favor of the East, which apparently the West had objected to, thinking it an underhanded way to avoid the question of papal authority in Illyricum. Or at least that's what Arsenius seemed to be saying.

"Your mother asked me to intercept any correspondence coming this way from Constantinople. She thought we might discover something like this, and now we have. You must make a statement in the strongest possible terms, Imperator, voicing your opposition."

Placidius opened his mouth to reply but stopped short. "Wait. My mother asked you to intercept any correspondence of mine coming from Constantinople?"

Arsenius couldn't conceal a certain gloating satisfaction. "Yes, and she requested that all correspondence of any sort pass through my hands before being handed on to your curator of correspondence, Liberius. We live in dangerous times."

Placidius felt his temper rising. "Then why wasn't I informed of this?"

"Were you not? Liberius was supposed to inform you."

"Liberius! He knows nothing about any of this. He claims you were interfering with his duties by withholding my correspondence from him."

A sneer curled Arsenius's lip. "That sniveling worm. I told him I was to review all your correspondence first. He was to inform you of it. We mustn't tolerate such incompetence. That wretch! I'll have him whipped."

"That won't be necessary," Placidius said. "He misunderstood. That's all."

"Misunderstood? Bosh! He's a disaster. I swear I don't know how he got promoted into his position. I will punish him."

"I said that wouldn't be necessary," Placidius repeated firmly.

Arsenius grumbled something under his breath.

Placidius frowned at him. "Now about this letter," he said. "Where did it come from?"

"I haven't the slightest idea," Arsenius said. "Where did *you* get it from?"

"Cyrus gave it to me."

"He's a clown. I don't approve of him."

"Be that as it may, he gave it to me. But he says he doesn't remember who gave it to him. He thinks it may have been you."

"Nonsense."

"Well then, where did it come from?"

"I don't know, but all correspondence is supposed to pass through me." Arsenius thought it over for a moment. "Liberius must know something about this. Something he's not saying. But I have ways of dealing with him. Believe me, Otho will make him answer."

Placidius sighed. "Liberius knows nothing about it. I've already questioned him."

Arsenius harrumphed.

"I'm afraid someone is trying to influence me by writing this letter in the guise of my mother," Placidius said.

Arsenius raised his brows. "Who?"

"I have no idea, but the person depicted in these pages cannot be her."

"Why not?"

"Because this person is cruel and heartless. She's not at all like my mother."

"Are you sure about that?"

"What are you saying?"

Arsenius raised his hands. "Forgive me, Imperator. I meant nothing by it. It's just – well... is the depiction of her the only thing that makes you suspicious of the letter's authorship?"

"No. There's more. My mother has been preparing to pass this letter on to me for months, as a way to guide me after I become fully invested, after I marry. But a few weeks before my departure it went missing. I received no reports of its recovery, and then, as soon as I departed Ravenna and was well on my way, it reappeared – when she was not around to corroborate it."

"Hmm, that does sound suspicious. Is there any part of the letter that strikes you as inauthentic?"

"What do you mean?"

"You said it was written to guide you. What kind of advice does it provide? Does the advice seem valid to you?"

"For the most part, yes."

"Then she probably wrote it. I mean, If someone were trying to mislead you, the advice would be dubious."

"Would it be?"

"I think so."

Placidius pondered this.

"Your mother knows what she's doing, she and Aetius together. They can be counted on to give you sound advice, and as a young emperor there is much you can learn from them. If you ask me, the letter is authentic, and you should trust what it's telling you."

Placidius's temper flared. "So that's it? That's all you have to say on the subject? Are you not troubled by the fact that a suspicious piece of correspondence made its way into my hands without being examined by you? A moment ago, you were jealous of your prerogatives. Now you seem ambivalent."

"Ambivalent? I'm the furthest thing from ambivalent. Let me assure you, no one is more concerned about your safety than I am, but I cannot do my job if I'm not permitted to exercise my full authority."

Before Placidius could answer back, Arsenius plunged ahead. "As I've told you before, there are people in this camp who were not properly vetted. They have not been entered into the official register because they have not been examined by me. I've asked you repeatedly for permission to interview them, but you've refused. I'm sorry, Imperator, but I cannot be held accountable for those whom I have no control over."

Placidius knew Arsenius was referring to Candida and her entourage. They had been appended to the imperial retinue without going through the proper channels. Arsenius had asked to interview them, but Candida had refused, calling it an unwarranted intrusion into her privacy. Placidius had agreed.

Arsenius assumed the part of the unfairly aggrieved. "I'm good at my job," he said. "I was princeps officius[2] with Aetius for many years under the most trying circumstances and nothing of this sort ever occurred. Perhaps that's because Aetius was firm on the subject of security. Aetius is not lax – never has been. He's a man conversant with the details of everything around

---

2. Chief of staff of a military commander or highly ranking official

him. You would do well to emulate him. You would have much less cause for concern."

The blood rushed to Placidius's cheeks. In his view Aetius was a conniving two-faced scoundrel. For Arsenius to hold him up as some sort of paragon infuriated him.

Arsenius folded his arms and waited.

He's waiting for me to lose my temper, Placidius thought. *Aetius told him how to get under my skin, and he's hoping I'll erupt. But if I overreact, Aetius will come to his defense, which will make me look weak and ineffectual. I can't afford to be compared unfavorably with Aetius. Not now. Not when I'm just about to come into my full power as emperor.*

Placidius seethed and swatted at the fly again. "What is that rank odor?"

"Slop for the pigs," Arsenius said. He was sorting the papers on his desk.

"It's disgusting."

Arsenius paused and sniffed the air. "Is it?"

"You know it is."

Arsenius shrugged. "I've smelled much worse on the battlefield. After the slaughter. After so many good men have lost their lives in service to Rome."

Arsenius was baiting him, but Placidius refused to take it. He had time on his side. After they got to Constantinople, he would marry Licinia Eudocia and become fully invested, and then he would deal with Arsenius and his puppet master Aetius. It would be among his first official acts as emperor, to deal with insolent subordinates like them. First Arsenius.

Then Aetius.

He couldn't wait.

Honorius was a degenerate. He had given himself over to a life of drunkenness and debauchery. Worse, he had consigned the running of the Empire to a handful of scheming subordinates and turned his back on his responsibilities. So much of what I blamed him for – the refusal to negotiate honestly with the Goths, the silence at the news of my pregnancy, the sending of Constantius to pursue and harass us – were the ideas of others, planted in his head and endorsed indifferently by him as he raised himself momentarily out of his depravity to sign this document or that.

Perhaps a part of his insecurity stemmed from his personal appearance. Unlike Stilicho or Aetius, Honorius did not cut a dashing figure. He was oddly effeminate in a pudgy, matronly sort of way. His eyes were hooded and dull, and his lips thin and colorless. He walked slightly bent over like an old man. It was easy to see how others thought they could control him, and he rarely disappointed them.

When I told him he was making a mockery of our father's legacy, he seized me by the arm and steered me into his bedchamber where he presented me with a spectacle I would not soon forget. On the floor below us were dozens of writhing figures, girls and boys, naked and entwined, egged on to the most appalling acts of depravity. Honorius confessed he liked to watch them as he pleasured himself. He was proud of his licentiousness and presented it to me as if it were a great accomplishment. He told me our father had never achieved such glorious extravagance, having squandered his privileges in the dry and tedious business of governance. He was dead serious.

Do not, my son, let the power of your position corrupt you. Honorius was not the first emperor to slide into degeneracy. There were Caligula, Nero, and

Commodus before him, each reviled in his time and denigrated posthumously, their names erased from statues and monuments, their property confiscated. Yet Honorius was the first Christian Emperor to have sunk to such lows. Having witnessed it, I wondered how he could justify his behavior and still call himself a man of faith.

He attended chapel daily, maintained the high holy days, and conferred with the Pope. Yet in his private life he was unapologetically grotesque. It was said of him that his refusal to sleep with his first wife had made of him an ascetic. But this celibacy in marriage, which he carried on into his second marriage, distorted his mind into the conviction that no woman was worthy of congress with his lordly flesh. He was not without sexual appetite. Quite the contrary. Rumors abounded of his having lost control, raped a girl, and then killed her to expunge his guilt – not over what he had done, but over the defilement of his person by her unworthy flesh.

You would have thought your uncle would have spent many hours in penitence over such heinous sins, but somehow he felt absolved in the eyes of God. At first, I thought this bizarre, but then I came to understand how he had arrived at such a twisted conclusion.

My enlightenment came when my brother sent for the Pope to take my confession. At the time, only a month after my return to Ravenna, I was restricted to my quarters, virtually a prisoner in the palace. Honorius had sent for Pope Innocent to hear my sins. Supposedly I had committed a grievous error in marrying Ataulf, who was an Arian Christian and therefore deviant because he did not share our Nicene creed. I was guilty by association.

At this time, Pope Innocent was at the height of his power, having extended papal authority beyond Rome to the provinces, where he dealt with any opposition with a reflexive severity. In the course of things, he had run into the teachings of a monk named Pelagius. Pelagius had been preaching that moral perfection could be achieved through human will, an idea many Christians found attractive as it placed moral shortcomings in the hands of the sinners and provided an incentive for improvement. But the Church didn't like it because it flew in the face of the Church's teachings on original sin.

According to the Church, original sin is the sin borne by all of humanity due to Adam's rebellion in Eden. All men are tainted with original sin from birth and can only be absolved the grace of God. Grace, as you know, is the free and unmerited favor of God bestowed to all humanity by Christ's sacrifice on the cross. It cannot be cajoled or pleaded for. It is a gift given by God. Pelagius's assertion that human beings can achieve moral perfection through will alone was interpreted by the Church as a demonstration of pride and a refutation of God's divine grace. Therefore, it was deemed heretical.

As it happened, the teachings of Pelagius represented a challenge to the Pope's authority in parts of the Empire where he was trying to extend his influence. So, the Pope condemned Pelagianism with the utmost severity and reaffirmed the Church's teachings on original sin, which, in the view of some, implied that man's sinfulness was utterly beyond human control.

Hence, a person like Honorius, who had given himself over to depravity, could take comfort in the belief that his wickedness was out of his control and not the result of his own choices. What's more, he was certain God would reward him in heaven for supporting the Pope against Pelagius and by championing divine grace and the concept of original sin. Honorius was quite content with this in-

terpretation of things. What he was not happy with was the immorality of his sister having married a heathen barbarian and having borne a mixed-blood child.

Pope Innocent was the pontiff who had been presiding in Rome when the Goths put the city under siege. It was he to whom the pagan senators had appealed and begged to be allowed to sacrifice to their old gods. The Pope had granted permission for this heresy, but when it came to a Princess of Rome marrying a Christian of a sect he considered unorthodox, he was unyielding. As far as he was concerned, I had sinned and needed to ask for God's forgiveness.

He allowed it was a weakness of my sex, made worse by the pressures of my captivity. Having been abducted and forced into unspeakable acts by uncivilized barbarians against my will, I could be forgiven, but I would have to show some humility. I tried to correct him. I told him I had married Ataulf of my own free will and had not been forced into it. He chose not to hear me. He repeated the fiction that I had been forced into the marriage and embellished the story with lurid details of beatings, rapes, and humiliations at the hands of my captors. He told me my baby had been a bastard and was a black mark against me, but he assured me I need not feel any remorse as long as I expressed repentance and made a heartfelt confession.

In the end, I thought it best to go along with him, not because I agreed with anything he said, but because I recognized I could not regain a position of influence unless I played along. So, I went down on my knees and prayed for forgiveness, all along fingering the amulet around my neck, taking strength from it.

After hearing my confession, he grew earnest and grandfatherly and opined my reputation might be entirely rehabilitated if I were to marry a man of unblemished reputation. I showed no enthusiasm for this, but it did not take him long to pass on his opinion to Honorius, who seized upon it with great enthusiasm. He had just one man in mind.

I tell you, Placidius, the Pope could not have devised a better punishment if he had beaten me with his bishop's crop. At that moment, there was perhaps no one in the Empire I detested more than your father. Remember, he was the man who had urged Honorius to betray us. He was the one who had driven us from Narbo and pursued us halfway to the coast. He was the one who had forced the Goths back into servitude as federates, humiliating them and planting the seeds of years of enmity yet to come. He was a beast and a liar, and I despised him.

But in my brother's eyes, Constantius would make an ideal husband. After all, Honorius still had the line of succession to consider. His strange peccadillos had brought him to a place where he had no child of his own, and he didn't want the Empire to fall into the hands of a stranger after he was gone. I was something of a renegade, and he certainly wasn't going to countenance my having conceived a child with a Goth, but I was still the best chance he had of producing an heir to keep the principate in the House of Theodosius. The only question was how to get me to bear the kind of child that would be acceptable. He believed he had the answer in Constantius.

Constantius was the most recent in a string of advisers that had won my brother's favor and been praised by him. Because Honorius had a distaste for the day-to-day rituals of his office he was always looking for someone to run the government for him and to make the hard choices. Because he realized that others might perceive this as a dereliction of duty on his part, he was at pains to convince anyone who would listen how great his deputy was, a figure above reproach, brilliant and worthy.

First he elevated Olympius, and after him, Jovius. He granted each man extraordinary autonomy and extolled their talents and abilities. He endorsed each of their opinions, ratified each of their decisions, permitted each of them to run things unencumbered until each man stumbled into a crisis for which he could not escape accountability. Then he turned on them, blaming them for all that had gone wrong, as if the fault were entirely theirs and not his. Whereupon he would find some new favorite, and the whole process would start over again.

His most recent pet was Constantius, an unusual choice given my brother's tortured relationship with Stilicho. As a boy, Honorius had despised Stilicho, and once Stilicho was eliminated, I never imagined Honorius would make himself subordinate to a general again – but he did so in promoting Constantius.

And it didn't take Constantius long to learn he could manipulate the Emperor. He praised and cajoled him and let him believe every good thing was his doing and nothing bad was ever his fault. As is so often the case with those who achieve power through happenstance, Honorius required constant reassurance. Those who gave it to him were deemed astute and perceptive. Those who didn't were considered dangerous and stupid.

Constantius had already achieved great success as a general. He had vanquished the usurper at Arelate. He could rightly take credit for preventing Honorius from being overthrown. But he also took credit for driving the Goths off the Italian peninsula and thwarting the ambitions of Jovinus, neither of which he had much to do with. But he was most celebrated for having rescued me, the poor princess, from the evil clutches of the barbarians.

In those first few months after my return to Ravenna, the public was abuzz with news of Constantius's glittering heroism. Rumor had it that having slain Ataulf in hand-to-hand combat, he had held Wallia at sword point and forced the concessions resulting in my release. Whether these were just the wild imaginings of an overwrought public or deliberately put about by Constantius to bolster his reputation, I never knew, but I would not have put it past him. In any case, the public adored him, and when news of our impending nuptials was announced, they applauded it.

I suppose at some level I should have been grateful for the way your father had spun things, for if the public knew the truth about me, they would have marked me as a traitor. Nevertheless, I loathed him for the way he had treated the Goths, and, as I got to know him, my contempt only deepened.

Your father was not a good-looking man. He had bulging eyes, a long neck, and a broad head. He slumped forward when he sat and shot glances right and left like some dull beast alerted to danger. His manner was sullen and downcast, and he was quick to anger in a grousing, petulant sort of way.

It was something of a surprise that such an unattractive figure should be regarded as a hero in the eyes of the public, but then I observed him in the presence of the Emperor, and I saw how he had won them over. He was charming and affable, quick to laugh, and sociable. He was cheerful and good-natured. He put his personality on and off like a suit of clothes. It was an astonishing trick.

Yet when he got me alone, he did not attempt to conceal his true nature. He regarded me with the open-mouthed covetousness of a panting dog. He declared he was quite unprepared for my beauty and said it would be difficult to restrain himself until our wedding night. Then he tried to take me.

When I batted his hand away, he regarded me under lowered brows and chortled. He commented how the Goths had taught me bad manners. He grabbed me behind the neck and forced his mouth on mine. I fought him off, twisting away and dealing him a blow to the neck with my elbow that left him choking and spluttering. When he collected himself, he promised he would teach me at thing or two about male superiority. It was only a matter of time. Then he left.

Oh, Placidius, how can I convey to you what a woman feels under the threat of such an attack? It is the threat that another human being, a man, can make you feel numb, mutilated, broken, invisible, and ashamed – render you voiceless and oppressed like a slave, and weigh you down with self-loathing. This is what your father had tried to do to me, and I'm ashamed to say he eventually succeeded. But not then. At that moment I still believed I could hold him off.

I waited for his return, determined to scratch his eyes out, but he didn't come back. Instead, he sent me a small gift and begged my forgiveness. When I saw him next, he was in the company of my brother and displayed the affable charm everyone found so captivating. Our wedding day was fast approaching, and he was concerned about who would conduct the ceremony. Pope Innocent had taken ill, and the clergyman chosen to replace him was a man whose views were not well known to me. "Let me speak to him," I said. "I'll take the measure of him."

Well, they were both surprised that I would take the initiative on such a thing; they had not expected me to speak up. The whole exercise was designed to show how kind and considerate Constantius was to his betrothed. As a woman I was supposed to be docile and silent. When I spoke up, they were caught off guard. Before they could object, I ordered the chamberlain to make the arrangements.

When you are without friends in a hostile place, you must look for every opportunity to cultivate allies. I knew nothing about the chosen clergyman and had no reason to believe I could win him over, but I needed to try. Fortunately for me, he proved to be worth the effort – very much so.

His name was Sixtus, and he had been the Deacon of Valentia. He was a big man but gentle, as his name implies, which means scraped or polished. He had a certain softness about him, as a well-made statue does through rigorous chiseling. He was as brawny as a wrestler and as gentle as a lamb.

As a youth, Sixtus had been kidnapped by Saxon pirates but had escaped and returned to his homeland, where he had worked for several years in a quarry. He lifted and carried stones, before joining the Church and rising to a position of prominence. When Venerius became bishop, Sixtus was called to Mediolanum to act as his bodyguard. When Venerius died, Sixtus moved on to Rome, where he served in the same capacity for Pope Innocent. He was there when the Goths sacked the city.

Today Sixtus is the Pope in Rome, but in those days he had no such lofty ambitions. He was content to remain anonymous, for at that particular time many men who shared his views were being vilified and exiled. You see, Sixtus was secretly a Pelagian.

He would not have revealed this to me had I not met with him and informed him that Constantius and the Emperor were concerned about his worthiness to conduct the ceremony. He seemed disappointed and a little hurt. He apologized and said he would withdraw if there were any concern about his capacity. I explained it was not a question of competence. Rather, his doctrinal proclivities were the issue. Again, he offered to bow out. He did not wish to give offense.

I asked him in the most mild and reassuring manner if there were any cause for concern. He became shy and evasive, demonstrating the bashful reticence of a maid, this brawny man who could have lifted up a millstone. I reminded him I had married an Arian and had not rejected his views, so it was unlikely I could be offended by anything he could tell me.

"Yes," he said, "but you had no choice but to marry the barbarian."

Now I was faced with a decision. Should I risk my reputation by telling him I had married Ataulf of my own free will? Or should I keep it under wraps

*and lose the opportunity to gain his confidence? As I say, I needed allies –
desperately. I decided to take the chance.*

*He seemed not to believe me at first, and when gradually he did come around, he
tried to change the subject, as if he had been drawn into a dangerous conspiracy
and wanted no part of it. But one cannot unhear what one has heard, so when
he tried again to excuse himself, I told him I had made myself vulnerable to
him and asked if he would do the same for me.*

I said, "If I cannot trust you, I must consider you a threat."

*With that, his face fell. He gathered himself and told me all about his involve-
ment with Pelagianism.*

*He insisted the monk Pelagius had never intended to cause offense by broad-
casting his views. Pelagius was a devout Christian and obedient to the authority of the Church. His views had been misrepresented by his followers and
distorted by his opponents. He had never rejected the concept of original sin
and meant only to say that every human being is capable of vice or virtue
because if not, then he cannot choose virtue and cannot be responsible for
himself before God. It was a conclusion arrived at by common sense and one
shared by the Early Church Fathers. It was not a deliberate attack on orthodoxy
as Pope Innocent would have it.*

*As an aside, I disagreed strongly with the Pope's argument that people are
incapable of change without the intervention of divine grace. Of course, people*

can change, and it is not heresy to say so. If I did not believe people could change, I would not be writing this to you now.

In any case, it seemed clear to me that Pope Innocent was seizing on a small issue of doctrinal disagreement to rid the Church of his rivals and extend his reach into bishoprics that had not formerly been under his influence.

Sixtus was not willing to go that far; he did not want to criticize the Pope. The Pope had been good to him and had given him many opportunities for advancement. But at the same time he did not want his patronage of Pelagius to be exposed.

I told him his secret was safe with me. My report to Honorius and Constantius would be full of nothing but praise for his fitness to conduct the marriage ceremony. But I had another problem. I told him I did not want to get married, especially not to Constantius.

He dropped his head as if he had just received some sorrowful news and sat there for some time in an attitude of despondency. When he lifted his head again, he told me he wanted to introduce me to someone, a woman of impeccable virtue who might be able to help me with my problem. And so, I became acquainted with Melania, one of the most extraordinary women I have ever met.

Slowly but surely I was building a core group of trustworthy people, friends who I could rely upon to stand by me through thick and thin and ensure I was never alone. If you are alone in the world, Placidius, you are powerless.

Even if you have power by virtue of your eminence, you are vulnerable without friends.

As emperor many people will claim to be your friends who are not. They have an agenda. They view you as a means to an end. But they do not care about you. Some are expert at making you believe they care, but they will betray you without a moment's thought if it serves them. Beware of them. They are all around you.

Friends and allies are the framework that buttress your power and strengthen it. But detecting them and sorting them out from the pretenders can be a challenge. Your uncle certainly could not. As self-absorbed as he was, he never realized that bootlickers like Olympius and Jovius were using him. Constantius was too.

By the time I arrived on the scene, Constantius had already persuaded Honorius to elect him to the consulship twice. And now with me as his wife, Constantius would have nearly as much power as the Emperor himself. If at any point Honorius had opposed him, I have no doubt Constantius would have slain him without a second thought, for Constantius had something Honorius did not have. Constantius had friends.

It's worth examining the kind of people who have friends. Constantius was one. Aetius is another. Even though we may not like a person, we must not let our prejudice prevent us from learning what they have to teach us. Constantius, with his ability to manifest friendly charm in the blink of any eye, attracted people to him. It was a performance to be sure, but one he had perfected.

As for Aetius, his charm is natural. He has a genuine curiosity about others that makes him likable. He strives to understand how they feel and achieves a sympathy with their views that makes him agreeable. And he doesn't stop there. He opens up and shares his feelings. He lays himself bare. In this way he cultivates a familiarity that makes others confide in him. In this he is remarkable.

I know you dislike Aetius. God knows I have done nothing to discourage you in that regard. Aetius is deeply ambitious and shrewdly political, and his methods are often questionable, but his warm-heartedness is genuine. It's a part of who he is, and it's something we can use to our advantage, if we take the right view of it. Aetius has much to teach us. Believe me. He does.

Ah, but how to tell friends from enemies. That's the question. Among those who are close to you at the moment, how many truly care about you? Who is your friend? As I said before, I have devised a method for getting at this, but for it to work we must acknowledge our purpose.

As Augusta and Augustus, we rule for one reason – to further the fortunes of the Empire. Anyone whose motives align with ours is our friend, even it means occasional disagreement. On the other hand, those who tell us only what we want to hear, those who cajole and flatter us, are only trying to get what they want from us.

The most genuine are those who follow a course of action that, although it may be detrimental to them personally, serves the good of the Empire. They are as rare as jewels, and as beautiful. Melania was once such. But when I speak of her beauty, I don't mean beauty in the physical sense, for she was as pitiful to look at as a starved dog. Her beauty came from within and glowed all around her. It emanated from her extraordinary commitment to God. One might say, from her holiness.

Sixtus accompanied me to the domus[3] where Melania was residing. She and her husband, Pinianus[4], were traveling through Italia on their way to Palestine to build a convent. They had spent the last six years in Africa, where they had lived a monastic life free of worldly temptations, laboring dutifully, and praying to God. They had little use for arcane squabbles over points of religious doctrine and even less for the trappings of aristocratic society. They had given up everything to live the life of ascetics, and they had given up much.

Being recently returned to Roman society, I was unacquainted with their story, but as Sixtus explained it, they were minor celebrities. They were talked about in glowing terms by the citizens of the towns and cities, compared favorably to Paula and Marcella and the other disciples of Jerome who had given up their wealth and status to become followers of Jesus. They were the frequent subject of heartfelt sermons and held up as shining examples of Christian piety, something anyone could aspire to, not just the wealthy.

---

3. Roman domicile or home

4. Pronounced pin-ee-ah-nus

Melania was the granddaughter of Valerius Maximus Basilius, the vaunted proconsul of Achaea and the prefect of Rome, and one of the most powerful landowners in all of the Empire. Her grandmother was Melania the Elder, one of the wealthiest citizens of the city. By the tender age of thirteen, Melania was a devout Christian and looked forward to a life of poverty and chastity, but her parents wouldn't hear of it. To persuade her otherwise they married her off to her cousin, Pinianus, a pagan, and immersed her in a life of extravagance.

As the daughter of a pedigreed Roman family, she had a duty to produce heirs. Reluctantly, she did what was required of her, but her two children died in infancy, and when her parents died soon after, she did the unthinkable. She persuaded her husband to convert to Christianity and gave away her fortune, at the same time freeing the family's eight thousand slaves.

News of this spread like wildfire through Italia. Not since the days of Paula and Marcella had a woman of such high aristocratic standing given up so much to embrace a life of poverty. It was a sensation, and people flocked to see her.

But Melania and Pinianus did not remain in Italia for long. They departed for Africa. They founded separate monastic communities for men and women and consulted with renowned theologians such as Jerome of Antioch and Augustine of Hippo.

Six years later they were back in Rome preparing for their journey to Palestine when news of their arrival spread. Large crowds gathered outside their modest dwelling to see them. Soon it got to be too much, the noise and commotion. They asked the Church to find them some quiet place where they could pray in silence. The Pope sent Sixtus.

Sixtus arranged for them to lodge in an opulent villa on the outskirts of Mutina, the last place on earth anyone would expect to find them. That's where I came to meet with them.

Sixtus had sent a message ahead announcing my coming and including some details about my predicament. When I heard of it, I was annoyed. I had told him my story in strictest confidence. He apologized and explained that they were not impressed with wealth or power - they had even refused to meet with Pope Innocent – but they would help me if they thought they could do some good.

The villa had a spacious atrium centered upon a long crystalline pool, clean white mosaics, and walls painted with colorful frescoes. The triclinium[5] had gold trimmings and vessels of silver and amber. Fruit trees, climbing vines and colorful statuary filled the peristylum. But I found Melania and Pinianus in a drab gray cubiculum[6] at the back of the house. The room had formerly been a servant's quarters.

When we entered the room, they were on their knees, heads bowed in prayer. We waited until they were finished.

---

5. Formal dining room

6. A small room in a room home, typically a bedroom

When Melania looked up, I was struck by her appearance. Her face was drawn and sallow, her eyes sunk in her head. Her hair hung lank and bedraggled beneath a soiled veil made of sackcloth, and her skin was covered with dust. Pinianus didn't look much better; both were dressed in rags. Still, there was something vibrant and alive about them as if they radiated divine energy. I could see why people were so taken with them.

Melania began without preamble. She went right to the crux of my dilemma. She said that if Constantius wanted to marry me, I must submit, for the Bible teaches us women are subordinate to men, much in the way men are subordinate to God. I failed to see how her advice could be of any help to me and looked to Sixtus with a pained expression.

Melania saw the look on my face and asked in a quiet, sympathetic way why I objected to marrying Constantius, whether it was a preference for another man, or the longing for a different, better life, one closer to God.

I told her Constantius was a brute who intended to take me against my will.

She thought about it for a moment. Then she said, "God would not have it so."

I agreed.

"This Constantius, he is powerful. But is he sanctified?"

I wasn't quite sure what she meant by that and looked to Sixtus for help. He explained, "Is he a man of God?"

"He's a Christian," I said.

Sixtus shook his head. "No. Not like that."

I was confused.

Pinianus tried to clear it up for me. "The question is: Is he obedient to God? Does he strive to be Christlike?"

"He performs the rituals of the Church, if that's what you mean."

They exchanged a dissatisfied glance.

"And you, dear," Melania asked, as she leaned toward me, "are you obedient to God?"

I chose my words carefully. "I try to be," I said, "although I fall short much of the time."

"As we all do," Melania said.

"In you, I see the lineaments of genuine humility," Pinianus said.

"Humility is the foundation of obedience," Melania said. "Do you intend to build upon it?"

I said that I did.

"Then you must strengthen the foundation first."

"How?" I asked.

"The way of humility is this: self-control, prayer, and acknowledging that you are inferior before God."

"Fine," I said. "I can do that."

"Can you really?" she asked. "Many people claim to want to be sanctified, but it's not simply a matter of following rituals. You must make a commitment before God."

"Through fasting and prayer," Sixtus said.

"Yes, and by putting away the things of this world," Pinianus said.

"And by taking a vow of chastity," Melania said.

"A vow of chastity?"

"You must vow to remain celibate as a measure of your humility before God."

"But I am to be wed."

"Marriage should not be a barrier to your commitment to God. Many Christian women are celibate in marriage. I for one."

I looked at her in surprise.

"Yes," Sixtus said. "It's one of the things people find most fascinating about Melania. It's a measure of her faith."

"And her humility," Pinianus added.

"Many women are inspired by Melania and have vowed to emulate her," Sixtus said.

"The popularity of celibacy is growing," Pinianus said, "particularly among women who are married."

Suddenly it all came clear to me. They were telling me to make a public vow of chastity before marriage. Once Constantius heard of it he would almost certainly call off the wedding. I couldn't help but smile.

Melania gave me a warning look. "It is not solely for your own purposes you do this. It is not solely to escape a union you find distasteful. You practice humility to draw closer to God. In so doing you sanctify your husband to whom you owe a duty."

Pinianus added, "'If a woman finds herself married to a man who does not believe in God, she should not divorce him. For the unbelieving husband is sanctified by the believing wife.' These are the words of Saint Paul."

"Yes," Melania said. "Pinianus knows of what he speaks. He was the unbelieving husband once, and my piety sanctified him. Now he has grown closer to God as a result."

I looked from one to the other. It was clear what they were telling me. They wanted me to marry one of the most powerful men in Rome and convert him by fasting, praying, and withholding sex. It wasn't just about thwarting his appetites. It was about making him a better person.

"I'll do it," I said.

Melania frowned. "This is not something to be taken lightly, Galla Placidia. It requires faith and courage. You must call on God. You must pray with great intensity. If you fail, it will go even harder on you than if you had never taken it up at all."

I told her I understood, but I was being glib. I had not really considered what it meant. They had given me the answer to my problem, and I was satisfied. Constantius would call off the marriage as soon as he heard. I was sure of it. He didn't really know me. He just wanted to sleep with me. And he didn't need me to help him climb the ladder of power; he was already doing that without me. If he couldn't have me sexually, he would reject me, and my troubles would be over. I was sure of it.

But I was wrong.

Chapter Eight

I was married to your father in the year of his second consulship mere weeks after my meeting with Melania and Pinianus and only days after my public vow of chastity.

On our wedding night, he tried to take me in spite of my vow, but I was one step ahead of him. I arranged to have a detachment of the papal guard stationed outside my door, and when I screamed, they rushed in and restrained him.

Word of this was passed on to the new pope, Zosimus, who had ascended to the papacy after the death of Pope Innocent. Zosimus admonished Constantius, warning him that to violate my vow of chastity would be a grievous sin. He told him that a detachment of the guard would now become a permanent fixture outside my door, as much to protect me from him as to protect him from the loss of his good reputation.

Constantius was frustrated, but there was little he could do. My vow of chastity had caused a great public sensation, and the public were behind me one hundred percent. If Constantius were to defile me, they would turn against him, which would make it hard for him to build support for his policies.

But I wasn't gloating. A wise victor recognizes that no victory is ever total. Every win is but a single triumph in an ongoing war, and today's enemy can be tomorrow's friend if the situation is handled wisely.

Understand this, Placidius. There is no better time to befriend your enemy than right after he has been defeated. It must be handled delicately. You must honor his failed effort to dominate you and make him believe he could have prevailed if fate had not intervened. This is particularly true if you are a woman.

No man wants to feel like he has been bested by a woman. On the other hand, women are particularly well practiced in the art of false humility. Soothing the fragile egos of wounded men is a skill we're taught from an early age. We pretend to be weak and docile, so men can feel powerful. We give up a bit of our agency to keep things calm and orderly, for a man who feels demeaned loses his judgment and acts irrationally. But my willingness to make peace with your father also had an ulterior motive. I wanted to make sure I remained close to the seat of power.

Call it hubris if you like, but it is not hubris to seek the reins of power if the person in charge has demonstrated little interest in doing so, if he shirks his duty or rejects good advice, if he takes the easiest path forward because he doesn't want to be inconvenienced. Had Honorius demonstrated even an iota of interest in governing the Empire as he should have it would've been different, but he didn't. He only cared about himself, about feeding his appetites and indulging his impulses, and no one could not convince him otherwise.

As a woman so close to the seat of power, my influence as the sister of the Emperor should have been greater than it would have been as the wife of a Consul. At least, on paper, that's how it seemed, except that Honorius had only contempt for me. He had forced me into marriage with a man I despised in order to punish me. Yet he was counting on me to produce an heir. Consequently, when he got word of my vow of chastity, he was upset with me.

I recognized that without the promise of an heir to keep him at bay, my usefulness to my brother was at an end, and I would be in grave danger. I needed to move quickly to prevent him from coming after me. So, I took on the role of the good wife and resolved to do what I could to support Constantius's ambitions.

Under the rules of succession, there was no way I could ascend to the throne myself, even though I was closest in blood. On the other hand, if Constantius were to ascend, I could exert considerable influence through him. As it was, sharing the consulship with Honorius and marrying his sister had brought Constantius within a hair's breadth of wearing the purple[1], but if Honorius were to die unexpectedly, the emperorship would pass to a distant cousin, bypassing us both. We had to eliminate that possibility.

I got Constantius aside and spoke to him about the need to fortify our position as regarded the succession. To achieve this we needed to work together. My idea was to encourage Honorius in his customary inclination to relinquish power to a favored subordinate. Constantius was certainly in a position to take

---

1. In Rome wearing the color purple was restricted almost exclusively to the Emperor. Thus, references to "wearing the purple" are references to being the emperor

advantage of that, but he could not achieve real parity with Honorius unless he was proclaimed co-emperor.

Needless to say, Constantius was suspicious of my motives. He was a man steeped in ideas of male supremacy and not the type who would readily assent to working with a woman. Still, he had to admit I had outmaneuvered him in the bedroom, and, as the daughter and sister of emperors, I possessed a special appreciation of the political intrigues surrounding the throne.

In time and by degrees, I persuaded him, but it was not without complications. As is so often the case with men who are guided as much by their cocks as their brains, he could not separate my desire to assist him with my desire to fuck him. He thought my willingness to work with him for our mutual benefit was a veiled attempt to disavow my chastity and sleep with him. It was pathetic. He began appearing at my bath clad only in a loincloth, begging to be admitted. I ordered him away.

I was more concerned with what we were planning. My scheme to marginalize Honorius owed a great deal to what I had learned about the power of the Church to influence things. My experience had taught me that public declarations of religious piety and the fine points of Church doctrine could influence the behavior of powerful men as effectively as bribery.

We needed to make Honorius feel uncomfortable with his depravity because this was something he was unlikely to give up willingly. He was besotted with it. Many were the times I could not get an audience with him because he was preoccupied with his perversions. Constantius was no more successful than I, even when he had pressing military matters to discuss with him. Even with the Goths fighting on our behalf now, Hispania was slowly slipping away. Yet Honorius was unavailable. For the good of the Empire, we needed to elbow him aside.

But Honorius had no intention of sharing power with us. In his mind, it was enough to shift all his responsibilities onto Constantius and make him answerable for any failures that might occur. For him, it was the best of both worlds, and it allowed him to cling to the idea that he was intellectually his consul's superior.

As deluded as that was, it wasn't the extent of my brother's self-deception. He also believed himself morally superior, not only to Constantius but to others. He had become convinced that his depravity was perfectly acceptable in the eyes of the Church. He had reached this bizarre conclusion after hearing Pope Innocent hold forth on the dangers of Pelagianism. The Pope's diatribe convinced Honorius of his powerlessness to do anything about his wicked proclivities and gave him the excuse he needed to go on wallowing in his sins.

Fortunately for us, Pope Innocent had passed away, and Pope Zosimus had taken over. The new pope was a kind and unassuming man, not well prepared for the discord that Innocent had stirred up. He was willing to listen impartially to both sides of an argument and deplored narrow-mindedness and fanaticism.

We needed Pope Zosimus to soften the Church's stance on original sin and walk back some of his predecessor's fiery rhetoric. If we could do that, Honorius might begin to feel like the degenerate he truly was. Weighed down with the burden of his sin, he might shrink from public view and abdicate more of his power to Constantius. Then, when the time was right, Constantius would ask to be named his co-emperor, and Honorius would accede because no one else would be able to shield him from the derision he would face if censured by the Church.

Constantius was in no position to influence the Pope, but I was. Through my friend Sixtus I was in contact with those members of the clergy who took a sympathetic view of Pelagianism and could be counted on to petition the new Pope. They were already about this business when their efforts were buttressed by the appearance of a presbyter named Caelestius, who came to Rome to ask Pope Zosimus to retract Innocent's condemnation of the Pelagians.

Caelestius argued that the views of the Pelagians were not so far afield from standard Church doctrine and that they had never been intended to cause offense. He suggested the Pelagians had been singled out by Pope Innocent as a way to marginalize them politically. Caelestius was modest and unassuming and assured Pope Zosimus that he was only making his appeal on behalf of the persecuted and had no other motives.

Pope Zosimus believed him. He sent a letter to the African bishops, who had taken up the persecution of the Pelagians with zeal, and admonished them to stop.

Constantius and I saw things coming together in our favor. However, the African bishops were not so easily deterred. They struck back, alleging Pope Zosimus had been deceived by Caelestius who was clinging to heretical ideas and trying to debase Church doctrine.

Confounded and annoyed, Pope Zosimus replied that he had not yet reached a decision on the matter. And then Honorius stepped into the breach. Recognizing what it would mean for him if Pelagianism were deemed acceptable by the Church, he made a public declaration against it. That was enough for Pope Zosimus, who disliked the bickering and didn't want to appear to be in opposition to the Emperor. He changed course, endorsed the condemnation of the Pelagians, and reaffirmed the Church's teachings on original sin. It appeared we had been thwarted, but then something unexpected happened. Pope Zosimus died. He had been on the papal throne less than a year.

His most likely successor was an archdeacon named Eulalius, a man whose views on Pelagianism were generally favorable. We met with Eulalius secretly and urged him to move quickly before his enemies could organize against him. He did so and within a fortnight he was elevated to the papacy by a conclave of prelates in Rome. But the anti-Pelagian forces, hearing the news, reacted by holding an election of their own. They elevated a man named Boniface, a staunch opponent of Pelagianism.

With a pair of rivals claiming the papal throne, the threat of violence hung in the air, so the prefect of Rome, with the approval of the Emperor, ordered both men out of the city to keep the peace until the matter could be resolved. It was decided to hold a synod of the bishops to settle the matter.

Constantius and I met to discuss how we could best influence the outcome. Sixtus had persuaded us that if we were successful in getting all the bishops to attend, the weight of opinion would fall in Eulalius's favor. We wrote to each of them in turn, urging them to come to Rome for the synod. Then, Eulalius sabotaged his chances.

Thinking himself legally elected, and confident of his confirmation, he reck-lessly flaunted the prefect's order to stay out of the city and went to the Lateran Basilica to conduct Easter services. Hearing this, Honorius condemned him, canceled the synod, and declared in favor of Boniface. Constantius and I were foiled again, but if you cannot reach your objectives by one avenue, you can choose another.

As popular as Constantius was, the possibility of simply having him pro-claimed by the army and daring Honorius to deny him occurred to us. Still, it would have been risky. If we did not have the weight of public opinion behind us there could be a backlash. But if we could arrange to have Constantius proclaimed at the height of his popularity, it would improve our chances. The ideal occasion would be a triumph, which meant a resounding military victory would be needed.

We certainly didn't lack for enemies. The Alans, Suebis, and Vandals were running amok in Hispania and needed to be suppressed. Of the three of them, the Vandals seemed the biggest threat. Having originated in Scandinavia, the Vandals had migrated south through Dacia and settled in Pannonia before being driven westward by the Huns. They had crossed the Pyrenees and settled in northwest Hispania but were considered a minor threat until the stars aligned in their favor.

In accordance with the peace agreement the Goths had struck with Constantius, Gothic troops had accompanied the Romans south to expel the Alans from Baetica. In the course of things their combined forces killed the Alan king and drove the Alans from Baetica. Leaderless and in disarray, the Alans went looking for allies to help them. The Vandals agreed to come to their aid, but on one condition. The Alans must bow to the sovereignty of the Vandal king and have no other king before them. The Alans agreed, whereupon they ceased to exist as a separate tribe and became one with the Vandals. Now the Vandal tribe was twice as large and commanded an army of tens of thousands. They marched on Baetica, overpowered the combined forces of the Romans and Goths, and retook the province.

By the time Constantius and I were looking around for a place where he could make his mark, the Vandals were assembling on the southern coast of Hispania and gazing covetously across at Africa, the breadbasket of the Empire. But Constantius was unconvinced the combined forces of the Roman field army in Hispania along with the Goths would be enough to drive them off. If we were to win the victory we needed, we were going to need some help. We arranged a meeting of our top military advisors where it was proposed we call on the Huns for assistance.

Everyone looked at each other in disgust, but no one dared dismiss the idea. We talked about it for some time and eventually the proposal was adopted. But it was a mistake in so many ways I don't even know where to begin.

Worse yet, it would come to impact me personally in ways I could not have imagined.

It was a decision that would change my life forever.

Placidius made his way through the camp flanked by two of his body-guards. He should have had more but he didn't like to flaunt his superiority. Candida considered it pretentious. As he walked along, people rose to greet him. They bowed their heads in deference. He nodded in return as he had seen his mother do, but he never felt as if he was carrying it off with the same gravitas. He worried people were laughing behind his back.

He couldn't stop thinking about the letter. The most recent part was more in accord with what he knew of his mother. She had always been focused on the Church, and she had worked quite closely with his father when he was alive. The cooperative, almost business-like nature of their relationship had been commented on by those who knew them. So, it rang true. Yet a lot of the letter still struck him as unlike her. The part where she had been so repelled by his father that she had taken a vow of chastity. He had never heard of this – and whatever vow she had made had obviously not lasted. His sister Justa had been born less than a year and a half later.

The other incongruous part was where she had advised him to follow the example of Aetius. His mother despised Aetius. She only tolerated him be-cause she had to. She would have gotten rid of him if she could have. For her to be advising him to model himself after Aetius seemed unlikely. Aetius had maneuvered his way into power through coercion and deception. He had forced his mother into promoting him to his present position. She had never really trusted him. How could she? He had threatened to make war against her, not just once, but twice.

Placidius continued on his way through the camp, nodding right and left, trying to look regal and commanding. They were encamped along the banks of the Sava River beneath a gathering of low, rolling hills, just north of the mining town of Domavia[2]. It was a moderately wooded area dotted with slender, pyramidal spruce trees. Beneath one such tree, Candida and her retinue were being entertained by a magician. Placidius recoiled in horror.

The magician wore silk robes and a conical cap. He was throwing dice and gesturing emphatically with his arms. The audience was leaning forward, watching the dice roll. Placidius could not make out most of what the man was saying but he heard him pronounce the name of the groom Stephanus. The audience, a group of about ten, exploded with laughter and clapped their hands. The groom, Stephanus, obviously the butt of some joke, hung his head in affected humiliation. The audience jeered. The magician grinned.

Candida draped her arm over groom's back in the most companionable manner and whispered something in his ear. She ruffled his hair.

Placidius marched into the gathering and demanded to know what was going on. The magician bowed and withdrew. The retinue broke up and slunk away. Only Stephanus and Candida remained.

"This is not acceptable," Placidius railed at them.

Candida produced a dazzling smile. "Oh, Placidius. Calm down," she said. "It's nothing to get excited about."

He grabbed her by the arm. "Who gave you permission to bring a magician into the camp?"

She winced and tried to twist away.

"Who?" he repeated, tightening his grip.

Jaw set, Stephanus tried to intervene, but Placidius's bodyguards blocked him, and he backed away, scowling.

---

2. Modern day Gradina in Bosnia and Herzegovina

"What were you thinking?" Placidius demanded of Candida. "You know full well outsiders are not permitted in the camp, especially not magicians and divinators. Are you trying to undermine me? Have you thought about what Arsenius would make of this?"

She raised her chin, defiant, and refused to look at him. She shook herself loose from his grasp.

In the next instant his mood shifted from annoyance to awkwardness and then to a kind of repentance. He asked her if she was all right.

She lifted one hand to deflect him and stalked away. He went after her. She was headed for her tent. He caught up to her at the door. She turned on him.

"*You* mad at *me*? Ha! That's a laugh! If anything, *I* should be mad at *you*! Oh, you have some nerve, Placidius, embarrassing me in front of my friends." She swept aside the flap and ducked inside. He followed.

Inside the tent, two attendants were tidying up. Candida snapped at them to get out. They sidled past and scurried away.

"You too!" she barked at Placidius. "Get out!" Tears welled in her eyes.

Placidius was at a loss. He couldn't permit her to speak to him like this, but at the same time he wanted to apologize. His anger and jealousy had subsided. He felt awkward and foolish. He tried to explain.

She scoffed and showed him the back of her hand. She went to her couch and lay down, propping herself up on one elbow. She twisted a strand of hair absently around one finger and chewed her lip.

"I don't know why you have to be so mean to me. I'm not doing anything to you. I'm just trying to have fun. It's all your fault, really. These people. My God. Talk about boring. All they ever do is sit around arguing about religion and politics. It's enough to drive a girl out of her mind."

Placidius started to say something, but she cut him off.

"I told Stephanus I needed some relief – some entertainment. He had gotten wind of a traveling magician hereabouts. I told him to bring him here because if I have to listen to one more conversation about the heresy of Nestorianism or the pre-incarnate nature of Christ, I'm going to kill myself. The magician was good. Everyone was having a good time. Then you had to come along and spoil everything. Thanks a lot."

"Outsiders are not permitted," he said.

She rolled her eyes. "You and your rules. If you were going to be such a stickler about who is and who is not permitted into the camp, you should've let me choose my own retinue. My secretary, for example. He's a good enough fellow. But he's old enough to be my father. My cook, my steward and my other attendants, they're like decaying old philosophers. All they do is sit around all day yammering about heterodoxies and heresies."

Placidius held up his hand. "Wait. What did you just say? Did you just say you didn't choose your own retinue?"

"Right, Placidius, as if you didn't know. I suppose I should be grateful because you allowed Stephanus to come along. One person out of nine. And now you won't even let me talk to him because you're jealous of him! Let me express my heartfelt gratitude to you, oh Imperator. You're so-o-o generous."

She lay back on the couch and folded her arms tightly across her chest and stared at the ceiling. Her chin began to quiver, and her eyes began to tear up. "I know what you're doing," she said with a hitch in her throat. "You want me all to yourself. You think of me as a pet or a toy. You want to be able to take me out and play with me whenever you feel like it, and the rest of the time you don't care about me at all. Here she began to sob. I'm miserable and lonely, and you ... you... don't... care."

He went to her and tried to comfort her, but she pushed him away. He stood back and fidgeted.

"I should never have come here," she said. "I don't know what I was thinking, agreeing to be your mistress. You don't really love me. You just want to fuck me."

"That's not true," he said. "I do love you. Please don't say such awful things."

"It will only get worse when we get to Constantinople. Then you'll get married to your cousin and forget all about me."

"No, I won't. I promise."

"Rumor has it she's beautiful, the most desirable woman in the East."

"She's nothing special. I assure you. Besides, I'm only marrying her for political reasons."

"Because your mother wants it. That's the truth." She sniffled and wiped her nose with the back of her hand. "Your mother hates me."

"My mother doesn't hate you. She hardly even knows you. Look, we have to do this to bring the two halves of our dynasty together, to unite the Empire. It was agreed to a long time ago when we were children. It's political. That's all. Love has nothing to do with it."

Candida pouted. "You didn't fight for me. When your mother said you had to marry your cousin, you didn't fight for me."

"What are you talking about? My mother and I quarreled bitterly over it."

"But why would you? If you can have me as your prostitute and her as your wife."

"I never thought of you that way."

"You only ever think of yourself. You never think of me. I'm nothing but a whore to you."

"Don't say that."

"Well, I don't have to be a party to it. When I get to Constantinople, I'm going to leave you. You won't have me to distract you anymore. You can concentrate on your new wife. That's what you want anyway." She got up and began to take off her clothes. "Please go away now," she said. "I'm going to take a nap."

"But I don't want to go."

She untied the sash from her tunica[3] and tossed it aside. "Stop gawking at me. You don't find me attractive anyway. Compared to your new wife I'm a repulsive monster."

"Don't be absurd. Nothing could be further from the truth."

"It's my body. Isn't it? I'm too flabby, like some fat old wench." She pulled her tunica up over her head and stood before him dressed only in her loincloth and strophium[4].

In Placidius's eyes she was insanely desirable, lithe and sensual like the depiction of a nymph in a fresco. She turned her back to him and unwound her strophium and released her breasts. She covered her nipples with her hands and looked back over her shoulder at him.

"Please go away now," she said. "I'm sorry it didn't work out between us, but I can't be with a man who thinks so little of me." She loosened the folds of her loincloth and let it fall to the floor.

Placidius couldn't hold himself back. He slipped his arms around her waist and began to kiss her. She slithered away. "Please leave me alone now. I already told you. I can't be with someone who thinks so little of me."

---

3. A woolen undergarment

4. A band of cloth worn around the breasts, serving as a sort of brassiere

He tried to grab her again, but she flitted away. "To not even let me be with my friends. I can only imagine how you'll be in the future. You'll be worse than Arsenius, and I'll be miserable."

He threw up his hands in frustration. "All right. Okay. You can be with your friends."

She gave him a sly smile. "Even Stephanus?"

"Even Stephanus," he said with sigh.

She opened her arms wide and gave him a come-hither look. He took her in his arms and kissed her hungrily on the mouth. She kissed him back. He backed her up against the edge of the couch and tipped her back. He stripped off his tunic. He was fully erect. She made a tiny cry when he drove himself inside her. For a moment, they were lost in the heat of passion. Then he began to flag.

At first, he wondered if he could be imagining it. He moved faster, hoping to coax it back. Then knowing it was softening, he began to pound away with a mindless intensity bordering on hostility. A moment later his cock popped out of her like an oyster squeezed between two fingertips. He collapsed on top of her with a groan. She pushed him off and stood up.

"You see," she said. "That's what I'm talking about. You think I'm hideous."

"Oh no," he said. "Don't think that. Please. Don't think that."

She crossed the room and opened her travel chest. She rummaged around in it, producing an amphora of wine. She poured the wine and drank it. She sat naked on the chest, one leg dangling over the other. She fiddled idly with the gold clasp on the trunk's lid.

He tried to explain, but she said she didn't want to hear it. She took a long, appraising look around her quarters and wrinkled her nose in contempt. "I hate this place," she said.

"Why, what's the matter?"

"My pillows and cushions are trash," she said. "They're not even worthy of a plebian."

He surveyed the furnishings in question. "They're not so bad."

"And it's not just the pillows. All my furniture is junk. Other people have better—Cyrus, for example. He has a table and chairs, so he can eat sitting up. All the smart people eat sitting up these days in case nobody told you. What good is a couch anymore? It's a thing of the past, a relic. It's junk is what it is. It just goes to show what you think of me. You secretly look down on me, don't you?"

This time he didn't take the bait. He was alerted to something she had just said. "How do you know what Cyrus has for furniture?"

She dismissed this with a wave of her hand. "I don't know. I was in his tent for some reason. Or maybe I wasn't. Maybe I saw the servants carrying it in. What does it matter?"

She put back the wine and started getting dressed.

He narrowed his eyes at her and sat up. "Let me ask you something."

She was wrapping the strophium around her breasts.

"Do you really care about me? Are you really my friend?"

She glanced up. "What are you talking about?"

"If I wanted you to do something for me, for the good of the Empire, would you do it?"

"Like what?"

"I don't know. Anything."

"It would depend on what it was."

He nodded slowly.

She tilted her head to one side and looked at him. "What are you getting at? What's going on in that suspicious little mind of yours?" She wriggled into her tunica and began to tie the sash around her waist.

"Who selected your retinue?"

She looked up. "Huh?"

"You said you had not been permitted to select your retinue. You said it had been selected for you. Who did it? Who selected your retinue?"

"Don't be silly. You did, of course. Who else would have done it?"

"It wasn't me, Candida."

"Well, then I don't know who. But I can tell you one thing. I'm getting tired of being interrogated. Please go away now. I'm annoyed with you, and I'd rather be by myself."

"No one knows who brought them here," Placidius said. "They were attached to the caravan without anyone's knowledge – at your request. And Arsenius hasn't been permitted to examine them."

Candida grimaced. "Ugh, that horrible Arsenius. He's such a tyrant; he's always trying to intimidate people. He tried to accuse Stephanus of stealing horse feed from the supply wagon. Did you know that?"

"Well, did he?"

"Did he what?"

"Did he steal horse feed from the supply wagon."

"Don't be ridiculous."

"Look, it's only natural that Arsenius would be suspicious of them if he hasn't been permitted to examine them. Maybe you should rethink your refusal to have them interviewed."

"Never. Arsenius hates me. He'll reject them all and send them home."

"Suppose he does. Why should that bother you? You said you didn't like them. You said they were boring. You called them decaying old philosophers."

"It's true. They're insufferable, but they're the only friends I've got. If he sends them home, I won't have anyone to keep me company, and then what am I supposed to do, sit around all day, staring at the wall, and waiting for you to show up? Forget it. Leave my retinue alone. I won't have them bullied by Arsenius."

"But, Candida, you don't even know who selected them for you. We don't really know who they are. They could be a danger to you. We must examine them if for no other reason than to find out who brought them here."

"I won't hear of it."

"You may not have a choice."

She glared at him.

"And you cannot bring outsiders into the camp," he said, "especially not sorcerers and divinators."

"He was a magician. That's all."

"Magicians are an affront to the Church."

"Oh, look at you, suddenly worried about the Church."

"There are rules, Candida. You must follow them."

Defiance flashed in her eyes. "And what if I don't? What are you going to do, are you going to have me arrested? Are you going to have me tortured? Are you going to have my tongue torn out?"

"Don't be so dramatic. Be realistic. None of this is asking too much of you."

"That's what you think. But you think only of yourself. You never think of me. You're a liar. And you don't keep your promises."

Placidius sighed. "Now what are you accusing me of?"

"You promised me you wouldn't interfere with my friends, and now here are you are doing it again."

"I never said any such thing."

"You did too! Right here. Just a short time ago, when you were slobbering around trying to fuck me. Or did you conveniently forget about that as soon as you got what you wanted?"

"I remember what I said. I said I would not try to prevent you from speaking to Stephanus."

"You said you would not interfere with my friends."

He dropped his chin on his chest. "All right, have it your way. But this doesn't end here. I'm not through with you. Someone brought strangers into this camp, and I intend to get to the bottom of it. Prepare to have your retinue interrogated. I'm sorry but we all have to make sacrifices for the good of the Empire."

She made a little cry of juvenile petulance and stamped her foot. "I hate you!" she said. "I command you to leave this tent at once!"

He spread his hands wide and gave her a sad smile. "You cannot command me, Candida. I'm the Emperor. No one commands me."

"No one except your mother!" she flashed back. "No one but your mother and Aetius!"

His eyes went cold.

She stormed out.

He knew it would be a mistake to go after her, but he couldn't help himself. Her defiance excited him. Her resistance cast a spell on him. He was bewitched by her.

He pursued her to the groom's tent. He stood outside the tent and shouted for her to come out to him.

There was a rustling within and the flap was thrown back. The groom Stephanus emerged. He stood a foot taller than Placidius and was broader through the shoulders and back. He looked like a legionary, square-jawed with an aquiline nose and thin lips. He drew himself erect and folded his arms. "She's not here," he said in a deep voice.

"Let me see for myself," Placidius said. He waited for Stephanus to step aside. An awkward moment passed. Finally, Stephanus grumbled something under his breath and let his pass.

Placidius looked inside the tent. Candida was not there.

"She's with Isaac," Stephanus said. "She always goes to him when she's upset."

"How do you know she's upset?"

"I saw her. She went hurrying across the camp in tears. But if I hadn't seen her, I would've known anyway from all the shouting and carrying on. It sounded to me like she was being beaten."

"I do not beat her," Placidius said.

"She claims you beat her. She says you try to force yourself on her."

"She lies."

"Does she?"

Placidius didn't have to suffer this sort of insolence from a lowly horse wrangler, a mere groom. He could have him arrested and whipped. But Stephanus seemed unstable, and the guards were nowhere to be found. He decided not to provoke him. He decided to try reason.

"Candida embellishes the truth to get attention," he said. "If you know Candida, you know that. The truth is we had an argument, but I didn't hit her. I never hit her. And I certainly didn't force myself on her."

"I saw you," the groom said. "When the magician was here, you grabbed her by the arm."

"Did I?" He didn't remember. "All right. Maybe I did. But that's as far as it went. I never hit her."

"That's not the way it looked," Stephanus said, then something in him shifted and he suddenly seemed to recognize who he was talking to. He averted his eyes.

Sensing he was getting the upper hand, Placidius said, "I can't be responsible for your misperceptions."

Stephanus lowered his head. "Forgive me, Imperator. I spoke out of turn. I'm sorry. It's just – well, I cannot stand it. My father used to beat my mother. It gets me here." He tapped his knuckles on his chest.

"I understand," Placidius said. "Think nothing of it." He was grateful and relieved to be able to offer forgiveness to a man who only a moment ago had been threatening him. It made him think of himself as strong yet tolerant, the kind of man who would make a good ruler, the kind of ruler people looked up to and admired. "Just see that it doesn't happen again," he said.

"It won't," Stephanus said. "And by the way, you're right."

Placidius was surprised. "Right about what?"

"She lies."

Placidius knew he should let it go. He shouldn't be standing here conversing with someone who was so far beneath him. But he was curious. "What do you mean?"

"We're not lovers. It's not true."

Placidius was at a loss for words.

"Don't get me wrong," Stephanus said. "I do care about her. My family has served hers for years. We've known each other since we were children. But that's as far as it goes."

Placidius tried to reply but his words came out as a croak. He cleared his throat and tried again, "She never told me that."

"When you asked her to come with you to Constantinople, she asked me to come along, to be a part of her retinue, so she could have a familiar face nearby, someone her own age. The others are all older than her."

"Why would she say that?" Placidius asked. "I mean, if you're not."

Stephanus shrugged. "You know how she is."

Sadly, he did.

"I'm sorry to have argued with you," Stephanus said. "I lost my head. I hope you'll forgive me."

Placidius was still pondering what he had said about them being lovers.

"It's just – well, I thought you should know, so you wouldn't get the wrong idea."

Placidius glanced up. "Tell me something," he said. "If you're so close to her, what do you know about her retinue? Do you know who selected them?"

"I thought it was you."

"No."

"Then it must have been Arsenius."

"Arsenius doesn't know anything about them. That's why he insists on questioning them."

Stephanus looked glumly at the ground.

"Is there something wrong?"

"It's just – well, I hate to think of those poor people getting hauled before Arsenius. He's such a hard man, and they're such good and decent people, a bit tedious at times, but well-meaning for the most part. He's so stern. He acts like he thinks everyone should bow and scrape before him, like he's the emperor, and not you."

Placidius bristled. "Arsenius is trying to protect me."

"Of course he is," Stephanus said. He toed the ground. "I'm sorry. It was presumptuous of me to speak that way."

"Yes, it was."

"Forgive me, Imperator. Sometimes I have trouble controlling my tongue."

"This conversation is at an end," Placidius said. "You will not speak to me again unless you have been granted official permission. Is that clear?"

"Yes, Imperator. Are you going to see Isaac?"

Placidius turned back. "Huh?"

"Isaac, her secretary. I assume you're going to see him now, since that's where she most likely is."

"What did I just say?"

He reads to her," Stephanus said. "That's how he calms her down. Poetry mostly, but Isaac has all kinds of material. He's a well-known writer himself. Did you know that? He's working on a panegyric[5] in praise of his patron."

Placidius sighed and rolled his eyes. "And why should I care?"

Stephanus turned up his hands. "I'm surprised you didn't know."

"Didn't know what?"

"Who his patron is."

"Who?"

"Isaac is writing a panegyric in honor of our Master of Soldiers, the honorable consul Flavius Aetius."

For the second time, Placidius's throat went dry.

The delegation of the Huns arrived on the fifth day of Martius in the year of the second consulship of Constantius. I remember the day well because it was the day Quirinus[6] came to town attended by great acclaim for his startling feats of magic. Both Honorius and Constantius were eager to see him do his tricks. We had heard the rumors that he had turned a woman into a mare and made a statue weep real tears. They arranged a private performance for us.

The Church was not pleased. Magic of this sort has always been considered wicked, the work of the devil and against God. Sixtus was especially aggrieved and asked me to do something to stop it, but I couldn't see what. Honorius and Constantius were looking forward to it like little children on Saturnalia.

The Hun delegation consisted of some two dozen men, a coarse and fearsome looking bunch with slanted eyes, scarred faces, and misshapen skulls. I had heard the Huns deliberately disfigured their children as infants, binding their skulls to achieve the bulbous craniums they consider a sign of beauty. The scarring was also deliberately inflicted, but their slanted eyes, it was said, were

---

6. Pronounced queer-eye-ness

something they were born with, a common trait in the part of the world where they originated from.

The Huns were ruled by a king named Charaton who had gone some way to uniting the disparate bands of mercenaries employed by both us and our enemies at various points in the past. Stilicho had used the Huns in his defeat of Radagaisus, and Honorius had used them to oppose Alaric's first invasion of Italia. But the Huns had switched sides and fought alongside the Goths in their advance on Rome, and banded together with the Sciri in their unprovoked attack on Moesia. In fact, Hun warriors were found on both sides of just about every conflict, forever on sale to the highest bidder. Charaton aimed to bring an end to their marauding ways and bring them together as a unified nation, a prospect as terrifying as it was preposterous. The Huns were simply too venal. They would never be able to coalesce into a single cohesive unit.

Fortunately for us, they were as united as they were ever likely to be, making it easier for us to negotiate with them. We knew that if we could buy their cooperation, the weight of their contribution would be on our side, no matter what our enemies could come up with to oppose us.

Charaton had not joined the delegation. He had sent several of his top aides along with a handful of advisors and translators. We met them in the great hall of the imperial palace, but Honorius was late in showing up because he was attending a performance of the magician Quirinus, who, it was said, had astonished everyone by making a ball roll uphill.

When the Huns heard this, they were annoyed. They thought they had been snubbed and threatened to end the embassy on the spot. Frantically, Constan-

tius dispatched a courier to call the Emperor away from his entertainment, but Honorius refused to come. So, I went to get him.

I found Honorius side by side with the magician bent over the entrails of a goat. The magician was practicing divination, a terrible sin in the eyes of the Church, tantamount to consulting with the devil. My brother was trying to ascertain who would succeed him on the throne by reading the web of capillaries in the viscera. When I entered the room, instead of taking offense at the interruption, he greeted me like a long lost friend.

I told him the Huns were waiting in the great hall and were threatening to leave if he didn't come at once. He finished with the magician and accompanied me back. As we turned the corner into the room, he put his arm around my shoulder in a strangely companionable manner.

"I have always loved you, Galla," he said.

We came upon a scene of tumult. The Huns had grown tired of waiting and were starting to leave. Constantius was pleading with them to wait just a little while longer. The sight of our approach incited him to redouble his efforts as he scurried along beside them.

"Look," he said, "the Emperor has come." In his desperation, he stepped in front of them, and they collided with him.

There was a moment of confusion, and the Huns drew their swords. Constantius reeled back. The guards, seeing the consul in danger, rushed up to protect him. It looked as if there was going to be bloodshed, but then somebody in the Hun delegation shouted out a name.

"Ayboric."

It means "white wolf."

A lone figure dressed in rags, a stinking patchwork of decaying rodent skins, approached from the opposite side of the room. The man's face was concealed in a tangled nest of unkempt beard. His eyes were red-rimmed and burning with anger. He strode up and interposed himself between the combatants, arms spread. I noticed something familiar in his deportment, an impression that deepened when I heard his voice.

He spoke to the Huns in their language and then turned to Constantius and addressed him in fluent Latin. He said that a gift of some sort would be required to atone for the insult, and to be quick about it.

My mouth dropped open. I could barely believe my ears.

Constantius asked what would satisfy.

"Gold," the man said.

Constantius pursed his lips and nodded.

The man in the rags looked at the Emperor, and then he looked at me. Our eyes met for just the briefest of moments, but it was enough.

It was all I could do to keep from throwing myself into his arms. At last, he had come. The man I had been waiting for all those years.

My absent one. My beloved. He had come.

Chapter Nine

We had been little more than children when we first met. I was fourteen. He was a year older. He had come to our villa outside Rome to accept his promotion to the rank of tribune of the imperial palace. He was awfully young for such an important position, but he was descended from the aristocracy on his mother's side and was the son of a famous general, a man, it was rumored, of barbarian blood.

Stilicho had invited him to the villa to receive his promotion. After the ceremony was over, Stilicho was so taken with the boy he decided to ask him to stay on with us for a few weeks. Stilicho found him bright and ambitious. Perhaps he saw something of himself in him.

Honorius watched them from afar and was jealous. True to his boorish nature, he snubbed the boy when they were introduced and avoided him thereafter.

My beloved hardly even noticed; he was starstruck by Stilicho. He considered him one of the greatest generals who had ever lived, on a level with Julius Caesar. He had been reading Caesar's memoirs at the time, and in the three weeks he stayed with us at the villa he went to Stilicho often to discuss salient points in the narrative. Stilicho was not a man easily swayed by flattery, yet he could not resist the boy. They talked and talked. The boy's enthusiasm was contagious.

I felt it too. Through him I first began to take an interest in politics. He was as ardent about it as some men are about chariot racing. He couldn't get enough.

We were introduced upon his arrival, but he barely noticed me. Later, after he had been there a week, he came upon me while I was sitting under a plane tree by the bank of the river, reading. He startled me. When he spoke, I nearly jumped out of my skin. It was far from the last time he would surprise me.

He laughed freely in the relaxed and easygoing manner that young people have in each other's company. When he saw I was cross with him, he apologized. He had not intended to scare me. To this day, I still don't know whether that was true or not. He asked me what I was reading. When I told him Catullus, he became interested. He said Catullus was one of his favorite poets. He especially liked the way Catullus related the concept of fidelity to the relationship between lovers. It was an idea more commonly employed in referring to faithfulness between allies.

"It's not so different, though, is it?" he asked and gave me an impish smile.

I told him I thought there was a great deal of difference; love involved more than commitment. There was consideration and affection, for example, and a genuine interest in the well-being of the other.

I could tell he was surprised by my answer. He probably expected a more measured response from a female, something reticent and self-effacing, a com-pliance with his views. He recovered, however, and countered that fidelity between allies was not without consideration and affection. He said the best alliances were cemented with a genuine interest in each other's well-being.

"To the extent it serves your own," I said, "But once your self-interest diverges from your ally's, the commitment is broken."

"It is not so with lovers?" he asked.

"I should hope not," I said.

His eyes twinkled and he smiled.

A few days later he approached me again. I was coming out of the workroom where I had been spinning at the loom. When he saw me, his face lit up. He asked if I would walk with him.

We walked through a late summer meadow, brushing our hands over the tall reeds of grass. Dragonflies swooped and darted. He told me he had a friend who was considering becoming a hostage to a barbarian tribe. The friend was from a good family and his parents were being tactful in their response. For political reasons, they had to appear to be in favor of the arrangement, but at heart they were worried and didn't want him to go.

Despite his parent's misgivings, his friend wanted to do it, and he was inclined to endorse his friend's decision, but after talking to me, he had been having second thoughts.

"Me?"

"It was what you said about fidelity, about it being self-interested. It got me thinking. I started wondering if it is possible for a hostage to be trustworthy to his captors while remaining faithful to his own people."

He saw that I was confused, so he tried to explain. "The purpose of a hostage is to keep the peace between potential combatants. Hostages are not exchanged unless both sides share a common objective, namely peace. To the extent a hostage strives to achieve that objective, he is being faithful to both sides. As long as his captors are sincere, they have a genuine interest in each other's well-being."

"Yes, I can see that," I said.

"But you also said that once a hostage's self-interest diverges from his captors', he must break his commitment to them in order to remain true to his people, which would make him untrustworthy."

"I said all of that?"

"Didn't you?"

"I was speaking of allies."

"If a hostage and his captors share the same interests, are they not allies?"

"It think it's a bit more complicated than that."

"Is it?" He waited for my answer.

I had to think about it. I had not expected to be engaged in an intellectual discussion with him. Women of fourteen rarely are. Men don't usually grant them the privilege, no matter how well educated they are. But he was different. He wanted to know what I thought. He seemed to be hanging on the answer, as if what I thought really mattered to him.

"Well," I said. "For one thing, allies aren't bound to each other by coercion. With hostages, the threat of violence hangs over them. If either side breaks the peace, the hostage suffers."

He nodded slowly, taking this in.

"Also," I said, "the purpose of a hostage exchange is to curtail existing hostil-ities. With an alliance, there are no hostilities. The two parties come together as partners."

"Which makes it all the more devastating should the alliance be broken."

"Yes. Of course."

He pondered this a moment. "I'm not convinced there's much of a difference. In either case, both sides declare a common interest and seek fidelity to achieve it."

A slight breeze lifted a strand of hair across my face. I brushed it away. "If it is strictly a question of fidelity, then I see your point."

He looked at me and seemed to see me for the first time. His pupils widened.

I blushed.

The breeze lifted another strand of hair across my face, but, before I could get to it, he took it between his thumb and forefinger and placed it gently behind my neck. "There," he said.

My heart skipped a beat.

"Come, sit with me," he said. He took me by the hand and led me to a fallen trunk. We sat looking out at the meadow. He scratched at the ground with a stick. He mused over the importance of knowing your enemies, about how a hostage was uniquely positioned to achieve such intimacy. He took it as a given that it was far more important for a man in a position of leadership to know his enemies than to know his friends. But to achieve such a level of goodwill, consideration and affection had to play a part, and it had to be real.

"But how can it be authentic if self-interest can so easily destroy it?" he wanted to know.

"Perhaps," I said, "you can convince yourself that your self-interest and theirs are the same."

He chewed on his lip. "Is that what lovers do?"

The question came out of nowhere and took me by surprise. I blushed and looked away.

He apologized for embarrassing me. He said, "As regards fidelity between lovers, as Catullus frames it, is that what lovers do? Do they convince themselves that their self-interests are the same?"

I refused to look at him. "I don't know," I said.

He lifted my chin with his finger. "Yes, you do," he said. "I want to know what you think. When we first met, you said fidelity between allies was easily broken when their interests diverged, but you claim it's not the same between lovers. I'm wondering how lovers are different."

I refused to answer.

"Please," he said. "You've been reading Catullus. I want to know what you think."

I could feel him watching me and waiting. He wasn't going to relent. With a force of will I overcame my embarrassment and said, "I suppose lovers are different because their interest in each other's well-being is greater than their interest in their own."

He drew back with a look of surprise. "Is that right?"

"Have you never been in love?"

"No. Have you?"

"No."

He went back to tracing lines in the dirt with the stick. "I'd always thought of it as sudden, unbidden thing – Cupid's arrow and all that – but the way you speak of it, it's at least somewhat intentional."

"Somewhat, I think, but first there's the bolt; before everything comes the bolt."

"Cupid's arrow."

"And the desire to do all, to give all to your lover."

"Which requires some intent."

"Perhaps a little. But it's not so difficult, if you are in love."

He glanced up. "You speak as if you know, and yet you say you have never been in love."

I felt the heat rising to my face. "I've read a lot of poetry, Tibullus and Sulpicia."

"You take much from a book."

"I suppose I must if I want to learn anything. I'm too young to know much by experience."

"I'm just like you. I read a lot. There's so much to know. One just has to make a nuisance of oneself."

"You are not a nuisance," I said.

He smiled.

I looked down at what he had been scratching in the dirt. He had drawn the figure of a dog, the ancient symbol for fidelity. "What will you tell your friend?"

"I'll tell him I made the acquaintance of a very bright girl, one whose advice I'd like to consult in the future– if she'll permit me."

"It would be uncouth of me to refuse so gallant a request."

Ours eyes lingered on each other's for a long moment. I was smitten.

The next day we walked out again, and each successive day thereafter for more than a week. We talked and talked. He was endlessly fascinated with the question of devotion, how one could give oneself to another to such a degree that the well-being of the other became more precious than his own. He thought it somehow divine, although he was an indifferent Christian.

We often held hands, but he never tried to kiss me. Then one day he told me something that stunned and appalled me.

Prior to his coming to the villa, he had met a woman in Rome, a lady of high aristocratic standing, the wife of a senator, who had fallen in love with him. She had been pursuing him aggressively with flattery and gifts. She was an older woman and unattractive. Her lust for him grew more intense the more he refused her. Finally, in desperation, she promised him preferment if he would sleep with her. She insisted it was within her power to make it happen as her husband was infatuated with her and would do whatever she asked of him. She promised to make him a legate, which would make him one of the youngest men ever to attain that status. From there it would be a short step to the Senate.

He was excited at the prospect. "Do you see what this means, Galla? If I go along with her scheme, I can be promoted out of my position as tribune in less than a year. I can become a man of influence before I'm thirty. By the time I'm forty, I'll be a senior senator. Who knows? I may even become a prefect. Oh, I tell you, Galla, if I can attain such a level of prestige in such a short period of time, I'll be in a position do great things for the Empire. What do you think?"

I thought he possessed a talent for leadership, and I told him so. But my heart was broken. I was a lovestruck girl, and I had read more into the relationship than was there. In the moment I couldn't believe his affection for me was so easy to discard in favor of something so mercenary and sordid. I began to cry.

He seemed surprised at my tears and begged me to see the logic of it. What he was doing was for Rome. He cared nothing for his would-be paramour; he was much more devoted to me. But the good of the Empire must come first. It would be no small task returning Rome to its former glory. We had to be prepared to make sacrifices.

I agreed and told him to go ahead. But I was devastated.

The next morning he rode into the city and didn't come back until late in the afternoon. When he did, he sought me out. He told me had spoken to his would-be paramour about my misgivings and together they had come up with a solution.

I was embarrassed. I hadn't meant to get into the middle of things. It was none of my business.

But he insisted he must have my approval — he thought so much of me — and he was sure I would like their idea. What he said next shocked me. They wanted me to join them, to participate in their lovemaking, the three of us together.

I couldn't believe it. The whole idea was disgusting. I was a good Christian and would never be a party to such debauchery.

He could see how I had taken it. His enthusiasm dimmed and faltered. He lowered his head and said he was sorry. He said he wouldn't go through with it. He could see I was jealous, and he didn't want to hurt me, so unless I agreed to participate, he would refuse the offer, even if it prevented him from achieving his ambitions.

I suppose I should have seen the clever game he was playing. I suppose it must have crossed my mind. But you have to understand, I was just a girl of fourteen, and the thing I really wanted more than anything was for him to love me. So, there he was, telling me he would sacrifice everything not to hurt me, and there I was, refusing to help him because of some petty religious compunctions and because the whole idea made me uneasy. Suddenly, I felt selfish and ashamed, and I gave in. I told him I would go along with it.

To his credit, he didn't exult or beam, but remained earnest, considerate, and asked repeatedly if I was sure because he didn't want to pressure me unless I was absolutely certain. I told him I had thought it through and decided he was right; we would need to make sacrifices – both of us – if we wanted to achieve our ambitions for the Empire. He looked at me as if he were seeing me for the first time. He took me by the shoulders and kissed me, a quick, congratulatory kiss, broken with a smile, and he was off to make the arrangements.

We agreed to meet the woman at a public place and from there to retire to her chambers for lovemaking. I was terribly nervous. I was still a virgin and didn't know what was about to happen. Serena had never discussed sex with me. What little I had gotten I had gleaned from books and from the idle talk of slaves, and it struck me as somewhat less than appealing.

My beloved arrived first, and we waited together on a stone bench before the Basilica Aemilia. His bright confidence was gone, and he sat hunched over, rubbing his thumb across his lip, and looking around apprehensively. People passed this way and that, going about their business. He studied their faces. Once or twice, he made a start as if he were going to speak to one or another of them but thought better of it and sank back.

At length, an old woman approached us, her hand outstretched – a beggar, a filthy old hag. I was about to give her a coin and shoo her away when my beloved stopped me.

"What are you doing?" he asked. "Show some respect. This is she."

I looked at him in disbelief.

"You see," he said. "I told you. She is nothing compared to you. Your jealousy is entirely unjustified. Oh, and she is not nearly as bright as you either."

I turned my eyes to her. She had seen me take out the coin and was pressing forward, her eyes fastened on it. "But, but – she's a beggar," I said.

"Yes," he said. "Did I not tell you she begged? She won't leave me alone. She has such insatiable needs."

It was then I heard the suppressed laughter in his voice. When I swung my eyes to him, I saw him biting his lip, trying to keep from bursting out.

This was too much for him, the utterly confused look on my face. He threw back his head and whooped. The poor startled woman recoiled in fear, which only fueled his hilarity. He fell over, holding his sides, shaking with laughter as tears ran down his cheeks.

I was furious, yes, but more than that, I was hurt, not only because he had made me the butt of his joke, but also because he had gone to such elaborate ends to bring it about. You see, there was no wealthy aristocratic woman. He had made the whole thing up. It was incomprehensible. How could someone who claimed to care for me treat me so cruelly?

But he had a ready answer. He maintained he had devised the whole thing as a way of testing me. He was curious to see if I would act in accordance with my beliefs. He wanted to see if I would put his interests ahead of my own as I had declared lovers were wont to do. He was still exploring the question of fidelity, how deeply it could go, whether a person could give himself over to it utterly and then pull back. This is what he wanted to know. This is what he needed to be convinced of. And I had convinced him.

"But you've made a fool of me," I said.

"And I apologize. Let tell you, I would not have tried it with another girl. I only chose you because I knew you would have the penetration to comprehend it once I explained it to you." He cocked his head and gave me a sympathetic smile. "Don't take it so hard, Galla. You and I both want the same thing. It's the same thing Stilicho wants, the same thing your father wanted, the same thing Caesar was striving for – the triumph of Rome. But make no mistake, we live in challenging times. We no longer possess the strength to dominate all our enemies with arms alone. To prevail, we must play them off against each other. Enlist allies. Embrace adversaries. Betray friends. It will be a shifting landscape from now on, and the man who truly grasps fidelity and can employ it like a fine instrument, for good or ill, will be the master of them all." He studied my face for any signs of forgiveness.

I refused to look at him.

That's when he stepped up and took me in his arms. "I'm sorry," he said. "I didn't think you would take it so hard."

Implicit in his words was the suggestion that my petulance was a failing on my part, that I was a disappointment to him and would never be otherwise if I didn't do something to persuade him differently.

"You're right," I told him. "It was a necessary thing for you to. It just that — well, it took me by surprise. I didn't see it coming. I'll have to learn to be more observant in the future."

He held me at arm's length and grinned. "Galla, you are one of a kind." Then he pulled me close and kissed me. It made feel warm all over, like I was truly loved.

I would be lying to you if I said he did not worry me. The mind that can conceive such things and devise stratagems to hone them is more than a little dangerous. Perhaps it was this very danger I found so beguiling — along with the intelligence and passion he appeared to possess in such great quantity.

The friend he had spoken of was a fiction. It was he who was considering becoming a hostage. The position he was about to relinquish, tribune of the imperial palace, was a rank no lesser man would have given up. But for him, it was all part of the same ambition – the forensic curiosity about the meaning of fidelity, the callous trick he had played on me, the abdication of an important military post to undertake a role best suited to those with far less promise. He wanted to get as close to his enemies as possible, the better to understand them, so he could develop a rapport with them that he could use to his advantage — and to the advantage of Rome. He would become a hostage. It was the thing he wanted more than anything — even more than me.

He came to me on a stormy night with the news, my beloved. He would be leaving on the morrow, and we would not see each other for a very long time. He promised he would be back, and when he came, he would take me away from whatever situation I was in, no matter how difficult or dangerous, because by

then he would have achieved his goals, and few would be the men strong enough to withstand him.

"Just don't get married," he said. "Wait for me. I'll come for you. When you most need me, I'll be there." He was serious, and I believed him utterly.

It was a hot summer night. A storm was coming. In the distance, the lightning flashed and rippled. Occasionally, a bolt would come zigzagging out of the ether as if Jupiter himself were flinging it earthward with great violence. I was upset, so he suggested we go for a walk. The wind was gusting and soon it would be raining. He gently chastised me for being intimidated and took me by the hand and led me into the storm.

He spoke excitedly of his coming departure. He was looking forward to it. The Goths had agreed to send three young men in exchange for him, sons and nephews of notable figures. He was flattered by the quality of the people they were sending. It was an honor, and he planned to tell them so. He meant to win their approval right from the start.

The first raindrops began to fall, plump, chilly drops that splatted and ran. I shivered, and he drew me against him. He kissed the crown of my head. He apologized for everything he had made me go through. He regretted the pain he had caused me, but he hoped I had learned something from it. "Men will try to deceive you," he said, "to manipulate and misguide you. You must not let them. You must stay one step ahead of them. You must use your intelligence to outwit them."

I looked up at him with tear-filled eyes, and he kissed me, slowly and deeply.

Just then the heavens opened up and the rain came down. I tried to move to cover but he held me back. All around us, the lightning flashed. I began to fear we would be struck. I urged him to seek shelter. He threw back his head and laughed. In the stark white glare of the lightning, his face was garish and mad.

Then he released me and strode out into the downpour, arms raised, chin lifted. He called for Jupiter to strike him down. "Throw down your bolts, mighty Jupiter!" he bellowed. "I dare you!"

The lightning flashed, making a sizzling sound, followed immediately by an enormous clap of thunder. He laughed and stretched out his arms. I pleaded with him to stop but my voice was drowned out by the beating rain.

"Jupiter is a false god!" he cried. "And our God in heaven will stay His hand lest I give the credit to a pretender. Ha! Looks like I have the advantage of both of them!" He threw his arms skyward and again the lightning flashed, and the thunder boomed.

I was terrified at his blasphemy. I tugged at him and begged him to stop. He looked at me with an affectionate expression and allowed me to draw him off. We took shelter under a weeping willow.

"You shouldn't say things like that," I gasped. "You shouldn't presume to know the will of God."

"Why not?" he laughed. "The bishops do it, and the presbyters. They claim to know the will of God. Why can't I?"

"God can destroy you for speaking like that. Stop it."

His reply was lost in a boom of thunder. He gave me that impish grin of his and took me in his arms. We made love under that willow, the rain streaming down its long branches and dripping steadily on the ground. There was pain in the course of our love, and euphoria too, and when it was over my heart belonged to him.

The next morning he was gone. I wept bitterly. And in the years after I thought of him often, standing in the storm, his arms outstretched, defying the heavens. He was vain and reckless, but he was utterly captivating.

I was sure he would come for me, but I was deluded. For I had not yet learned the crucial lesson we must all learn if we are to avoid crushing disappointment, the crucial lesson I have been trying to impart to you.

Too often we see the world not as it is, but as it is colored by our convictions. For most men, it is of little consequence, but as rulers it is incumbent on us, before we decide on great and momentous matters, to make a wise and judicious pause, and review, with honest scrutiny, those prejudices of the mind which may communicate an unfair bias, causing us to decide not as things are, but as we wish them to be. We do ourselves no favors by refusing to face up to the truth.

When he didn't come for me at Rome, when I discovered he was no longer among the Goths, the last vestiges of my girlish naiveté vanished. The promise he had made, that he would come for me and spirit me away when I needed him, turned out to be false. Even so, I couldn't stop thinking of him, and when I found out he had been sent along by the Goths to act as a hostage to the Huns, I worried about him, for I had heard the Huns were vicious and cruel.

But I let go of any hope of rescue from him. As Alaric and his people took me into captivity, I realized for the first time that I was on my own. Still, I wasn't afraid. I had the courage to carry me through, and I credited him for that. In the short time I had known him, he had given me strength.

Later, when I was married to Constantius and we were plotting his rise to become co-emperor to Honorius, I had all but forgotten my beloved. It had been twelve years since I had seen him last and for all I knew he was dead. It appeared all his talk of achieving great things was little more than the exuberant ramblings of an over excited teen. He was a hostage and had been for many years, while I had grown in stature and influence until I sat but one remove from the throne. We were two different people by then, and his sudden reappearance in my life as Ayboric the White Wolf caught me off guard. I had to do something about it.

I sent word for him to meet with me in private to discuss the proposed alliance. I did not inform Constantius. I dismissed my servants , telling them I would not need their services for the evening, an unusual measure that risked rousing their suspicions, particularly those of my personal attendants: Spadusa, Elpidia, and Leontius.

He met me in my rooms. He had aged beyond his years, the consequence of arduous labor, harsh conditions, and frequent abuse. His eyes were wrinkled at the corners and his skin was embedded with grime. He wore a mass of tangled blonde beard that hung to his waist. It was the feature that gave him his Hunnic name, Ayboric, the White Wolf.

He met me in my rooms. He had aged beyond his years, the consequence of arduous labor, harsh conditions, and frequent abuse. His eyes were wrinkled at the corners and his skin was embedded with grime. He wore a mass of tangled blonde beard that hung to his waist. It was the feature that gave him his Hunnic name, Ayboric, the White Wolf.

He bowed his head in deference, but I told him to look up, and when he did, his eyes burned with the same animal intensity, the same expression of vision and purpose I had known as a girl. I went to him and touched his cheek. "What's happened to you?"

Without missing a beat, he said, "I've been cultivating fidelity."

I offered him a comfortable couch, but he preferred to sit on a hard wooden bench beneath the window. He sat with his knees spread and his palms pressed down on his thighs as if he meant to get up at any moment. He wore a tunic of rodent skins sewn together and trousers made of goat hide. His boots were of sheepskin, embroidered with circular plaques and colorful beads. They were nearly worn out at the toes. The smell of horsehair and animal dung hung about him. He asked me why I had summoned him. His tone was brusque, almost demanding.

"I've been waiting for you," I said.

"Have you?"

"Well, of course I have," I said, a little put off by his gruff manner.

He shook his head. "Fine," he said. "Here I am."

I went to him, a little too quickly, and he flinched, raising his arm, as if he feared I was going to attack him.

"What's wrong?" I asked. "Are you afraid of me?"

"Not afraid," he said. "Just cautious."

"But I'm your friend."

He lowered his arm. "All the more reason."

I looked past him out the window at the distant marshland and gathered my thoughts. "I was in Rome during the sack. I waited for you. I was sure you were going to save me."

"I was no longer with the Goths by then," he said. "They had sold me on to the Huns at your brother's request."

"I had no idea," I said.

"Did you not?"

I took exception to his accusatory tone. "Of course not. I thought you were dead."

He scoffed. "You're lying."

My temper boiled over. "You're right," I told him. "I didn't think you were dead. I thought you were content where you were, making friends with your enemies, cultivating fidelity."

"So, you left me to rot."

He was incorrigible. I was hard pressed to hold my temper . "I left you to your agenda," I said. "Remember that? You were going to bend the Goths to your will. You were going to win their hearts. Apparently that didn't work. They put Rome under siege three times before they sacked it. They ran wild through the countryside burning and pillaging. They took me captive."

"I thought you loved me."

"Don't play the wounded child with me. I'm not fourteen anymore."

He looked deflated. "I hardly recognize you," he said. He looked at the floor.

I reached out and touched him. "They didn't hurt you, did they?"

He put his hand on mine. "Not badly."

"What do we do now?"

"I want to come home, please."

It was a lot to ask. Constantius and I were just barely getting along; our fragile alliance was precarious at best. To go to Constantius now, right after the embassy, and make an appeal on the White Wolf's behalf, would raise eyebrows. Questions would be asked.

"Galla," he said. "Why didn't you wait for me like I asked? Why did you get married?"

"I waited as long as I could. After such a long time, I thought you were dead."

"I'm sorry," he said. He hung his head. He might have been crying.

"Don't be so hard on yourself," I said. "We were children. Saying childish things."

"I meant every word of it."

"That was a long time ago. We were young."

He let his eyes linger on mine – those intense blue eyes. They still burned with determination inside his ravaged countenance. "You've grown more beautiful with age. You are more alluring than ever. "

I felt myself blushing like a schoolgirl. He had that effect on me. I relished it almost as much as I resisted it.

He closed his hand over mine. "I hope Constantius values what he has."

I took my hand away. "Constantius is disappointed."

"For God's sake, how could he be?"

"I am out of his reach. I have taken a vow of chastity."

He began to laugh. "Surely you jest."

I answered him without humor. "I am a woman of piety. I have committed myself to God."

He took a moment to digest this. "Do you mean to tell me you have not consummated your marriage?"

"No."

He shook his head and chuckled to himself. "My goodness, I feel so privileged."

I tried to slap him but he caught my hand as quick as a cat. "Nuh-uh, be nice. You don't want to be the kind of ruler who punishes a man for speaking honestly."

"I am not a ruler. I am merely the wife of a consul."

"For now," he said, letting go of my hand. "But something tells me you're making other plans."

"You know nothing about me," I said.

"Bring me back, Galla. I can help you. You're obviously in need of good counsel."

"How dare you."

"You've lost sight of the important thing."

"More important than saving the Empire?" I shot back.

"If that's your plan, you're certainly going about it in a peculiar way."

"If you have something to say, say it."

"Celibacy," he said. "It's counterproductive."

I dismissed this with a snort.

"Look," he said, "being a devout Christian is all well and good, but refusing to bear children works against the good of the state. Already the army is having trouble filling its ranks. What will it be like in a generation or two if this continues? Do you think Hun women are refusing to have children? Or Goths? Or Vandals? Celibacy reduces our numbers and weakens our hold on power. It makes us vulnerable to being replaced — by outsiders."

"I've heard that argument before."

"I suppose you have. But have you heard it from the man you love?"

I drew myself up. "You presume too much."

"Do I?"

I struggled to maintain an air of dignity. In spite of his ragged appearance, he was as handsome as ever, perhaps even more so. He had filled out from his lanky fifteen-year-old frame and was muscled and sinewy. He patted the bench beside him. "Come sit beside me, Galla."

"I think it's time for you to go."

"You sent the servants away so we could be alone."

"I wanted to speak to you in private."

"About the Huns."

"Yes."

"You're making a mistake."

"I don't think I am."

"With the Huns," he said. "You're making a mistake. You think you can use them to drive the Vandals out of Hispania. It's a bad idea. The Huns are ungovernable. I advise you to end the embassy at once, give them the gold they want, and be done with them."

I lifted my brows. "I'm surprised. I thought you would want a stronger alliance with your captors."

"Not everyone makes a good ally, Galla. The Huns are bare-faced extortionists. Worse yet, they're insatiable. They'll bleed you dry. And if you ever stop paying them, they'll desert you — or, worse yet, they'll turn on you."

"Stilicho used the Huns against Radagaisus with no ill effects."

"True, but Constantius is not Stilicho. It will take a very strong leader to keep the Huns contained, and that man is not here – not yet."

I smiled at his presumption. "I suppose you're the only one who can control them. What a surprise. No doubt this will require a high military command for you and a free hand in dealing with them."

"I know them. Can you say the same thing about Constantius?"

"I must say, your arrogance is breathtaking."

"Not arrogance. Experience."

I gave a little laugh. "I thought you had been ground down by your captors, abused. How did you put it? Left to rot."

"Just because it's been difficult doesn't mean it's been unprofitable. You see where I am now, acting as a key translator for the embassy. It's not because they don't have other hostages who can speak the language. They favor me. They trust me."

"You've been cultivating fidelity."

"I have."

"And so the time has come to see if it's been fruitful. Is that it?"

"You are perceptive, Galla."

"And you are condescending."

He pulled me to him and gathered me in his arms. I struggled for just a moment. We were face to face.

"I've dreamed of you every night for years," he said. "The thought of you kept me alive." He bent down and tried to kiss me.

I braced myself against his chest. "Let me go."

He pressed his lips on mine. I turned my head and pushed him away, but he wouldn't stop. I pummeled him with my fists, but he persisted. He kept after me, kissing me on my neck, my cheek, my eyes. It was like an attack, yet I did not summon the guards to expel him. My distress had become a kind of exhilaration. I felt myself beginning to weaken. I was on the verge of surrendering. And then, abruptly, he released me. He crossed to the door.

"I will inform the Huns that the embassy has been called off, the offer is withdrawn. Ten pounds of gold ought to suffice to compensate them for their trouble. You will not see me again."

He put his hand on the latch.

"So that's it?"

He turned back.

"You show up here and threaten me, and then, when you don't get what you want, you just walk out?"

He looked puzzled.

"I had taken you for a better negotiator."

"Are we negotiating?"

"Not in a way I find satisfying."

He stepped back up to me. "What would satisfy you?"

I put my hand behind his neck and drew his mouth to mine. I kissed him, hungrily, urgently. We made love.

What a stupid mistake! One of the dumbest mistakes of my life. I had thrown away my chastity like a ceremonial garment. I had let my heart rule my head. I was as foolish as a teenaged girl.

I tried to convince myself he would stay. I tried to delude myself into believing he would rescue me from my horrible marriage. But in the morning he was gone. He had gone back with the Huns to the foothills of the Carpathian Mountains.

The proposed alliance was called off. The idea of mounting a military campaign against the Vandals was abandoned. Constantius and I were going to have to come up with a different way to win the public over to our side and marginalize the Emperor.

Very soon thereafter, however, our scheme became moot. Within a month it became clear to me that I was pregnant.

I was sick with dread, terrified of what would happen if Constantius found out. I dashed off a letter to my beloved and told him I was carrying his child. I begged him to come back. I told him I would make all the arrangements, no matter the risk. I promised him a juicy military commission if he would come. I didn't want to be Augusta anymore. I didn't care about Honorius or Constantius or the politics of Rome. My only concern was the survival of the child.

I should have known better. It was all wishful thinking.

A month later, I received his reply. He was gracious. He said he admired my bravery. He told me what he saw: a woman clever, resourceful, courageous, enterprising, and above all, resolute in the face of danger. Clearly, a strong sense of responsibility for the Empire ran in my blood. I would be the one to save Rome. He was sure of it. But I must be patient and endure. Now was not the time for him to answer my summons. Things had changed. His advice against the alliance had increased his capital with the Huns. He was finding new ways to cultivate fidelity. He would remain where he was.

I was devastated. His selfishness and cruelty were beyond belief. How could a man who claimed to care for me treat me so badly? I harbored a burning resentment against him for years. But it didn't last. With time and distance I began to understand why he acted as he did, and I came to forgive him, although for political reasons I have let others believe I continue to despise him.

Nothing could be further from the truth. Quite the contrary. His shrewdness and cunning were invaluable to me.

I wouldn't be where I am today without him.

I suppose you know who he is by now.

My beloved is Aetius.

Chapter Ten

"Aetius! Preposterous!"

Placidius hurled the codex to the floor.

"My mother didn't write this. Somebody is trying to manipulate me."

He called for Isaac, Candida's personal secretary, assigned to her retinue without his knowledge, without Arsenius's knowledge, a clear security risk. The man stood before him with his head bowed as a light rain pattered the roadside. The imperial caravan had been halted and the Emperor's litter lowered. Staff and officials looked on; Stephanus watched from the back of the crowd.

Isaac was a short, stocky man of advanced years with large knotty hands and wide simian feet. His sandals were unfastened at the ankles and the sash that held his tunic hung at his sides. Placidius took offence.

"What is the meaning of appearing before me in this slovenly manner?"

"I'm sorry," the man said. "It's the Sabbath."

"What are you talking about? It's Saturday."

"A thousand pardons," Isaac said. "I'm a Jew."

Placidius recoiled as if he'd been slapped. "A Jew!"

"Yes, Excellency. I do apologize, but my faith will not permit me to work on Saturday. That's the reason my garments are unfastened."

Placidius struggled to process this. "Not permitted to work? Who gave such an order? Not I, certainly. Not Arsenius. And what are you talking about? Fastening your garments is not work."

"The Torah says it is."

"The Torah!" Placidius pressed his hands to his face. "Oh, for the love of God! Who let this Jew into my camp?"

No one replied.

"Who sent you here?" Placidius demanded. "You're not enrolled in the official register. You're not legal without examination. Did Aetius put you up to this? Did he plant you in my entourage to spy on me?"

"Aetius is my patron, but—"

"Aha! Now the truth comes out. Aetius is your patron."

"Correct, Imperator. The Master of Soldiers hired me—"

"To write a verse – a panegyric in his praise."

"Correct, Your Excellency."

"With the intention of presenting him in a favorable light."

"Of course."

"This isn't the first time, is it?"

"I don't know what you mean."

"You've written about Aetius before. You've burnished his image. You've sought to glorify him."

"I've never written about him before now. This is the first time."

Placidius picked up the codex and shook it at him. "Are you denying you wrote this?"

Isaac craned his neck forward and squinted at it. "If I'm not mistaken, that's the letter written to you by your mother, the Augusta."

"Ah ha!" So you know about this!"

"I do. I was the one who passed it on to Cyrus."

"Cyrus?"

"Yes. I gave it to him to deliver to you."

Placidius hesitated. Something didn't add up. Cyrus told him he couldn't remember who had given it to him, but how could he have forgotten a character like this?

"Where did you get it from?" Placidius demanded.

"It was delivered to me by a trading party heading east."

Galla's recommended method of posting confidential correspondence – or so the letter said. On the other hand, if someone else wrote the letter – this scheming heathen perhaps – he would know enough to buttress his credibility by claiming merchants had delivered it.

"Let me get this straight," Placidius said. "You're telling me you were sent here by Aetius, but he did not give you this letter to deliver?"

Isaac scratched his temple, then shook his head. "I'm sorry. Perhaps I gave you the wrong impression. I never said Aetius sent me here. I only confirmed that Aetius is my patron and that I am writing a panegyric for him."

Placidius set his teeth. "Well then, who sent you here? How did you end up in my entourage?"

The Jew remained calm. "I was assigned, along with my wife, to the retinue of Candida. We were appointed by Cyrus on the recommendation of Justa Grata Honoria."

Justa!

His older sister, the bane of his existence. Justa would've been first in the line of succession had she been born a male, but her gender disqualified her for the imperium, something she had never come to terms with. She resented Placidius's ascendancy and never let him forget it. She considered herself disparaged, not only in the eyes of the government, but also in the eyes of their mother, who she suspected of favoring Placidius, which may well have been the case, although not for the reasons she reckoned.

Until her recent conversion, Justa had been practically unbearable. Her temper tantrums were the stuff of legend. She would disappear for days on end, keep company with low, unsavory people, get drunk, and turn up at the palace, noisy and rambunctious and spoiling for a fight. It was an act that got old fast, and Galla had grown weary of it to the point where she could barely conceal her contempt when her daughter behaved like that.

But everything had changed recently. After a particularly galling incident in which Justa's behavior had brought shame on all concerned, Galla had exiled her to Constantinople to live in a convent. When Justa came back after a year and a half, she was a changed person. But Placidius wasn't buying it. Experience had taught him not to trust Justa. And now it appeared his skepticism was warranted. She had involved herself in the selection of Candida's retinue. But why? Was she trying to plant someone near him with the intention of hurting him? Was she trying to kill him? It seemed a stretch. But Justa never lacked for surprises. Just when it appeared she had done every outrageous thing she could think of, she found a way to take it even further.

And what about Cyrus? What had she to do with him? Placidius could not recall a time when he had ever seen the two of them together. In fact, as far as he knew, they were strangers to each other. Yet it looked as if they had collaborated on the matter of the letter. Without dismissing Isaac, he summoned Cyrus before him. This time he was not going to let the waggish *adiutor* use his nimble wit to weasel out of a thorough grilling.

But he was disappointed. Cyrus was not present.

"Where is he?" Placidia asked.

"He has taken leave," Isaac said. "He had pressing business in Ravenna. He departed yesterday."

"Without permission?"

"Oh no, Imperator. He wouldn't have left without permission. Arsenius granted it."

Placidius pressed his hands to his eyes and groaned. When he lowered them, he saw the Jew still standing before him.

"May I go now?" Isaac inquired.

"Yes, of course," Placidius said. "Go. Leave. Do whatever you like. Everybody else does." Then he thought better of it. "Hold on. You're here illegally. You must be examined. Report to Arsenius and submit to his authority. I will not have people milling around me who have not been examined."

"As you wish," the Jew said.

"And tie up your tunic," Placidius called after him. "It doesn't matter what day it is."

The bearers raised the litter onto their shoulders and the caravan started forward. The rain had stopped. Placidius reclined on his pillows and flipped through the pages of the letter. The manuscript had been written by a woman, of that, he was certain. No man could articulate a woman's sensibilities with such accuracy. *Justa*, he thought. But then he rejected the idea. His sister didn't possess the patience or aptitude to carry off such a complicated ruse. *No, someone else had written it – someone brighter – someone more experienced. But who?*

A movement outside the litter caught his attention. The big groom Stephanus was hustling along beside him, waving his arms like he was shooing away a bird.

"See what this fool wants," Placidius told the guard.

The guard went and came back. "He wants a word with you, Excellency. He says it's urgent."

Placidius rolled his eyes. "He realizes I'm the Emperor, doesn't he?"

"I think so."

Placidius sighed. "Tell him to come up."

Stephanus fell into stride beside the litter.

"All right," Placidius said. "You have my attention. What has Candida done now?"

"Nothing. This has nothing to do with Candida. It concerns Cyrus – and Arsenius."

"What about them?"

Stephanus looked around apprehensively. "It's highly confidential, Your Excellency. I think I should speak to you privately."

Placidius was annoyed. He ordered the litter stopped and lowered. Then he ordered the guards and bearers to move back. Only after they had moved out of earshot did it occur to him that he was making himself vulnerable.

Stephanus came closer and leaned in. "You were misinformed, Emperor."

Placidius edged back as if the intrusion offended him.

Stephanus didn't take the hint. He leaned in closer. "It's not like Isaac said. Cyrus didn't take leave like he told you. He was dismissed, sent home. By Arsenius."

Placidius pretended indifference. "Arsenius is authorized to release whoever he wants. He's my chief of staff."

"Yes, he's authorized to protect you, but in this case, I suspect he may have been protecting himself."

Placidius narrowed his eyes at the big groom. "What are you getting at?"

"Cyrus and Arsenius quarreled, something about sticking to the plan that had been laid out for them. Arsenius accused Cyrus of going off on his own and endangering the whole enterprise. Then he lost his temper and ordered him to leave the camp."

Placidius tried to downplay the news. "I'm sure it's nothing to be alarmed about. Anyway, I'll look into it. Is that all?"

"One other thing," Stephanus said. "When you speak to Arsenius about it, could you keep my name out of it? You know how he is. He might overreact, and I don't want him accusing me of crimes I didn't commit. I've already been down that road with him."

"What do you mean?"

"He accused me of stealing feed from the supply wagon, which was not true, and he's been watching me ever since, waiting for me to slip up. If he finds out I informed on him, I'm afraid he'll have me expelled or worse. He might even turn me over to Otho."

"I wouldn't worry about that," Placidius said. "Otho's job is to interrogate anyone who might be a threat to me. He's not called upon to prosecute minor crimes like petty theft. You're not a threat to me, are you, Stephanus?"

"Of course not."

"There you see. Nothing to worry about."

Stephanus had lost some of his color. "May I go now, Emperor?"

"I want to ask you something," Placidius said.

"Yes, Imperator."

"You're part of Candida's retinue. I wonder, have you heard anything about Justa having a part in selecting it?"

"Justa?"

"Yes, my sister."

Stephanus lost a little more of his color. "No, Imperator. Nothing whatsoever."

"You wouldn't be lying to me, would you?"

Stephanus gulped. "Never, Imperator."

Placidius looked for something more, an eye twitch...a nervous gesture...a lie. He saw nothing but the groom's vacuous stare.

"You may go now," Placidius said.

Stephanus hastened away as if he'd been stung.

Placidius cut a look at his Nubian bearers. They had drawn closer and were standing near enough to have heard some of what was said. They were tall, strapping men. He had never spoken to them except to bark orders. He wondered if they could understand Latin. He doubted it. Still, he needed to be more circumspect. He was getting close to exposing a conspiracy, and who was in on it was anyone's guess.

He gave the signal to move on. The bearers stepped into position and raised the litter in a single smooth motion with nary a tilt or list. He began to glide forward over the hard earth. He reclined on the cushions with the codex in his lap. They were in a low grassy region that bordered the Drinus River and defined the southernmost reaches of the Pannonian Plain[1]. North of here the Huns grazed their herds. From now on, his soldiers would have to be especially vigilant. The Huns were unpredictable and dangerous.

They were under new leadership. Their late king, Rugila[2], had been struck dead by a lightning bolt, and a pair of unruly brothers had come to power, Bleda and Atilla. They were an enigma. Whether they would be more or less amenable to working with the Romans remained an open question, although it seemed unlikely they could be more of a menace than Rugila had been.

---

1. Modern day Hungarian Plain

2. Pronounced Roo-gil-ah

As if the threat of a Hun attack and the possibility of treachery in his midst were not enough, something else was gnawing at Placidius's consciousness. He couldn't quite put his finger on it. It had something to do with what he had learned about Justa from Isaac. He picked up the codex and began thumbing back through the pages.

Where was it? Where was it?

When he found it, he gasped.

"Within a month it was clear to me that I was pregnant."

He dropped the codex into his lap.

Pregnant...Galla and Aetius had had a child together.

He spoke the next words out loud.

"Justa is Aetius's daughter."

I can imagine what you're thinking now, Placidius. You think there's no way I wrote this letter. You're thinking, "My mother can't stand Aetius. She squirms under his thumb and only abides him until she can find a way to oppose him. Aetius is her enemy. Aetius turned her against Bonifacius and executed her worthy master of soldiers, Felix. He orchestrated the downfall of the noble Sebastianus and threatened Ravenna with the martial strength of the Huns. Aetius is a snake best dealt with by cutting its head off. Aetius is not her friend. Aetius is not her companion. This letter is a lie, written by someone else to make Aetius look good." But I tell you, Placidius, nothing could be further from the truth.

The value of Aetius to me is beyond measure, but, like all good colleagues, his worth lies not in how he eases the pressures of my office, but in how he divides it up into in manageable pieces, never giving me more than I can handle, and taking the rest upon himself. Yes, he has made things difficult for me at times, but always to my eventual benefit. Unlike so many others, he has never failed to understand me. He has always believed in me, valuing my courage and intelligence when others did not.

Know this, Placidius, your most reliable counselor will probably not be someone who tells you what you want to hear, but rather someone who vexes and challenges you, someone who makes you see reality even when looking at it is difficult.

Has there been deception? Yes, of course. Deceit is a tool in our arsenal, best wielded with skill. Deceit employed clumsily can lead to disaster. Ah, but how to acquire such skills? I'm afraid there's no other way than to learn it in the heat of battle when everything is hanging in the balance and one wrong move can ruin you.

The truth is Aetius could have rescued me from my difficulties. He could have allowed himself to be recalled when he received the summons. Together we could have fled to Aquitaine and taken refuge with the Goths. From there, we could have raised an army and marched on Rome. But that would have been a disaster.

I may have carried the future heir to the throne in my belly, but I had already learned there were no guarantees. If Honorius refused to recognize our child, our play for power would have been regarded as little more than a coup, and the people and the Senate would have joined the Emperor in opposing us.

No, if there was any hope of seeing the child legitimized, it lay in making Constantius believe the child was his, and for that to succeed, it would be best for Aetius to remain where he was. Aetius knew this, even if I did not.

I know it's hard for you to hear, but the thought of sleeping with your father made me sick. Nevertheless, I steeled myself and did it. I seduced him, but he wasn't stupid. He knew right away something was wrong. He probably deduced the truth, that I was pregnant by a lover, but he had no idea who it was and probably didn't care. All he knew for sure was he had gotten the advantage of me at last. And he would use his advantage to even the score for the way I had made him suffer.

His retribution took the form of abuse. He forced himself on me. If I resisted, he beat me. If I cried out, his brutality got worse. He was careful not to leave marks. He knew the news of my failed vow would soon become public and he didn't want anyone to think I had been taken against my will. In any case, he knew I would not dare to claim any such thing. If I did, he would kill me.

Any trace of our previous collaboration vanished. He hated me, not only for the way I had treated him, but also for the way he had been forced into conspiring to keep a secret that, were it known, would have made a cuckold of him and a bastard of the heir to the throne.

Honorius, on the other hand, was thrilled. When he figured out what had happened, he congratulated Constantius in full view of his staff. Later Constantius made me pay for the way the Emperor had embarrassed him by forcing me into an act I cannot in good conscience relate here. Suffice it to say, your father was conversant with the behavior of men who prefer the company of others of the same sex.

When news of my broken vow got out, the public was scandalized. They reacted as if I had affronted each of them personally. I was spoken of as a criminal and a whore. A statue of me was defiled. When I appeared in public, they shouted profanities at me and spit on the ground.

For all of us in a position of notoriety, it sooner or later comes as a surprise to learn just how strongly the public feels they have a stake in our conduct. Every little thing we do elicits a response whether we notice of it or not. When their reaction is favorable, we accept it as a compliment and think little of it. But when their reaction is hostile, it can be difficult to endure. Many were the nights I sat alone in my room and wept, more distraught at the sneering mockery of the public than at the contempt of my husband.

Those were dark days. I was alone and wretched. I felt empty and drained. I slept long hours. Some days I couldn't get out of bed. My servants thought me mad and kept their distance. It was awful. As the child grew inside of me, I contemplated taking my own life.

During this time, word reached me of the death of my old friend King Wallia. He had been succeeded on the throne of the Goths by his capable second in command, Theodoric, who had once tried to spirit me away to safety and who had suffered on my behalf. By all accounts he was a wise and judicious leader, Theodoric, and the Goths were fortunate to have him. But for my part, it meant my old ties to the Goths were severed at last. I felt it as a loss, which only added to my sadness. My only comfort in those long, bitter hours was the amulet Emilius had given me in Rome. I prayed over it, and it gave me strength.

The months dragged past, and I came to term and gave birth. From the beginning, your sister was trouble. She was feverish, sick, and bawled incessantly. She could not be soothed. To make matters worse, Constantius took one look at her and turned away in disgust. The Emperor was also visibly disappointed, for I had given birth to a girl.

I named her Justa Grata Honoria. I said, "This one, born of bitterness and strife, will be a trial." My prediction was only too true.

After that, I thought Constantius would have been finished with me. He was offended by what I had produced. Yet my failure to give him a son who could inherit the throne only spurred him on to more vigorous efforts. This time there be no doubt as to the child's paternity.

As for me, I was but a means to an end. He treated me like chattel. He threw me down and took me like an animal. He didn't deign to look at me. My hatred for him grew until I began to think of ways of killing him. Had I carried out those fantasies, I surely would have been put to death, but I was desperate. I was imprisoned with a screaming, inconsolable infant, and prey to an ugly, pitiless brute. Adding to my suffering was the knowledge that Aetius had refused the summons I had sent to him. He would not be coming back. I was alone. At that moment, I was prepared to do anything.

One day came a knock at my door. It was Sixtus. When he saw me looking so despondent, he knelt before me and took my hand. He blessed me and took my confession. It was a great relief, and I wept on his shoulder as he held me. I have never been more appreciative of another human being, not even Ataulf when he rescued me from the sea.

Sixtus forgave me my broken vow; he forgave me my adultery and my bastard child; and he pressed me to consider my predicament. He knew the exercise of contemplating my plight could lift me from the dregs of despair. He urged me to reflect honestly on what I wanted for myself and to say it out loud. I told him. I wanted Constantius out of my life, even if I had to murder him.

To his credit, he didn't reject this as preposterous. Instead, he said he would think it over it and get back to me later. When he returned, he had some very specific suggestions about what could be accomplished.

Let it never be said that Sixtus is not loyal. It's one of the reasons I nominated him as pope and supported his candidacy so vigorously.

At the inquisitive age of thirteen, you asked me why I spent so much time and energy on Sixtus. I told you then that he was the best man for the job and deserved to be elevated, but the truth is far more profound. Sixtus and I have always supported each other. From the start, our relationship has been characterized by mutual regard and a genuine interest in each other's well-being. Between us exists fidelity of a kind I have only enjoyed with one other person, and she is far away from me now.

When Sixtus came back, he had a suggestion. It was no surprise he had devised a plan that would aid him in his purposes as well. Concord is best achieved when both parties reap the benefits. The only one who would suffer would be a minor personage, the incorrigible magician Quirinus, who was a sorcerer and a practitioner of evil. The plan was inspired. It held out the promise of ridding me of Constantius forever without actually doing him any harm. And it nearly succeeded – before it failed and triggered unintended consequences of a kind I could never have foreseen in a thousand years.

Beware the magician, Placidius. He is a perpetrator of evil and an offense to God. He dazzles you with divination and spells to weaken your piety and make you vulnerable. If he is near you, he is the author of your woes and must be eliminated.

Quirinus would not leave well enough alone. He knew the Church considered him a threat, but when Honorius summoned him back to the palace to perform more magic for the court, he came happily and with great fanfare. He was surrounded by a carnival as if in defiance of the Church. Sixtus loathed him.

Sixtus had troubles of his own. He had never really shaken the rumors of Pelagianism that dogged him. He had been a good and devout priest, but he was on the wrong side of the controversy. To advance in his calling, he needed to convince the most influential theologians, men like Augustine and Jerome, that he could be trusted. Cracking down on Quirinus would give him the opportunity, but he was going to need some help.

The problem with simply condemning Quirinus publicly was the likelihood that Honorius and Constantius would come to his defense. They were big fans of the magician and continued to ask him to perform in spite of the Church's condemnation of him. If we were to succeed, we needed to make them uncomfortable with the magician.

Sixtus found the answer in an old law. It had been rescinded by the Emperor Julian nearly sixty years before. It stated that a woman could divorce her husband with no restrictions on a second marriage if her husband were to be condemned of paganism. Julian, who was himself a pagan, had struck the law from the books. Through successive principates, it had been forgotten. But now, if it could be brought back, it could be the answer to our problems.

This was going to require pulling some strings. The Senate still retained power to make law, but only with the Emperor's approval. However, with an indifferent ruler like Honorius it was easy enough to get measures past due to his lack of interest. Thus, I traveled to Rome to confer with my old acquaintances in the Senate. These were the same men who had been in power when the Goths sacked the city nine years before. I was at pains to persuade them I was still a woman of deep piety in spite of my broken vow.

They weren't buying it, but it didn't really matter. Some of them were avowed pagans; most of the others were Christians in name only. Their only real devotion was to wealth and power. Having the sister of the Emperor petitioning them was sufficient to persuade most of them to cooperate. Yet some of them were more obdurate. Among them was Symmachus[3].

Symmachus was a member of one of the most powerful families in Rome. He had in his employ a clerk by the name of Joannes for whom he had great aspirations.

Symmachus wanted to know what consideration he could expect in exchange for his cooperation in reinstating the law. He perceived correctly that the law could be used to justify a divorce action against Constantius. He knew if my marriage were to end and I were to remarry, my new husband would effectively become regent to the future Emperor on Honorius's death, a position of great power. Symmachus wanted a say in who my future husband might be.

He told me in no uncertain terms he wanted Joannes. The idea was absurd, of course, but I made no objection against it. I knew that when Honorius died I would likely be the mother of the heir. I would be regent and could do whatever I wanted and Symmachus couldn't stop me. Hence, I consented to his absurd condition and got the law passed. The whole process took a few months, and by the time it was over I was pregnant again. This time the child inside me was you, my son.

You were born on the fifth day preceding the nones of Iulius in the year of the consulships of Flavius Monaxius and Flavius Plinta. From the moment I saw

---

3. Pronounced si-mach-us

you, I was awestruck. I had never seen such an adorable infant, not even my darling Theodosius. Your appearance changed everything.

The rules of custody under Roman law are clear. Should a couple divorce, the man will retain custody of the child. To divorce your father would mean losing you. I couldn't bring myself to do it. I told Sixtus I had changed my mind, and we canceled our plans.

He was disappointed, but he understood, and the matter would have ended there, except for two things. First, Constantius, who I had hoped would leave me alone once he had gotten the son he wanted, continued to abuse me. If anything, his cruelty intensified. I began to worry that if I didn't get away from him soon, he would murder me. Second, the magician Quirinus returned at the Emperor's request to celebrate the birth of the heir, flaunting the immunity he had gained by Honorius's favor.

The Church wanted him stopped. If the magician were permitted to go on practicing the black arts, it was feared he would sooner or later corrupt the Emperor, making him into a tool of the devil, which would bring the wrath of God against us all. Sixtus was prepared to take the lead against Quirinus and condemn him publicly regardless of the consequences, but I cautioned him to wait, for if Honorius took offence, it could end badly for Sixtus. Besides, I had stumbled on something that might offer a way out.

I came upon it in a conversation with a lawyer, and it surprised me. As it turned out, my position as sister of the Emperor put me in a unique position. Normally, a woman who divorced her husband would have no custodial rights after the child's third year, but the sister of the Emperor, whose offspring could become heir, could stay with the child as long as she remained close to the Emperor. In other words, in the event that I divorced Constantius, if Honorius chose me to be his adviser and companion rather than Constantius, I could retain custody. But if he chose Constantius, I could lose my son and also my life. My way forward was clear. If I wanted to survive, I was going to have to ingratiate myself to Honorius.

You were the thin edge of the wedge as far as that was concerned. He was ecstatic about your birth and couldn't get enough of you. I brought you around at every opportunity to visit with him. Even when he was off engaging in his debauchery, he would return quickly when he heard we were waiting for him. During these visits I would try to be warm and friendly in a way I had not been with him before. I tried to be sisterly, as I had seen other women do.

Our relationship warmed, and he began to become affectionate with me. When we were talking, he would place his hand on my arm or lean in close. He sometimes let his gaze linger on mine longer than was comfortable. His behavior began to make me uneasy, but I pressed on anyway. There was simply too much at stake.

About this time, the African bishops – Augustine, Auerilus[4], and the others – sought to resist the jurisdiction of Pope Boniface in hearing the appeal of a certain Apiarius[5] of Sicca, who had been excommunicated for heresies including Pelagianism. The African bishops were of the opinion that the Pope had no jurisdiction over their excommunication of the prelate and could not

---

4. Pronounced aw-reel-ee-us

5. Pronounced ap-ee-ar-ee-us

overturn it. The Pope, finding himself on shaky ground, knew his authority could be undermined if priests serving under him were revealed to be secret Pelagians. To protect himself from criticism, he began to make inquiries.

Sixtus's situation was increasingly tenuous. He had to do something to deflect attention from his past, and he had to do it while Quirinus was still around. Sixtus meant to declare his condemnation of the magician no matter the consequences. I told him I would not let him do it without me. We would proceed with the original plan. We would use the accusation of sorcery against Quirinus as grounds to begin divorce proceedings against Constantius.

Our complaint took Constantius by surprise. Not knowing that the law had been reinstated, he had never considered how his patronage of Quirinus could be construed as paganism and used as grounds for divorce. His first reaction was to dismiss it with a laugh. Yet he quickly realized that the more he disparaged the charges, the more he drew the censure of the Church, and the weaker his position became. Naturally, he was angry, for I had outmaneuvered him again.

As for Sixtus, the plan worked perfectly. The Church Fathers championed his condemnation of Quirinus. His willingness to take a public stand against the magician was regarded as courageous, a bold defiance of imperial authority, and one bolstered by the enlistment of the Emperor's sister on the Church's behalf. The Church Fathers rallied to Sixtus's defense, shielding him from any accusations of Pelagianism.

Emboldened by their support, we made a public pronouncement against the magician and called for his arrest on charges of sorcery and black magic. We waited to see how Honorius would react. If he chose to defend Quirinus, he would be taking a stand against the Church, which would give me the grounds I needed to divorce Constantius. But if he gave in, he would be relinquishing a measure of his authority to the Church and endorsing the execution of a court favorite.

I don't know whether Constantius got to him first, but Honorius didn't react with the defiance I expected. Instead, after a few days' cool deliberation, he deemed the charges reasonable and had the magician arrested. A few days after that, Constantius also came out publicly against Quirinus. He claimed he had been laboring under a spell and promised to back the Church in whatever it wanted to do to the magician.

Our plans were upended. Without Constantius's defense of Quirinus, I lacked the grounds to divorce him.

As if to drive the point home, Constantius arranged for Quirinus to be tortured into a confession. The magician was chained to a wall and whipped without mercy. Constantius forced me to watch. It was horrible. I cringed at every crack and cry. When I returned to my room afterward, I threw up. The next morning Quirinus was put to death.

Afterwards I was racked with guilt. It occurred to me that the crimes the magician had suffered for, namely divination and the performance of miracles, were practices routinely performed by the Church. He had suffered torture for something his oppressors did with impunity, and it didn't seem right.

When I voiced my misgivings to Sixtus, he gathered my hands in his and said, "When the Church performs miracles, they are for the glory of God. When the magician performs them, they are for his own profit, without God. Those who act apart from God act contrary to his will. They are agents of the devil and must suffer the consequences."

This was not unlike what Stilicho had said about the good of the Empire, how it must come before all things – how we must measure the morality of our actions by whether they are good for Rome. Those who act contrary to the Empire's best interests are the enemies of Rome, no matter their status or station. Replace the word "God" for the words "the good of the Empire" and essentially Sixtus and Stilicho were saying the same thing.

In other words, as long as God and the good of the Empire share a common purpose, everything is forgivable. But if they should ever diverge... well... I didn't want to contemplate what that might portend.

From time to time in recent years, you've questioned my generosity to the Church. You've expressed concern over whether it's the best way to expend our resources. My attempts to explain it to you in the past fell on deaf ears, so I stopped trying. I realized that until you were able to hear my story and understand my motivations, you would not understand.

Now you begin to see. We must enlist the Church as our ally. Its power is growing all the time even as our own power declines. It profits us nothing to pretend otherwise.

You may not want to hear this. You may cling to the conviction, as your uncle did, that the Emperor is more powerful than any civic institution. But that's not true, and it hasn't been for some time. Our power extends only so far as the other institutions of government permit it. If you make the mistake of turning them against you, you will see how vulnerable you are. The wise strategy is to curry their favor. Grant them those things that will keep you in their good graces. It will make you stronger. It's the best way to invest your resources.

Long years of bitter experience have taught us how dangerous it can be to rouse the army's wrath. Even now, with a powerful and charismatic leader like Aetius at the helm, the threat of usurpation is constant. The Church is similar. Don't underestimate its power. Handled correctly it can be a formidable ally. Its hierarchy is functional and efficient, unlike the state bureaucracy, which is bloated and corrupt. What's more, the Church is the voice of the people. It represents their interests in a way that the Senate ceased to do centuries ago. In a very real way the Church is a government in and of itself and can take over and assume power should the Senate and imperium dissolve. Enlist the Church's power in your favor and you will do well. Get at cross purposes with it and you will suffer.

Honorius and Constantius underestimated the Church and very nearly stepped into the trap we had set for them. At the last minute they saw how vulnerable they were and skirted the calumny they would have brought on themselves had they chosen to defend the magician. In the end, Constantius averted my attempt to divorce him, and Honorius continued to receive the good opinion of the Church in spite of his depravity. But I was not without some victories as well.

Although I failed in my attempt to divorce Constantius, I succeeded in winning new allies. The African bishops, ever on the lookout for new ways to leverage power against their rivals, embraced both Sixtus and me as like-minded enemies of paganism. Their endorsement resonated throughout the episcopal hierarchy and won us the approval of everyone from the lowest clergy up to the Pontiff himself.

In addition, my intrepid stand against Quirinus had won me a much-needed reprieve from the public, whose harsh derision of me for having failed to keep my vow seemed inexhaustible. It says a lot about the influence of the Church when you realize my condemnation of a sorcerer did more to earn the people's pardon than the fact that I had given birth to the heir. Times were changing. Yet the public's good opinion of me wouldn't last. Before a year was out, I would again be the object of their contempt, but this time not as a result of my weakness but because of a betrayal by those closest to me.

I didn't see it coming. At that time all my wariness was focused on Constantius and Honorius. I knew they wanted nothing more than to punish me for having forced their hand on the matter of Quirinus. What's more, Constantius had figured out by then what my purpose had been in condemning the sorcerer and was determined to dissuade me from trying anything further along those lines in the future. But neither man dared be explicit in their hostility.

The high regard in which I was held by the Church kept them at bay. Constantius even removed himself from my presence lest he lose his temper and do something he would regret later. Honorius, as a way of getting back at me for my interference, elevated Constantius to a third consulship and then went a step further to twist the knife by naming him co-emperor.

Ironic. This was exactly what Constantius, and I had been striving for when we were trying to ensure the succession. In many ways we had achieved our goals, but Constantius's elevation now benefited me not at all. I would be lucky if I got through the year alive. Oh, how I longed for Aetius to come back and save me. But it was not to be. I was on my own, and I was going to have to think of some way to extricate myself from the situation I was in.

Then, as is so often the case if you are patient and vigilant, an opportunity came along. Our cousin in Constantinople, Theodosius II, was now twenty years old and a formidable ruler in his own right. He had sat quietly by as Honorius raised Constantius to consul three times, an exceptional promotion for a person who was not of royal blood. But Theodosius II was not about to tolerate Constantius's being elevated to co-emperor, a move over which he had not been consulted and one he was entitled to appraise as emperor of the East. He refused to endorse the promotion.

Constantius was indignant. He vowed to win Theodosius's approval by reason or force. He sent an embassy to Constantinople to discuss the matter while assembling an army at the same time. The whole idea was rash and ill-considered. With the Vandals marshaling their strength in southern Hispania, the last thing we needed was a civil war with the East. I went to Honorius and tried to reason with him.

I asked him to forget his resentment toward me and think about the good of the Empire. If Constantius started a war against our cousins in Constantinople, the barbarians would surely seize the opportunity to strip away more territory from the West. And if the Vandals invaded Africa, they could cut off our grain supply and starve us to death. He had to put a stop to this.

"It's Theodosius who must put a stop to it," Honorius came back. "Either he must endorse Constantius or suffer the consequences."

"Don't be so pigheaded," I said. "Think about it. A war with the East would be a dangerous distraction that could lead to our downfall."

"I doubt it," he sniffed.

"Why doubt it?" I asked. "Is it because Rome has carried on for almost two thousand years? Is it because it seems inconceivable we could fall? Is it because you've convinced yourself God favors us? But what if you're wrong? What if God is angry with us and wants to humble us? What if the Pelagians are right? What if we can correct our moral shortcomings through human will apart from divine grace, and our failure to do so has offended God?"

He shot to his feet. "Silence! You blaspheme!"

"If you let this happen," I said, "you'll go down in history as the Emperor who brought down the Empire. Is that what you want?"

To his credit, he didn't lash out, but slumped back in his throne and brooded on it.

I made bold to go on. "Theodosius feels slighted because you didn't consult him. Unfortunately, you can't do much about that now. But you can allay his wounded feelings by seeking his approval for one more elevation, one he'll find more appealing."

He eyed me distrustfully. "Go on."

"Name me Augusta. It's the answer to all our problems."

He threw back his head and laughed. "Ah, Galla, you scheming little bitch, Constantius warned me you would try something like this."

"If Constantius warned you, it was because he could see the logic of the idea and hopes to discourage it, but that doesn't make it any less reasonable. Listen to me. Theodosius dislikes the idea of elevating a person who is not a member of our dynasty. He's concerned about the long-term survival of our gens. By elevating me, he'll be reassured the dynasty will go on."

"Young Placidius's birth ought to convince him of that."

"Children die, Honorius. If little Placidius doesn't make it to manhood, the house of Theodosius will be at risk."

"Then you'll have another son."

"Will I? Do you think Constantius wants to have another child with me? He hates me. The greater likelihood is that he'll kill me and marry another. Then their child will become the heir."

The point hit home. Honorius rubbed his chin and ruminated.

I got up and said, "Theodosius realizes this, which is why he won't endorse Constantius. You can put his mind at ease. Elevate me and prevent a war."

He scoffed. "You're only trying to protect your own skin. As Augusta you would be beyond your husband's reach."

"If I'm the Augusta, the house of Theodosius will remain intact."

"Are you willing to have another child with Constantius?"

"I'll do what's best for the Empire."

He thought it over. "I'll give you my decision later."

I didn't have to wait long. Before the week was out, he made me Augusta.

The title of Augusta is formidable. It bestows upon women of dynastic privilege a status near to divinity. The wife of an emperor is strong, but an Augusta is untouchable to all but the Augustus himself. Constantius was only a co-emperor. Honorius was the Augustus. By making me the Augusta, my brother gave me a status greater than Constantius himself.

Constantius raged at Honorius. As co-emperor, he believed he should have been consulted. But Honorius pointed out that, if that were so, then Theodosius should probably have been consulted in the decision that elevated Constantius to his position. Better to leave well enough alone. Together, Constantius and I would be Augustus and Augusta. It was best for all concerned.

Constantius stormed out and continued his preparations for war. The Empire trembled on the verge of conflict with the East. Then fate intervened.

In the late summer of that year your father took ill and within a fortnight he was dead. No one knew what befell him. Some thought it was the fever – he was sweating profusely and shaking all over, although it was late in the season. Others thought it was something he ate. Still others suspected he had fallen victim to some dastardly deed. In any case, he was gone, and with him went his reckless plans for war with the East. I must confess I was relieved.

I'm sure it's difficult for you to hear me write of your father in these unflattering terms. As a child you were always led to believe he was brave and wise, a hero. But the things we learn as children are different from the things we must accept as adults. You are no longer a child, Placidius. You deserve to know the truth.

I can tell you this much. Your father was a well-respected military commander to most everyone but me. Having been on the receiving end of his aggression, I could never forgive him, but from the perspective of Rome his hostility against the Goths was justified. It was as a ruler he failed.

His success led him to overreach, to aspire to a position for which he was unqualified. As Augustus, he was even more stubborn and petulant than Honorius. He disliked the job and chafed under the obligations it entailed. He whined bitterly, as if he had been asked to dig a ditch in the rain. None of the emoluments of being emperor made it palatable to him.

It doesn't serve us to put our personal feelings ahead of the Empire as your father did. The job of Augustus is not a license to indulge yourself. Managed properly, it is more restrictive and confining than most people think. As Augustus, you must be prepared to make sacrifices and listen to those who know better. Above all, do not do unnecessary things that endanger the Empire to feed your good opinion of yourself. It's a recipe for disaster.

In the absence of Constantius, Honorius and I became Augustus and Augusta — brother and sister. And we might have ruled together effectively had your uncle not succumbed to his weaknesses. You see, Honorius's voyeuristic perversions had continued unchecked all this time by Church or public con-demnation. They stemmed from the peculiar notion that no ordinary flesh was worthy to touch his own. Intimacy with anyone below him he considered sordid. As a result, by the time of his thirtieth-seventh year, he had grown tired of watching others and was hungry for human affection.

Even before I was elevated, it must have occurred to him that, as siblings, we were peers. Even while Constantius was still alive, he had begun to warm to me. As previously described, he would draw close to me and touch me in ways I found unsettling. Now, with Constantius out of the way and my status nearly equal to his own, my brother's attentions intensified.

He would sit uncomfortably close with his thigh pressing against mine. He would reach over to where my hands were gathered in my lap and insinuate his fingers until I opened them. In public, he insisted on walking side by side, his arm around my waist. He would turn to me with a loving gaze. From time to time, he would try to kiss me.

In private, he never attempted liberties that could be considered excessive. I knew the day was rapidly approaching when his practice of withdrawing to his private quarters to pleasure himself would prove inadequate, and he would try to force himself on me, but I tried not to be too prudish. For the first time in my life, I had achieved a modicum of control over him, the one person who had always been my chief antagonist — the one who had executed Stilicho, the one who had stood idly by as I was besieged, the one who had left me un-ransomed among my captors, the one who had refused to recognize the legitimacy of my child, and the one who had forced me into marriage with a man I despised and nearly brought the Empire to ruin — I was within sight of having him in my thrall, and I didn't want to lose the chance. But my plans were dashed by betrayal from an unexpected quarter.

Considering all we have to contend with in the rivalry for power – senators and bishops, generals and kings – we must also beware our servants for they too have the capacity to bring us down.

To understand what happened, I have to take you back a few years. I hope I have your attention, for I have an important point to make.

When I returned to Ravenna from the Goths, I came away with a small retinue of servants. They were good people and kind. They bolstered my spirits at a time when I was confused and afraid. They were friends to me at a time when I had no others.

When I got to Ravenna, I was outfitted with a full retinue befitting my position. The new retinue resented the rapport I enjoyed with my Gothic servants. As full-blooded Romans, they considered the Goths beneath them and began scheming to get rid of them. Chief among these conspirators were three of my closest attendants. They provoked public brawls between my Gothic retinue and common street thugs, hoping to discredit them. They accused them of theft and debauchery. In general, they tried to play on the popular perception that all Goths were filthy brutes prone to criminal behavior.

When I got wind of their mischief, I called the three troublemakers before me and gave them a tongue lashing in full view of the household. They were embarrassed and contrite, but secretly they were seething with resentment and determined to get even.

When Honorius began to make his public displays of affection towards me, they saw their chance. They put it about that our private liaisons went far beyond the innocent touches and caresses so often seen in public. They reported that as soon as we got behind closed doors, we shed our clothes and indulged in feverish lust, that Honorius performed all kinds of deviant acts on me, and that we laughed at the impotence of the Church to do anything about it.

These rumors incited outrage among the public. They called me a seductress and accused me of ensnaring my brother in sin. The Church, which had been my champion, condemned me as a Jezebel. In Rome, among the Senate, there was talk that I had gone too far and brought shame and opprobrium on the Empire, and that my brother had displayed a shameful moral weakness ill befitting an emperor.

Honorius, who had felt his influence with the army beginning to slip the moment Constantius died, worried some powerful general like Castinus might try to overthrow him. To lessen the pressure on him, he ordered me to take my children and go to Constantinople where I could take refuge with my nephew, Theodosius II, whose impending nuptials would give me the excuse I needed to go without the appearance of fleeing in ignominy. To further distance himself from me and demonstrate we were not romantically involved, he stripped me of my title.

Oh, Placidius, how our fortunes ebb and flow. At last, I had the full power of the Augusta within my reach when I lost it and was reduced to the status of an ordinary citizen. I was driven from Ravenna in shame and rendered an outcast, but I did not give up. The greatest test of courage is to endure defeat yet soldier on, for the final victory goes not to those who win the battle, but those who win the war.

And a war it was. I had no illusions about that. My life had been one long struggle to see the most capable people in power. And I wasn't done yet.

I had a few things working in my favor. For one thing, the heir apparent was in my charge. For another, I was by now keenly aware of the fickle attitude of the public. Having risen and fallen in their estimation more than once, I had every reason to believe my reputation might again be rehabilitated once they had grown jaded with their newest darling.

Fortunately for me, events were already underway. Soon, yet another usurper would undermine the stability of the Empire and garner the people's disdain. It would take two full years for the whole thing to unfold and in the meantime I would live in Constantinople with you and your sister and our cousins, Theodosius and Eudocia and little Licinia.

You don't remember those years. You were too young to have any memory of them. But I will relate them to you now. They were not as you've been led to believe, and it's important for you to know the truth of what happened. Until you do, you cannot know the real purpose of this letter.

Change, Placidius. It's never easy. But those with the strength of character to do it are those who should lead us. And those who do not — well...

Chapter Eleven

It had been our intention to travel to Constantinople by land. A sea voyage would have been faster, but Honorius claimed he lacked the money to finance such a journey. It was a curious thing, for the imperial coffers were overflowing. Still, Honorius pleaded poverty and demanded we go by land. We went with a diminished retinue and a truncated guard. Naturally, I was suspicious.

There was a party of malcontents in Rome who had come together around the newly appointed master of soldiers, Castinus. These men had long chafed under Honorius's rule but had been held in check by Constantius until now. With Constantius gone, they began to assert themselves.

When the scandal of our alleged incest came to light, they made their move. They took Honorius aside and warned him that the army was disgusted by what they'd been hearing and were about to revolt. The soldiers were only restrained by the good offices of Castinus and the other generals, who, they were at pains to tell him, only wanted to protect him from the insurrectionists. Even so, unless they could offer the rank-and-file soldiers something to appease them, their obedience could not be guaranteed. Honorius wanted to know what they wanted. They told him they wanted my death.

I knew none of this at the time. I only learned it after subsequent events brought it to light. The only thing I knew at the time was that a firestorm of public outrage was building against me. When Honorius ordered me to go to Constantinople and take my children with me, I didn't object. I only became suspicious when I was told I had to travel by land without proper protection.

If we had taken the land route, we would have been ambushed and slaughtered by the agents of Castinus. You see, even then he was planning to overthrow Honorius and seize power. Castinus knew that as long as you, Placidius, remained alive, he would always have to contend with a legitimate claimant to the throne, so he was plotting to kill us both.

Fortunately, we had a champion in Bonifacius, a capable military tribune who had been enlisted in Castinus's nefarious plot, but who secretly opposed it. Bonifacius had always been a stalwart supporter of the House of Theodosius and deplored would-be usurpers like Castinus who believed themselves craftier than they actually were. Bonifacius arranged to have a ship outfitted to take us to Constantinople. He paid for it in secret and didn't tell anyone – even us – until the last possible moment.

On the morning we were to depart, I received a courier who informed me there had been a change in plans. We would be traveling by sea with a proper guard. I didn't know who our secret benefactor was, but I was perceptive enough to recognize we had one. I jumped at the chance, and we set sail.

Always be on the lookout for unexpected allies, Placidius. For every groveling sycophant who pretends loyalty, there is a genuine advocate who believes in your worthiness and will brave lions to protect you. Bonfacius was one such.

On the morning we departed, the seas were calm, but by afternoon the wind was howling, and the waves were rising to frothy peaks. The sky grew dark, and the rain slanted down. The ship began to veer and heel. Waves crashed over the deck. For a moment, it looked like we were going to be swamped, but the sailors brought the ship around and headed her into the surging swells. We rose and fell, the bow crashing through the troughs.

You and Justa clung to me in terror. To tell you the truth, I was afraid as well, but my fear was tempered by having endured something similar in the past, back in the days when Ataulf saved my life during the Goths ill-fated attempt to cross to Africa. Experience teaches us that nothing is as frightening as the thing we do not know, and for this reason every ordeal makes us stronger. Like a man who strengthens his muscles by stressing them with weights, our courage is bolstered by facing down threats. Gird yourself Placidius and go straight at the thing that scares you. Remember, nothing fosters bravery like experience.

As for me, I prayed to my patron saint, John the Evangelist, to deliver us from the tempest. I swore to dedicate a church in his honor if he brought us through alive. I gathered you and Justa against me and wedged us between some barrels. I lifted the amulet from around my neck and prayed over it. In time, the storm subsided.

We arrived in Constantinople under sunny skies. The storm had dissipated like a delusion that haunts us in the night and dissolves in the dawn. The sight of the city lifted my spirits. I had been born in Constantinople and had spent the first few years of my life there but had no real recollection of it. I must say it was more breathtaking than I imagined.

Unlike Rome, Constantinople has a freshness and vitality about it, it being a new city, having been mostly built within the past century. Unlike Mediolanum, it is well defended. Unlike Ravenna, it is not fetid or malodorous in the summer heat. Had it been my choice I would have remained in Constantinople forever. But I had other duties, and, in the end, I was not welcome there. Pulcheria had seen to that.

We were met at the dock by a party of dignitaries. The members of the royal family had not come out to greet us. Instead, they sent their regrets, explaining that they were entirely taken up in preparations for the royal wedding. My nephew, the Eastern Emperor Theodosius II, was engaged to wed a Greek woman of surpassing beauty, the daughter of a philosopher. Everyone commented on her wit and charm. Her name was Athenais[1] . She had been deliberately chosen for the Emperor by his older sister to be his bride.

We were driven down a wide, colonnaded avenue called the Mese, which is lined with handsome statuary, sculptures of Roman heroes like Caesar, Augustus, and Diocletian. We were shown the four-way arch of the Milion with the distances to all the major cities etched into its base. We saw the porphyry Column of Constantine, and the ceremonial square of the Augustaion. We viewed the Baths of Zeuxippus and the magnificent oval of the Hippodrome. Everything was new and pristine, not tired and shopworn as it is in Rome, not desecrated and vandalized and gone to seed.

Although I had heard of the wonders of Constantinople, nothing prepared me for its splendor. This is one of the benefits of travel — it connects our imaginations to reality. We begin to see things not as we imagine them to be,

---

1. Pronounced ath-en-ai-us

but as they really are. We gain an advantage over the all too human tendency for self-delusion. I urge you to travel far and wide, Placidius. For every journey is a lesson.

I was wrong about our cousins too. I had thought they would welcome us with open arms. Instead, they remained aloof and distant. They didn't even arrange an audience for our formal presentation until nearly a week after our arrival. I thought it rude and insensitive. I had effectively been exiled, a shameful come down from my former status as Augusta, which might have garnered pity from more compassionate relatives, but Theodosius and Pulcheria ignored me.

To make matters worse, you two children were upset by all the changes you were experiencing, especially you, Placidius. You have never been one to tolerate change easily. You like things to remain as they are.

For that first week in Constantinople, I was miserable, but I tried to make a virtue of necessity and embrace the novelty of being alone. My whole life I had been surrounded by people — guards, servants, colleagues. Being alone with my children was a unique experience for me, and I took something positive from it. I learned that being alone can give you a sense of independence, the feeling that you don't have to answer to anybody. In many ways, being alone makes you feel as though you have fewer problems than you actually do. It's an illusion, of course, but a welcome one after such a difficult stretch. I savored it. But it was not to last. Our audience with Theodosius and his sister Pulcheria was approaching fast, and I was about to learn they were not the warm, loving cousins I had imagined they would be.

Placidius set the letter aside and gazed up at the indentation of the pole in the ceiling of the tent. Already a spider was spinning its web there, stretching its strands into a glistening latticework. A fly bumped along the opposite wall. It zipped off at an angle and disappeared out of his field of vision. The air was hot and sultry. Outside was the loud whir of cicadas.

A servant was tidying up on the other side of the room. Placidius watched him. *Would such a lowly person have the audacity to start a rumor against me?*

He ordered the servant to get out.

Startled by the young emperor's cross tone, the servant stared open-mouthed, then scurried out.

Placidius lay back on his couch and knitted his fingers behind his head. He liked being alone. His mother was right about that. It made you feel as if you had fewer problems.

They had been on the road for more than a month now. It had been a long trek, more than 600 miles, but they were more than halfway to Constantinople. A sea voyage would've been faster, but the overland route was by design. Once they got to Constantinople and Placidius was married, his mother's regency would come to an end, and he would be fully invested as Western Roman Emperor. Even though he had technically been emperor since he was six years old, his mother had been making his decisions for him, which meant his full investiture would be like the elevation of a new ruler, and the people would be excited to see him and celebrate his ascension. Thus it was decided he should travel by land, to promenade across the countryside as a way of exhibiting his imperial presence to his loyal subjects. His advisers had anticipated large crowds would turn out along the route to catch a glimpse of him, but it hadn't turned out that way. Except for a few dozen gawkers who showed up near the larger settlements, the roads were mostly devoid of enthusiasts. Maybe they were afraid of the Huns.

Two years earlier, the Eastern Roman Empire had signed a treaty with the Huns at the nearby village of Margus establishing a boundary the Huns agreed not to cross. But the Huns were not to be trusted. They could violate the treaty at any time and cross the boundary seeking plunder. If they did, the Romans could do little to stop them. Garrisons in this region were sparse and where they did exist the soldiers manning them were second rate. If the people here were less than thrilled about the appearance of the young Emperor in their midst, it was perhaps understandable. After all, the Emperor was the visible representative of the Roman Empire, whose chief attribute to them was as a protector. Having failed them in that regard, maybe the Emperor was not someone they wanted to celebrate.

Placidius tried to put it out of his mind. Above him on the ceiling the spider continued its slow, methodical work. The fly zipped around in wild, erratic loops.

Placidius thought about what he had read. Maybe his mother had written the letter after all. The woman portrayed in its pages was beginning to line up with the person he knew. The way she spoke about her children. Her commitment to the Church. These were things he had experienced. One of his earliest memories was his mother's dedication of the Church of St. John the Evangelist in Ravenna. The dedicatory inscription read, "Galla Placidia, along with her son, Placidius Valentinian Augustus, and her daughter, Justa Grata Honoria Augusta, paid off their vow for their liberation from the sea."

Sixtus, who was deacon at the time, had been at her side. He remembered how warmly his mother had greeted him. They were old friends, just as she had written.

Even the troubling account of her rumored incest with her brother spoke to the truth. Placidius recalled a painful memory. When he was about ten years old, he heard another boy repeating the salacious rumor about the Augusta and her brother. Shocked, he confronted the boy and demanded a retraction. The boy insisted it was true. They fought, and Placidius got the worst of it. Appalled that anyone could slander his mother or lay a hand on his person, he went to his mother and demanded the boy be executed. His mother was calm and diplomatic.

She said, "We must not seek revenge on every lowly person who offends us."

This was during the time when Bonifacius had rebelled against her and enlisted the aid of the Vandals to support him, a betrayal of astounding proportions. Yet within two years of this treason, his mother had forgiven him and made him her master of soldiers. When she talked of forgiveness, his mother wasn't just talking. She meant what she said.

Yet this was the woman, as depicted in the letter, who condemned Serena and betrayed Emilius simply because they became inconvenient to her. This was the woman who, upon returning to Ravenna after her exile in Constantinople, tracked down the three attendants who had spread the rumors about her and had their tongues cut out. It was an appalling act of vengeance, difficult for a young mind to comprehend.

He remembered it well. As children, Justa reported the horror to him with wide-eyed excitement. She had been thrilled. He remembered being horrified. He wept bitterly and insisted it wasn't so. Justa called him a baby.

On the surface, his mother's forgiveness or revenge seemed arbitrary, but the letter told a different story; she always wielded her prerogatives for a purpose, to advance the good of the Empire, and maybe it was so. Still, there were things in the letter that just didn't add up. Her championing of Aetius, for instance. Or her contempt for his father. It all seemed designed to lionize Aetius and make Constantius look bad. It just didn't sit right with Placidius.

Maybe his mother had written the letter at Aetius's direction. Maybe she had done it against her will. And what to make of that revelation about his sister's parentage? Did Justa even know that Aetius was her father, and if she did, was it possible they could be working together to sabotage him? The information that Justa had been involved in putting together Candida's retinue demanded an explanation. He meant to get to the bottom of it. He had already sent word through an intermediary, without Arsenius's knowledge, to recall Cyrus. Once he got him in front of him again, he would grill him without mercy.

But the idea that his mother had been compelled to write the letter didn't accord with the palpable sincerity of much of it. For instance, that business about the amulet. That seemed real. He remembered his mother wearing it all the time when he was little. She had been partial to it. True, she had never spoken to him about it, but she obviously believed it to be a talisman of great spiritual significance because she often prayed over it. Besides, who would include such a detail if they were writing a letter to pursue an agenda. The amulet had no political relevance. It was a thing only his mother would consider worth mentioning.

Placidius was more confused than ever. His head hurt. He gazed up at the spider spinning its web. The fly swooped and darted, drawing ever closer to the threads.

He must've dosed off because the next thing he knew Candida was standing over him, shaking him awake.

"Get up!" she said.

"Wha...what?"

She was red in the face. "How dare you, Placidius! I know you did it. Don't try to deny it."

"Did what?"

"They'll die out there! They'll be murdered or starve!"

"I have no idea what you're talking about."

"Isaac and his wife! You expelled them from camp – a defenseless Jew and a poor afflicted woman who cannot speak. You must bring them back!"

"Slow down. I didn't expel anyone. I'm confused. Isaac has a wife?"

"Elpidia is his wife, as you well know."

"I don't know anything about it. Stop saying that."

"She's mute. She cannot speak. How's she supposed to beg for food? Did you think about that before you threw them out?"

"I didn't throw them out."

"And Isaac won't be any help when it comes to begging for alms. When they see he's a Jew, they'll deny him. They'll starve. Both of them. If the Huns don't get them first."

"Arsenius must be behind this."

"Oh, sure. Blame it on Arsenius. As if you didn't have it out for Isaac, the way you scolded him in from of everyone for observing the sabbath on Saturday. You want to see him humiliated, and you don't care if he dies. You hate him because he's a Jew! You hate him because he's my friend!" She was practically screaming.

He shook her by the shoulders. "Stop it! Get hold of yourself! You're hysterical!"

She twisted free of his grip, dropped to her knees, pressed her hands to her face, and sobbed.

He waited for the histrionics to pass.

When she had calmed down, he said, "I told you your retinue was going to be examined. They were assigned to the caravan without proper inspection. They're a security risk."

"But if the Huns find them, they'll kill them," she muttered miserably.

"Don't worry. I'll send someone to find them and bring them back."

She brightened instantly. "Will you?"

"Yes."

"Oh, Placidius," she cooed. She cuddled up next to him. "You're so good to me."

But he was deep in thought. "That's twice now."

"Twice?" she asked apprehensively. "What do you mean?"

"Twice Arsenius has expelled someone from this camp without consulting me. It's beginning to look like he's trying to get rid of people before I can question them."

Candida's brow crinkled.

"Something's going on here, and I mean to get to the bottom of it."

Suddenly Candida was solicitous. She petted his arm and played with his hair. "Relax, Placidius. You're jumping at shadows. No one is out to get you."

Placidius mulled it over. "Cyrus colluded with Justa to pick your retinue. Isaac was among those they selected, and Isaac is working for Aetius. Now come to find out Isaac brought his wife along. None of these people were properly vetted, and now they're being sent away one by one before I can question them."

"You're being irrational," she said, which was rich, coming from her.

"I don't trust Arsenius," he said. "He and Cyrus have been plotting something."

Candida studied him carefully. "Who told you that?"

"I have my sources."

She rolled her eyes. "I know what's making you act like this. It's your mother's letter, isn't it? It's putting all kinds of crazy notions into your head."

He squinted at her. "How did hear about my mother's letter? I never spoke to you about it."

"Oh please, Placidius. Everyone's talking about it. They say you're obsessed with it." Her eyes sought out the codex lying on the couch. "That's it. Isn't it?"

He stood in front of it protectively. "It's none of your business."

She began to laugh. "You really are full of yourself, aren't you? You see assassins lurking around every corner. I swear you're one of the most insecure people I've ever met. Fortunately, I can forgive you your flaws. Can you say the same thing about the woman you're about to marry?"

"Leave her out of this."

"I'm just saying, maybe you'd be a better ruler married to a woman who understands you, that's all."

He showed her the palm of his hand. "We've been through all of that. I don't want to discuss it further."

"Why? Are you afraid I might have a point?"

He eyed her warily. "How long have you and Cyrus known each other?"

She looked at him incredulously. "For the love of God, Placidius, what are you talking about? Cyrus and I don't know each other. I've seen him around the camp, but we are not friends. Acquaintances at most. Who told you such a thing? I hate it when people tells lies behind my back."

"The last time we spoke, you confessed you had been inside his tent."

"I never confessed any such thing?"

He gave her a dour look. "Well, were you? Inside his tent, I mean."

She sighed. "Elpidia showed me the inside of his tent. I was curious about his furnishings. I couldn't believe he was permitted to have a table and chairs when you wouldn't let me have them."

"Elpidia showed you the inside of Cyrus's tent. Why would Elpidia have access to it?"

"Because she's on Cyrus's staff. She's one of his assistants."

Placidius pressed his hands to his face and groaned. "Elpidia is a member of your retinue, and she's on Cyrus's staff?"

"No. Elpidia is *not* a member of my retinue. Isaac is. They just happen to be husband and wife. Elpidia is one of Cyrus's personal assistants, which could explain why he chose Isaac to be on my retinue, so the two of them could be together." She was giving him with a wide-eyed, don't-you-get-it-now look and holding out her hands.

Placidius lay back on his couch with a heavy sigh and gazed up at the ceiling. The spider was still at work, but the fly was nowhere to be found. The cicadas buzzed with an incessant drone. He felt a headache coming on.

"I want you to hear this," Candida said, producing a sheet of parchment from the folds of her stola. "Elpidia wrote this before she left. She was sorry for any trouble she caused, but she was scared. Listen to what you've done to that poor woman with your unfounded suspicions and your cruelty."

Placidius slowly closed his eyes. "Go on," he said. "If you must."

Candida read. "Fear not for us, my friend. We will make our way as we have always done, though we are but humble people of modest means. And we thank you for your friendship. It has been more than we could have hoped for. Sometimes support and compassion come from the most unexpected places. For every imposter who pretends sympathy, there's a genuine well-wisher who will stand in the breach to defend you. We know you did your best. Thank you for that." She lowered the letter and frowned. "Isn't that pathetic?"

"Is that all?"

"No. There's more." She read on, "Having fallen under unwarranted suspicion, we head off into this unknown country bearing the burdens God has given us. I, a mute. Isaac, a Jew. Some would say these burdens are of our own making, and perhaps they are. But we cannot be less than we are. We must be true to our convictions. You may ask, are we afraid? I would be less than truthful if I said we are not. But every ordeal makes us stronger. Nothing fosters bravery like experience." Candida lifted her eyes and gave him a reproachful look.

"Wait," he said, feeling the hair on the back of his neck stand up. "Read that again."

"I'm not done yet," she said sniffily and continued on. "Do us a favor and tell the Emperor we are sorry for any inconvenience we may have caused him. We didn't know we had not been properly examined. If we had, we would not have come. Nevertheless, we shall try to consider our circumstances in the best light. We shall pretend we have been sent away on an unexpected holiday, a pilgrimage perhaps, to some wild, exotic locale. I've never been to Moesia before, although I've heard it described. This will be an opportunity to see just how much my imagination accords with reality. I shall be able to see if I was right about it. This is one of the benefits of travel, to see how closely our imaginations match the truth. To see if we've been fooling ourselves."

"Give me that," Placidius snapped.

She evaded his outstretched hand.

"I want to see that parchment."

"I'm not done."

"Give it to me."

She twisted up the corner of her mouth. "Don't be such a bully. I'm still reading." She continued on. "I suppose the worst part is being separated from all those good people we met in the camp. Being alone will take some getting used to. But being alone is one of those things that also has a positive side—"

Placidius interrupted. "Being alone gives you a sense of independence. Being alone makes you feel as if you have less problems than you actually do."

Candida looked up at him, and then she looked down at the letter. "Wrong. That's not what it says. Now let me finish, will you?"

He lunged at her, going for the letter. She backed up and collided with the center pole of the tent. It shook the whole structure. The spider fell from its web and landed on Candida's neck. Placidius braced for a scream. But she didn't overreact. Instead, she tilted her head tentatively to one side and plucked it off with the delicacy of a naturalist. She held it up before her.

"Look at that," she said. "Someone has been spying on us." She crouched down and set it gently on the ground. It began to scurry away. Placidius squashed it underfoot.

"By the gods, Placidius! Why did you do that?"

"I don't like vermin in my tent."

She fixed him with a withering glare.

He snatched the parchment from her and began to study it. He took it over and compared it side by side with the codex. The handwriting was different.

Candida stood watching him, arms folded tightly under her breasts.

"Did you find what you're looking for?" she asked.

"It doesn't mean she didn't write it," he said. "She could have dictated it."

"How could she have dictated it? She's mute."

"Her husband could have transcribed it." He stabbed his finger at the parchment. "The advice here, it's almost identical."

"You're imagining things."

"Am I?"

"Elpidia didn't write your mother's letter," Candida said. "Elpidia is a good woman. Isaac is a good man. They were kind and decent to me when you were being insecure and irrational, and now you've driven them off."

Placidius eyed her distrustfully. "Earlier you called them decaying old philosophers and complained they were boring."

"Really, Placidius? Are you going to throw that in my face now? By God, you're cruel."

"I'm only repeating what you said."

"Let's talk about what *you* said. You promised me you would not interfere with my retinue, and then you did. Now you've exiled two of my best friends. Sent them out to die. I don't know if I can ever forgive you."

"Don't be so dramatic. I already told you I'm bringing them back. I intend to question them further, without Arsenius."

Candida stamped her foot and made a little cry. "You're horrible! You're a tyrant! Browbeating two innocent old people!"

"Oh, drop it, Candida. I'm tired of your act."

She buried her hands in her face and wept.

"Make no mistake, Candida," he said, trying to keep his voice even. "I intend to discover who wrote that letter purporting to be my mother, and if I find out you had any part in it, you'll be punished."

She lifted her head with a look of disbelief. Her eyes were dry. She'd obviously been faking it. "You'd really hurt me?" she asked with a wounded expression. "Me, the only one who understands you?"

He didn't dignify that with an answer.

"I love you in the only way that you can be loved. What other woman would be willing to go to such lengths for you? Before you do anything to me, you should think about that."

She stood watching him, waiting for his answer.

He turned his back on her.

A moment later she stormed out.

He stood rooted to the spot, still holding the parchment from Elpidia, struggling against the impulse to go after Candida, to bring her back. Every fiber of his being yearned to retrieve her, to return things to the way they had been before he had started reading his mother's letter.

The old Placidius would have given in to his impulses. But circumstances had changed, and he needed to change with them. He needed to be more like his mother. He needed to adapt. Otherwise, he might not make it to Constantinople alive.

Placidius wrote out an order to have Isaac and Elpidia brought back. He gave the order to a servant to take to Arsenius and a little while later

Arsenius answered back. Placidius had to read the message twice to make sure he understood it correctly. Placidius sent for his chief of staff.

When Arsenius showed up at his tent, he seemed annoyed.

"How can I be of assistance, Your Excellency?"

"Sit down, Arsenius. I want to talk to you about something."

Arsenius could barely contain his impatience. He took hold of a curule chair[2] and stabbed it into the ground so it was facing the emperor and sat down heavily in it.

Placidius eyed him disapprovingly. "I want to speak to you regarding Isaac and Elpidia. It says here you sent a search party after them."

"That's right. I wrote the note you have in your hand."

"I can see that. I'm not questioning whether you wrote it or not. I'm trying to understand why you would send a search party to bring back two people you just exiled."

The response was sharp. "Who told you that? I didn't exile them. I was in the process of interrogating them when they ran off."

"Ran off?"

"Yes. Ran off. Took flight. Bolted. You get the idea."

Placidius rubbed the back of his neck. "Why would they do that?"

"Well, if I had to guess, I'd say it had something to do with the old Jew's wife. Apparently he didn't want me to interrogate her."

"What makes you think so?"

"Simple. After I finished questioning him, I asked him to send her in, and that's the last I saw of them. The funny thing is I was rather inclined to

---

2. A chair with curved legs forming a wide X, and with no back and low arms, traditionally used by a magistrate when addressing inferiors

believe the old guy. He struck me as trustworthy. He's writing a panegyric on Aetius. Were you aware of that?"

Placidius said he was.

"I had no reason to suspect him of anything, but then he let it slip that his wife was traveling with him. I asked him if she was entered into the register. He said he didn't know, so I looked her up. She's not. She's working for Cyrus, and she's not in the register. That made me suspicious, so I asked him to send her in, which was when they ran off."

"That's not the story I got," Placidius said.

"Something doesn't add up," Arsenius said. "I suspect Cyrus is behind this. Which is why you shouldn't have acted without consulting me first."

"I beg your pardon," Placidius said.

"Look, if you had come to me first I would have cautioned you against granting him leave, and we wouldn't be in this mess."

"I didn't grant him leave!" Placidius shouted.

"You didn't?"

"No. In fact, I was informed you had thrown him out. I intended to talk to you about it."

Arsenius bent forward with his elbows on his knees. He rubbed his hands together. "This is bad. Very bad. Someone is trying to sow mistrust between us. Divide and conquer. We can't let them get away with it. Look, Imperator, you're going to have to trust me. For your own safety and security, you're going to have to let me do my job."

"Let you do your job?"

"I've been put here to protect you. Don't get in my way."

Placidius bristled. "I'm not getting in your way."

"We're being manipulated," Arsenius went on. "Fed false information. Who told you I threw him out?"

Placidius hesitated. He promised Stephanus he wouldn't betray him. He tried to change the subject. "We'll get to the bottom of this after Cyrus is arrested and brought back."

"You sent someone to bring him back?"

"I did."

"Without informing me?"

Suddenly Placidius felt self-conscious. "Well, I..."

Arsenius threw up his hands. "Oh, for the love of Christ! This is just what I'm talking about. How can I protect you if you keep going behind my back?"

Placidius's face reddened, half in shame, half in anger. He was still trying to suppress one emotion and drag up the other when Arsenius pointed to Elpida's note lying on the couch. "What's that?"

Placidius snatched it up. "It's a note from the Jew's wife to Candida. It's a farewell note."

"It's evidence," Arsenius said. "Hand it over." He made a curling motion with his fingers.

Placidius held it back. "It's private," he said.

Arsenius shook his head in dismay. "You're being manipulated. Someone is plotting behind your back. And you want to withhold evidence from the person in charge of protecting you?"

"It's nothing. It's just a sentimental note between two women."

Arsenius leaned forward. "What's on the back?"

Placidius turned the parchment over. There was indeed writing on the back, but he couldn't make heads or tails of it.

Arsenius noticed his incomprehension. "Still struggling with Greek, are you?"

Placidius took umbrage. "How dare you."

"As emperor you'll be presented with a lot of documents in Greek. You should try harder to learn the language — to avoid being misled."

Placidius fumed. His mother had badgered him incessantly to learn Greek, but he had rebelled against it. He didn't like being told what to do.

"Give it to me," Arsenius said. "I'll translate it for you."

Placidius reluctantly handed it over.

Arsenius read it carefully. His brow knitted. "Hmm. That's odd. It's a formal statement of religious belief, a confession of faith."

"Huh?"

"It's a proclamation on the tenets of Nestorianism. Here, let me read it to you."

"'Jesus Christ is not identical with the Son but is personally united with Him, and lives in Him, sharing a single human nature.'"

He turned the parchment around and showed it to Placidius. Beneath the text was a short list of names. The writing was sloppy, hurried. "Signatures," Arsenius said.

Placidius had never heard the term before.

Arsenius explained, "People write down their names. It's supposed to stand as a written endorsement of the contents of the document by the people who put them there. It's supposed to be as valid as an oath."

Placidius had a hard time comprehending this. *How could the writing down of a name be as valid as an oath?*

Arsenius went on. "Whoever signed this document was declaring their belief in the tenets of Nestorianism, and they were doing so under oath."

Placidius scratched his chin. "Nestorianism. Isn't that a heresy."

"Anathema," Arsenius confirmed. "And look at the signatures."

Placidius bent closer to look at the names. There were at least a dozen of them, none of which he recognized.

"Skip the rest and look at the one at the bottom."

Placidius drew back in shock.

The last signature on the page was larger than the rest. It said Flavius Placidius Valentinianus.

Someone had signed his name.

When matters are out of our control, we must face facts. One of the most difficult things for any sovereign to do is to admit we are in the dark. As head of state we are the arbiter of last resort, so naturally people look to us for answers. But just because we are the ultimate decision makers doesn't mean we are equipped to render a proper verdict on everything that comes before us. Often we find ourselves in the dark, and it behooves us to say so and not pretend to be more knowledgeable than we are.

This is especially true when we feel threatened. The tendency is to lash out, to act without thinking, which almost always makes things worse. We must resist the temptation to overreact. A good ruler, when faced with an inscrutable threat, acts with restraint and awaits his opportunity.

I know you Placidius. You are impulsive by nature. You must try to overcome this shortcoming. It will do you no credit and may do you harm. This will require you to make a conscious change. I believe you are equal to the challenge. This is not about us and our individual appetites. It is about what is best for the Empire.

After almost a week in Constantinople, we were finally called to meet the Emperor. The occasion was a formal presentation with Theodosius and his court, quite different from the cordial familial greeting I had expected. In fact, there was nothing warm about it at all.

I stood in the middle of a cavernous hall with my children at my side. Theodosius sat on his throne. He was stiff and imposing. He nodded solemnly at us as if we were foreign dignitaries from some newly discovered land where word of his majesty had not yet penetrated.

His sister Pulcheria sat beside him in a simple wooden chair with her hands folded in her lap. Her gaze was appraising and imperturbable. Despite her modest trappings, she was the Augusta of the East, and thus the equal of her brother in every way, save one – she was a woman.

Pulcheria was straight-bodied and pale with an odd little twist about the mouth. Her eyes were faintly slanted. At first glance, one might have mistaken her for shy or demure, but on further observation what was taken for shyness was revealed as smug detachment. She did not speak. Instead, she deferred to her brother. Only when an awkward silence prevailed did she look at him with a heavy-lidded gaze meant to prod him along. He was a dull fellow, your future father-in-law. I trust the intervening years have sharpened his wits.

Theodosius observed that we had come to Constantinople for reasons other than to celebrate his wedding. He heard we had been driven out of Ravenna by scandalous rumors of grotesque perversions shocking to Christian minds. He asked if there were any truth to the rumors. I assured him there were not; I was the victim a vendetta. He seemed satisfied, but Pulcheria kept on eyeing me. There was a long uncomfortable pause. At last, she said, "Grass rarely grows on a beaten path."

I acknowledged the truth of the aphorism but kept my head bowed and waited for the interrogation to pass. When I looked up again, she was still glaring at me. I would be lying if I said she didn't unnerve me. After a spell, I grew irritated. This had gone far enough. She was my niece, seven years my junior, not my inquisitor. I returned her glare. Neither of us flinched. The seconds drew themselves out. The room filled with an uncomfortable silence.

Pulcheria had ascended to her position through guile at the age of fifteen. She had taken over the role of regent from the powerful praetorian prefect Anthemius, a man of considerable talents, who she had forcefully removed from his position on the basis of his not being related by blood to the Emperor. This was the selfsame Anthemius who had long ago provoked Stilicho to conceive his plan to seize power for himself, a scheme that was aborted when Stilicho was killed.

Contrary to what Stilicho believed, Anthemius was neither corrupt nor incompetent. In his seven years as regent to young Theodosius, he had done much to increase the fortunes of the East. He had made peace with the Persians, bolstered the grain supply, filled the imperial coffers, and undertook the construction of the formidable walls that now surrounded the city. He was popular with the people, the Church, and the army. But when Pulcheria took aim at him, his days were numbered. One day he vanished. Pulcheria claimed he was enjoying his retirement on a remote island in the Aegean and refused to discuss the topic further. She was made regent and shortly thereafter proclaimed Augusta by a compliant Senate. She was fifteen. Theodosius, her younger brother, was twelve.

Pulcheria's sway with the Senate owed a lot to her influence over the Emperor. As a young sovereign, Theodosius was known to be friendly, jovial, and naïve, susceptible to those who would manipulate him. Pulcheria transformed him. She taught him how to behave like an emperor, how to walk and talk properly, how to ride his horse, how to sit on the throne, how to wear his robes and speak with dignity, and above all, how to be circumspect and guarded. By all accounts, the change in him was remarkable. The Senate, ever appreciative of decorum and stability, was grateful. They rewarded Pulcheria with the role she coveted and endorsed her brother's nomination of her as Augusta. She was nothing if not daunting, and now she was glaring at me, trying to make me crumble. I would not give her the pleasure.

As it happened, however, Justa chose that moment to misbehave. She was just five years old and must've sensed the hostility in the air. She began to whine and cry. My efforts to silence her only provoked her to greater fits of temper. By then I had broken off my staring contest with Pulcheria and was trying to appease her when Pulcheria's voice rang out like a clap of thunder. "Out!" she cried.

Justa gaped in horror. Tears ran down her face; her mouth froze in mid-wail.

"Remove that child," Pulcheria commanded.

The guards closed in around us. Poor little Justa rotated her head on her shoulders and looked at the men towering over her. When they reached down to take hold of her, she whimpered and clung to my leg. I told her to go with the nice men and assured her she would be all right. They dragged her away kicking and screaming. It was cruel, I admit it, but what else could I do. I regretted it ever after.

"The other one can stay," Pulcheria said. "He seems like a nice, well-behaved little boy." She paused. "I like well-behaved boys."

I looked down at you by my side. You were a little agitated by what had befallen your sister, but I gave you a bright red ribbon to play with and you were content.

Theodosius asked me how long I planned to stay. I told him I would return to Ravenna when Honorius recalled me.

"How long do you think that will be?" he asked.

"When the scandal dies down."

He waited.

"In a year or so," I said.

"Of course, you may stay with us," Theodosius said. A modicum of sincere graciousness seeped out from behind his imperious posturing. "You may live with us in the palace. But you must understand we do things a little differently here."

"We are pious people," Pulcheria said. "We respect God and the Church."

This was her way of saying she would brook no further scandals from me. She was warning me that if I proved as sinful as my reputation, I would be exiled – or worse.

I was not about to argue or make a case for my innocence. Clearly, they had already made up their minds – or at least Pulcheria had, which amounted to the same thing. My situation would be best served if I restrained my emotions and didn't make things worse. I was a princess, yes, and a former Augusta, but at the moment I was at their mercy. I bowed my head and said, "Of course."

The audience was at an end, but as we were preparing to leave, Theodosius spoke up. He was about twenty years old but looked a good deal younger, rather like an overgrown schoolboy. He was pudgy about the face with weak eyes and a thick neck. His belly was prominent, but his legs were spindly, and his arms were thin. He said, "You will be attending the wedding, I assume."

I told him I had been planning on it.

He looked to his sister. Something unspoken passed between them. Then he addressed me in a stiff, formal manner. "We will select your attire for you."

It was all I could do to hold my tongue. The idea that I could not be trusted to dress myself was offensive and probably meant to be. I nodded my acquiescence.

There comes a time, Placidius, when we must acknowledge our powerlessness, when our titles and trappings are meaningless because someone else holds the advantage. To get through such times, we must recognize our helplessness and surrender. There will be opportunities to right the wrongs against us in the future, but for now we must be patient. Don't think of it as a humiliation. For by humbling ourselves we can get the distance we need to assess the situation, the better to act when the opportunity arises.

They may regard you as weak. But at the end of the day their underestimation of you is a vulnerability that can be exploited, so for the time being you must be patient.

Chapter Twelve

The marriage of Theodosius and Athenais was a lavish affair as you may well imagine, and something similar to what you will experience when you and Licinia wed, although without the attendant unpleasantness I hope.

At first, Pulcheria was quite proud of what she had put together. She had assembled the guest list and seen to every detail. She had ordered the decorations, chosen the vestments, and selected the food for the banquet. As mentioned earlier, she had even selected the bride. Everything about the wedding wore her imprint, and she promised a ceremony on a scale unseen in the city since my father, Theodosius, wed my mother, Galla, thirty-four years before. The public thought it glorious.

They loved a good show, and they loved Pulcheria. Whenever she appeared in public, they cheered her. She was hugely popular, ostensibly for her vow of chastity. Yet behind their enthusiasm for her abstinence there lurked more selfish motives. They adored her because she was generous. Her charity was unrivaled. She channeled huge amounts of money through the Church for distribution among the poor, funds that might have gone to amassing a large inheritance for her children had she borne any. Both she and Theodosius were celibate, and it was presumed they would remain so. To the public this meant their largesse would continue unencumbered. Hence, whoever married into this barren arrangement would be expected to be equally abstemious or earn the public's rancor.

Athenais was from Athens. Her father was a famous Greek philosopher and very wealthy. They were not Christians but practiced the pagan religion of old, a failing that would have disqualified her for marriage to Theodosius had she not had other outstanding qualities.

She first came to the attention of Pulcheria over a matter involving a stolen inheritance. For years, Athenais had been a devoted daughter and taken care of her father as he grew old and feeble. As a result, her father valued her above her siblings and promised her she would inherit more than them when he passed. But when he died all his wealth was left to her brothers, under mysterious circumstances, and she was left destitute.

After exhausting all other means to achieve justice, Athenais appealed to the Augusta. Pulcheria, ever mindful of her public image, agreed to hear her case. On first seeing her, Pulcheria was struck by her extraordinary beauty. It fit the one prerequisite Theodosius had set out for her in choosing a bride for him. He had written: "I want you to find me a young girl, very comely, the most beautiful ever seen in Constantinople. And if she isn't marvelously good-looking, I have no use for her."

Even more to Pulcheria's liking, Athenais seemed shy and demure, which in Pulcheria's mind meant she could control her. She wasted no time in putting her to the test. She laid out for Athenais the conditions she had to agree to before she could marry Theodosius. First, she had to convert to Christianity. Second, she had to change her name. Third, because Pulcheria considered female chastity the highest Christian virtue, she had to remain chaste, even after they were married. Athenais agreed.

Pulcheria couldn't have been more pleased. She assured Athenais her sacrifice would win the public's favor and make her wildly popular, which it did. But there was another reason behind Pulcheria's requirement that Athenais remain chaste. Pulcheria was only twenty-two-years-old. She intended to remain in power for decades to come. If Athenais were to give birth to an heir, it would threaten Pulcheria's hold on power the moment the child was conceived. Keeping the royal couple childless ensured Pulcheria would remain the Augusta for as long as her brother remained alive.

Pulcheria presented Athenais to Theodosius, and the instant he laid eyes on her he approved his sister's choice. She was even more beautiful than he had hoped for. The wedding was on.

Athenais was baptized within the week and submitted to a name change. Henceforth, she was to be called Eudocia[1], which means "well satisfied" in Greek – ironic to say the least. In any case, no one ever called her by that name. We royals almost never call each other by our ceremonial names. No one ever calls you Valentinian III, for instance. You are always Placidius to us. By the same token, Eudocia was never called Eudocia, nor was she called by her original name, Athenais. Rather, she was called Eustacia[2], after Saint Eustace, a Christian martyr burned to death for refusing to worship the pagan gods.

---

1. Pronounced yoo-doe-see-uh

2. Pronounced yoo-stay-see-us

Eustacia was remarkably well educated for a young woman. Her father had taught her rhetoric, poetry, and philosophy. She knew the Socratic virtues. She was well spoken and could recite poetry. She had strong opinions. But she was also shrewd and diplomatic and knew when to speak and when to hold her tongue. She let Pulcheria believe what she wanted to believe, unwilling to do anything that would jeopardize her opportunity to wed Theodosius and gain a share of power. She bided her time.

I first met her ahead of the wedding as she was being primped and adorned. She wore a belted white tunic and a traditional orange veil. There were ribbons in her hair. She was stunning, a dark-haired, brown-eyed beauty. She had a sculpted figure, dancer-thin, a long, slender neck, and well-proportioned, delicate features. Her thin crescent brows lifted slightly when she smiled, her dark lashes batted, her lips parted, and her flawless teeth dazzled. She was gracious in the manner of someone impeccably schooled in the social graces, yet she surrendered nothing of the modesty for which she was renowned. In a moment, she had sized me up and recognized me as a potential ally. It took me only a little longer to perceive her value to me.

It happened after I had withdrawn to take my place among the wedding guests in the basilica. I suddenly realized I had dropped the satchel of hazelnuts I had brought with me to shower on the newlyweds with after the ceremony, and so I returned to the room. Eustacia had sent her attendants away and was alone. She was sitting with her back to the door, her head turned slightly away. She had a knife in one hand. She was cutting off a lock of her hair. When she was done, she placed it in a small metal pan with some incense and burned it.

I knew at once what she was doing. She was making a nuptial offering to the goddess Athena. It told me everything I needed to know about her. She had not entirely succumbed to Pulcheria's demands. She was still a pagan, covertly defiant, her own woman, and courageous, all qualities I would find to my advantage should I find myself at odds with Pulcheria. I abandoned my hazelnuts and returned to the congregation.

The wedding was magnificent. The basilica was adorned with flowers and tapestries. The windows were covered with ornate patterns of thinly sliced alabaster through which the afternoon light made clever shapes and shadows. The bride and groom wore wreaths of gentians and periwinkles. Pulcheria appeared arrayed in a shimmering stola of Oriental silk and presented the wedding contract, which the bride and groomed signed with due solemnity. Then the matron of honor, a handsome woman of forty years, asked for the exchange of gifts. Eustacia gave Theodosius an engraved ring. Theodosius gave her a Bible. The matron joined their hands and called for the exchange of vows. They did so silently, as is the custom, and when they were done, all repaired to the great hall for the wedding banquet.

There were more than two hundred guests in attendance, some traveling from as far away as Britannia. We dined on roasted lamb, oysters, and dormice. We drank honeyed wine. An orator delivered a panegyric in praise of Theodosius and Pulcheria, an honor orchestrated by Pulcheria herself, which nevertheless made her blush at its glowing adoration. Another orator said a few words in honor of the bride. There was music and entertainment. Everyone was light-hearted and dancing and having a good time. In the midst of the festivities Eustacia stood up and requested the guests' attention. She wanted to read a poem she had written. Pulcheria was instantly on guard. This had not been in the plans.

The poem was a panegyric on the Roman victory over the Persians. Harmless on its face, it was laced throughout with oblique references to the bride's paganism. Pulcheria sat stock-still throughout, her hands folded primly in her lap as a vein throbbed silently at her temple.

It was the first volley of Eustacia in defense of her newly conquered bastion. She was serving notice to Pulcheria that she was not just going to roll over and take it. As I sat there in the clothes Pulcheria had picked out for me, I couldn't help but smile.

It didn't take long for Pulcheria to strike back. Two weeks after the wedding, at the Augusta's urging, the Senate passed legislation that tightened the restrictions against paganism. Like everything Pulcheria did, her actions had the dual purpose of undermining her enemies while simultaneously increasing her own status. She was nothing if not economical.

The people of Constantinople applauded the confiscation of property belonging to the so-called apostates. They praised the restrictions that barred pagans from joining the military and the civil service and celebrated the edicts that denied them the protection of the judiciary. I tell you, Placidius, it is the mark of a true tyrant when the basest instincts of the public are used to pursue a personal vendetta. Pulcheria was making it clear, she was not to be trifled with.

Eustacia was shocked at the viciousness of her sister-in-law's retaliation. She dared not be too transparent in her paganism now and had to sit on her hands as friends and family were hounded and persecuted. Among the victims were her two brothers, who, you will recall, were the original reason Eustacia had appealed to Pulcheria. She had come to Constantinople to seek redress for the misappropriation of her inheritance by them. On the pretense of exacting justice for Eustacia, Pulcheria had the two men imprisoned and threatened them with torture if they did not give back the money. The only problem was they no longer had the money. They had wasted it on ill-considered enterprises and were destitute. Pulcheria had no sympathy for them. She accused them of having donated it to an illicit cult and clapped them into the dungeon to await a visit from the interrogator.

Eustacia deplored her brothers for their avarice, but she didn't want to see them hurt. She pleaded with Theodosius to have mercy of them, but he deferred the decision to his sister. The two brothers were brutally whipped.

Eustacia retired to her chambers, where I expected to find her distraught, but having gone there to offer my sympathy, I was surprised to find her sitting calmly by the window, gazing out at the Bosporous. When she saw me standing in the doorway, she greeted me with a smile and patted the seat next to her.

"Come, sit next to me, Galla, and commiserate."

I did.

We sat looking out at the boats going back and forth across the strait. She said, "I have a fairly good idea of what will happen next. She will make a public announcement that she has recovered my inheritance. She will make a great show of giving it back to me. The public will applaud her, and I will be expected to make a show of gratitude. Then she will declare I have no need for it now, as I am the wife of the Emperor and have all the riches I could ever want. She will tell them I have decided to donate it to the Church. They will cheer her — and me."

"You seem to apprehend her quite well."

"I was introduced to a lot of different kinds of people while I was growing up. My father was sought out by the rich and famous for his penetrating intellect. I am not unfamiliar with those who make an art of currying the public's favor, although Pulcheria is on another level when it comes to her willingness to demolish her rivals."

"What are you going to do about it?"

"Play along. Let her believe I have been vanquished. That's what she expects, and she shall have it, for a time."

"But only for a time."

"People obsessed with their public image have a difficult time believing that others aren't as well. They tend to regard them as either dangerous or stupid."

"And you prefer to be thought of as the latter."

"I am not willing to show my hand yet. I don't want her to feel threatened by me, like she does by you. She doesn't know what to make of you. She can't understand why you did what you did."

"I made a mistake."

"Really, Galla? Are you that careless? Somehow, I doubt it. Deep down, you knew the cost, and you were willing to pay it. I think you showed great courage. In fact, I consider you an inspiration."

"What are you saying?"

"I'm considering breaking my vow."

I hadn't seen that coming and was taken aback. Her marriage was only a few weeks old. Her vow of chastity was freshly minted. To break it now, so soon after having made it, would imply a lack of self-control and a weakness of character. It would incite a great public outcry against her, but she knew what she was doing.

She put her hand on mine. "I'm only telling you this because I believe you can be trusted, and, frankly, I could use your advice. You violated your oath of celibacy. You risked public humiliation to achieve something better. Was it worth it?"

I hesitated. "Well, it gave me my children. It gave me Placidius and Justa."

"It gave you the heir."

"Yes."

"Well, that certainly is momentous. But was there anything more?"

"It gave me influence over Constantius – or would have, under different circumstances."

"Different circumstances?"

I looked away.

"Oh, I see," she said.

"But your situation is quite different," I said. "Theodosius will be the father. No question."

"That's the plan," she said. "But will he go along with it?"

"Do you really think his sister has that much influence over him? She can't be in bed with him. Can she?"

"She's always with him — in his head."

"You're a beautiful woman. How could he resist you?"

Eustacia gave me a sweet smile.

I felt myself blushing.

"It will cause a great scandal," she said. "The public will attack me."

"And the Church will jump at the opportunity to vilify you."

"But I will have the heir," she said. "And I will have Theodosius. He will be in my thrall, and not in hers."

"But she will still have the Church, and she will still have the people, and she will use them to ruin you."

"Not if I'm the Augusta?"

"Do you really think you can get him to take the title from her and give it to you?"

She smiled and batted her lashes. She pulled the top of her palla down to expose the tops of her breasts.

"Ah, the temptress."

"Eve with the apple. I will offer him a bite of the forbidden fruit, and then I will snatch it out of his reach. Until I get what I want."

I was impressed. She was clever and brave, and she knew her own mind. Believe me, had these words issued from the lips of some lesser person, I would have discouraged it in the strongest terms, but I believed Eustacia could make it happen.

She drew her palla back up around her shoulders and retied her sash. "I've been watching them. Pulcheria's ability to control him owes less to her strength than to his weakness. If she can manipulate him, so can I."

"Don't underestimate her."

"I won't. That's why I'm confiding in you." She leaned in closely enough for me to smell her perfume and feel the warmth of her skin. She whispered in my ear, "Surely, it has occurred to you how much I risk by sharing my plan with you. After all, we hardly know each other."

The thought had occurred to me, but I had not given it proper consideration, given that I was so thrilled by her combination of beauty and daring.

She went on. "I am prepared to offer you something in exchange for your discretion, something you desire."

"What is that?"

"Illyricum."

Well, to say I was surprised would be putting it lightly. I hadn't expected her to be acquainted with the political dispute between East and West over the status of Illyricum, although on reflection, I don't know why. She was Greek, which is in Illyricum after all, and due to her father's fame, she knew people in politically connected circles in Athens.

"Would you like that?" she asked.

"Well, of course," I said. I began to feel like an honored guest who was being offered a rare delicacy from a platter. "But how? Why?"

"Because I need your help and guidance. Because I'm not sure I can do this alone. And because we both want the same thing, which is to see Pulcheria put in her place.

"We're going to have to be careful."

"Agreed. She's treacherous and cunning. Everything she does is for a political reason. Do you know why she chose me to marry Theodosius?"

"Because of your beauty."

"Ostensibly, yes, but there was more. She told Theodosius – out of earshot she thought, but I could hear them – that by marrying a Greek they would strengthen their hold on Illyricum. She said of me, 'Her father is a famous philosopher, renowned throughout Illyricum, very popular with the people,' which is true. Later I learned the Prefecture of Illyricum is a matter of dispute between the two halves of the Empire. Originally under the jurisdiction of the West but loaned to the East by Emperor Gratian to assist them in putting down the Goths, it was withheld by Constantinople after the war and never returned. The West wants it back. Meanwhile, the East is trying to tighten its grip on it. By marrying the Eastern Emperor to the daughter of a popular Greek philosopher, Pulcheria is hoping to strengthen their claim."

I thought back to Stilicho and the way he had spoken about Illyricum, how vital he considered it for the future of the West. He was planning to go to Constantinople and overthrow Anthemius to get control of it. That had been his plan and the reason he had wanted me to go along with him, to lend him legitimacy. The East was never going to relinquish it otherwise.

"Theodosius is a simple man," she said. "He doesn't care a whit about Il-lyricum. It's a source of potential trouble for him. He'd just as soon return it to the West and be done with it. It's her. She wants it. He only hangs on to it to appease her. When Illyricum is returned to the West, he will be relieved. Only she will be disappointed."

I had to admit she was probably right. Theodosius wasn't canny enough to be invested in a place he had never set eyes on. I told her I would help.

She clapped her hands like an exuberant child. She beamed and wrapped me in her arms. It was not the reaction I had expected. She had about her a certain childish innocence in spite of the fact that she was clever and cunning. I found her enchanting.

She held me at arm's length and looked me in the eyes. "I don't want to get too far ahead of myself. I don't want to act impetuously. Tell me what to do first."

I gave her an indulgent smile and patted the back of her hands. I advised her to proceed with caution, and not to assume her influence over Theodosius was stronger than it was. She needed to test it first. I suggested she use her feminine wiles to see if she could persuade him to defy Pulcheria and release her brothers from custody. If she could accomplish that, we would be ready for the next step. She agreed.

A week later we met again. It turned out better than we had hoped. Instead of begging and pleading with Theodosius, as she had done before, she enticed and beguiled him, bringing him to a fever pitch of lust before pulling back and making her demand. The next day her brothers were released. What's more, they were given good government jobs at a distant border outpost where Pulcheria's wrath was unlikely to reach them. Eustacia was thrilled.

"Oh, Galla, I knew I could count on you. Your advice was priceless!" She kissed me.

Our next move was going to be riskier, an attempt to make Theodosius complicit in the loss of her chastity. If he balked, our entire scheme would fall apart; if he reported her advances to his sister, we were ruined. To make it work, Eustacia was going to have to affect irrepressible ardor for her new husband, make him believe she was so smitten with him she could not keep her vow, convince him that if he did not take her at once she would have to seek relief somewhere else. We both laughed aloud at that, wondering how anyone could have such feelings for Theodosius, and giggling at the peculiar weakness for sexual flattery shared by all males, and how they bristled at the threat of a more potent rival.

Theodosius was no exception. He surrendered at once. He made only the meekest objection on religious grounds, then consummated his marriage with gusto. In the following weeks, she visited him over and over again, hoping to become pregnant by him before Pulcheria found out. No success. Then Theodosius's guilt got the better of him and he revealed everything to his sister.

Like a coldblooded assassin, Pulcheria went on the attack. She denounced Eustacia as a sex-mad degenerate who had led the Emperor into sin and error. The public, secretly titillated, pretended outrage. Eustacia was heckled and spit upon. The Church labeled her a pagan and an infidel. She was refused Holy Communion. She was officially censured. Yet she bore it all with quiet dignity. She had taken a chance, and it had gone wrong, and she was prepared to suffer the consequences.

In private, we discussed what she needed to do to build back her reputation. I gave her my opinion, and she listened, but she had already figured it out. She would have to do as Pulcheria had done, and as I had done, in a certain sense, when I had condemned the magician. She would have to give the public something to satisfy their thirst for revenge. Executing a Jew or two would have done the trick, but she was too tenderhearted for such brutality. She left it to me to come up with something.

The Church would be easier to placate. A substantial monetary contribution to the bishop with the instruction that it be distributed to the poor but with no official oversight would be more than enough to soften their criticism. Sadly, however, she didn't have the resources for such generosity. She was not the Augusta. She didn't have access to the imperial treasury as Pulcheria did, which was why we decided to implement the second part of our plan without delay.

Eustacia would try to persuade Theodosius to proclaim her Augusta. She would entice and elude him. She would titillate and rebuff him. She would flirt with other men and drive him insane with jealousy. She would dangle her precious fruits just out of his reach and ask him if he really loved her, and when he professed his passion, she would demand he prove it.

He promised he would. He swore he would proclaim her. She took him at his word and had pity on him, pathetic creature that he was. She figured it couldn't do any harm to have sex with him every now and then; he was her husband, after all. Besides, giving him a taste would keep him enthralled. But her generosity had consequences. Within a month, she was pregnant, and then things got complicated.

Eustacia gave birth to a daughter who she named Licinia Eudocia, a lovely child, sweet and gentle, with a mild temperament. It made me envious because my own experience was so radically different. Justa was uncontrollable. At six-years-old she was willful and manipulative. She threw tantrums. She was mean and vindictive. She wanted to go home. She hated Constantinople and couldn't understand why we had to stay there. She cursed the servants and railed against her tutors. She pulled the legs and arms from her dolls. She threw the cat out the window. I seriously thought about giving her away but couldn't bring myself to do it. In spite of her horrible behavior, I still loved her. Every time I looked at her I saw something of Aetius.

Unbeknownst to me, at that very moment Aetius was trying to get recalled. When the Hun king Charaton died, Aetius's effectiveness as a hostage came to an end. The king's successors, a pair of brothers named Octar and Rugila, were not as enamored of him as their predecessor had been, and Aetius felt he had gotten everything he could get from them. He had lived as a hostage among Rome's enemies for the better part of seventeen years; his insights into their minds and motivations were complete. Few knew more about the Huns and Goths than he. Even the Emperor recognized that, so Aetius got his wish and was recalled.

When he got back to Ravenna, he was appointed governor of the imperial palace, effectively one notch above the rank he had relinquished when he had gone away as a boy. If Aetius resented the menial assignment he had been given, he never said so. In any case, his star was about to ascend. Events were unfolding. He was destined to become one of the most influential men in the Empire, much to my grief I might add. But I knew nothing about it at the time, cloistered as I was in the imperial palace at Constantinople.

Following the birth of Licinia Eudocia, Pulcheria changed tactics. She had failed to prevent her brother from siring a child, and now she would have to contend with an heir. Being a girl, Licinia Eudocia posed no real threat to her, but a boy child could swiftly marginalize her, so she began to work to persuade Theodosius to grant her unprecedented access to the as-yet-unconceived child, much in the manner of a regent. She had legal documents drawn up legitimizing this peculiar arrangement, and Theodosius signed them without Eustacia's knowledge.

The scheme nearly worked. The following year, Eustacia gave birth to a son, and Pulcheria quickly asserted her rights. Eustacia was taken by surprise. She was embarrassed and disappointed. She had taken Theodosius at his word when he promised to proclaim her Augusta, but the minute a son was born, he brushed her aside and confirmed Pulcheria's ascendancy.

Eustacia could barely contain her anger. "My father taught me to be smarter than that," she said. "How could I have been such a fool?"

But fate dealt Theodosius and Pulcheria a blow. The child died in infancy. All their scheming to relegate Eustacia to irrelevancy came to naught. If they wanted another boy now, they were going to have to go through Eustacia, and she was not about to cooperate with any arrangement destined to give Pulcheria parental rights. Eustacia barred Theodosius from her bedchamber until he tore up the documents empowering Pulcheria and proclaimed her Augusta as he had promised.

Pulcheria fought back. She urged her brother not to give in. She reminded him he was the Emperor, the most powerful man in the East, and Eustacia was his wife. He was within his rights to take her sexually anytime he liked. But Theodosius was not the sort of man who forces himself on women. Caught between his sister and his wife, he simply gave up and refused to discuss the matter any further, which left the status quo in place.

"I believe we've reached an impasse," Eustacia complained as we strolled through the gardens one afternoon. "I'm afraid I've squandered my opportunity to control him."

I stopped and took her by the hands. "Buck up. You're not done yet. I've been thinking it over and I have a solution, something that will put Pulcheria in her place and get you what you want."

She looked at me curiously. "Go on."

"You and I have similar aspirations. You want to become Augusta of the East, and I want to return to Ravenna and become Augusta of the West again. But for either of us to get what want we must win back the approval of the people. Correct?"

She nodded.

"It's simple. We betroth the children. We promise Placidius and Licinia Eudocia in marriage."

She halted in her tracks. I could see the wheels spinning in her head, adding it all up, seeing the exquisite beauty of it. She turned to me, eyes wide. She had worked it all through to its obvious conclusion.

"She will not risk a civil war, will she?"

"She would be a fool if she did, for it would expose her as the self-serving schemer she is."

Eustacia made a little squeal of delight. She threw back her head and shook her fists. "Oh, Galla, I love it! It's brilliant!"

She knew the announcement would prompt diametrically opposed reactions from Constantinople and Ravenna, which we could use to our advantage.

In Ravenna, the news would be celebrated. Honorius would welcome the idea of the two halves of the Empire being brought back together through marriage. He would be thrilled at the notion of his heir, the future Emperor of the West, being situated to make a claim to the throne of the East. His people would exult at the prospect of the Empire being reunited under their emperor's leadership. As the author of such a union, I would be lionized.

But in Constantinople, Pulcheria would be mortified. A marriage between our two children would threaten her grasp on power. It would make the East the junior partner in the arrangement. What's more, it would render the whole question of Illyricum irrelevant. To her, such a marriage would be unacceptable, but to oppose it would be nearly impossible.

On the face of it, a marriage reuniting the Empire was what everyone dreamed of, both East and West. The division of the Empire 130 years ago during the reign of Diocletian was undertaken to create stability and ensure a peaceful transition of power, and it did to a degree. But over time the two halves had begun to drift apart, politically, culturally, and, most importantly, economically.

With its capital situated on a narrow neck of land surrounded on three sides by water, the East found it easier to defend its territory against invasion, which meant it didn't have to spend as much on defense. As a result, the East had built up vast reserves of wealth. The West, on the other hand, had been compelled to move its capital three times, from Rome to Mediolanum and finally to Ravenna, in an effort to locate a more defensible position. It had fought numerous wars to repel barbarian invasions. The resulting instability had led to repeated attempts at usurpation, more wars, instability, and a treasury that was seriously depleted.

Reunification now would give the West access to the bountiful treasury of the East and allow the West to expand its armies and refurbish its defenses. After driving back its enemies and establishing dominance over its territory, the glory that was Rome could be resurrected and carried forward into the future.

In the minds of every Roman, East and West, this was a thrilling proposition. No one wanted to believe the Empire's best days were behind it. In the heart of every Roman the prospect of reunification was a dream fervently to be hoped for and aggressively to be pursued. To oppose it would be political suicide, and Pulcheria knew it.

The cherished love of her people, which she had done so much to build, would have been lost in an instant. Moreover, any opposition to the betrothal, without an alternative heir, would have been considered madness. To suggest that the future ruler of the West was not worthy to marry the daughter of the Emperor of the East would have left the impression that the East felt itself superior to the West, an insult that could be grounds for war. No, Pulcheria had little choice but to appear to be in favor of the betrothal, even as she worked frantically behind the scenes to avert it. Her most obvious counter was another child, a boy. But she would have needed Eustacia's cooperation. Murder was not out of the question, but Eustacia employed loyal bodyguards loyal and had a taster to sample her food.

In the end Pulcheria was forced to negotiate, a distasteful alternative because it meant she had been outwitted and would have to surrender something to get what she wanted in return. What she gave up was her opposition to the title. She went to Eustacia and offered to give her the title of Augusta in exchange for another child — once the child was born. But Eustacia would not be fooled a second time. She had seen the value of future promises. She demanded to be named Augusta first, and then she would see about having another child.

Pulcheria thought it over. To neutralize the threat to her power, she needed a child, and she needed it to be a boy. So, she agreed to name Eustacia Augusta at once, but only if she dropped the idea of a betrothal between the two children. Oh, and there was another sticking point. Pulcheria had no intention of giving up the title she already had. If Eustacia wanted to become Augusta, it could be done, but she would have to share the title with Pulcheria.

This was wholly unprecedented, two Augustas at once – in the same household – with equal power. Eustacia wasn't totally opposed to the idea, but she needed to make sure Pulcheria wasn't engineering things so her own seniority conferred greater authority. If Eustacia was not equal to Pulcheria, then the title of Augusta was meaningless. Eustacia insisted she be allowed to submit the agreement to a lawyer of her choosing. Pulcheria consented, the agreement passed muster, and the deal was struck. Within a fortnight Eustacia was named Augusta, and the East effectively had three heads of state: Theodosius, Pulcheria, and Eustacia.

Theodosius was welcomed back into his wife's bed. The idea of the betrothal was abandoned, and it looked as if everything had been resolved to the satisfaction of all parties. But then an event a thousand miles away turned everything on its head.

My brother's affliction came on without warning. His ankles and feet began to swell. He grew dizzy, fatigued, and had trouble focusing his vision. Those who tended to him said his breath was foul. He itched all over. Within a fortnight of falling ill, Honorius, Emperor of the Roman Western Empire, was dead.

News of his death reached us by the swiftest possible courier. Even so, a week had passed, and the situation in Ravenna had grown critical. With no one in place to assume the throne, rivals began to jockey for position. Even before his passing, Honorius's enemies had been plotting to overthrow him. His sudden, unexpected death had only served to move up the timeline.

Chief among those seeking to seize power was Castinus, the duplicitous general who had convinced Honorius to exile us. And Castinus had friends in high places.

Everyone knew that you, Placidius, should have been proclaimed immediately upon your uncle's passing, but you needed the imprimatur of the Emperor of the East, and for some reason Theodosius dawdled. A day went by and then another. News of Honorius's death had reached us on a Tuesday. By Friday you had still not been proclaimed. Finally, I lost patience and went to Theodosius to get some answers.

I was led into the reception hall and made to stand in the same place I had stood in two years earlier when we first arrived in Constantinople. Just as then, Theodosius sat on his golden throne and tried to look firm and imposing. Pulcheria sat in her wooden chair by his side, hands folded primly in her lap. The only difference was that this time my lovely Eustacia sat on the other side of the Emperor. She was regal and radiant. She was now Aelia Eudocia, the Empress and Augusta of the East.

Theodosius asked me the reason for my coming, as if he didn't know. I told him it was vitally important for him to proclaim you emperor without delay. He regarded me with dull interest. He looked aside at Pulcheria. She leaned forward in her chair and said, "Placidius is too young to rule. If he were to be proclaimed Emperor of the West, he would need a regent to rule on his behalf. It would have to be someone we could rely on, someone we could trust. We've been racking our brains trying to think of someone, but we cannot. Tell me, Galla, can you think of someone?"

I glared at her.

She gave me a smug look and sat back.

I swung my eyes to Eustacia in desperation. She opened her mouth to speak but Pulcheria cut her off.

"Silence!" she snapped.

She turned her icy eyes on Eustacia and said, "You may think yourself my equal, and technically you are, but whichever of us has the weight of the Emperor's approval enjoys an advantage the other must respect. Theodosius agrees with me that Galla is unfit to be regent. She's a sinner and a sneak. She'll be lucky if she doesn't end up convicted of some heinous crime and driven from this city in disgrace. Your opinion is overridden. Our combined voices cancel yours out. If you persist in trying to object, it can only be regarded as insolence worthy of punishment. Do you understand?"

Eustacia was rendered speechless.

Theodosius turned to me. "You realize, Galla, if no emperor is named, I, by rights, become Augustus of the entire Roman Empire, East and West. As I understand it, you are in favor of reunification, so you should not object."

"To be sure," Pulcheria said. "It was Galla's plan to betroth the children as way of knitting together the two halves of the Empire through marriage. But that would have taken fifteen years. This accomplishes the same objective at once. God must be smiling on us. Eh, Galla?"

I was seething, but I managed to hold my temper. Letting our emotions run away with us is never to our advantage. I said, "You can't possibly hold the entire Roman Empire together under a single ruler. You don't have the strength. You will be overthrown in the West, and more provinces will fall to the barbarians. Is that what you want?"

"We will enlist allies," Pulcheria said, "which is why even now a messenger is on his way to the Master of Soldiers, Castinus, to see if he would be willing to act as our vice-regent in Ravenna. As it turns out, we are not in need of your advice. We have the situation well in hand."

If I were going to erupt with anger, that's when I would have done it, but I held my fury in check. "You know Placidius is the rightful heir," I said evenly. "He is entitled to be proclaimed emperor of the West."

"Entitled?" Pulcheria sneered. "You dare speak to me of entitlement? We are entitled to run our family and dominion as we see fit without the meddling of some conniving outsider exiled for depravities offensive to God and cast up on our doorstep like some pathetic waif."

"Yes," I said in cold, measured tones. "And I am entitled to take what's mine." I turned on my heels and stalked out.

But I had acted without thinking. I was in no position to make good on my threat. In my impulsiveness I had ceded the advantage to Pulcheria and given her the excuse she needed to have me seized and taken into custody — and you along with me, Placidius.

I acted rashly and put us both in jeopardy.

If it weren't for Eustacia, we might never have made it out alive.

Chapter Thirteen

"What do you know about this?"

Stephanus looked down at the paper and shrugged. "I told you it means nothing to me — a jumble of religious gibberish as far as I can tell."

Placidius tried to exude an air of menace, but he had a hard time sustaining it. The handsome groom really did seem ignorant of the matter. Placidius got behind him and hovered there. Stephanus sat at the table with the confession of faith laid out before him. He started to turn around.

"Don't look at me," Placidius snapped. "Look at the paper. Tell me how my name got there."

"I haven't got the slightest idea."

Placidius considered calling a guard over – the big burly fellow – to knock Stephanus around a little, but it seemed too much, so he decided to try a different tact. He walked around the table, sat down across from Stephanus, and folded his hands. "I know you lied about Cyrus's dismissal."

"I only told you what I heard."

"You tried to deceive me. You wanted me to think Arsenius and Cyrus were plotting against me, didn't you?"

Stephanus affected a wounded air. "I was only trying to help. I knew you were angry about Candida – maybe you were jealous, I don't know. I wanted to set the record straight. I needed you to know there was nothing between us. To be honest, I was hoping to get into your good graces. When I overheard the messenger misleading you about what happened to Cyrus,

I thought you would want to know what I had heard. Apparently, I was mistaken. I'm sorry. I meant no harm by it."

Placidius tried to convey an impression of harsh intolerance, but the groom's contrition touched him. No one had ever asked him for mercy before. It would be a shame to earn the enmity of such a person, especially if he really was trying to help. He needed to know more.

"Bring the clerk to me," he said. "I will question him directly."

"I will do so gladly if it will restore your faith in me."

"Bring him to me. Then we'll see."

When Stephanus returned, Placidius was surprised to find that the clerk in question was none other than his curator of correspondence, Liberius.

"This is not the clerk," he said.

"Unfortunately, I am the clerk," Liberius said. He brushed the hair out of his face with the back of his hand. "I was recently relieved of my duties as your curator of correspondence. Arsenius sacked me. He accused me of incompetence. He said I had failed to inform you of the arrangement by which he was to see all of your correspondence before it reached my desk. He stripped me of my duties. Then he beat me. Now I'm nothing but a clerk."

"He beat you?"

Liberius nodded. "He and his man, Otho. They said I needed to be taught a lesson."

Placidius became indignant. "This is unacceptable. He doesn't have the right."

"It was my fault," Liberius muttered. "I should have been clearer when I spoke to you earlier. I left the impression that he was deliberately trying to undermine me — overstepping his authority. Of course, he was not. He's Arsenius. He can do whatever he wants."

"He most certainly cannot!"

Liberius dropped his chin on his chest. His hair fell over his face. He spoke quietly under his breath. "Well, I shall not offer my opinion again. I've learned how things work around here. I will not make the same mistake twice."

"Let me ask you something. It's important. Did you hear Arsenius quarreling with Cyrus?"

"I don't want to say."

"I don't care what you want to say. Tell me. I command it of you."

Liberius shot a nervous glance at Stephanus. "I will not forswear what this man told you earlier. Perhaps we can leave it at that."

"We most certainly cannot. Now answer me. Did Arsenius quarrel with Cyrus before dismissing him?"

Liberius stared miserably at the ground. "Don't make me do this. I'm innocent of anything." It sounded like he was on the verge of tears.

Placidius hated to torture the poor fellow, but he needed answers. "Arsenius told me he had been given a note informing him I had granted Cyrus leave. What do you know about that?"

"I don't know anything about any note."

Placidius frowned mightily. "Well, we shall see about that. We shall ask Cyrus directly when he gets back."

The clerk looked up. "Cyrus is coming back?"

"He's being brought back whether he likes it or not. We will get some answers when he gets here. I promise you that."

"I wouldn't count on that," Stephanus uttered under his breath, but then Liberius shot him a warning look, and he clammed up.

"Speak up," Placidius ordered. "Out with it."

Stephanus gave him a rueful look. "The last time I told you something in confidence, you accused me of misleading you. Maybe I ought to just keep my mouth shut."

"Don't be foolish. Go on."

Stephanus gave him a doubtful glance and plunged ahead. "All right, but I'm only telling you this because I think you should know, and it might benefit you."

"I'm listening," Placidius said.

"Very well. What I heard was—"

"Don't say it!" Liberius interrupted.

Placidius rounded on him in anger.

The timid curator gulped. "I'm sorry, Imperator. Forgive me."

"Hold your tongue or I'll give you reason to be afraid."

"Yes, Imperator."

Placidius turned back to Stephanus. "I'm running out of patience with you. Speak."

Stephanus shot a quick glance at Liberius and went on. "The talk around camp is that Cyrus won't be coming back. They say he knows too much, he and the others."

"The others?"

"The Jew and his wife. You will never see any of them again. When the search parties come back, they'll report them missing, and that'll be the end of it."

Placidius narrowed his eyes. "What is it that they know? What are they hiding?"

Stephanus shrugged. "I don't know. Whatever it is, someone around here considers it dangerous."

"Who exactly is someone?"

"I don't know," Stephanus said. "I'm only telling you what I heard."

Placidius turned to Liberius. "What do you know about this? Tell me now or I'll have you crucified."

Liberius began to weep.

"Is it Arsenius?" Placidius demanded. "Is he behind this?"

Liberius dropped his chin on his chest and nodded.

"Ah ha!" Placidius cried. "Finally! The truth!"

"He'll kill me," Liberius groaned.

Placidius tapped his finger on the confession of faith lying on the table. "What about this? Is he behind this as well?"

Liberius said nothing.

"Out with it!" Placidius shouted.

"I don't know!" Liberius sobbed. "I don't know! Maybe."

Placidius tugged on his lip as he pondered this.

"I suggest you hide that document until you find out who's behind it," Stephanus said. "It's evidence. If it falls into the wrong hands it could vanish."

"Evidence of what?"

"Evidence of a plot against you," Stephanus said.

Placidius brooded. "What about the letter from my mother? Do you think Arsenius is behind that as well?"

Stephanus raised his hands. "Whoa there. I never said anyone was behind anything. I want to be perfectly clear about that."

Placidius scowled. "Nonsense."

Stephanus pointed at Liberius. "He's the one who mentioned Arsenius."

Liberius stretched his hands out before him in a pleading gesture. "I never accused Arsenius of plotting against you, Imperator. You asked me if

Arsenius considered Cyrus and the others a danger to you, and I said yes. Which he does. But that's all."

Placidius set his teeth. "I'm getting tired of this. Someone wrote my mother's letter, and I'm pretty sure it wasn't my mother, so who wrote it?"

"If I may make bold to speak," Stephanus said, "does the letter seem to paint anyone in particular in a favorable light?"

"It does," Placidius said.

"That may be your answer."

Placidius stroked his chin and thought it over.

Stephanus cleared his throat. "Imperator, we have made ourselves vulnerable by speaking to you in this way. If Arsenius finds out, he will send Otho to interrogate us, and I think you know what that means."

"I do."

"I hope you will not allow your good and faithful servants to be brutalized."

"I'll keep this conversation between us."

Relief washed over Stephanus. "Thank you, Imperator. We owe you our lives."

The groom and the ex-curator waited. After a few moments, Placidius blinked and looked at them as if remembering they were there. "You may go," he told them.

After they were gone, he stood in the doorway of his tent and looked out at the encampment. He went back inside, picked up the confession of faith and hid it among his personal belongings at the bottom of his traveling chest.

A commotion outside brought him back to the present. He emerged from his tent to find the search party coming back. They were bringing bad news. Contrary to what Stephanus had speculated, Isaac and Elpidia had not gone missing. They had been tracked down and brought back. A wagon bearing their lifeless bodies creaked into the common area and ground to a halt. Curiosity seekers gathered around it. Placidius elbowed them aside. What he saw made him flinch.

The two bodies lays face down in the wagon. The bed of the wagon was glazed with their blood. Their throats had been slashed. They had been deprived of their purses. The feet of the dead man were shod with sandals unfastened at the ankles. The woman was wearing a peasant's dress. Placidius turned away.

The official report blamed it on the Huns. Placidius didn't believe it for a second. Someone had tried to silence them. Someone who resided in this camp.

The night of my fraught meeting with Theodosius and Pulcheria, in the wee hours before dawn, Eustacia came to my room and urged me to gather my children and come away with her. She had overheard Theodosius giving the order to have us arrested.

I wasted not a moment. Gathering you and Justa, we followed her to the home of a wealthy widow who was taking a great risk in hiding us. She clearly resented having been imposed upon, but Eustacia paid her handsomely, so she went along with it. But once Eustacia was gone, she turned aloof and treated us dismissively, as if you were not the presumptive emperor and I was not your regent. She treated us like common filth, which made me angry, but I didn't say anything.

We had missed our breakfast and were hungry. Justa asked the widow for something to eat, and the widow acted as if she had asked her for her last coin. In a fit a pique the widow dug up a stale, half-eaten loaf with an air of disgust and threw it down in front of her. Justa cried for more, but the widow spurned her, which provoked Justa to a tantrum.

The house was filled with Justa's screaming when a small boy appeared at the door and reported a search party was going from house to house, looking for us. The widow barked at Justa to shut up, then she went to the door and peered out. Justa picked up the piece of bread and threw it at her. The widow stomped across to her and struck her.

I acted without thinking. I seized the widow by the throat and drove her against the wall. The back of her skull struck the wall, her knees buckled, and she sagged to the floor. I might have killed her, but the soldiers came pounding at the door. I froze, my hand raised to strike. I looked around, my faculties instantly sharpened.

My first thought was for you, my son. If the soldiers seized you, I would never see you again.

You were standing off to one side, watching the goings-on with a bemused expression, inured to frantic scene Justa had brought on.

I lifted you in my arms and headed for the rear of the house. At the same time, I took Justa by the hand and dragged her along. True to her nature she tried to resist. She threw herself to the floor and flailed her arms and howled. I knelt beside her and begged her to get up, but she was in the throes of a tantrum and could not be reasoned with. The pounding at the door got louder. Then the soldiers started trying to break down the door.

Fate was staring me in the face. I had no choice. I had to let her go. I had to abandon my little girl in order to save my son. Maybe if circumstances were different I would have chosen differently, but it was more than just you, Placidius. I had the future of the Empire to consider.

Having fled the Goths during the sack of Rome, I was no stranger to narrow escapes. One thing I knew: misdirection was our friend. Justa's pitiable wailing served to keep the soldiers' attention focused on the front of the house while you and I slipped out the back. Later I learned they had kicked down the door only to discover a woozy old widow and a distraught six-year-old throwing a fit. Realizing their mistake, they had rushed out the back in hot pursuit of us, but we were gone.

We took refuge in a xenodochium[1], a shelter for the sick and dispossessed, a place of horrible noises and nauseating odors. Hundreds of people were crammed together in a single room, many suffering horrible diseases. Physicians were circulating among them and administering treatments. A man next to us went into a seizure and died. Another screamed in agony. In that awful netherworld, no one recognized us, and we remained there for two whole days,

---

1. A charitable institution run by the Church typically comprising an orphanage, an old people's home, and physicians' services; the earliest form of a modern day hospital

huddled together, and living off the charity of those good Christians who ran the place.

After leaving the xenodochium, we took refuge in the home of a kindly old monk who had been recommended to us by the physicians. He was one of those whose unquestioning obedience to imperial authority was unbreakable, and knowing you were the heir to the throne of the West, he was eager to help us in any way he could. I sent him to look for Justa, and in the course of his search he got news of the West, news that was later fleshed out by my own inquiries.

It seemed events had moved too quickly for Theodosius and Pulcheria. Before their generous offer to make Castinus vice-regent reached his desk, he proclaimed an emperor of his own to replace you. The man he chose was a civil servant by the name of Joannes. This was the selfsame Joannes who Senator Symmachus had insisted I wed in exchange for his help in reinstating the law against paganism several years earlier. I don't know whether Joannes had been Symmachus's secret lover in the past, but he was clearly a man well favored for his tractability. In other words, he was the puppet of powerful men, men of influence who could rally the support of the Senate and the Church. Joannes was proclaimed with great fanfare, although the people of Rome were lukewarm to the idea of backing a usurper in the absence of the legitimate heir.

This startling turn of events presented Pulcheria and Theodosius with a dilemma. Should they back the new regime or reject it? They had never intended to replace you, Placidius. They had only wanted to prevent me from becoming your regent. To back the usurpers against you meant ratifying the overthrow of our dynasty and sanctioning the end of the House of Theodosius in the West. They would not do that. They owed it to our ancestors to keep it going.

No, the only thing to do now was to take the fight to the West. The East had the military assets to defeat the usurpers, and among its leadership were two of the finest generals in the entire Empire, East or West, Ardaburius[2] and Aspar[3]. But if the aggression of East against West were interpreted as a power grab by Theodosius to extend his own sovereignty, the citizens of the West would back Joannes, and the war could drag on for years, weakening both halves of the Empire.

Pulcheria and Theodosius had to face facts. As much as they hated to admit it, the only way to defeat the usurpers and keep the people of the West happy was to restore the rightful heir to the throne. If the war were characterized as a fight to restore you, many of the soldiers in the ranks, who might otherwise be inclined to resist, would give in. While, at the same time, a war of restoration would sow dissension among the enemy's troops and weaken him.

It was really the only option they had, but to make it a reality they had to find us and make amends for the horrible way they had treated us, and I did not trust them, so we remained in hiding.

To show he was sincere and draw us out, Theodosius announced he was proclaiming you Caesar in absentia. But it wasn't enough. I had been the Augusta. I knew the importance of titles. So I waited, intending to force his hand. Finally, Theodosius gave in. In the autumn of that year, just after your fourth

---

2. Pronounced Ar-duh-buhr-ee-us

3. Pronounced As-par

birthday, he made it legal. He named you "most honored boy." To assassinate a most honored boy would be an act of regicide for which even an emperor like Theodosius could not escape condemnation. To assassinate his mother would be almost as bad. We now had the legitimacy we needed to come out of hiding.

Still, I was cautious. I sent word first to Eustacia. She met me in the great urban square called the Augustaeum. She looked haggard and drawn. The weeks spent agonizing over what to do about Castinus had taken their toll on her. As you might expect, she was on our side all along.

From the start she had pressured Pulcheria and Theodosius to proclaim you emperor of the West with me as your regent. They had threatened to have her arrested. But when Castinus proclaimed Joannes, they came around to her point of view without ever acknowledging her good judgment. They insisted on treating her like an adversary. Without me around for support, she began to grow weary and despondent. Seeing me now was the first respite she had had from them in weeks.

I hated to see her that way. All her childlike exuberance was gone. I suggested we repair to the Baths of Zeuxippus where I could soothe her. Eustacia ordered the general public out so we could have the place to ourselves. We sent our servants away and then disrobed and immersed ourselves in the steaming water of the caldarium.[4]

---

4. Hot plunge bath in a Roman bathhouse

She was standing waist deep in the water, looking off into space and enjoying the feeling on her skin. I came up behind her and started to scrub her back.

"Justa is missing," I said. I explained how I had lost her when the soldiers broke in.

She began to cry. Her shoulders hitched and she took little convulsive snatches of breath. I turned her around to face me. I held her close. She wept unreservedly. It had finally gotten to her, the ceaseless battle with Pulcheria, the scheming and backstabbing. Eustacia was smart; she understood things, but at bottom she was just a sweet, good-natured philosopher's daughter from an ancient city where people still believed in things like principles and ethics. She was unprepared for Pulcheria's unscrupulousness, the doggedness of her vendetta, and the lengths to which she was willing to go to get the upper hand. Eustacia felt responsible for what had happened to Justa because she had set me at odds with Pulcheria and turned her against me. She apologized and begged my forgiveness.

I kissed her, petted her, and told her it was not her fault. I assured her I had already come into conflict with Pulcheria before we had even met. Besides, everything would turn out for the best. I would find Justa, we would return to Ravenna, and I would become Augusta again. The day would come, I assured her, when our children would reign in peace and harmony without Pulcheria's meddling. The day would come when Pulcheria was stripped of power. I had said this in an attempt to calm her, but it had the opposite effect.

"Stripped of power?" Eustacia looked at me with tear-filled eyes.

"Yes," I said. "This is not over. Pulcheria must pay for what she has done. She has gambled the future of the Empire in the pursuit of a personal vendetta against us. It's inexcusable."

"I don't know if I can do this anymore," she said. "It's exhausting."

"Be strong," I said. "There's one more act to play out. We must betroth the children as planned. When they grow up, in thirteen years time, they'll become Augustus and Augusta, and Pulcheria's influence will be diminished."

"But that assumes . . ." Her voice dropped off and she tried to find something to look at other than my face.

Now my hand was at my brow. "Do you mean to tell me you're pregnant again?"

"No. Not yet. But soon perhaps."

"Oh..." I stopped, but I had not been able to keep the disappointment out of my voice.

She looked up at me with pleading eyes. "Please, Galla, try to understand. After you've gone back to Ravenna I'll still be here with them. I can't fight them forever. Sooner or later I'll have to give them what they want."

"Leave," I said. "Desert them. Come away with me to Ravenna. I'll protect you."

She gave me a long wistful look and touched my cheek. "Dear Galla," she said. "Wonderful Galla. I wish I could, but I have my daughter to think about. Theodosius loves little Licinia. Believe it or not, he truly loves her, and if I try to take her away from him, he'll come after us, and you'll find yourself at war with him. It's not worth it. I won't do that to the Empire."

She was so good — and sweet and fine. She was everything I might have been had I been born in another place and time. I told her I understood and would not pursue it further, and I meant it. Much as I longed to see Pulcheria put in her place, I loved Eustacia and didn't want to see her hurt.

We spent the better part of the afternoon in the baths, washing and consoling each other. We both knew that our time together was coming to an end. We were prisoners of our roles. Nothing could ever give us the kind of lasting bond we desired. I would be heading home to Ravenna to fight a war against the usurper Joannes, and she would remain here, subjugated to a bitter, vindictive rival she had lost the will to fight. Or at least that's what she had led me to believe.

When Eustacia got back to the palace, Pulcheria was waiting for her. She pointed an accusatory finger.

"I know what you've been doing," she said. "It's immoral and an affront to God. The Church Fathers will be informed, and a suitable punishment will be imposed on you, a grueling ordeal of fasting and self-flagellation. And if you do not comply in a manner satisfactory to me, your sin will be reported to the public and what little remains of your reputation will be destroyed.

Any protest was futile. Pulcheria had already made up her mind. Eustacia might have submitted quietly had it not been for the obvious fact that her sister-in-law's attack was aimed less at her than it was at me. It was a final, desperate shot, a cheap and cowardly blow meant to communicate that she had won, and not I.

I learned all of this in a letter Eustacia sent to me in which she expressed outrage at the way she was being treated. She had changed her mind. She would not let Pulcheria get the last word. She would agree to my proposal after all. We would betroth the children.

We made the announcement publicly. There was no way for Pulcheria to head it off. The people were thrilled. They gathered in the Augustaeum to cheer us on. Behind closed doors, Pulcheria raged. She called it a betrayal and vowed to make us pay.

Indeed, from that day forward Eustacia became the target of her sister-in-law's inexhaustible vengeance. Pulcheria got to Theodosius and poisoned him against her with scurrilous reports of adultery, deviancy, and indiscriminate lust. Eustacia's relationship with Theodosius deteriorated until he refused to share a bed with her any longer. The prospect of another son faded. All hopes of the Eastern Empire producing a successor to Theodosius ground to a halt.

But Eustacia was not finished. She gave as good as she got. She was not without resources; she was still an Augusta. Like her adversary, she dipped into the imperial coffers to endow churches and to perform acts of public charity and won a growing number of supporters as a result. In addition, she pushed for the restructuring and expansion of education in Constantinople. She wanted a more classical curriculum. She succeeded in rescinding the harshest laws intended to persecute Jews and pagans. Among her supporters, she cultivated a substantial power base from which she retaliated against her rival with a few well-placed rumors of her own, the most effective of which was that Pulcheria had broken her vow of chastity, not once, but countless times. The public lapped it up like pigs at a trough.

In the end, the two adversaries settled into a dismal stalemate, which is the situation you will find them in today. They barely speak to each other. They reside at opposite ends of the palace and are at pains to stay out of each other's way. As a result, the worst of their hostility has subsided. Still, I must warn you, if there's anything that can bring Pulcheria's vindictiveness to a head, it's the thought of my interfering in their lives again, which is why I'm not coming with you to Constantinople; I would not want to do anything to interfere with your nuptials.

Hopefully, everything will go off without a hitch. Pulcheria has given no sign she will try to stop the marriage. After all, she and Theodosius must give Licinia a way to someone in marriage, and Licinia's was always bound to be a political union, so strengthening the ties between East and West seems as good a purpose as any.

But I would be remiss if I didn't make clear the kind of adversary you're dealing with. Pulcheria is capable of anything. Don't underestimate her. Stay on your guard. Carefully watch anybody who comes into your camp, for they may be agents of hers sent to harm you. Listen to those with experience. Take their advice. Don't defy those who want to help you just because they know better than you. This is one of your greatest flaws. Try to overcome it. Try to become a better person. Try to change.

Hear me, Placidius. One of the most difficult things for any sovereign to do is to admit a lack of control. Humble yourself. Permit yourself to be led. But always keep your eyes and ears open. The world is a dangerous place for people like us, and if we cannot trust those whose job it is to protect us, we make ourselves prey to those who seek to pull us down.

Placidius almost wished he hadn't read the last part. It annoyed him. How dare his mother make him an unwitting proxy in her war with Pulcheria. Didn't he have enough trouble already without having to worry about yet another threat, this one from a previously unknown source? But then it occurred to him he was being silly. The letter was a hoax, an invention designed to manipulate him. To allow himself to get rattled by it was to play into his manipulators' hands — whoever they were.

Still, the woman in the letter did bear a striking resemblance to his mother, more like an exaggerated version of her, to be sure, but weirdly authentic. It was as if the writer had taken aspects of her character and magnified them to suit their own purposes. His mother had never complained about her relatives in Constantinople — at least not with any real conviction. Sure, she had been critical from time to time, but who is not critical of their relatives? But the woman in the letter appeared locked in an ongoing struggle with her relatives for the future of the Empire, a struggle in which he was now to play an important part.

Still, he suspected someone was trying to deceive him.

But to what end? No one had to persuade him to marry Licinia. He had already consented to the marriage before leaving Ravenna. Why send a long letter afterwards to convince him? And then there was the letter itself. So far it had remained pretty close to its stated purpose, to advise him in his upcoming role as Augustus. As a cautionary guide, its counsel seemed reasonable. Keep your friends close and your enemies closer. Seek allies where you can find them. Recognize when things are out of your control. Don't be afraid to be led. It was all very reasonable, even if a bit fussy in a motherly sort of way. And all that stuff about being patient, reading the situation carefully, and awaiting your opportunity didn't square with someone trying to trick him.

Try as he might, he could not shake the sense that the letter might be genuine. If it was, he needed to be careful. He had been warned, and he didn't have a lot of people around he could trust. There was Candida, of course. But what about Cyrus? He had thought Cyrus was his friend, but apparently he had been wrong. Had he been more on his toes he would've gotten to know Cyrus better, gotten closer to him, not been so taken in by his wit and charm. He could not make the same mistake again.

He called for Stephanus.

When the groom arrived, Placidius greeted him in a friendly manner and invited him to sit down. He poured him a cup of wine and asked him about his family and background. Stephanus was instantly on guard. To ease his mind, Placidius turned the topic to Candida. He asked how she was. He had not spoken to her since their latest row. It had started when she confronted him as he was being borne along in his litter. She had stood in the road, blocked his bearers, and insisted they put him down.

He could have had her punished for that, but he let it go. *Don't do unnecessary things that endanger the Empire to feed your good opinion of yourself.* It was good advice.

He had stood in the road with his subjects looking on and suffered the brunt of her attack. She was furious about Isaac and Elpidia. She blamed him for their deaths. If he had not sent them to Arsenius for examination, they would still be alive. She would not let it happen again, she shouted. She would not permit any more of her retinue to be examined.

Placidius let her rant. When the last of her verbal barbs ran out, he looked at her calmly and said, "Is that all?"

She stamped her foot and stormed off.

It felt great to get the advantage of her. It was exciting, even titillating. He went after her and cornered her in her tent and made rigorous love to her. He was so proud of himself afterwards he was walking on air.

Having established his dominance, he felt he could be charitable. He told Stephanus to give Candida a message from him. "Tell her I've halted the examinations."

"Oh, thank you, Imperator. She'll be grateful for that."

But Placidius had another motive for halting the examinations. He wanted to assert control over his headstrong chief of staff Arsenius. If

Arsenius could not examine Candida's people, he could not expel them, and if he could not expel them, he could not track them down and kill them. Then perhaps Placidius could get to the bottom of the plot against him.

"I want you to do something for me, Stephanus? Can I count on you?"

"Of course, Imperator."

"I want you to make some inquiries around the camp, see if anyone has arrived here who shouldn't be here."

For a fleeting moment he thought he caught a glimpse of dread in Stephanus's eyes.

"I'm at your service, Imperator."

"You may go now."

Stephanus rose to leave.

"I like you, Stephanus," he said. "I trust you. I hope you won't let me down."

Stephanus looked confused and worried.

"I consider you my friend," Placidius told him.

On his way out, Stephanus ran into Arsenius coming in. Stephanus bowed slightly and moved aside to let Arsenius pass. A look of mutual disgust passed between them. Then Stephanus went out.

"What is he doing here?" Arsenius demanded.

"He's my assistant."

Arsenius rubbed his eyes and shook his head. "Imperator, listen to me. You can't make him your assistant. He hasn't been examined. Look, someone is plotting against you. You can't have people around you who haven't been approved."

"Leave that to me."

"The man is a criminal. He was caught stealing feed from the supply wagon."

"He was falsely accused."

Arsenius reddened. "Says who?"

"Says me. Based on my own examination."

Arsenius's jaw tightened. "This is not a game, Imperator. These are serious allegations; a lying thief is capable of other transgressions. A proper examination requires skill. There are ways to go about it, time-tested methods."

"I've heard about these time-tested methods," Placidius said cynically.

Arsenius thrust his chin forward as if ready to let fly with an angry retort but caught himself. He crossed the tent and stood looking at the opposite wall, rubbing the back of his neck. "I know you don't trust me," he said. "You don't even like me. It seems obvious you've set yourself against me, which makes it hard for me to do my job. But I consider it my duty to protect you. What's more, I believe it's in the best interests of the Empire to make sure you get to Constantinople alive." He turned and faced Placidius. "Your survival is crucial to the fate of the Empire. That's how I see it. So, I will do my job, even though you try to thwart me at every turn. I will do it for your mother, if not for you."

"For my mother?"

"Yes. She would have it so."

"And for Aetius as well?"

Arsenius lips parted. Placidius felt he had struck a chord.

Arsenius said, "Is there some reason you believe Aetius is a threat to you?"

"You mean other than the fact that he looks down on me and considers me unfit to be emperor?"

Arsenius sighed. "For the sake of argument let's assume you're right. Let's assume Aetius thinks you lack the maturity to rise to the challenges of the job. It doesn't matter. Aetius respects the line of succession. He would not do anything to undermine you."

Placidius scoffed.

"As your master of soldiers, Aetius commands the army," Arsenius pointed out. "If he was really as treacherous as you think he is, he could've overthrown you years ago. His restraint should tell you where he stands."

"Aetius would never oppose my mother. His restraint is all for her. How he feels about me is another matter."

"Believe me. His feelings about you are the same as my own. He believes you are vital to the future of the Empire."

Placidius drew himself up. "Where is Cyrus?" he asked. "I thought you were bringing him back."

"I'll admit it's been taking longer than expected to track him down. He must've escaped far to the west. He must've ridden away at great speed, almost as if he were running away from something."

"Or in a hurry to report something."

Arsenius eyed him churlishly. "Do you really think I'm plotting against you?"

"I don't know what to think. When he gets back, I want him delivered to me first. You are not to question him before me. Is that clear?"

Arsenius grimaced.

"You may leave now," Placidius said.

Arsenius held his ground.

Placidius raised his eyebrows. "I'm sorry. Did you not hear me?"

"We have not yet addressed the matter I came to speak with you about."

"Go ahead, then. Speak. I don't have all day."

Arsenius closed his eyes and took a deep breath. He dragged his hands down his face. "Look," he said, "we should not be halting the examinations. It's a mistake."

"I have given the order."

"I'm aware of that, but someone is plotting against you. We are in dangerous territory here. We should be increasing our vigilance, not relaxing it."

"From now on, I'll do the questioning. There will be no more expulsions without my permission."

Arsenius nodded. "I see. So, you think Isaac and Elpidia were falsely accused and driven out so I could track them down and kill them."

"I find it curious that they were slain before they could be questioned."

"I questioned them."

"Yes, you and your heavy-handed methods frightened them. They ran away to avoid being tortured and were killed. By whom or what, I don't know, but you drove them out as surely as if you had banished them."

"They were not threatened by me."

"Your reputation is threat enough. They were afraid of what you might do to them, you and Otho, so they fled. You should've been alert to that possibility. What's more, you should've realized how vulnerable they were, a Jew and his mute wife. You should've considered what might happen to them if they were alone out there."

"I didn't know she was a mute, not then."

Arsenius was on the defensive, and Placidius took pleasure in goading him. "I find it hard to believe you were so negligent. It almost seems like you wanted them to run away, like you wanted them on the road where their lives would be at risk. A mute and a Jew, wandering the countryside alone, seeking alms. They were a tragedy waiting to happen."

"I am not your enemy. I am trying to help you, Imperator."

"A pair of helpless transients in a land menaced by the Huns. Easy prey."

"I am not guilty of what you're accusing me of."

Placidius chuckled. "Very well, let's say you're not. Let's say you didn't order them killed. Let's say they were slain by the Huns. The result is the same. They were silenced, eliminated."

"Fine. I agree, but before you satisfy yourself that I'm to blame, I wonder if you've considered another possibility. Maybe they were murdered by someone else in this camp, somebody with the motive to silence them."

Placidius feigned contempt for the idea, but the implication struck home. In fact, he had not considered it.

"I have good evidence that Isaac and Elpidia were part of a plot."

Placidius waved the accusation away.

"Yes, it's true. Whoever killed them did so to silence them, to keep them from being questioned, so they wouldn't reveal the truth. It could have been someone with a score to settle against you or your mother."

"My mother? What has my mother ever done to earn such enmity?"

Arsenius gave him an exasperated look.

"She has never been anything but a kind and generous to her subjects," Placidius said, "and they adore her for it."

"Not all of her subjects."

"What are you talking about?"

"When I heard the name of the Jew's wife, I became suspicious. When she fled rather than submit to questioning, my suspicions deepened. Then when I heard she was a mute, it struck me. Elpidia was here with the intent of doing you harm. Make no mistake about it."

"I don't understand."

"Elpidia was the name of one of your mother's servants when you were young. Along with two other servants, she gave voice to a horrible, scandalous rumor that drove your mother from Ravenna in shame. Your mother was justifiably furious, and she had Elpidia punished for her betrayal."

"How?"

"She employed one of those time-tested methods you find so distasteful. She had her tongue cut out."

Placidius felt woozy. He had to sit down.

Arsenius adopted a conciliatory air. He was completely at ease now, having regained the advantage. "You must be careful," he said. "The world is a dangerous place for people in your position, and if you refuse to put your faith in those whose job it is to protect you, you make yourself vulnerable to those who wish to do you harm."

Chapter Fourteen

We began at once to prepare for an assault on the West. We would strike against Castinus and Joannes on two fronts, one army led by Ardaburius, who would advance by sea, the other, led by his equally capable son, Aspar, would take the land route, traveling west through Noricum to strike at Ravenna from the north.

My children and I would go with them. We would not remain behind awaiting the outcome as might be expected but would travel with the army on campaign. This was for two reasons: partly to be present when the usurpers fell – so there would be no question as to who was to ascend next — but also because Pulcheria and Theodosius had made clear to us we were no longer welcome in Constantinople.

Before we could start, we had to find Justa. She had been missing for a month. The kindly monk who had given us shelter had tried to find her, but to no avail. And then, mere days before we were to leave for Ravenna, she turned up, residing in the home of a legionary of the palatini[1] , a widower living alone.

She had been brought there by a pair of prostitutes who had come upon her wandering the streets behind the Hippodrome, a seedy district notorious for its

---

1. A soldier of the palace guard

vice. They had tried at first to keep her in their brothel, but the environment there was no place for a child, and so they took her to the home of one of their clients, a cheerful, genial fellow well regarded for his generosity. He was happy to take her in, but persuading him to let her go was another matter.

The monk visited him and informed him that the child was none other than Justa Grata Honoria, the daughter of Galla Placidia, Augusta of Rome. The man shut the door in his face. The monk continued to knock, but the man refused to open up. After some time, the man stuck his head out of an upstairs window and shouted down at the monk, accusing him of trying to steal the child away for some depraved reason and threatening to come down and cut him to pieces if he didn't stop.

It seems Justa had told her benefactor that she was the daughter of a barbarian ambassador who had come to the city to negotiate with the Emperor. She explained she had been left in the care of a wealthy widow while her father went about his business, but the widow had died and her father had returned home without her, so she had wandered the streets alone until the prostitutes found her and took her in. It seemed too extravagant a tale to be invented by the mind of a six-year-old, so her benefactor believed her. But I knew the kind of deceit Justa was capable of. She was devious beyond her years and liable to scheme against those she believed had wronged her. I told the monk to go back and try again.

He stood at the door and shouted up at the window, trying to get the man to open up. When at last he did, he emerged angry and brandishing a club. The monk fell back in a stumbling panic and landed on his backside in the mud.

At the time, I was coordinating the assault with Ardaburius. I asked him to pull rank and send an officer from his headquarters to pry the child away from her benefactor. He sent a deputy of the magister militum[2], but even then the man resisted. Exasperated, I decided to go myself. I did not go alone. I brought a number of armed soldiers with me.

The man met me at the door, his sword drawn. Justa was just behind him, peeking out from behind his hip. I ordered her to come out at once, but she whimpered and claimed not to know me. Annoyed, the man demanded to know what kind of a monster I was to frighten a child. I told him I was Galla Placidia, Augusta of Rome, and the child's mother. I ordered him to hand her over. He raised his sword to threaten me, and my protectors rushed forward. A brief, bloody fracas ensued, and the man was killed.

Justa watched all this with wide, staring eyes. When it was over, she rushed to her benefactor's side and threw herself down on his body. I snatched her up by the arm and tried to drag her away. She struggled and fought, wailing that I was not her mother and that I was trying to kidnap her. She appealed to anyone who would listen. She kept saying the same thing over and over until I pawned her off onto some servants and told them to put her to bed. Then I went to my room and wept.

I tell you no one has done more to break my heart than Justa. It's as if she has been put on this earth to torment me for all the ways I've fallen short as a parent. I have no illusions when it comes to my deficiencies in this area. I know I've made mistakes when it comes to being a mother to you and your sister, none greater than my decision to spirit you away to safety and leave Justa behind

---

2. A soldier serving under the master of soldiers

when we were being menaced by the agents of Pulcheria and Theodosius. In choosing you over her, I fixed her in the conviction that she was not wanted, and nothing I could do from then on could convince her otherwise. Her resentment would haunt me for years.

After this unfortunate episode, our preparations for the assault on the West continued apace. We moved to Thessalonika where we assembled our forces. Aspar was for setting out at once, but Ardaburius observed that Joannes was experiencing some difficulties in governance and advised restraint. He remarked to me, when his son was out of earshot, how the young are always too eager to fight when wisdom teaches that a little forbearance may allow the enemy to weaken himself, increasing the chances for success. Good advice, which I commend to you.

In his role as emperor Joannes was reportedly having his share of problems. First, his praetorian prefect in Arelate was slain, which led to an uprising there. Then the Church was put off when he instituted a policy of tolerance to all Christian sects, including the Arians. Finally, the public grew disillusioned with him when he was seen in public with an older man said to be his lover, a man who had earned the scorn of the commons by advocating for a reduction in the grain dole.

That's always the problem with puppets. The thing that makes them good puppets, their tractability, makes them poor rulers, for they have few sound opinions that have not been put there by someone else. They're vulnerable to the slightest manipulation and prone to act without thinking. Joannes had been a mere civil servant, elevated to the purple by Castinus and Symmachus. He was clearly out of his depth. What had begun with proclamations of greatness rapidly turned into a fiasco.

Joannes's biggest problem came to him courtesy of Bonifacius. You will remember Bonifacius. He was the one who helped us escape Castinus's murderous plot against us by arranging a ship to take us to Constantinople. Well, after we left the West, Bonifacius went to Africa to entrench against an expected Vandal invasion and while he was there Honorius died and Joannes was proclaimed emperor.

Good Bonifacius, ever loyal to the House of Theodosius, rebelled against Joannes and sought to weaken him by cutting off the grain supply. As a political move it was astute and confirmed our high estimation of him. Remember this: the support of the people correlates with the fullness of their bellies. When Joannes was proclaimed, there were games and banquets. The sideboards groaned, and the wine flowed freely. The people cheered him, and the mere mention of our names brought laughter and jeers. Yet as soon as the grain supply was cut off, as soon as the bakers stopped baking bread, and the biscuits were snatched from the mouth of their children, the public grew restive. They muttered under their breaths and cursed Joannes for his stupidity. As time dragged on, they grew nostalgic for the rule of the Theodosians. "Where is Galla?" they asked. "Where is young Valentinian, the rightful heir?"

Ardaburius advised us to hold back and let the cancer eat away Joannes and Castinus. The army in Gaul had already turned against them. The Church despised them. And the people hated them. Seeing their political capital draining away, Castinus urged an invasion of Africa to break Bonifacius's grip, but that enterprise floundered due to a rebellion in the ranks. That's when we struck.

We set forth from Thessalonika with thirty thousand men. Half our force departed by sea. The other half went by land. We accompanied the latter force, headed by Aspar, through the very country in which you are now traveling. We had every expectation of success. But then things started to go awry.

Ardaburius's fleet was dispersed by a storm at sea, scattered across the Adriatic like so many grapes from a sack. Forces loyal to Joannes captured Ardaburius's flagship. The general was taken prisoner. A galley nearby witnessed the calamity. News of it reached us halfway to Ravenna.

Aspar was beside himself with grief, presuming his father slain. He wanted to throw his forces at Ravenna in a fit of revenge, but his advisors cautioned against it. With half our forces scattered to the wind and the element of surprise lost, we were at a disadvantage. Even now, it was argued, Castinus and Joannes were marshaling their forces to counterattack. We should withdraw, they said. We should return to Thessalonika and draw up a new plan.

Aspar came to me. He was itching to confront the enemy and pay them out for their effrontery, but he didn't want to overreact and ruin our plans. If it was better to go back to Thessalonika and regroup, then he would do it, although it grieved him to do so.

I liked him. In spite of his youth, Aspar demonstrated great maturity. He had been taught well. I told him to let me think about it for a spell, then I would come back to him with my opinion. He agreed. I went off by myself and prayed over the amulet. I held it to my lips and kissed it and lifted my eyes to heaven.

It may occur to you that my faith in the amulet was misplaced; perhaps you think it had brought me nothing but misery and misfortune. After all, I had been taken prisoner by barbarians, lost a beloved child, was forced into a horrible marriage, stripped of my title, and driven from the capital in shame only to become the target of a vicious, malevolent shrew determined to destroy me. Hardly a chronicle of fortuity. Yet I had come to believe it was all to my benefit. It had made me the woman I was — strong and resilient with the presence of mind to be a formidable regent, and in time to provide you the guidance you needed to be a formidable emperor.

Don't ask me why I had such faith in it. After all, it had been lifted from the neck of a suicide and carried to me by a man I subsequently betrayed and condemned to death. It should have been polluted by the taint of those sins, but it seemed to exude a power that diminished them to insignificance, a power of goodness that communicated, not a world without hardship, but a world where God's will would ultimately prevail. I believed in the amulet and trusted its guidance, and I'm glad I did.

I went to Aspar and gave him my opinion. We should press forward toward Ravenna. We should take the fight to the enemy. Castinus and Joannes were as weak as they would ever be, and if we waited we might miss our chance. Delighted by my decision, he ordered his army to muster. We resumed the march.

In the meantime, wholly unexpected events were unfolding in Ravenna. Contrary to what we had feared, Ardaburius had not been executed but was working behind the scenes to turn things to our advantage, an advantage that would have been lost if not for the amulet.

Never underestimate the weakness of your adversary. It is an odd thing to say, I know, because you are more commonly cautioned to beware of his strength. Yet to assume he is strong when he is weak is to give him power he has not earned. Joannes was weak – weaker than we ever imagined. He was afraid of us, afraid of what might happen to him if he did us harm and then found himself at our mercy. What's more, he was afraid of the East, afraid they would come in behind us. Even if he and his ilk succeeded in holding us off for now, the East was more powerful than the West, had more resources and men, and should hostilities drag on, would almost certainly gain the upper hand and vanquish them. So, he began to hedge against that possibility.

He did not kill Ardaburius when he could have – or arguably, should have. He let him survive, hoping we would see his act of mercy as a sign that he was someone with whom we could bargain. He held out an olive branch, hoping to end the conflict with as few negative consequences for himself as possible. He was in over his head, a lowly civil servant raised to the purple by a venal, grasping scoundrel canny enough to realize erecting a tractable puppet was less risky than taking the throne himself. But the puppet was losing heart.

Ardaburius, captured at sea and imprisoned at Ravenna, read the situation correctly. Seeing his chance, he complained of discomfort in his confinement. He requested the princely courtesy of being permitted to walk the court and streets of the city until the discomfort was resolved. He assured Joannes it would accrue to the benefit of his good reputation if he would permit him such a liberty. He promised he would not run away. Incredibly, Joannes granted him permission.

Had Castinus known, he surely would have forbidden it, but Castinus was away, mustering troops for the upcoming fight with Aspar. His armies were still at Mediolanum, deep within Italia. He was awaiting reinforcements from the north and didn't want to engage until he knew the reinforcements had arrived. He was hoping to catch us in a vise, which was why Aquileia[3] was entirely undefended when we entered it, the first sign my intuition had been right.

We occupied Aquileia with no resistance, and some of the citizens, seeing it was Galla Placidia and her little boy, the future Emperor Valentinian III, celebrated our arrival. What had looked to be a long, grueling ordeal was beginning to look rather effortless, and it was about to get easier. For unbeknownst to us, at that very moment, Ardaburius was walking the streets of Ravenna, chatting with the soldiery, winning them over with his charming personality. He convinced some of them that Joannes didn't really want to be emperor and that Castinus was an incompetent fool – both of which were true. It didn't take much persuading to get them to defect to him.

It was just the beginning. Those first few defectors went back to their quarters and told their fellow soldiers that a powerful force had come from the East to reinstall Galla Placidia and her son, the rightful heir, and that Joannes was doomed. Steadily, their numbers grew. Meanwhile, Joannes was oblivious to all of this. Holed up in the imperial palace, receiving dispatches from Castinus about troop dispositions and the status of the approaching reinforcements, he was blind to the subversion going on under his nose.

---

3. A Roman city at the head of the Adriatic 150 miles up the coast from Ravenna

We were encamped at Aquileia less than a week when we received word that Ardaburius had won over a large portion of the army in Ravenna and we should move at once, sending a body of troops by sea to approach the city through the marshes while the remainder swept down the shoreline and assaulted the city from the north. Aspar was thrilled to do as his father asked.

We went aboard a galley, part of the amphibious assault force, while Aspar led a company of troops by land.

The weather was perfect. We approached the coast in the dark and saw the flame of a torch in the distance. The coastline along Ravenna is a labyrinth of marshes, bedeviling to anyone who doesn't know it. The torch was held aloft by a man on a barge sent by Ardaburius to guide us. He poled along ahead of us and showed us the way through the grassy channels. The flickering orange flame veered, curved, and doubled back in a slow, erratic pattern as we slowly made our way in. After a while, the channel narrowed, and we disembarked.

The man on the barge poled back out again. He was going to bring the next galley in. Behind us at sea, lay fifteen more galleys, the bulk of our army. Each galley would be led in succession through the marshes to the base of the city walls where we would assemble to besiege the city.

We continued on foot, led by a local, who knew that sodden ground well. With each step, water would well up around our shoes and threaten to suck them off. Our escort knew the patches of dry ground where the tufts of reed grass grew, and as we drew nearer to the city, these became more prevalent until we found ourselves hopping from one to the next like rabbits. You children considered this great sport and giggled with delight, and so infectious was your laughter, broad grins were elicited from the soldiers who accompanied us. Eventually, we reached the walls of the city.

The sentries atop the walls took note of our presence but didn't shoot down at us, a measure that would've met with some success had they tried it since digging into the sodden soil was out of the question. Rather, they stood and observed as we assembled, hour after hour, each newly arrived galley bringing more men and arms until we stood more than five thousand strong at the base of the wall.

When we were assembled and ready to strike, our ranking officer called up to the sentries and announced that Galla Placidia had arrived with her son, the Augustus Valentinian III, who was emperor by right of succession. We had come to assume the throne.

The sentries discussed it among themselves. After some disagreement, one of their number stepped to the edge of the ramparts and demanded to see us.

The officer flicked a worried glance in our direction and declared we would not expose ourselves to their arrows. If they wanted to see us, they would have to throw down their arms.

The sentry mulled this over and came back, "If they are actually present, we will open the gates for them, if not, we will fight."

This gave the officer pause. He looked to me for direction. I stepped forward. I looked up and said, "I am Galla Placidia, empress of Rome, your former Augusta and current regent. My son Valentinian is here with me. We intend to take what is ours."

"Let me see the boy," the sentry shouted.

"My son is a child. I will not expose him to danger. You will have to take the word of his mother, who was once your Augusta and will be again."

The sentry hesitated.

I scowled up at him. "What gives you pause, man? Do you doubt that I am who I say I am, or do you dislike taking orders from a woman? If it's the latter, you might as well go ahead and fight because I will be giving you orders for some time to come. My son is a child. I am his regent, so I will be your commander-in-chief for the foreseeable future. Now open these gates. I command you."

The sentry took a step back as if he'd been slapped. He walked down the ramparts and discussed it with his fellows. They stood huddled together, shooting anxious glances back at us. I don't know whether it was disgust with Joannes or fear of what we might do to them if they refused, but at last they came to a decision. They disappeared behind the ramparts and a few minutes later the gates swung open.

It was largely a bloodless affair. Apart from a few skirmishes here and there, there was little resistance. As we approached the city center, Ardaburius strolled up to us with a broad grin, arms spread, as if he were the prefect of the city welcoming us like a group of visiting dignitaries. We repaired to the palace.

Joannes was not there. After turning over the diadem and scepter, he had thrown himself on the mercy of Ardaburius, whose clemency, he was told, would depend on the safe arrival of Aspar. Joannes was clapped in irons and led away, his cries of despair having more to do with his overwhelming sense of remorse than with any torture inflicted on him.

Joannes was not tortured for the simple reason that he had nothing worthwhile to tell us. He was a tool. Nothing more. Castinus was the real villain. And Castinus wasn't through with us yet. Fortunately, information about his plans were not hard to come by. Officers who had defected to our side eagerly gave them up.

Castinus was marching east from Mediolanum with about three thousand men, which was about three thousand less than we had in Ravenna given the combined forces that had defected to us and the troops we had brought with us. It looked like we could easily defeat them. But then we learned something that surprised us.

Castinus was reportedly receiving reinforcements from a hitherto unknown source, the former governor of the palace, whose familiarity with the barbarian armies was unprecedented. It was said he had lived among them as a hostage for many years and had cultivated their trust to the extent he could call on them for assistance. On his say so alone, an army of six thousand Huns was now advancing south to link up with Castinus's army and cut off Aspar before he could reach Ravenna.

If I didn't know already the identity of this remarkable person, the nature of our approaching enemy would have told me as much, for the adversary we now faced was no halfhearted puppet, but a man of ruthless courage.

Yes, Placidius, I am speaking of Aetius.

To be perfectly honest, Joannes was not a bad fellow. People liked him. He was friendly and generous, difficult to anger, quick with a joke. He tended to give others the benefit of the doubt, a good comrade. But these are not the qualities of a good emperor. A good emperor must be stern and imposing, aloof to the point of inscrutability, calculating in the execution of policy, pitiless in the application of justice. A good emperor is not the most popular man at the party.

But Joannes made a lot of friends, and among them was Aetius. As governor of the palace, Aetius came into contact with Joannes many times, and Joannes went out of his way to be friendly and approachable, a stark contrast to his predecessor Honorius who was chilly to the point of rudeness. Joannes conversed with Aetius openly, expressed an interest in his opinions, and invited him to dinner. Those dinners were carefree, congenial affairs consisting of a mix of high and low officials thrown together without regard to status and encouraged to express themselves freely.

At one of those dinners, Aetius's intimacy with the Huns came to light. Generally, people knew he had spent a good deal of time among the Huns, but many former hostages have little to show for it other than a low opinion of themselves and disinclination to discuss the experience. Aetius was different. When one of the dinner guests expressed the view that the Huns were nothing but a bunch of mindless savages, he took issue and asserted that the Huns were master manipulators, clever and resourceful, secure in their talents and confident in their abilities. He reminded everyone how the Huns had enriched themselves many times over with the gold they had extorted from their so-called betters. He advised them how Rome's purposes would be better served by reaching out to the Huns rather than by treating them as pariahs.

Many of the guests scoffed, but Castinus took notice. He had been searching for a solution to the problem of disaffection in the ranks. Bonifacius's embargo of grain from Africa was beginning to pinch. The public was unhappy, and the army was beginning to doubt its leadership. With an invasion by the Eastern Roman army imminent, Castinus needed to do something to instill confidence. An alliance with the Huns was the answer.

After dinner, Castinus took Aetius aside and asked him if he could persuade the Huns to join an alliance. Aetius assured him he could. And so, a diplomatic mission was arranged.

You might wonder if Aetius ever considered the possibility that by helping Castinus he would end up opposing us. Of course, he did. But remember, this was the opportunity he had been preparing for all his life. Castinus had told him if he could arrange an alliance with the Huns, he would be promoted to the rank of comes rei militaris,[4] one rank below a general. Aetius didn't hesitate.

Now I know what you're thinking. If he truly cared for me, he would not have agreed to fight against me. Ah, but if it were only so simple.

One thing you must learn if you're going to be effective as Augustus: no one can achieve any long-lasting influence without a power base, which is why you must be careful about who you grant such a privilege. Generals and bishops can turn against you. Court favorites can undermine you. Spouses and siblings can betray you. But none can do so without a power base, one they will almost certainly assemble with your full awareness since it is very difficult to do so in secret. It may be a group of likeminded people. It may be others in their calling. It may be a portion of the public drawn by stirring rhetoric and acts of charity. And in the case of military men, it will almost always be disaffected soldiers or ambitious allies.

Take a look around. Who has the most friends? Who is the most liked and admired? He is the greatest threat to you. It is not the man who is despised or feared. Intimidation and fear make poor disciples. The man with the sparkling personality is the man you must worry about it, for he can get others to follow him — and turn them against you.

---

4. Count of military affairs

Aetius has this quality. He is winning. People like him. It's not deliberate. He does it without thinking. It's natural with him. And yes, it can be irritating.

With a man like Aetius, it's best to recruit his talents rather than to fight them. You don't want to get into a long, drawn-out struggle with a man like Aetius. The longer it goes on, the longer others will have to measure you against each other, and you will suffer by comparison.

By sending Aetius to enlist the Huns as allies, Castinus, fool that he was, had given him the power base he needed. Castinus was unpopular. He lacked charisma, which was why he had made the likable Joannes his puppet. Had Joannes not been taken prisoner, had his army not revolted, Castinus would have fallen in time, for Aetius would have usurped him.

Then what would Aetius have done? It is a matter of conjecture. He tells me he would have restored you to the throne as the rightful heir. But of course, he would say that. If his motives were so pure, he would not have supported our enemies in the first place. The truth is Aetius never misses a chance to turn things to his advantage. You must beware of this and try to keep him in harness. We are far better off with him as our ally than as our enemy.

It won't be easy. With Aetius, you must stay calm and keep your cool. He'll try to rattle you. He's like an unruly child, constantly testing your limits. If you show him weakness, he will make a fool of you. Act with dignity and repose but be firm. Never let him ride roughshod over you. Always demonstrate a willingness to listen, and make sure to embrace the best of his ideas. He is brilliant and would make a great emperor. His contributions are shrewd and perceptive. As hard as it is to swallow, he really does want the same things we want. And he always acts in the best interests of the Empire.

I can hear you now. "My mother is deluding herself. She actually believes that a man who marched sixty thousand bloodthirsty Huns to depose her was acting in the best interests of the Empire." But it's true. Aetius was aware I would need a powerful master of soldiers to be an effective ruler, someone who knew me, someone who could anticipate my needs and inspire the army on my behalf. What I was doing was unprecedented. Rome had never been ruled by a woman before. Without him, I would have faced repeated attempts on my life. Within a month, a dozen would-be usurpers would have sprouted like flowers in the spring. But with him at my side those contenders were discouraged.

Yes, I needed a powerful master of soldiers, and Aetius intended to be that man for me, but he was also aware that the optics of my defeating him would undermine his legitimacy. He couldn't just capitulate. What's more, he couldn't simply turn the Huns around and send them home. If Aetius were going to persuade them to relent, he was going to have to pay them off, and for that he needed a large amount of gold, which he could only get from the imperial coffers. From his perspective, there was only one thing to do: fight us to a standstill and then offer a truce, the terms of which would pay off the Huns and make him the new master of soldiers.

Two weeks after we toppled Joannes, Aetius and the Huns attacked Aspar's army from the rear. It was a bloody fight with the loss of many lives. But even before it started, Aetius had sent a courier to me offering terms.

To say I was furious would be putting it lightly. In the fog of war, I could not perceive what I would later come to understand, that he really had no choice if he were going to achieve his objectives. In the moment I could not adjust my perspective to see the larger politics of the thing. I saw it only as a slap in the face. My younger self was asserting herself, the bookish girl, dazzled by the handsome and exuberant young rake, intoxicated by his dreams and aspirations, only to discover he was an arrogant rogue. Consequently, I spurned his offer.

My first act as regent was driven by my heart and not my head, and it was a mistake. It's a lesson I shall share with you in the hope you will not make the same mistake. When you are wed and have assumed your full powers, you must grow up fast. You cannot be the same nineteen-year-old Placidius who left here for Constantinople. You cannot indulge your petty resentments. You cannot be stubborn and mercurial. You cannot give vent to your temper. You must become Valentinian III, regal and restrained. You must accept things your younger self would have found objectionable; you must accept things, not for your own sake, but for the good of the Empire. You must find it within yourself to change.

I acted petulantly and as a result many men lost their lives. Only after the fighting dragged on for days and thousands lay dead did I see the error of my ways. I sent Aetius a message. I was prepared to discuss terms with him. He answered back saying he preferred to meet with me in private. I agreed. A truce was declared, and he came to the palace.

Believe me when I tell you I was itching to get even with Aetius for what he had done, but I had already overreacted and needed to stay calm, so I swallowed hard and watched him as he approached me in the audience chamber flanked by a military guard bristling with arms. He grinned broadly and greeted me with a flourish. I sniffed contemptuously and turned away.

For our private parlay we retired to an anteroom of the great hall where ceremonial vestments and imperial regalia were stored. I refused to do him the honor of meeting him in a more formal setting. I preceded him into the room and stood in the center as he closed the door. He turned to me and gave me that impish smile. I walked up and slapped him across the face. He barely flinched. His blue eyes still sparkled, but his smile melted away. "I suppose that was for the child," he said.

"That and everything else," I said. "I ought to have you whipped."

"The Huns wouldn't like that."

"How dare you threaten me with the Huns."

He gave a little twist of his mouth, as if he had just gotten the joke and didn't find it funny. He crossed the room and sat on a stool. He hunched over and combed his fingers through his beard – he'd started growing it again to make himself more amenable to the Huns.

"Oh, Galla, Galla," he said. "You always do this. First your heart and then your head. In that order. Always."

"Watch your mouth, or I'll make you regret it."

He looked up from under his lashes. "Really? Are we going to play at this? Very well. Here's the part where I tell you that you cannot threaten me. You express great outrage. I persist, and then you grudgingly accept our equality. Then we begin to talk, using our heads, not our hearts, and we make progress. Shall we begin?"

I called for the guards.

Four burly soldiers entered the room and awaited my orders.

Aetius sat back, arms folded, smirking. "Go ahead, Galla, have me arrested. Throw me in the dungeon. Whatever it takes to make you feel like you're in charge. While I'm down there, I can visit Joannes. He's a friendly enough fellow, much more accommodating than you."

I looked daggers at him.

He waited. He inspected his fingernails. He crossed his legs. The cocky teenager whose self-assurance I had once found so disarming sat before me now an arrogant ass. I tell you I could have strangled him, but I held my emotions in check. I dismissed the guards, and we were alone again.

He stood up and began inspecting the imperial regalia on the shelves: mantles, standards, spears, a jeweled scepter with an orb. He picked it up and weighed it in his hands. "So, all of this is yours — at last."

"They belong to Placidius. I'm just the regent."

"Just?"

"What do you want from me, Aetius?"

"I want to be master of soldiers."

"No."

He shook his head dolefully, a faint smile on his face. "Be reasonable. The Senate and the people will want to be reassured we've put our differences behind us, that we're working together for the good of the Empire. Otherwise, they might become anxious."

I laughed. "When I find myself in a position where I have to reward disloyalty to keep the peace, you'll be the first on my list. In the meantime, I think I'll look elsewhere."

"Don't be so flippant, Galla. Your situation is insecure. The Senate cannot be trusted. Remember, they supported your usurper. Symmachus and Argicola and that lot, they're not above trying it again. They think you're weak because you're a woman."

"You're probably right, but I fail to see how appointing the former governor of the palace as magister militum[5] will convince them otherwise. As far as they're concerned, you're an unknown."

"An unknown? I assure you they will know me well enough if I set the Huns on them."

"You'll have to get past Ardaburius and Aspar first."

"Be serious. Ardaburius and Aspar aren't going to stay here forever. As soon as the dust settles, they'll go back to Constantinople. And after Castinus and his followers are purged, the position will be open. No one will make the slightest objection when you proclaim me magister militum."

---

5. Master of soldiers

"You want me to be serious? Very well, let's be serious, Aetius. The politics of the situation are delicate. I'm a woman ruling on behalf of my six-year-old son. Naturally, some people are skeptical. Do you really want me to begin my reign as Augusta by permitting myself to be bullied by a duplicitous scoundrel — a man who once claimed to be my champion."

He was still holding the scepter. He turned it contemplatively in his hands. "I am your champion, Galla. I have always been your champion. Too bad you've grown so cynical."

"Cynical? What could possibly make me cynical? Could it be the way you impregnated me and then refused to come to aid when I was slandered and beaten? Could it be the child you gave me, for which you refused to take responsibility? Or maybe it was the way you threw in with my enemies against me? Or could it be the way you have delivered the Huns to my doorstep and used them to coerce me into giving you a position you're not deserving of? You will have to forgive me if I'm just a little bit cynical."

He smiled to himself and looked down at the scepter. "I don't want this," he said. "I really don't. I'm better off with a sword."

"Well, at least you're correct about one thing."

He held the scepter out to me. "Take it," he said. "It's yours. You'll do it justice as long as you have it, which I fear won't be long if you don't listen to what I'm telling you."

"Ah, I see. I can't do this without you. I need the guidance of a big, strong man, preferably a genius, like you."

"Someone will try to overthrow you."

"Someone. But not you."

"Not me. But someone. The army and aristocracy are full of opportunists who think they have what it takes to rule the Empire. Fools like Castinus and Joannes. They're everywhere, and they may succeed in ousting you, but they'll never be your equal. You're the best qualified person to rule the Empire right now. I honestly believe that. But you must be protected. You cannot command the army without a strong master of soldiers behind you. The rank and file will not take orders from a woman, and a mere political appointee will not have the prestige to control them. You need me, Galla. I'm here to look after you so you can reign without the fear of someone trying to depose you."

I laughed. "Right. The only one I'd have to worry about would be you."

"I've already told you what I want, and it's not this." He tapped the scepter in the palm of his hand.

"I hate to disappoint you, but I've already made up my mind. Flavius Felix will be my new master of soldiers."

He winced as if he'd been stung. "Felix! But he's nothing but a conceited boob!"

"Felix has commanded an army in the field, and he's married to the daughter of Julius Agricola, a man with great influence in the Senate. By making him my master of soldiers, I will settle my differences with my former enemies so we can move forward and put all this unpleasantness behind us."

He sulked. "You will move forward from nothing if the Huns burn down your capital."

"Your capital too, let me remind you. You're still a Roman at heart, even if you wield the barbarians like a club to bludgeon us with."

"Ah, yes. The barbarians. That's something we have in common, Galla, this intimacy with the barbarians. You and I – not Flavius Felix. Not any of these privileged creatures with their silk robes and soft hands. They represent the past. We represent the future. Don't make the mistake your brother did. Don't start thinking that the only good Romans are the ones who can trace their ancestry back to the Republic. Those of us who feel a kinship with the barbarians will be the ones who save Rome, not them."

"I can make you a dux of the comitatenses.[6] That's the best I can do."

---

6. Leader of a Roman military unit

"Don't insult me. I will walk out." He pointed at the door with the scepter.

"I can you make you a comes[7] in Britannia if you like."

"Please. You can't get rid of me that easily."

"All right then. Pannonia. Pannonia will put you near your pals the Huns."

"I don't have to be near the Huns to command their loyalty. I can call on them whenever I like. Would you like me to call on them now?"

"This is growing tiresome. You cannot be my master of soldiers. What do you want to be instead? Name it."

"I want to be your partner. I have only ever wanted to be your partner. Think of what we can accomplish together, Galla."

"I generally try not to partner up with those who attack me."

---

7. An imperial official with his own staff. The title eventually evolved into medieval title "count"

"Come on, Galla. I didn't attack you. I only threatened you. I had to get your attention, didn't I?"

"With six thousand Huns?"

"I could never do you harm. I think you know that. I had to get your attention because I didn't think asking you politely would've gotten me very far. Am I right?"

"I guess we'll never know."

"I was advancing on Ravenna with the Huns when I heard Joannes had abdicated. I could have sent them back, but I decided to use them to strengthen my hand." He put the scepter on a shelf. "You're a woman who knows the importance of bringing all her resources to bear on a problem. Can you blame me?"

"Don't patronize me, Aetius. You didn't send them back because you wanted to strengthen your hand. You didn't send them back because it was not possible for you to send them back without paying them first. So come on. Out with it. How much are they going to cost me?"

"Your astuteness never ceases to amaze me, Galla."

"You forget, Aetius, I was on the other side of this transaction once. There was a time when I needed a concession from an emperor to keep a barbarian army at bay. When he refused to provide it, Rome was sacked, and the Empire was weakened. I will not make the same mistake again. And I won't see more of our soldiers slain needlessly."

"Quite right."

"Here's what I have for you: I can send you to Arelate to become the magister militum of Gaul. It may not be all you had hoped for, but it's quite a promotion for a governor of the palace, and it's far better than being executed for treason."

"You intend to make me subservient to Felix."

"Yes, although I doubt it will keep you in check."

He gave me that impish grin of his. "You aim to set me a challenge. Fine. I'll take it. Overcoming obstacles makes me stronger. I shall consider it a gift. But I must say I'm hurt you don't want me here with you in the palace. We could keep each other company." There was a twinkle in his eye. He took a step toward me. "My affection for you has never slackened, Galla. You are still the only woman I've ever loved."

I raised my hands and backed away from him. "Not this time, Aetius. The last time I ended up pregnant and abandoned. That was a challenge. You may go now, but before you leave town, you may go to the treasury and draw whatever you need to pay off the Huns. I trust you won't take more than is necessary."

"I'm not a thief, Galla."

"We shall see about that."

He made a pouty face. "When will I see you again?"

"When I have need of you."

He started to go.

"Wait," I said. "Aren't you forgetting something."

He seemed at a loss.

"Your daughter," I said. "Wouldn't you like to see her?"

He seemed thrown.

I frowned. "Well, if you'd prefer not to —"

"No. No. I'd like that very much."

"I'll make the arrangements."

"Shall I confess to her that I'm her father?"

"Better not. She's been through more than her fair share of trauma and I don't think finding out her father has been threatening her mother with the Huns will console her very much. Let's just keep it between us for now."

He gave me a winning smile, made a slight bow, and withdrew.

I stood looking after him with a wistful smile. I must confess, I felt a twinge of regret at seeing him go. He was incorrigible to be sure, but he was also correct. I was going to need help ruling the Empire and it was going to have to be someone I could trust. The only question was whether he was the one.

Early signs were not good.

Oh, and by the time I had made arrangements for him to visit Justa, he had already gone.

Chapter Fifteen

Placidius read over the last part again and shook his head. The authenticity of the letter was becoming increasingly hard to deny. Whoever had written it had done an admirable job of making it seem genuine. Here at last was the Galla he knew, calmly weighing the politics of her reign, navigating rivalries, offering concessions, trying to maintain a delicate balance between tolerance and passivity — and, most of all, working hard to thwart Aetius's insatiable ambition.

And yet it could not be true, for Elpidia had written the letter. She had crafted it in league with Cyrus in order to mislead him. But why? What were they trying to get him to do? In what way could the letter be seen as an attempt to make him do something he might otherwise refuse? It was baffling.

Was Aetius involved? That seemed unlikely now. The Master of Soldiers had not come off very well in the letter's depiction of him. Of course his mother's criticism had been tempered by her tendency to make excuses for his inexcusable behavior. Still, Aetius would have looked better had he authored the letter himself. His insufferable ego would have seen to that.

What about Arsenius? Could Arsenius have played a part in its composition? It seemed a stretch. After all, Arsenius had discovered Elpidia's true identity, and his surprise upon discovering who she was had seemed genuine enough. Still, he might have feigned surprise to divert attention from his own involvement. It remained possible he had killed her to keep her from revealing the truth about the letter.

And then there was Candida. She had been his lover for two years, but did he really know her? She was the daughter of a minor official in a mid-level administration post in Rome. He had first made her acquaintance when she came to Ravenna to attend a banquet with her father. The banquet was to honor a group of senatorial landowners who had orchestrated vast increases in tenant rents. The benefits of this scheme were supposed to redound to the Emperor in the form of generous bribes meant to dissuade him from inquiring too deeply into their paltry tax contributions. His mother had urged him to play along.

Placidius had smiled and nodded and demonstrated gratitude to the nobles, but he found the whole affair tiresome and thought that if this were to be his lot in life he would rather be anything other than an emperor. Then, he saw Candida. She was not beautiful in any classical sense; her eyes were rather too large, and her mouth had a peculiar tilt to it. Her hair tumbled down freely on both sides of her moon-shaped face, more or less untended — one might say messy — and honey blond in the sunlight. Yet she had a coltish charm seen in women of a certain age, a reckless zeal made more dangerous by her apparent naiveté. He was intrigued.

He approached her beneath a columned portico with an architrave inscribed with the names of his ancestors. She was flirting with two older men, gently chiding them for their forwardness and pretending embarrassment at their flattery. When he approached, they departed self-consciously. He fumbled his way through an awkward introduction. She laughed at him but urged him to go on. There was never any question about who was in charge.

Right from the start she hooked him. She enflamed his infatuation with gushing admiration and long, moony gazes. She clung to his arm, giggled at his jokes and feigned interest at his most insipid observations. When he got her alone, she practically flung herself at him, and when he took her to bed, she guided him into her with a well-practiced hand. She was no virgin, but by the time he learned about her many and varied assignations, they had achieved such a level of familiarity that she could rebuff his questions without fear of consequences.

She wielded her prerogatives freely. She was frequently demanding, often aggrieved. She used sex as both carrot and stick, and the more she vexed him, the more he wanted her. Soon she was talking freely about becoming his wife. Consequently, when she discovered he had agreed to marry his cousin, she threw a fit. She overturned furniture, tore down drapes, and smashed precious keepsakes. She threatened to leave him. He begged her not to go. It was embarrassing, as he reflected back on it now, the way she humiliated him. She made him follow her around in full view of the guards while she ignored his pleas for forgiveness. She played him like a lyre. But she ran into a more formidable adversary when she ran up against his mother.

His mother had insisted on Placidius marrying his cousin with a rigidity he found surprising. In the past she had been susceptible to an impassioned plea, weak, almost a soft touch. The demands of her children rarely went unsatisfied. Tears and tantrums almost always got results. But when it came to the question of his marrying his cousin, she was as immovable as a rock. She dismissed his love affair with Candida as a childish lark and rejected the idea of her becoming his wife as a sick joke. He remembered thinking he didn't know this brittle, demanding version of his mother. It was almost as if she was channeling someone else. It was almost as if Aetius was speaking through her.

His sister Justa witnessed the row. She was sitting by the window sewing when the argument broke out. She kept quiet and smiled to herself. Placidius hated his sister. Although she had changed since coming back from Constantinople — she was much less open in her contemptuousness now, more sly and cunning — she was still dangerous, and he didn't trust her.

For the next few days, Placidius refused to cooperate with his mother. The royal entourage was assembled without his cooperation. Arsenius was assigned as his chief of staff. Cyrus was assigned as his first deputy, which was surprising since he had no qualifications to recommend him for such a position. Placidius figured Cyrus had been included as a sop, a concession from his mother to make him feel better about going. Cyrus was a cut up. Cyrus made him laugh. He considered Cyrus his boon companion.

Placidius continued to sulk and resist for more than a week until the caravan was assembled. Eventually, as news spread that the Emperor was preparing to depart for Constantinople, the public forced his hand. They were thrilled, not only because it foretold a peaceful transition of power, but also because it portended the knitting together of the Empire and the end of the difficult, often fractious relationship between East and West. In the end, Placidius had no choice but to give in, for to do otherwise would have risked disappointing the public.

He went to Candida and broke the news. The expected outburst ensued. To appease her, he offered to bring her along, but she refused. She demanded he stand up to his mother and say he had chosen a different woman to be his wife. He begged her to be reasonable. He tried to explain the political risk of appearing to be in opposition to his mother, but Candida wasn't listening. Finally, after a good deal of drama, she gave in, but on two conditions. First, if she was going to travel with him, she insisted on being accorded a place of honor, and, second, she would have her own retinue. She would not be treated like a concubine.

Placidius agreed, which immediately brought him into conflict with Arsenius. The idea that a peripheral contingent had been attached to the royal entourage without his consent irritated Arsenius. He complained to Galla, which peeved Placidius, who tried to have him sacked. But Galla wouldn't hear of it, and the matter remained unresolved as the caravan rolled out of Ravenna on its way east to Constantinople.

Curiously, Galla had made no attempt to stop Candida from joining the caravan, probably another conciliatory gesture on her part. Galla was no stranger to concession and compromise, a trait often attributed to her softness as a woman and frequently characterized as a flaw. But the Galla of the letter explained it differently. How had she put it? *Sometimes you have to sacrifice your allegiance to fulfill your duty.* As his mother saw it, her duty was to achieve the reunification of the Empire through the marriage of the two halves of the house of Theodosius. If she had to concede her son his temporary infatuation with a girl beneath him, so be it. In any case, she knew that any further opposition on the matter of Candida would only make him hostile to the advice she was about to give him in the letter.

Once the issue was put to rest, however, Placidius had to admit his mother had a point. Candida could be a problem. She had never really acted in the best interests of anyone other than herself. She was petty and manipulative. She cared nothing for the Empire and even less for him personally. He could not ignore the fact that she had been close friends with Elpidia and Isaac. She had also enjoyed some vague, shadowy relationship with Cyrus. He could only hope she wasn't hiding something. He was going to have to question her.

But when he called her to his quarters, she refused to come. He could make her come, but that would only result in another ugly scene. For once he decided to be strategic. He would let her believe she had regained the upper hand. He would let her think he was so smitten with her she could demand anything she wanted from him and get it. What had the letter said? *Sometimes you must humble yourself to get some distance and assess the situation properly.* If Candida thought she still controlled him, she might well let down her guard and reveal something incriminating. But he had to act fast. If Arsenius got to her first, she might be driven from camp before Placidius had a chance to get to the bottom of things.

He sat down and wrote out a note. He apologized for being so high-handed with her. He expressed remorse for what had happened. He hoped she could forgive him. He missed her. His heart ached for her. She meant everything to him. He laid it on thick.

He called for Stephanus and handed him the note. "Take this to Candida."

Stephanus bowed and began to withdraw.

"Wait," Placidius said. "Is there any news?"

"News?" Stephanus asked. "News of what?"

"You remember. That thing I talked to you about."

Stephanus looked perplexed. Then it came to him. "Oh, that! No, Imperator. No one has come into the camp who shouldn't be here."

"Not even a messenger?"

"No one."

Placidius eyed him suspiciously. "Are you sure?"

"Yes. Quite."

"Very well then. Keep looking."

Stephanus went out. The tent flap fell back into place.

Placidius stared after him. An idea began to form in his mind. He waited a few minutes, then swept back the flap and followed him at a distance.

It was dusk and the setting sun cast the distant Haemus Mountains[1] in shadows of purple and red. Placidius crossed the camp with his hood drawn up over his head to avoid recognition. He followed the groom to Candida's tent. Inside, the lamps were lit. He could see the shapes of two silhouettes against the goatskin walls. He could hear the murmur of earnest conversation punctuated by sporadic laughter. He crept forward, the better to listen. Candida was reading his note aloud, mocking it.

"Won't he be surprised when he finds out?" she said. "I wish I could be there when Arsenius finally tells him." More laughter.

He heard Stephanus say, "Yes, and he asked me again if anyone had come into the camp."

"What did you tell him?"

"Nothing. Why would I say anything? If I put him off for long enough, he'll forget all about it. A more scatterbrained person I've rarely met."

"I don't know why you don't just tell him," Candida said.

"What, and miss the opportunity for more laughs? No, let's just wait and see what happens."

"Is he still around?"

"So I hear."

"It would be wonderful to see him again. He was amazing. He fairly took my breath away."

A knowing chuckle. "You know what your problem is, Candida? You get excited too easily. How about this? How does this make you feel?"

There was a brief silence followed by giggles.

"Stephanus, stop it! Someone might hear us."

"Oh, come on, my saucy little Empress, let me show you the magic."

---

1. The Balkan Mountains

It grew silent. Placidius leaned in. Then he heard it, the brusque, rhythmic moans of a woman in the throes of passion.

His blood began to boil.

One thing I've learned is that powerful men can never be fully appeased. Nothing is ever enough for them. They'll always want more. In the end, you can never satisfy them, but you can slow them down, make them work hard for every concession, and draw them out. Some men are worth the effort because their hunger for power can eventually be diverted to constructive ends, but others will not be happy until they bring you down. These must be eliminated. The trick is telling which is which.

When the war was over, Aetius cashiered the Huns with three hundred pounds of gold taken from the treasury. Thereafter they withdrew to the territory they had claimed for themselves on the plains north of the Sava in the province of Pannonia. At that time, they were still ruled by a pair of brothers, Octar and Rugila, but before long Octar would be slain in battle, after which Rugila would rule on his own for several years until he was struck dead by a lightning bolt. After that, a new pair of brothers would come to power, a pair that even Aetius would have difficulty controlling. They were Bleda and Atilla.

In Ravenna, it was time to settle accounts with those who had betrayed us. Joannes was mounted on a donkey and paraded through the streets to be spit on and reviled. He lost all sense of dignity and wept openly as he was led to a platform before a jeering crowd, where his hands were chopped off with an ax.

It took several blows to sever them completely. The crowd roared their approval. Poor Joannes, who had once been the favorite of the masses, fainted from the blood loss and had to be revived for the final act. He was brought to the infield of the Hippodrome, stumbling and drained of color, where he was lashed to a stake in the infield and pelted with stones before being decapitated. It was an ugly business, but necessary.

As for Castinus, he ran away like a coward and went into hiding. Later I learned he was living under an assumed name in the suburbs of Carthago[2]. I could have had him arrested and brought to justice, but to what end? The message had already been sent. Any potential usurpers already knew the cost of treason. To seek retribution on Castinus would have been nothing more than self-indulgence. Listen Placidius, it avails us nothing to punish our enemies for our own self-gratification. It is indecent, not to mention risky.

I tracked down the three attendants who had started the rumors against me in Ravenna, the vile gossip that had stripped me of my title and driven me from my homeland in disgrace. I had them arrested and brought before me.

I planned to make an example of them. But it was not necessary to punish them all. One would suffice. I ordered them to draw straws. The loser, I deprived of her tongue. The others, I let go. By this method, news of my clemency was spread alongside reports of my severity. It is always best this way. You want the public to like you, your associates to respect you, and your enemies to fear you. Punishment meted out wisely gives you the best opportunity to achieve all three at once.

---

2. Modern day Tunis in Tunisia

In the fall of that year, you were proclaimed Augustus in the presence of the Senate. It was a somber proceeding full of rituals and formalities. During most of it, you played with a figurine of a horse I had given you. When they put the purple robes on you, you looked chagrined as if you might cry, but I petted you and gave you your toy and you were content.

At the same ceremony I was formally granted the title of Augusta and pro-claimed regent. Justa, who had been made to watch the whole thing quietly from the back, got nothing.

I named Felix my Master of Soldiers and recalled Bonifacius from Africa to promote him to commander. I named Aetius the commander of the Army in Gaul, a higher rank than comes, in order to appease him and make sure he didn't stir up any more trouble. With this promotion Aetius stood in the same relationship to Felix as Bonifacius did, which is to say they were his immediate subordinates and co-equals. This arrangement would cause me no end of headaches in time, but at the moment it seemed prudent.

Aspar and Ardaburius returned to Constantinople, Bonifacius returned to Africa, and Aetius went to Gaul. The Empire went about its business. In Rome there was one last notable who needed assuaging, a mere formality as I saw it. In due course, however, it would prove to be the thorniest issue of all, for the Church was in transition.

During our time in Constantinople, Pope Boniface passed away, and a new pope, Celestine[3] , became pontiff. He had come to power through the influence of the African bishops, that group of authoritative theologians, including Cyril of Alexandria and Augustine of Hippo, who were determined to dictate the direction of the Church. To them the Nicene Creed, established by the Council of Nicaea, was the only legitimate profession of faith, and any other form of Christianity was heretical. They condemned their rivals with righteous fervor and attacked them with expulsions and anathemas, even going so far as to condone violence against them. While such brutality might have suited the purposes of the African bishops, it created enmity and discord among the people of Rome and inflamed tensions at a time when I was trying to heal the wounds of a civil war. I could not have it. I called for a meeting with the Pope.

Celestine was a short, thickset man with a squashed-in nose and pinched lips. He seemed to be fighting a cold. He was wheezy and rheumy-eyed. He had the sniffles and kept wiping his nose with the embroidered sleeve of his dalmatic.[4] He was accompanied by a nervous clerk who took notes on everything that came out of our mouths and stopped repeatedly to brush the hair out of his face.

Celestine was calm and respectful. He paid proper deference to me as Augusta and made no sign that he thought himself superior to me merely because I was a woman. But I had heard that he was not to be trusted.

---

3. Pronounced sell-ess-teen

4. Long, wide-sleeved tunic often worn by clergymen

He had been a bitter opponent of Joannes's policy of toleration toward the Arians and had worked to undermine the Emperor by supporting acts of violence against the Arians. Arian churches had been vandalized and desecrated. Arian prelates had been harassed and beaten, all without the Emperor's sanction. Finally, in an attempt to legitimize the persecution of his rivals, he had sought special dispensation from the Emperor to continue the violence. Joannes ignored him.

Now he had become Pope, and a new emperor had taken the throne, and he wanted an answer to his appeal.

He asked if I had any particular sympathy for the Arians, knowing full well that I had lived among the Goths and had been married to an Arian. Still, he persisted and feigned ignorance, so I decided to make it clear. I told him I was in no way troubled by the fact that people had different interpretations of Christianity and saw no benefit in setting people against each other to establish the dominance of one creed over another.

Celestine observed that the tolerance of heresies tended to weaken the Church and asked what I intended to do to promote the true religion. I told him I meant to endow a church in gratitude to my patron saint for having saved me and my children from a storm at sea. He complimented my generosity but appeared to expect more. I told him I also intended to help restore churches throughout the realm that had fallen into disrepair. He nodded his approval. When I didn't immediately offer more, he rubbed his chin and turned to the clerk. "Give me the book," he said.

I expected him to produce a Bible but instead he brought forth a book bound into a codex and authored by Augustine, the powerful theologian and bishop of Hippo. It was entitled The City of God.

I was familiar with it. Sixtus had explained it to me. During the time I was in exile, it had become quite popular among the clergy in Rome. It spoke of a conflict between the City of Man, inhabited by those who embrace the cares and pleasures of the mortal world, and the City of God, inhabited by those righteous enough to put away earthly pleasures and dedicate themselves to the faith – the faith as interpreted by the Nicene Fathers. As Augustine told it, anyone who denied the Nicene faith was on the wrong side of God and wicked.

Pope Celestine stood before me and held the book out to me. He asked if I was literate. I told him I was. He handed it to me.

"It has proven powerful guidance to those who seek righteousness," he ex-plained.

I took it.

"Persons of the highest standing have assimilated its message."

I was sure they had.

"Persons both in the clergy and in government."

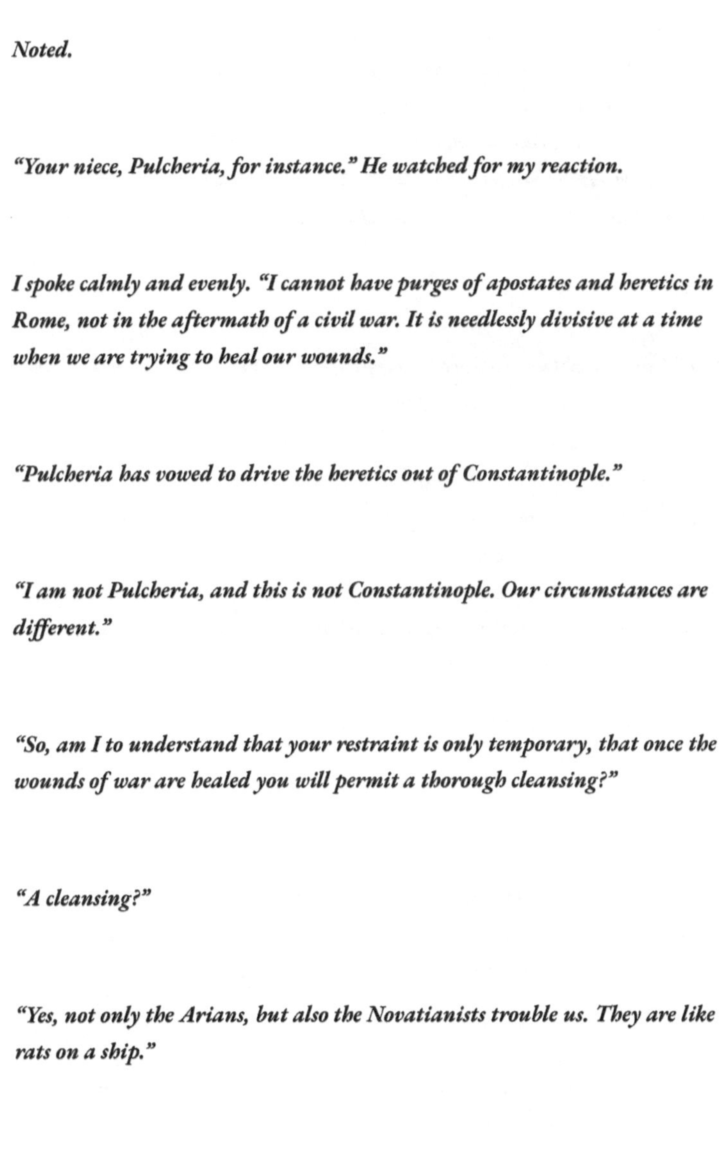

Noted.

"Your niece, Pulcheria, for instance." He watched for my reaction.

I spoke calmly and evenly. "I cannot have purges of apostates and heretics in Rome, not in the aftermath of a civil war. It is needlessly divisive at a time when we are trying to heal our wounds."

"Pulcheria has vowed to drive the heretics out of Constantinople."

"I am not Pulcheria, and this is not Constantinople. Our circumstances are different."

"So, am I to understand that your restraint is only temporary, that once the wounds of war are healed you will permit a thorough cleansing?"

"A cleansing?"

"Yes, not only the Arians, but also the Novatianists trouble us. They are like rats on a ship."

"The Novatianists?" This was the first time I heard that sect mentioned, and I was surprised. The Novatianists were a nearly two-century-old Christian sect. Having refused the right of baptism to those who had renounced their faith under persecution, they had been declared heretical and suppressed. Over the course of centuries, their numbers had dwindled away to practically nothing. If there were more than five hundred practicing Novatianists in the entire Roman Empire, I would have been shocked. And Celestine wanted to persecute them.

"No," I said. "I will not approve the persecution of a minor Christian sect whose continued existence poses a threat to no one."

I saw a flicker of contempt in his eyes. The clerk was writing vigorously. Celestine wiped his nose with his sleeve. "How regrettable," he said. "Frankly, I had hoped that the elimination of the apostate Joannes would lead to more righteous leadership in Ravenna, something more akin to what we see in the East." He was trying to goad me.

I said, "Social strife does not serve us."

He cleared his throat. He wiped his nose. He said, "Pulcheria's advisers are all men of God. There is not a single one who is not exactly what he claims to be. I wonder, can you say the same about the men who guide you?"

He was alluding to Sixtus. He was making it clear that he knew about Sixtus's past and was prepared to use it against him if I refused to cooperate. It annoyed me.

"Let me be clear," I said. "You will not persecute the Arians, the Novatianists, or anyone else. I will not permit it."

He bowed to me, but he did not pledge his obedience.

"This audience is at an end," I said. My tone was not cordial.

He withdrew taking his nervous note taking clerk with him.

Soon thereafter he made a public declaration of condemnation against the Novatianists in direct contravention of my wishes.

Yet I did not retaliate – not then. I understood that I had to proceed cautiously. The Church was as formidable an enemy as the army. I could not underestimate them. I needed to speak to Sixtus first.

During the years we had been away in Constantinople, Sixtus had risen to a position of prominence under Pope Boniface. When Boniface died and Celestine was made Pope, Sixtus was kept on in his former role, although he no longer enjoyed the warm personal regard he had had with his former mentor.

From the start, Pope Celestine's administration undertook to dig up whatever it could find against the prelates in its jurisdiction. It pried into their pasts, gathering information it could use against them should they prove uncooperative, and then made them toe the line in support of a policy of persecution. The template had been established by the patriarch Cyril, whose well-orchestrated purges had led to riots and bloodshed in the streets of Alexandria. When prelates objected or tried to resist, invariably some former association with a heretic, presumed innocent at the time, would be brought to light and used against them. It was under this hostile coercion that Sixtus found himself when I returned to Ravenna and got wind of Celestine's agenda.

"It's the African bishops, Galla, and it goes far beyond rooting out heresies. They mean to take control of the Church and dictate policy, for now and for the future. Anyone who opposes them will find themselves accused and condemned without trial."

We were in the nave of the Basilica of St. Paul Outside the Walls, a cavernous space some 450 feet long with vaulted ceilings one hundred feet high. We were on our knees with our heads down, surrounded by worshipers. It was perfectly silent except for the rustling of clothes and clicking of heels. When someone coughed, it echoed through the chamber like a shout. Sixtus thought it best to meet here to avoid suspicion; the Pope had spies everywhere.

"They are deliberately stirring up unrest," I whispered. "I won't have this city turned into another Alexandria. I intend to stop it."

Sixtus cautioned me. "They won't hesitate to move against you. Your power doesn't scare them. Orestes[5], the prefect of Egypt, thought he could intimidate them. He was nearly stoned to death."

The story of Orestes and his friend, the pagan philosopher Hypatia[6], was well known. It served as a cautionary tale about confronting powerful men of the Church.

Immediately upon being elevated as Patriarch of Alexandria, Cyril began persecuting pagans, Jews, and heretics. He closed the churches of the Novatians and seized their sacred vessels. He antagonized the Jews and incited public outrage against them by claiming they were plotting to destroy Christianity.

Orestes was the prefect of the city, the highest government official in the diocese, and he did not like what he was seeing. He asked Cyril to desist, and when Cyril ignored him, he wrote to the Emperor begging him to rebuke Cyril.

When Cyril learned of this, he wrote a letter of his own, not to the Emperor, but to Pulcheria. He complained of the prefect's interference with the Church. Neither man received an answer.

Cyril took this as approval for what he was doing and sought to teach Orestes a lesson. He arranged for a band of Nitrian monks to come to the city. These

---

5. Pronounced oar-rest-ees

6. Pronounced hy-pay-she-ah

monks had a reputation for violence. They instigated a mob against Orestes and accused him of being a pagan. The truth was Orestes had been baptized by the Patriarch of Constantinople and was a devout Christian. But it didn't matter. The monks surrounded Orestes and threw stones at him. He was struck in the head and fell to the ground. When the supporters of Orestes saw this, they retaliated. A riot broke out, and dozens of people were injured.

In the aftermath, Orestes had the instigators arrested. He dashed off another letter to the Emperor reporting what had happened and urging him to intervene. When Cyril got wind of this, he was furious.

One of the most prominent citizens of Alexandria was a pagan philosopher named Hypatia. She was the head of the Neoplatonic school at Alexandria and was well respected for her insights and wisdom. She had long been a friend of Orestes.

Within days of the riot, a rumor spread that Hypatia had persuaded Orestes to oppose Cyril even to the point of bloodshed, thus laying the blame for the riot at her doorstep, even though she had had nothing to do with it. Cyril stood in the pulpit and condemned her as a sorceress, whipping his followers into a frenzy. They formed and mob, broke into her home, and beat her. Then they dragged her to an open pit and stoned her to death with roofing tiles and pottery shards. Afterwards, to drive the point home, they mutilated her body and set it on fire.

Horrified at the violence and dismayed at the lack of response from Theodosius and Pulcheria, Orestes resigned his post and withdrew from Alexandria. The episode had ended in Cyril's favor. A strong message was sent to anyone who might consider opposing him: they could be killed.

From that day forward, Cyril continued to extend his reach through intimidation and violence even going so far as to insinuate himself into ecclesiastical politics in Constantinople. He promoted compliant bishops to do his bidding at apostolic sees throughout the East. He enlisted the alliance of Aurelius of Carthago and won the endorsement of Augustine of Hippo. Then he reached his grasping hand into the politics surrounding the elevation of a new pope after the death of Boniface in Rome. Celestine was his man. This was the point Sixtus was trying to make. Any opposition to Celestine was opposition to Cyril, and Cyril was too dangerous an enemy to underestimate.

"I advise you against it," he said. "Wait for a better opportunity. It will come; Celestine is ill. That cold he has been suffering from has never left him. When he dies, you can take action. In the meantime, cultivate allies among the prelates who oppose him. There are plenty of them, although at the moment they are bullied into silence. When the time comes to elevate a new pope, they will support your choice over whoever Cyril nominates."

"And shall I just let Celestine flout my authority? I am the Augusta. I cannot be seen to be so soft. I must do something."

"Yes," said Sixtus. "I agree. Negotiate with the Pope. Give him something that will appease him, but demand something in return. That way you can keep him at arm's length until you get a better opportunity."

I saw his logic and called at once for another meeting with Celestine. He appeared before me again with his false humility and his nervous note-taking clerk. I told him I had thought the matter through and decided to allow him to expel the Novatianists. In return, I asked there be no more persecutions, at least until the public had had a chance to recover from the trauma of the recent conflict.

He consulted with his clerk. They stood with their heads bowed and discussed it. Then he turned to me with a regretful expression and shook his head. It was not enough. He wanted to expel the Arians as well.

I have to tell you, Placidius, the idea of persecuting the Arians turned my stomach. The Goths were almost entirely Arian Christians, and they were as devoted to their religion as anybody, but it would never have occurred to them to tyrannize the few Nicene Christians living among them. I knew this for a fact because I was a Nicene Christian, and my faith was never an issue for them, not even when I was married Ataulf. So irrelevant was the question of our different religious beliefs, I even attended Arian mass without repercussion. But to the Nicenes, these minor differences were a provocation, and they were hell bent on rooting out the least little dissension. They want Christendom all to themselves.

"You may expel them," I said as I searched for a middle ground, "but you may not molest them or confiscate their belongings, and you may not destroy their places of worship."

Celestine gave me an aggrieved look as if he had been unfairly deprived of something. Again, he consulted with his clerk. They talked it over. At last, he agreed. *If they were permitted to expel the Novatianists and the Arians, they would curtail their violence for the time being.*

It made me heartsick to have to agree to such a grim compromise. I wondered what Theodoric would think when he heard that Galla Placidia, his former friend and colleague, had endorsed the expulsion of the Arians from Rome. The Goths were already restless. They felt they had been mistreated by Joannes and Castinus. There were rumors swirling that they were up in arms and ready to exact revenge by moving on Arelate. I decided to write Theodoric in hopes of mollifying him, but it was already too late. By the time my letter reached him, the Goths were on the move, and although I cannot say for certain, I suspect they were only validated in their resentment when they learned I had expelled the Arians from Rome.

In any case, Celestine went ahead. The churches of the Novatianists were closed and their belongings confiscated. They were banished and exiled. The Arians were driven out as well. Families were torn apart, reputations ruined. As ugly as it was, it was finally over. The Nicenes had done their worst, and the Empire had held together.

And then, not two weeks later, Celestine called for another persecution. I was incredulous. He was flouting my authority, daring me to stop him. I couldn't help but feel that he would not have been so brazen if I had been a man. I yearned to teach him a lesson, to make him pay for his defiance, but Sixtus urged me not to react. Doing so would only have played into their hands, he said.

Oh, Placidius, let me tell you. There will be times when you will want to strike out against your enemies even though prudence dictates otherwise. You must not give in to the temptation. You must hold back, get the measure of them, and bide your time. Powerful men will never be satisfied. They will always thirst for more. To get the advantage of them you must draw them out, use their avarice against them, and lead them into a trap.

In my case, the time was not right to strike against Celestine and his allies. I needed to take my time, and, with Sixtus's help, build a rival coalition to oppose them. Although it embarrassed me and made me look ineffectual, I rolled over and took it when Celestine broke his promise to end the persecutions.

In the end, however, it was the right decision, for it emboldened him to go further. Soon Celestine was aiming for bigger game. He intended to go after the Jews.

Meanwhile, the Goths' assault on Arelate took an unexpected turn. It ran up against an unexpected adversary in Aetius. Had Theodoric struck two months earlier, he would have found our defenses weak and disorganized, but his hesitation as he waited to see how I would react to the persecutions delayed him long enough to allow Aetius to organize a defense. A terrific battle ensued, and the Goths got the worst of it. Theodoric reorganized his forces and took another run at Aetius but was beaten back. Finally, he gave up and withdrew.

Reports had it that the Huns were the decisive factor. Unbeknownst to me, Aetius had kept a contingent of Hun mercenaries with him after the bulk of the Hun army had withdrawn to Pannonia, a contingent numbering a thousand. These Huns were credited with spearheading Aetius's forces. They penetrated deep into the Gothic defenses, sowing fear and confusion, until the Gothic middle collapsed, and their flanks disintegrated. The Goths had not seen it coming. They had never suspected the Romans could marshal so many Huns to fight for them. It was all down to Aetius.

At Arelate, Aetius was praised and celebrated. Paeans were written in his honor. Songs were sung. He was given a parade, which some characterized as a triumph[7], but this was treading on dangerous ground, for only an Emperor can call for a triumph. To declare one without the Emperor's permission comes very close to treason. Wisely, Aetius had the good sense not to call it that but referred to it instead as a "parade of appreciation" for his services. But if Aetius, the "hero of Arelate," demonstrated cautious restraint in that case, his diplomacy utterly failed him when I summoned him to Ravenna.

The purpose of the meeting was to discuss a new threat by the Franks on the Upper Rhine. As my new master of soldiers, and Aetius's immediate superior, Felix was present. It was my idea to send Felix, along with some supporting troops from Aetius's army to confront the Franks, but Aetius was against it. He saw no need to involve Felix when he could handle everything himself as Commander of the Army in Gaul.

---

7. The celebration of a military victory the centerpiece of which is a parade to honor the victorious military commander

Felix began to speak up, but Aetius cut him off. He said anyone with a clear view of the situation could plainly see that the Army in the Presence of the Emperor (Felix's army) must remain in the capital until the new Augusta's dominion was secure. "To pull them away now would be to invite rebellion."

Felix bristled and tried to pull rank, but Aetius ignored him and turned to me. He wanted to know whose bright idea it was to leave the capital undefended in the wake of a civil war. He didn't wait for an answer but allowed as it could not have been me. He knew me too well to think I would ever be so reckless. But rather than accuse Felix directly, he let the matter drop and said he would go to the Upper Rhine and deal with the Franks while Felix remained in the capital to look after my security.

Felix lost his cool. He pounded the table and ordered Aetius to desist.

Aetius smiled.

I was not stupid. I could see what was going on. Aetius was doing this for my benefit; he wanted to show me who was really in charge. He wanted me to know who should have been giving the orders and who should have been taking them.

Remarkably, Felix helped Aetius to make his point. After much discussion, Felix came around to Aetius's point of view. It was agreed. Aetius would go to the Rhine. Felix would remain behind.

But Aetius wasn't finished yet. After the meeting was over and Felix had gone, he took me aside and pontificated on another matter he considered of great importance.

Africa was hanging by a thread, he said. Bonifacius was making a mess of things, living a lavish lifestyle, claiming the prerogatives of a king, and growing dangerously complacent. He was being supported by a network of corrupt officials who were abusing the local populace and turning them against us. The troops were growing restless, and rebellion was in the air. To make matters worse, the Vandals were aware of what was going and were licking their chops. He urged me to dispatch him to Africa to rescue the situation before it got out of hand.

I sighed at his transparency and played along. "And what about the Franks?" I asked. "I thought you were going to the Rhine to deal with them? You can hardly be in two places at once."

"The Franks are doing the same thing they've been doing for the past seven years. Threatening the Upper Rhine is their favorite pastime. Confronting them today is no more urgent than it was yesterday. Africa, on the other hand, is on the verge of a crisis. I must go at once and take over or a Vandal invasion will be imminent."

"I see," I said. "So, you're planning to go there and take charge."

"Yes."

"And the Franks will wait for you to finish your business there before they press us any further on the Rhine."

"Don't worry. I will send someone to the Rhine to keep an eye on things."

"Not Felix?"

"Not Felix."

"And you will also maintain control over Arelate."

"I will."

"And you will take the reins from Bonifacius in Africa."

"It is imperative."

"That will give you quite a bit of territory to be responsible for, don't you think?"

He shrugged.

"If you had all that territory, you'd have more men under your command than Felix and Bonifacius put together, not to mention you'd have control of our grain supply. It seems to me, if you don't mind me saying so, that with so much territory under your control you could take over. You could get yourself proclaimed emperor."

He frowned. "Oh, Galla. You don't still suspect me of plotting against you. Do you?"

I laughed. "I'm sorry, I must have mistaken you for the man who used six thousand Huns to extort a military commission from me."

Aetius shook his head. "Be fair."

"Fair? What's not fair? I see you for what you are, Aetius. You're a conniving wretch. Am I supposed to ignore that?"

"Listen to reason. I'm speaking to you as my superior officer. The unrest in Africa is real. It must be addressed."

"I don't trust you."

"Why? Because of the Huns?" He sighed as if he was deeply put upon. "Listen to me. I was bringing them at the command of the Emperor to defend the Empire. I was just doing my job."

"Is that right? I didn't realize it was within the purview of the governor of the palace to make war."

"It is within the purview of all government officials to defend Rome."

"And I was the one you were defending it against. Correct?"

"Well, to be honest, I didn't expect you to show up so soon. I anticipated a protracted struggle. I was surprised to discover Joannes had been ousted so quickly. People thought highly of him. I thought he would rally the public behind him and resist."

"And suppose he had. Then what? You would have made war against me?"

"Maybe. To keep up appearances, you know. Until I had a chance to speak with you and see what you could offer."

"So, you admit it. You're for sale. The same thing you accuse Bonifacius of."

"I like to be among the winners. There's nothing wrong with that. Most successful leaders are good at reading fluid situations and changing course when necessary. I knew you would prevail in the end. You're smarter than the rest. Sooner or later it was inevitable you would be in charge. It was just a matter of making the best possible arrangement in the meantime, and I had six thousand Huns at my disposal, and we were negotiating, so I used them, naturally."

"Naturally."

"That's right. I would've been a fool to do otherwise. But if you think I would use the grain supply to strong-arm you, you don't know me." He looked at the floor and shook his head. "Frankly, it's a little insulting."

I couldn't help but smile. He was such a pitiable actor. "I'm not sending you to Africa, Aetius. You can forget about it. I need you in Gaul."

He sucked his teeth. "Do you know your problem, Galla?"

"I'm sure you're going to tell me."

"You're gullible. Just because someone does you a favor it doesn't mean you should trust them. Bonifacius is pulling the wool over your eyes. He knows you're loyal to him, so he's running Africa like it's his own personal fiefdom, which, in itself, wouldn't be a bad thing, except he's making a mess of it. Yes, he's for sale, but so are plenty of other people. The problem with Bonifacius is that he's doing it badly, fueling resentment and creating instability even as

the Vandals grow emboldened. Let me go to Africa and remedy the situation before it gets out of hand."

I wasn't worried. If Bonifacius was really a problem, I would've heard about it from someone else. But I had heard nothing. Obviously, Aetius was making it up. I dismissed him with a wave of my hand. "Leave me alone. You're beginning to bore me."

"Very well. I'll go. But promise me one thing, Galla. Promise me you'll look into it. See if I'm not right."

"Fine. I'll look into it."

"And don't delay. I can repel a Vandal invasion if need be, but it will cost a lot less in blood and treasure if we can stop it before it gets started."

I sighed. "If you insist."

At this juncture, the sound of tiny fists were heard pounding on the door. From outside came a shriek and some childish giggling. I nodded at the guard, who opened the door, and you and your sister came tumbling into the room. The two of you were engaged in a game of tag. You chased each other around, climbing the furniture and dodging in and out between the columns, laughing hysterically. Aetius stood back with his arms folded, grinning.

You were seven by then, and Justa was nine. You were both rambunctious and difficult. I should have taken a sterner hand with you, but I was greatly preoccupied as you can now appreciate. I had no sympathy for the assertion, voiced by some, that I should have been able to attend to my duties as a mother while running the Empire at the same time. I had servants for that.

I ordered you to stop but you ignored me. Justa chased you around behind a column and took advantage of the situation to bite you on the hand. You howled at the pain and injustice of it. I ordered Justa to come out from where she was hiding. She stepped out from behind the column, hands turned up as if she could not understand what had come over you.

You ran to my side, clung to my skirts, and wailed. I tried to calm you down. I asked to see the wound. You held your hand up to me. The indentations from her teeth were plainly visible. I rounded on her. "You bit him!"

"I did not!"

"I can see it!"

"He did it to himself...to get me in trouble."

The look that came into your face was something new to me. The rapidity with which you transformed from victim to aggressor was startling. You flew at her and struck her, knocking her to the floor. Then you flung yourself on top of her and began to pummel her. Aetius dragged you off with rather more force than I would have liked.

"Stop that!" he shouted. His voice was deep and hard, a man's voice.

You froze, petrified. Then you began to cry.

You were unaccustomed to being reprimanded by anyone, much less someone with Aetius's strict, no-nonsense bearing.

Aetius knelt down and helped your sister to her feet. He petted her head. He said soothing things to her. Then he swung back on you. "Don't you know you must never strike a girl? It's behavior unbecoming a prince. It's unmanly."

You gaped at him, mortified. No one had ever spoken to you like that before, and you were quite undone by it.

"Aetius," I said. "She bit him."

"I don't care if she did," Aetius said. "He must never strike a woman. It's cowardly and mean. He must start acting with more grace and dignity if he hopes to be emperor someday."

"He is the emperor," I reminded him.

"In name only, thank God. The boy has a lot of growing up to do. He must learn to comport himself properly. Otherwise, what kind of emperor will he be?"

You stopped crying and fixed him with an icy glare.

Just then your governess appeared, full of apologies, and led you and your sister away.

Aetius shook his head in dismay. "Galla, you really must spend more time with them. They are growing unmanageable."

"Oh, is that right? And just when am I supposed to find the time to do that?"

He looked at me in mild surprise. "I don't know," he said. "But it's your duty as a woman."

I was aghast. "My duty? Need I remind you, one of those children is yours? How about your duty? When have you ever visited your daughter? When have you ever spent any time with her?"

"I've been defending the Empire."

It was all I could do to hold myself back. I don't know whether he was deliberately trying to goad me or whether he was really that clueless, but it was less the words he said than the words he did not say, the words that hung in the air:

"You stay home and take care of the children, and I'll take care of the Empire."

I could have killed him.

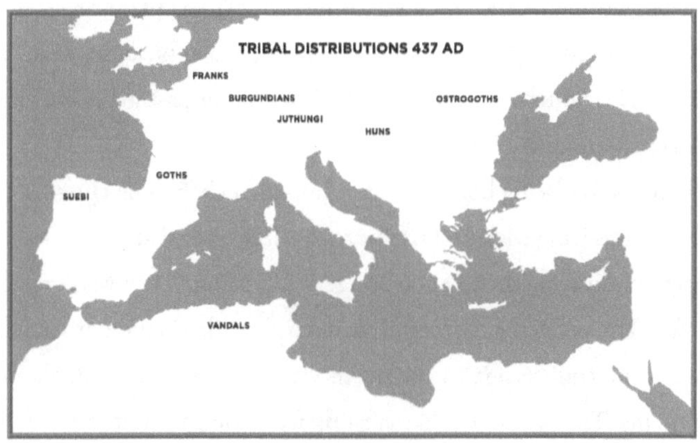

Chapter Sixteen

Placidius gazed out at the Thracian countryside. He remembered the incident well. It was a little hazy, but the letter had brought it back, his shock at Justa's unprovoked attack followed by the fear and loathing he felt toward Aetius. It was etched into his memory like a trauma, and it had formed the basis of his feelings toward the man who had come to play such a pivotal role in their lives. He despised Aetius, and his opinion had not changed in the twelve years since the incident had happened.

He weighed the codex in his hands. Anyway, one thing was for certain. Aetius had not written the letter. He would never have depicted himself so negatively, and if anyone had written it on his behalf, he would have changed that section to make himself appear more agreeable. Aetius was not behind the letter. No. If anything it appeared more and more as if Galla had written it after all. Notwithstanding Elpidia's knowledge of the contents, the letter appeared to be fulfilling its stated purpose, which was to provide Placidius with an unvarnished view of the past so he could make sound decisions in the future.

Placidius was being borne along in his sedan chair. The curtains were open. He was lying back on his pillows, his feet crossed at the ankles. The temperature was mild. A gentle breeze was stirring. They were traveling through Thrace[1], about a week out from their destination at Constantinople. The countryside to the north was hemmed in by the Rhodope Mountains. The peaks were like cresting waves on a tumultuous sea. The scent of pine filled in the air.

Placidius heard hoofbeats approaching and then Arsenius rode up alongside him with a look of agitation. Placidius set the codex aside and ordered his bearers to halt. He waited for the sedan chair to be lowered and then stepped out.

Arsenius was still sitting astride his horse, looking down at him. "I need to speak to you," he said.

Placidius took umbrage. "Get down," he said.

Arsenius looked confused.

"Dismount," Placidius said. "Is there something about the exercise of protocol in the presence of the Emperor that inconveniences you?"

Arsenius grimaced. "It's just—well, I have an important matter I want to discuss with you."

---

1. A Roman province largely made up of modern day southern Bulgaria and northern Greece

"I don't care," Placidius said. "I told you to get down."

Arsenius dismounted.

"You forget yourself, Arsenius. Unless someone has elevated you to Augustus, you owe me deference, not the other way around. Did I miss something? Have you been proclaimed?"

Arsenius turned red. He struggled to hold his temper.

"Walk it off," Placidius said. "Go over there. Take a deep breath, get control of your emotions, and when you're ready, come back and address me properly. We wouldn't want you to lose your head over this, would we?"

Arsenius did as he was told. When he came back, he exhibited a sullen compliance. "Excellency, may I have permission to speak?"

"Go ahead."

"I have received your order countermanding the directive I issued regarding the retinue of your friend. I must object in the strongest terms. If you will not permit me to examine them, then sending them home is the best way to safeguard you against any threat they may pose to you."

"They will *not* be sent home. That's final."

Arsenius breathed heavily through his nostrils and took another moment to collect himself. "But, Imperator, I fail to understand. There's evidence of a plot against you. I have asked you repeatedly for permission to examine them, and you've refused. Your friend, the young woman—"

"Candida. You may say her name. Candida."

"Very well, Candida. She approached me requesting permission to be sent home along with the rest of her retinue. Under the circumstances, I thought it best to let them go as it will remove them as a potential danger."

"Remove them how?"

Arsenius looked perplexed.

"Others who have been expelled from this caravan have never been heard from again. They have been removed from among the living."

"Excellency, I hope you're not trying to imply I had anything to do with what happened to the Jew and his wife? Tell me, who has been putting this slander into your head? Is it that criminal, Stephanus? I told you he was not to be trusted."

"You were right about him."

Arsenius was surprised. "I was?"

"I have reason to believe he's been hiding something. He needs to be questioned."

Arsenius breathed a sigh of relief. "Thank God. At last, you've come to your senses."

"Send Otho to my quarters. I will conduct the interrogation."

Arsenius grimaced. "But Imperator you are not qualified to interrogate him."

"That's why you must send Otho.

"Excellency, please listen to reason. Otho is not an interrogator. He is but an instrument in the hands of an interrogator — like a whip or a wheel. He has to be utilized properly."

"You've spoken of time-tested methods of getting at the truth. It seems to me Otho is the expert in that area. Send him to me and I will utilize him as you do."

Arsenius plowed his fingers through his hair. "At least allow me to be there to provide guidance."

"I prefer to do it alone, lest your presence influence the suspect's testimony."

Arsenius pressed his fingers to his temples. Then a thought came to him. He said, "That letter from your mother, where do you stand with it? Are you nearly finished?"

"Why? What business is it of yours?"

"None at all. It's just that, well . . . you said your mother was offering you good, practical advice. Perhaps she had something to say about a situation like this."

"I never said my mother was offering good, practical advice."

"Yes, you did."

Placidius racked his brain trying to remember if he had given Arsenius his opinion of the letter. Then he grew irritated. "I don't care to discuss the matter with you. Send me Otho. I will conduct the interrogation."

Arsenius set his teeth and turned to go. Then he turned back. "Pardon me, Imperator. May I ask you something?"

Placidius had already sat down in his sedan chair. It was sitting on the ground; the bearers had not yet lifted it onto their shoulders. Consequently, Placidius sat below the eye level of Arsenius, who stood above him.

"I'm curious," Arsenius said. "What did Stephanus do to rouse your suspicions?"

"He lied."

"Lied about what?"

"He told me no one had come into the camp when someone had."

"Who?"

"A certain traveling magician, a practitioner of divination."

"I had no knowledge of that."

"We shall see," Placidius said. He ordered his bearers to lift him up. He maintained steady eye contact with Arsenius as he was raised to his level. Then he ordered his bearers forward.

Arsenius watched him go with an exasperated expression.

Placidius picked up his mother's letter. He was smiling. He was quite proud of himself. He had stirred things up. Now he would see what bubbled to the surface. He leaned back on the pillows and continued reading.

To persecute the Jews has always been a cheap and easy way to win the approval of the public. A long tradition of persecuting the Jews dates back centuries and might rightly be called a convention of sorts. Back then, however, it was the pagans doing the persecuting. Today, it is the Christians, which strikes me as the height of hypocrisy.

The attainment of power is intoxicating. It blinds us to the suffering of those beneath us and leads us to regard them as mere instruments for the achievement of our purposes. It makes us forget. It's the only way I can explain how a group of people who were so recently the victims of persecution themselves could justify persecuting others. What's more, for a Christian to persecute a Jew, he must willfully overlook the fact that Christianity began as a Jewish sect, and that the suffering he now inflicts was once inflicted on him for the same reason. It's like the victim of a bully, having once attained the strength to fight back, embraces the methods of his tormentors and turns against his former fellow sufferers. It's shameful.

After the war to defeat Joannes and restore the rightful heir, Pulcheria and Theodosius received great public acclaim in Constantinople. They had done what was necessary to ensure stability, and the people of the East were grateful for it. But, as is always the case with these things, after a while the adulation began to wane, and Pulcheria began to worry. She couldn't stand the idea of not being the object of veneration, so she went after the Jews.

The Jews of Constantinople, well acquainted with the signs of an impending pogrom, were careful not to do anything that might be construed as resistance. Yet in spite of their hard-fought restraint, they were sabotaged by events that were out of their control – an uprising of the Jews several hundred miles away in Palestine – this gave Pulcheria the excuse she needed to attack them.

She publicly declared that agents of the Palestinian uprising were circulating in Constantinople, plotting the overthrow of the Church. She ordered a group of Jews arrested and beaten. She did it publicly. The good Christians of Constantinople ate it up. They had not witnessed such a demonstration of state-sanctioned brutality in years and couldn't get enough of it. This was better than the chariot racing. But not everyone was happy.

The new patriarch of Constantinople was a principled and upright man by the name of Nestorius[2]. He considered Pulcheria's treatment of the Jews an outrage and said so. Appalled at his impertinence, she called him before her to dress him down. When he refused to be intimidated, she changed tactics and tried to buy him off by dangling a hefty endowment to silence him, but he kept talking. He wanted the persecutions stopped and said so, publicly. Then he went further. He wanted the Jews compensated for their suffering. This was going too far.

---

2. Pronounced Ness-torr-ee-us

Pulcheria dashed off a letter to Cyril, the Patriarch of Alexandria, bemoaning her plight and asking for his help. She knew Cyril to be an unprincipled opportunist and presumed correctly he would seize the opportunity to replace Nestorius with a bishop more to his liking.

Nestorius was on shaky ground. Any clergymen bold enough to take up a position opposing the African fathers on a question of theological debate was putting himself in jeopardy, and Nestorius had done just that. Earlier that year, he had weighed in on the question of whether or not the Virgin Mary could be properly referred to as "the Mother of God."

The debate had gone back and forth between the bishops and theologians for some time, some asserting that God in Christ was born as a man and therefore Mary was properly fashioned the "Mother of God," while others held that God was eternal and therefore could not have been born and so Mary could not rightly be called His mother. In offering the alternative designation of "Christ-bearer," Nestorius sought to chart a middle course in an attempt to reach compromise. It turned out to be his downfall.

In a letter to the African bishops, Cyril accused Nestorius of trying to detach Christ's divinity and humanity into two separate beings by employing the title of "Christ-bearer," thus denying the reality of the incarnation. In other words, he said, Nestorius was declaring that Christ and God were not one being, which was heretical.

To any objective observer, the charge was ridiculous, but such was the power of the African bishops that they could make the most absurd allegations appear sensible. A number of prelates came out against Nestorius, and soon enough a groundswell was building for his removal as patriarch of Constantinople.

He should have capitulated. But Nestorius was not the sort of man to yield to an injustice. He fought back. Pulcheria denounced him. Other bishops followed suit. Nevertheless, he refused to surrender. Then Cyril, with Pulcheria's support, arranged to have him excommunicated. This was no mean feat because the Augusta of Constantinople and the Patriarch of Alexandria lacked the authority to excommunicate the Patriarch of Constantinople. Only the Pope could do that. So, Cyril reached out to his friend Pope Celestine with an idea.

If not handled delicately, what Cyril had in mind would certainly raise some eyebrows. He proposed nothing less than the handover of papal authority from Rome to Alexandria so Cyril could wield the power to excommunicate Nestorius without the Pope's involvement. It was a dangerous proposition because once the Patriarch of Alexandria assumed full papal authority, there was no guarantee he would ever give it back, running the risk that Church power might shift permanently from Rome to Alexandria.

But Pope Celestine was ever the creature of Cyril and the African bishops and would certainly do their bidding. He agreed but understood, as Cyril did, that some pretext would be needed to explain why Celestine didn't just excommunicate Nestorius himself. To be sure, it was an open question. But anyone who knew Cyril knew the reason why. Cyril couldn't be satisfied merely defeating his enemies; he had to humiliate them. Cyril wanted Nestorius to know he was the one excommunicating him. He wanted to rub his nose in it.

The pretext they came up with was a distraction in Rome, a distraction of such magnitude that Pope Celestine would be so preoccupied he would be unable to attend to his other duties. In particular, he would be unable to conduct the examination required to excommunicate an eminent bishop. Therefore, he would have to cede that responsibility to Cyril.

About that time rumors began to circulate in Rome that the Jews were desecrating holy relics and murdering Christian infants in their cribs. The Christian public lost their minds. There were riots in the streets. Synagogues were burned. Jews were set upon and attacked. This was exactly the kind of civil unrest I had been trying to avoid by bowing to Celestine's demand that he be allowed to expel the Novatianists and the Arians. But he reneged on the deal, and now I knew why. He had deliberately cooked up the disturbance in order to accommodate Cyril, and, by extension, Pulcheria.

I was roused to a towering pique and might have lashed out at them had Sixtus not stayed my hand. He warned me we had to tread lightly. If we made the wrong move now it could rebound on us. He explained the situation with Cyril and Nestorius in light of how Celestine figured into it. He made me see that I was not contending with Celestine alone but with the entire roster of African bishops. Should we incur the wrath of the African bishops we would not be able to forestall the transfer of papal authority from Rome to Alexandria, a transfer that, should it happen, could have long term ramifications for the power and influence of the Western Roman Empire as a whole.

"Alexandria is part of the Eastern Roman Empire," Sixtus pointed out. "It answers to the imperial authority in Constantinople. If the seat of the Western Church comes to reside in the East, Pulcheria and Theodosius will be able to exert power over you by way of their influence over them. You must not let

that happen; you must not allow papal authority to be shifted. But you must be careful. You cannot let them know you recognize the danger it represents. Cyril is hungry for power. He cannot be sated. Pretend ignorance. Say nothing about Pulcheria or Nestorius or the power of excommunication. Cyril and Celestine and the other African bishops already think you too soft. Let them go on thinking it. Do nothing to alert Celestine to your concerns."

This made sense, as far as it went, but there was a problem and I said so. "Pulcheria knows me. She'll think it suspicious if I don't do something to address a person who has defied me as publicly as Celestine has done. I must make some show of disapproval."

"You're right," Sixtus said. "Too much timidity on your part might ring false." He stroked his chin. "Very well, here's what you should do. Call Celestine before you to answer the charge that he betrayed your agreement but do nothing outwardly to punish him. Let him think he still has the advantage of you."

"Nothing outwardly?"

"I have nothing to say about what you do discreetly, nor do I want to know anything about it. I must be able to retain the ability to deny any knowledge of your motivations."

He was right, of course. His involvement needed to be kept secret.

There's a lesson here, Placidius. Never force an ally to squander his deniability. His ignorance may be a powerful weapon in your favor, especially if your purposes are discovered and you are held accountable. That way, even if all else fails, you will have an ally working behind the scenes to your advantage.

Hence, the plan I came up with to punish Celestine for his impertinence I came up with all on my own.

In the summer of that year, Aetius marched his army to the Upper Rhine and confronted the Franks. In just three months, he defeated them and slew their king, Chlodio. What many in Rome once considered a formidable enemy on the scale of the Vandals turned out to be no match for Aetius and his army in Gaul.

Once again Aetius was given a victory parade and crowned with laurels. Reports reached me that he had been offered the purple by his soldiers but had turned it down. This was a relief to me, as you might imagine, but when he returned to Ravenna, he was as insufferable as ever.

Felix wanted to discuss the Gothic movements near Tolosa[3] . Aetius wanted to discuss Africa. Aetius interrupted Felix and tried to change the subject. I

---

3. Modern day Toulouse, France

reprimanded him and told him if he interrupted again I would have him shown the door. He sulked.

In the weeks preceding this meeting, I had looked into Aetius's accusations against Bonifacius and found them groundless. Bonifacius had been doing good work in Africa keeping the Vandals in check. What's more, I had heard nothing about the corruption and discontent Aetius accused him of. But Aetius refused to let the matter rest. As soon as he had permission to speak again, he leveled the same charges against Bonifacius. This time, however, Bonifacius was present to defend himself.

The two men nearly came to blows. Bonifacius called Aetius a liar, and Aetius accused Bonifacius of incompetence. Bonifacius exploded. Aetius held his ground. Felix was helpless to stop them. It fell to me to end the quarrel. I could have pressed my hands to my ears and screamed at them to stop, but that's exactly what they would've expected to do, and if you want to get somebody's attention, you've got to surprise them.

I remained calm. I waited for them to stop barking at each other. Then I announced it was beyond my abilities as a woman to quell the rancor between two such powerful and headstrong men. Instead, I would appeal to a third party for adjudication. They probably thought I was going to call on Felix, but what I said next caught them off guard. I told them I would let the public decide.

The timing was perfect. With Celestine ramping up his persecutions, pressure had been growing on me to announce where I stood. Publicly, I had remained silent, but the longer I held back, the more the people began to suspect I was against the persecutions, which annoyed some and provided Celestine the opportunity to turn them against me. I had to do something to win back their favor.

Endowing a church is always a good strategy, but it tends to be short-lived. Almost immediately after being proclaimed, I had announced the construction of the Church of St. John the Evangelist in fulfillment of the vow I had made at sea. For several weeks, I enjoyed public acclaim, but then it quickly dissipated. By the time I actually dedicated the church, it was old news. I had announced other public works as well, but nothing got the public as excited as a good old-fashioned persecution, preferably one that entailed the destruction of property and the execution of a scapegoat or two. If I intended to distract the public's attention from Celestine's victimization of the Jews, I would need to provide them with something equally compelling.

I was privy to some intelligence the others didn't know. It had been my intention to reveal it at the meeting—in fact, it was one of the primary reasons I had called the meeting – but before I could get it out, Aetius started in with his antics. Now I could use it to my advantage. I had learned the Goths were on the move, intending to strike Arelate for a second time. We needed to send our strongest army to oppose them, but asking Aetius to do it would only invite more resistance — he was intent on wresting Africa away from Bonifacius and would hear of nothing else — so I decided to take a different route.

I told the generals we would meet again in the palace in two days' time whereupon I would announce a plebiscite to determine how we should proceed in Africa. Whatever the public decided was how we would proceed.

Aetius was all in favor of it. His recent victories in Gaul had sent his public approval through the roof. On the other hand, Bonifacius had been working behind the scenes in Africa. Public knowledge of his efforts was sparse. If the people were permitted to vote, Aetius would almost certainly win. But I took Bonifacius aside and urged him to take heart. I had some information that would sway the public in his favor.

Felix was confused. Worse yet, he was feckless. Aetius had been right about him. As a political decision, my appointment of him as master of soldiers had achieved its intended purpose: the aristocracy had been appeased, and there had been no murmurings against me from that quarter. But now Felix was becoming an impediment, and I needed to find a way to get rid of him.

Two days later we met in the palace. We gathered on the balcony overlooking the public plaza. A great throng of people had gathered to participate. I introduced each of the generals in turn. Aetius received the greatest ovation by far, followed by Bonifacius, and then, lastly, Felix, who as master of soldiers should have rated better than tepid applause.

I signaled for the crowd's attention. They fell silent. I announced my intention to ask their view on how I should deploy my generals. I explained the situation. The Vandals were building their forces in southern Hispania and threatening Africa. However, under Bonifacius's capable leadership they had been held at bay. There was no indication of an imminent invasion, yet there was still cause for concern. We could not let our guard down. A murmur went through the crowd. Aetius smiled behind his hand.

There was another matter, I announced. The smile fell from Aetius's face. I had it on good authority that the Goths were moving on Arelate. If we didn't act to stop them at once, we were in danger of losing Gaul. We had to hit them fast, and we had to hit them hard. This was why I had called the public together. I wanted their advice. I wanted the advice of the people. Whose army should I send? Should I send Felix to oppose the Goths in Gaul?

Except for a few scattered claps, the crowd remained silent. Should I send Bonifacius? More excitement, hardly a full-throated endorsement, but some middling support for the general safeguarding Africa. Should I send Aetius? The crowd erupted with a mighty roar.

I turned to Aetius. "It seems you are their champion. They want you to go to Gaul."

Aetius scowled.

I turned away from him and addressed the crowd again. I raised my hands for silence. The crowd quieted down. "Now, as regards the matter of Africa," I said, "who should be in charge there?" I wanted them to say his name, to get the feel of it in their mouths. "Bonifacius!" they cried.

I waited for their enthusiasm to subside, then I spoke to them again. "Thank you for your help," I said. "It shall be as you command." They let go another mighty roar. A thousand beaming faces gazed up at me. I had totally won them over.

The people are like a mule. You can coax and prod them all you want, and they may give you grudging compliance. Yet offer them a carrot once and they will come along gladly. Our forefathers understood this. They gave the people chariot races and gladiatorial battles and public baths, but today the Church frowns on all such blandishments. In their place, they offer lavish basilicas filled with shiny objects to dazzle the eye and cruel persecutions to appease the people's discontent. Celestine had stepped into the void after the fall of the usurpers and given the people something to get excited about. Until that moment, I had given them very little. Now, suddenly, I had bestowed the greatest gift of all: a sense of their own value to the place they called home.

I expected Aetius to request a private audience to excoriate me for my chicanery, but he left Ravenna without a word, and I did not hear from him again. The following spring, he marched his army against the Goths and defeated them for a second time.

The Goths would not attempt to take Arelate again, but they had not given up trying to extend their dominion. King Theodoric believed the Goths were entitled to all of southern Gaul as part of the agreement struck between Wallia and Honorius thirteen years before. If he could not pry it away from Rome using his army alone, he would enlist allies. He reached out to Genseric, the Vandal king, and offered his daughter in marriage to Generic's son. The offer was accepted, and just like that a formidable alliance was struck that threatened Gaul and put additional pressure on Bonifacius in Africa.

Yet, despite the threat, I had little choice but to turn my back on foreign affairs until I resolved matters closer to home. Celestine was still a thorn in my side, and until I defeated him, I could not give my full attention to matters abroad.

I summoned Pope Celestine to the palace. I was determined to make him answer for his impudence in delegating papal authority to Alexandria without my consent.

He was blithe and dismissive. His attitude demonstrated his low opinion of me. In his mind, I was a weak and ineffectual woman, unequal to the task before me. He had witnessed my appeal to the people on the matter of the generals and interpreted it as an act of desperation by someone overwhelmed by her duties. From his point of view, events were running ahead of me. He suffered from an all too common affliction among those in power – a refusal to see the world as it is. Celestine was blinded by his prejudice. Soon enough his blindness would be his undoing.

"I find it disappointing," I said, "that you would not think to consult me before making your decision."

"I was unaware that the principate had any jurisdiction in Church matters," he said.

"We do when it impacts our ability to govern."

He chuckled and shook his head. "It strikes me that this is a matter of interpretation, one that favors your intruding into our business whenever it suits you."

"Intruding?"

"Let us say 'inquiring into,' if that suits you better."

"It's not a matter of what suits me. There are customs and precedents to be followed."

"Well, if it's a matter of following customs, I feel affirmed in acting as I did. I am the Pope, the father of my people. As I understand it, it has been quite a while since you have had a father, Augusta, so perhaps you have forgotten. Fathers do not take orders from their daughters. It's unnatural."

"Need I remind you, I am the Regent, acting on the Emperor's behalf."

"A seven-year-old boy."

"Eight. We just celebrated his birthday."

"Am I to understand that an eight-year-old boy has strong opinions regarding the papal prerogative to excommunicate?"

"He has strong opinions about holding on to what belongs to him. You would not want to see him when he's deprived of things. He can put up quite a fuss."

"And my authority to excommunicate is one of the things that belong to him?"

"His ability to govern unencumbered by outsiders is one of the things that belongs to him. I'm afraid you have compromised that by ceding papal authority to Alexandria."

Celestine wiped his nose with his sleeve and cast a beleaguered look at his clerk, who was writing feverishly. "Well, if it's any consolation, I assure you it's only temporary."

"Until Cyril is able to settle his score with Nestorius."

Celestine was caught off guard. "You're acquainted with the matter?"

"Occasionally I hear things when I'm not weaving or reciting verse. Recently, I've been hearing a great deal about persecutions."

"Regrettable, but necessary. The Jews are a problem."

"Always."

"Yes."

"I thought we had an agreement."

"Did we?" He pretended ignorance.

It was all I could do to keep from lashing out at him in his smug arrogance.

He wiped his nose again. He didn't look well. He looked pale and drawn.

"You seem ill, Celestine. I hope you're having that looked into by a physician."

"I'm being attended by one of the best physicians in Rome."

"Yes. Herius. I know him. We met recently over a matter of mutual interest."

Celestine narrowed his eyes imperceptibly. "Is someone ill?"

"Oh, you know how it is. There's always someone suffering from some sort of malady. It's helpful to be acquainted with someone who can help with such things. Besides, I'm helping funding a new almshouse for him. He envisions something on the scale of what they have in Constantinople, a place where the physicians can experiment on the destitute in their pursuit of new treatments."

"That's very generous of you."

"I tend to help the people who are of assistance to me. Don't you do the same, Celestine?"

His smile lacked warmth. "Of course."

"Let me be blunt, Celestine. You are not of assistance to me. Quite the contrary, you are a hindrance. Bloodshed in the streets is not what I had in mind when I took the job of regent. I have problems enough with unruly generals and barbarian invasions."

"The Jews are a problem."

"Not to mention the Novatianists and the Arians and the Pelagians."

"Yes."

"*I want it stopped, Celestine. You are undermining my ability to govern.*"

He laughed. "Oh, the vanity. But I suppose it should come as no surprise; vanity in a woman is part of her nature. But I am a man. I owe my allegiance to God. Heresy will not be tolerated in my jurisdiction. End of discussion."

There was a long, heavy silence. Celestine wiped his nose with his sleeve and waited, a self-satisfied look on his face. He might have gone on waiting for a very long time, but his clerk broke in, unable to bear the silence. "We have a list!" he cried.

Celestine shot him a sharp look. The clerk blanched and stuck his head in his papers.

"A list?" I asked. "What kind of a list?"

"A list of heretics," Celestine explained.

"Uh-huh," I said. "On what basis are they accused?"

"Suspicious activities," he said.

"Oh, well," I said. "I suppose you can never be too careful when you're defending God — and his city."

I was referring of course to Augustine's book The City of God.

Celestine picked up on the reference instantly. "Ah, so you've read it."

"Sadly, I have not, although everyone else has, apparently."

Celestine frowned. "That's a pity. You should find the time. Augustine has much to teach a woman like you."

"Yes, I'm sure Augustine and the other African bishops would love to instruct an ignorant woman like me, but my time is taken up trying to keep the peace in a city wracked by strife, a city of man, as Augustine would fashion it."

Celestine nodded and smiled.

"Now about those heretics," I said. "I suppose they're given an opportunity to reform before they're exiled. After all, it would be the Christian thing to do, to give them a second chance."

"Naturally. We are not beasts. We encourage them to renounce their sins and express repentance. After they go through a proper penance, they are welcomed back into the fold."

"That's very generous of you."

"We are men of God."

"Very nearly Christ-like."

Now the clerk spoke up again. "You should read the book," he said. "It would help you appreciate the proper order of things."

I bristled at his interruption. It was one thing to be talked down to by the Pope, quite another to be lectured by a mere functionary. "Remove this person from my presence," I snapped.

Celestine acted as if he found my behavior tiresome. He wiped his nose and made ready to go, despite the fact that I had not given him permission to leave.

On his way out, I called out to him. He turned back. "That list of yours. I suppose you've made your subordinates aware of it, the bishops and prelates who work under you."

"Most of them. Yes."

"But not all. Certainly not those whose names are on it."

"If their names are on the list, I cannot be a party to their crimes. What happens to them is their own doing. Why do you ask?"

"Oh, it's nothing, really. It's just that we women are great makers of lists, as you may have heard. And sometimes our lists get misplaced. When they do, we are completely undone and don't know what to do about it. I think it's a good idea to share your list with others, should the original be misplaced."

He looked at me in bewilderment and went out, taking his nervous note taking clerk with him. But that impertinent functionary wasn't finished with me yet. After the Pope had rounded the corner into the hallway, he stopped in the doorway and looked back. He looked at me for a long moment, brushed his hair out of his face, and went out.

Is struck me that no one would dare be as brazenly insolent as that unless they were confident they could not be touched. He had powerful people behind him, that clerk, people I suspected who might go beyond just the Pope. Maybe even the African fathers themselves.

Placidius stopped, stunned. He began thumbing back through the pages and reread the parts about the nervous note-taking clerk. *Liberius!* he thought. His heart picked up a beat. The nervous note-taking clerk was Liberius! Liberius had been planted in the imperial entourage to further the agenda of the African bishops against his mother. But things had changed. The target had shifted. Now he, Placidius, was the one in their sights. Now they were coming after him!

Placidius looked up from the letter in growing comprehension. Liberius was the one who had told him that Arsenius had expelled Cyrus from the camp for not following orders. Liberius along with Stephanus. Together they had put the idea into his head that Arsenius was trying to silence anyone who might expose his role in the plot. They had begged him not to tell Arsenius, and for good reason. They were trying to mislead him, and they didn't want Arsenius to find out.

Placidius congratulated himself for having solved the puzzle. Later tonight, after they made camp, he would force a confession from Stephanus and confirm his suspicions. Liberius would come next.

Placidius dove back into the letter, hoping to learn more.

Cyril went through the motions of making a thorough examination into the allegations against Nestorius. It took longer than expected, given that the outcome was a foregone conclusion. Perhaps Cyril was wary of insulting the intelligence of the laity by acting too precipitously, but in the end he delivered his sentence. Nestorius was deposed and banished.

I'm quite certain Nestorius was as astonished as anyone that his mild proposal to refer to the Virgin Mary as "Christ-bearer" rather than "Mother of God" had been twisted into a criminal act worthy of excommunication, but it showed the power of the African fathers, and it spoke unmistakably to Pulcheria's involvement. She wanted Nestorius excommunicated, not only because he had possessed the unmitigated gall to stand up to her, but also because by now she recognized the advantage it would give her to have papal authority residing under her jurisdiction and not ours. But before Nestorius left Constantinople he got one last jab in against his nemesis. In his farewell sermon he attacked Pulcheria.

It was a measure of her growing self-importance that Pulcheria insisted on being referred to as "the bride of Christ" in public worship services, an advertisement of her piety and a reminder of her chastity, something she had been able to maintain while other, lesser women had failed. But Nestorius warned his congregation not to fall for this fiction. Pulcheria was hardly pure, he contended. She had slept with at least seven men.

The scandal shook Constantinople to its core. Pulcheria called Nestorius a liar and demanded a retraction. Nestorius dug in. When Pulcheria threatened to have him arrested, he went one step further and had her image removed from the mosaic above the altar of the Church of the Holy Apostles. When she found out, she was apoplectic. But by then Nestorius was gone. Condemned of heresy, excommunicated, and exiled, he left town and would never be heard from again. But that didn't stop Pulcheria from getting her revenge.

Nestorius had not been without his supporters. Some members of the Church had spoken out against his ill treatment, including more than two dozen bishops. Seventeen of them were accused of heresy and removed from their sees. And it didn't stop there. Any member of the public who expressed sympathy for Nestorius was deemed a heretic and required to denounce him publicly or suffer the consequences. A few resisted. They were beaten, stripped of their possessions, and banished.

This was completely disproportionate, and I was in the middle of drafting a letter of protest against it when I learned Pope Celestine was planning the same thing for the West. He announced he had a list of people in high places in Rome who secretly supported Nestorius. He was planning to expose them as heretics, but in the spirit of Christian mercy he would permit them to come forward and confess their errors. If they did, he might forgive them.

It was no coincidence that most of the people on his list were quite wealthy. Implicit in his demand that they confess was an unstated demand for money. Those who gave generously to the Pope would be forgiven. Those who did not would be condemned. What the Eastern branch of the Church acquired through theft, the Western branch would get through extortion. Then came the next revelation. My name was on that list.

I can't say I was surprised. Celestine had already demonstrated his shameless audacity. His willingness to defy me was by now well established. I knew he had a list; he had already threatened me with it obliquely. It was a simple step further to make it explicit. At that point I had had enough.

Less than a week after announcing the list, Celestine's health went into a steep decline. Although his demise was inevitable, it was far more precipitous than anyone expected. One day he was alive; the next he was dead. There were those who suspected foul play, but no one dared make any accusations. The man was sick, after all.

Within hours of his death, I had a number of his associates arrested. They were forced to relinquish the lists they had in their possession. Only a few had any. It seems Celestine had been distrustful of my advice to share them and had made only a few copies – my design all along. Never underestimate your ability to induce stubborn men to do what you want by advocating the opposite. I urged Celestine to make copies, so he did not. I wanted as few lists as possible so I could confiscate them as soon as I got the chance. I was almost entirely successful. Only a few slipped through my grasp. One was almost certainly in the possession of his nervous note-taking clerk, the one who had spoken to me with such impertinence. I sent my soldiers to arrest him, but when they kicked down the door, he was gone.

Not surprisingly, the list condemned both Sixtus and me. But no one would ever know it. I ordered the original and all the copies burned. Then I made a list of my own. If the people were so hungry to persecute someone, I would give them what they wanted.

I called for a public audience. I announced that I had come into possession of Celestine's list. The names on it were heretics. In keeping with the late Pope's final wish, I would see them stripped of their property and exiled. Then I read the names aloud. Every name on that list was a supporter of Celestine. Within a week they were violently impoverished and banished, their wealth confiscated.

The public got what they wanted. Papal resistance to imperial authority came to an end. The persecutions were halted. And now began the search for a new pope. I moved swiftly to nominate Sixtus, and then I smoothed the way to his rapid election. Before Cyril or the other African bishops could react, it was over. Sixtus was the new Pope.

One of Sixtus's first acts as Pontiff was to take back the power of excommunication from the Bishop of Alexandria. Wisely, Cyril didn't protest, perceiving that the instrument he had once wielded against others might now be wielded against him. In the end, he proved himself a bully and a coward.

Yet as good as it felt to get even with my enemies in the Church, I had no illusion that they had been vanquished. Pulcheria was their champion, and although she had come out battered and bruised, she was still in power and as vindictive as ever.

Beware of her Placidius. She is not to be underestimated. Like a vicious rodent chased from the larder, she is at her most dangerous when she is backed into a corner, and she is not happy that I've gotten the upper hand in this. I can promise you that.

She will attack again.

Chapter Seventeen

Placidius fingered the confession of faith on the table before him. He poured another cup of wine and slid it across to Stephanus.

Stephanus tipped it back. He watched Placidius over the rim of the cup. Then he set it down.

"Drink up," Placidius said. "Don't be shy. It's good wine."

Stephanus eyed him uneasily. "What about you? Aren't you going to join me?"

"I'm not feeling well," Placidius said, rubbing his stomach. "You'll have to excuse me. I've had quite a shock."

"A shock?"

"It's nothing," Placidius said. "Go ahead. Drink up. Enjoy."

Stephanus picked up the cup and drained it of its contents. When he set it down, Placidius refilled it. He pointed to the lute player in the corner. "Pleasant, isn't he?"

Stephanus glanced at the musician, a young man of slender build with a long beak-like nose and a jutting row of upper teeth.

Placidius slid the cup over. "The wine, the music…they're meant to calm you. Please don't be afraid. You're among friends."

"I'm not afraid," Stephanus said, but his eyes told a different story.

Placidius tapped the confession of faith. "What do you know about this?"

"I told you. Nothing. I never saw it before in my life."

"Someone signed my name to it," Placidius said. "Whoever it was clearly intended to implicate me with the Nestorians. Do you know who the

Nestorians are, Stephanus? They're a heretical sect condemned by the Church and reviled by Pulcheria and Theodosius, my soon-to-be in-laws. If they ever suspected I was a Nestorian, they would cancel my wedding to the Princess and invalidate our betrothal. Tell me, Stephanus, do you know anyone who would want to ruin my wedding plans?"

Stephanus looked worried. He started to object.

Placidius held up his hand to silence him. He pointed to the cup. "Drink up. It'll settle your nerves. Then you can tell me what you think."

Stephanus drank.

Placidius grinned. He was enjoying this. He liked seeing Stephanus squirm.

The wine had been Otho's idea, the wine and the soothing music. Placidius had wanted a more punitive approach, something that pinched and stung, but Otho explained that the purpose of an interrogation was to extract information, not to satisfy a thirst for revenge. The big man discussed it while paring his nails. He leaned against a chestnut tree with his legs crossed. "If that doesn't work, we can try something else," he said, holding up his hand with the palm out to inspect his handiwork. He was remarkably laconic for such a reputedly merciless interrogator.

Placidius was willing to bow to Otho's expertise, but he failed to see what he was supposed to do next if gentle persuasion didn't do the trick. The legionary tent where he was conducting the interrogation was devoid of so much as a flagrum[1]. For all the whispered talk about Otho's brutal methods the whole proceeding seemed disappointingly benign.

---

1. A short whip made of three leather straps

The lute player sat cross-legged on the floor. Placidius and Stephanus sat at opposite ends of a trestle table with the amphora of wine and the confession of faith between them.

"Candida is scheming to ruin my wedding," Placidius submitted.

"Oh, no. You're wrong about that," Stephanus averred. "She knows nothing about any of this." He pointed to the confession of faith. "I can tell you that with certainty."

"Well, you should know," Placidius sneered. "You're quite intimate with her, aren't you?"

"We're old friends. I've been her family's groom for years."

"Old friends," Placidius said. "Right." He picked up the document. "She brought this to me on the pretext of reading the note written on the back. She left it in my tent. But that's not all. She also left this." With a dramatic flourish, he produced the scroll she had left in his tent, the scroll he had cavalierly tossed aside, thinking it was beneath consideration. He set it in front of Stephanus.

"What is it?" Stephanus asked.

"It's the transcript of a sermon by Nestorius. In it, he rejects the title of 'Mother of God' for that of 'Christ-bearer,' a trivial ecclesiastical point, hardly worthy of consideration, except that it has been deemed heretical. And now, because of Candida, it can be found in my tent along with this."

He held the two documents up – side by side – and leaned forward with what he hoped was a menacing glare. "The two together are enough to accuse me of heresy. What do you have to say about *that*?"

Stephanus shrugged. "Nothing. What am I supposed to say?"

Placidius stewed. He wished he could lunge across the table and smack him across the face. He wished Otho was in the room to back him up. But Otho had instructed him to stay calm and keep Stephanus drinking. Then he had left him alone with the lute player to conduct the interrogation. Annoyed, Placidius poured Stephanus another cup of wine.

The lute player strummed his strings.

Placidius slid the cup over to Stephanus.

Stephanus begged off. "No, thank you, Imperator. "I've had enough."

"I insist," Placidius said.

Stephanus gave him a weary, put-upon look. "I suspect you're trying to get me drunk."

"I only want you to feel comfortable."

"You want me to lose my inhibitions and open up to you."

"I would hope you would be honest with me without the inducement of wine."

"I am always honest with you, Excellency."

"And yet you lied to me."

"Never."

"You did. You assured me no outsider had come into our camp when you knew full well someone had."

"But that was —"

Placidius banged his fist down on the table. "You lied!" he shouted. The cup of wine jumped and nearly toppled over. "You knew the magician had come into the camp from the east, but you lied to protect him!"

Stephanus turned up his hands. "It was a small thing. He was here to entertain us. Nothing more. When you asked me to identify suspicious persons who had come into camp, I thought you were looking for an official, a courier, a liaison, even a soldier, not a lowly entertainer. If you wanted me to root out every man or woman who has come into our camp over the course of our entire journey, I could have found plenty. Among the baggage handlers and husbandmen there must be dozens.

"Drink," Placidius said."

"But Imperator, I'm feeling queasy."

"Drink!" he shouted through clenched teeth.

Stephanus sighed and drank.

Placidius turned away in frustration. This was going nowhere. Otho's methods weren't working. If anything, Stephanus was becoming even more insolent. He needed some way to get through to him, something to show him he wasn't playing around.

He took another look around the tent. Nothing.

Then it occurred to him, *Maybe Otho is trying to undermine me. After all, Otho is Arsenius's man. If Arsenius is involved, maybe he doesn't want Stephanus to confess; maybe they're in it together.*

"Stay put," Placidius said.

He went outside in search of a branch.

He had gone no more than a few feet when Otho stepped in front of him. "What's happening?"

Otho was a big man, as wide as he was tall, with a shiny bald head and a face like a slab of beef.

"He's not cooperating. I intend to beat him."

"Stick to the plan."

"But he won't confess."

"Stick to the plan."

Stephanus stuck his head out of the tent. "I have to pee," he said.

Placidius rolled his eyes. "Very well but be quick about it. We're not done yet."

But before Stephanus could take another step, Otho stepped in front of him. "Go back inside."

Stephanus looked at the big man in distress. "But I have to go."

"Inside," Otho commanded.

Dejected, Stephanus went back into the tent.

At that moment one of the guards appeared and announced a request by the curator of correspondence, Liberius, to have a word with the Emperor. "He insists it's a matter of grave importance."

Ah ha, Placidius thought, *Liberius knows I'm in here with Stephanus, and he's worried I'll discover something, so he's trying to distract me.*

But before Placidius could answer, Otho interrupted. "The Emperor is busy. He's not taking any meetings right now."

Placidius looked at Otho and weighed how to respond. No one should be permitted to subvert his authority. It made him look weak. It made him look like he was not in charge. In the past, he would have corrected such impertinence, but now he hesitated. He turned to the guard. "Tell Liberius I'll speak to him later."

The guard went away.

Placidius turned back to Otho. "All right, what are we supposed to do now? He's not cooperating. Your approach is not working."

"It's working," Otho said. "Keep him drinking. Don't let him stop. And don't let him pee."

"But the man has to urinate."

"Don't let him pee," the big man repeated.

With a grunt of frustration, Placidius went back into the tent.

Stephanus was inside, standing with his hands between his knees. It was a ludicrous tableau, this handsome, strapping young man bent over and fidgeting like a schoolboy while a musician strummed melodic airs.

"Please," Stephanus said. "I really have to go."

"Sit down," Placidius said. He pointed to the table. "You can relieve yourself after you've answered my questions."

"But I've already told you, I don't know anything."

"Sit!"

Stephanus sat down and squeezed his knees together.

Placidius sat down across from him. "Now tell me the truth. Otherwise, I can't be responsible for what happens to you. About the magician, what was he doing here? Was he conspiring with Isaac and Elpidia? Were they up to something?"

"He came to entertain us. That's all."

Placidius poured him another cup of wine and slid it across to him.

Stephanus pushed it back. "I can't. I'll wet myself."

"Drink it!"

Stephanus shook his head.

"Drink it!"

Again, Stephanus refused.

Otho threw back the flap and entered the tent. He loomed up before them. All eyes turned to him. The musician stopped playing.

"Ask him again," Otho said.

"The magician," Placidius asked, "what was he doing here?"

Stephanus groaned "I don't know. I wasn't part of their clique. They were selected by Cyrus to be part of the retinue. I was picked by Candida. They didn't share their secrets with me."

"Ah, so they had secrets!" Placidius shouted. "What?"

"I told you, I don't know. They didn't tell me."

"Was Candida in on it?"

Stephanus swallowed hard. "I have to go. Please."

Otho's voice was chilling in its imperturbability. "Answer him."

Stephanus sighed. "You know how she is. She's not the type of person who can keep a secret. She's too emotional. If they were up to something, they certainly wouldn't have shared it with her."

Placidius leaned in. "And what about you, Stephanus? Can you keep a secret?"

Stephanus gave him a miserable look. "I had nothing to do with it. I already told you. Please, can I go? I'm about to burst."

Again, the calm menace of Otho. "You may not."

Stephanus squirmed. "Are you trying to humiliate me? Is that it? Because if that's what you want, I'll piss all over this floor."

Otho towered over him. "If you do, I'll break your neck."

Stephanus gaped at him.

Otho reached down and slid the cup of wine towards him. "Drink."

Perspiration gleamed on Stephanus's brow. He picked up the cup and drank.

Otho nodded at Placidius. "Go ahead."

Finally, this was beginning to look like a real interrogation. Placidius was excited at the prospect. He gave Stephanus a cold smile. "What do you take me for, a fool?" When Stephanus hung his head, Placidius seized him by the tunic and shook him. Stephanus looked around him in mild surprise like a man jostled accidentally by someone standing in a crowd.

"Candida planted these documents in my possession!" Placidius roared. "Do you mean to tell me she had nothing to do with it!"

"I don't know. Maybe they tricked her into it. Maybe they wrote the note on the back of the document because they knew she would read it to you. She's nothing if not predictable. She would be easy to manipulate."

"You're lying!" Placidius bellowed. "You're trying to protect her!"

"I'm not," Stephanus insisted.

"You're trying to protect her because you're in love with her. Isn't that true?"

"I swear I'm not."

"Then why are you fucking her!"

The color drained from Stephanus's face.

Placidius licked his lips and went eyeball to eyeball with him. He had him now. "Confess!" he shouted.

Stephanus dropped his chin on his chest. "All right. I'll admit it. I slept with her, but not because I wanted to. God knows I tried to put her off. But she's insatiable, that girl. She wouldn't leave me alone. She kept pestering me, and when I tried to avoid her, she threatened me with Arsenius; she said if I didn't give her what she wanted, she would report me to him. But I didn't want to. I was afraid of you, Imperator — afraid of what you might do to me if you found out. When I continued to put her off, she made good on her threat and reported me to Arsenius, saying I had been stealing from the supply wagon. What could I do? She was serious. I didn't want to get thrown out of the caravan. We're in Hun country. A person could get killed."

Placidius filled another cup and slid it across to him. "Drink," he said.

Stephanus looked at the cup as if it were poison. He picked it up.

"Wait," Otho said.

Hope lit Stephanus's eyes. Sensing a reprieve, he lowered the cup.

Otho turned to the musician. "Lute player, unstring."

Both Placidius and Stephanus watched, bewildered, as the musician carefully removed a single string. He handed it to Otho.

Otho turned to Stephanus. "Stand up."

Fear crept into Stephanus's eyes. "Why?"

"Stand up."

Stephanus got hesitantly to his feet.

"Lower your trousers."

Stephanus gaped. "Why?"

"Do it."

Stephanus complied.

"Remove your loincloth."

"But I—"

Otho struck him across the face.

Stephanus toppled over backwards and landed flat on his back on the floor. The linen of his loincloth darkened.

Otho snatched the amphora off the table and dashed the wine in Stephanus's face.

"Stop pissing!" he shouted.

When Stephanus didn't immediately comply, Otho grabbed him by the hand and began bending back his fingers. Stephanus howled, but he stopped urinating. Otho jerked him to his feet.

Placidius found all of this quite exhilarating. He was dying to get in some licks of his own but thought it best not to get in the way. Otho knew what he was doing.

"Take off your loincloth," Otho demanded.

Stephanus did as he was instructed. Instinctively, he covered his genitals like a bashful schoolgirl.

"Take your hands away," Otho instructed.

Stephanus held out his hands to the side. The look on his face was equal parts terror and misery.

Otho knelt down in front of him.

This was too perverse for Placidius. He thought he'd better say something. "What are you doing?"

Otho held the lute string between his thumb and forefinger. He stretched it taut. "Interrogating," he said. He leaned forward and began wrapping it around the shaft of Stephanus's penis.

Instinctively, Stephanus backed up. Otho seized him by the balls and began to squeeze. Stephanus cried out. Otho relented. He looked up at his victim. "Do that again and I'll crush them. Do you understand?"

Stephanus nodded mutely.

Otho continued wrapping the lute string around Stephanus's penis. When he was done, he got up and inspected his handiwork. He nodded, satisfied, then moved around behind him. He bound his hands behind his back with a length of rope he had brought with him. "Sit down," he said.

Stephanus sat down.

Otho looked at the musician. "You're finished now. You can leave."

The lute player scurried off, his face gone white.

Otho turned to Placidius. "Now we'll get some answers."

"What are you doing?" Placidius asked, unable to hide his anxiety.

"He's had a lot to drink," Otho explained. "He really needs to pee, but if he attempts to pee now, he'll have a problem. The lute string is cutting off the flow of his urine. If he pees now, the urine will back up, and the pressure will cause his cock to expand. The string will cut into his flesh and his cock will be sliced off as neat as you please."

"My God," Placidius murmured in horror.

Stephanus moaned. His eyes welled with tears.

"Go ahead," Otho said. "Ask him a question."

Placidius took a moment to gather his thoughts. He tried to muster up the same exasperated umbrage he had been feeling before, but now he felt only pity for the poor soul before him. "Who else is in on it?" he asked without much conviction.

"I don't know. I swear I'm not part of this. I told you."

"You're lying," Placidius said.

"I'm telling the truth! That's all I know!"

Placidius turned to Otho. "I think he's telling the truth. Maybe we should let him go."

Otho shook his head. "Interrogate him."

Placidius felt sick. He hated himself for being such a wimp. His mother wouldn't have been so spineless. She would have gotten answers. His mother had cut out Elpidia's tongue. She had looked on as Quirinus was flogged. She had watched as Serena was strangled. She had always done what was necessary, no matter how distasteful.

"It's cutting into me," Stephanus whimpered. Tiny beads of blood were forming along the edges of the lute string.

"Help me!" Stephanus cried. He rubbed his hands up and down the sides of his face.

Placidius started to move towards him, but Otho grabbed him by the arm. "Don't," he said.

Stephanus looked from on to the other of them in despair. Then he broke. The confession came out of him in a torrent. "It was Arsenius! He's behind it all! He's the one who planned it! He hired Isaac and Elpidia! He brought in the magician! He convinced Candida!"

Otho's face betrayed nothing. He stared at Placidius for a long moment, then, he got up and left like a man who had suddenly remembered he had an appointment.

"Untie me," Stephanus begged. "He's going to tell Arsenius."

Placidius didn't know what to do.

"Hurry up. Before they come back."

Placidius hesitated.

Then, as suddenly as he had gone out, Otho came back carrying a fresh amphora of wine.

Stephanus stared at him in horror. "No!"

Otho stepped up to him, caught his head in the crook of his arm, jerked his head back, and poured the wine down his throat.

Stephanus coughed and spluttered. Trickles of blood ran down his penis and sprinkled on the ground.

Placidius was paralyzed with revulsion.

Otho tipped up the rim of the amphora up and the wine ran back into the vessel. He looked down at Stephanus's wine-drenched face. "One last chance, then you drink it all. Who else is in on it?"

Stephanus's eyes bulged from his head. He said nothing.

Otho pried the man's jaw open. He raised the amphora.

"Liberius!" he cried. "He's in on it! He's the one!"

Otho released his jaw. "We're listening."

Stephanus looked from one to the other in a panic. "Liberius intercepted the letter from the Emperor's mother. He gave it to Elpidia so she could read it before it was passed on to the Emperor."

Placidius was stunned. "So my mother *did* write the letter."

"I'm not sure," Stephanus said. His voice was coming in gasps. "Neither were they. That's why they wanted to read it, to see if it was written by someone else. Plus they were worried it might implicate them. Elpidia kept it for several days before returning it to Liberius. She transcribed some passages."

"What do you mean Liberius intercepted it? Where did it come from? Who brought it here?"

Otho released Stephanus.

The beleaguered groom stood up and staggered over to a table, coughing and wheezing. He leaned against it and tried to untie the lute string.

"Tell me!" Placidius demanded.

Stephanus began to cry. Tears rolled down his cheeks. "It hurts so bad. It's cutting into me."

Suddenly one of the guards burst into the tent. He was out of breath. "Come quick," he said. "Something's happened."

"What?"

"Murder."

Otho rushed out. Placidius followed him. The guard brought up the rear.

A small group of people were clustered around a body in the woods. Placidius pushed his way to the front.

A man lay face down on the ground, a gaping stab wound in his back.

"Turn him over," Placidius said.

It was Liberius.

Placidius's blood ran cold.

"They got to him," Otho said, his voice devoid of emotion.

Placidius knelt down beside the body. "Who did this?" he asked. He wheeled on the bystanders. "Who did this?"

The people in the crowd looked at each other in confused hesitation. Some drifted back. Others turned to go.

"No one goes anywhere until I get some answers!"

They stood rooted in place, heads bowed. No one said anything.

Placidius picked out a man whose expression struck him as devious. He tried to interrogate him, but to no avail. Then he remembered Stephanus.

They had left him alone in the tent with the lute string still tied around his penis.

When he got back to the tent, the scene that confronted him made him physically sick.

The groom was slumped over the table, his skin oyster gray, his mouth hanging open, his eyes staring vacantly into space. Blood had trickled down his legs. On the floor at his feet his severed penis lay in a spreading pool of blood, a mute and grisly accusation against the incompetence of his interrogator.

Sometimes problems beset you and threaten to overwhelm you. You must resist the urge to overreact. You must keep a level head about you. The measure of an effective ruler is restraint. Perhaps a good way to think about it is that God is testing you. This is your chance to prove you're worthy of Him.

God knows I've been tested. In those days, Celestine wasn't my only concern. In the fall, I received a letter. It was a strange letter written by Bonifacius to his friends in Rome. It was intercepted by my spies. It spoke of his absolute sovereignty in Africa and boasted of his ability to seize power whenever he saw fit. Although his words were plainly treasonous, I thought I saw the hand of Aetius behind them.

Aetius was mopping up after his successful campaign against the Goths in Gaul and could not be recalled to Rome to answer for his duplicity, so I sent him a message reprimanding him and cautioning him against any more tricks. I knew he would never be satisfied until he evened the score for the way I had embarrassed him. He wrote back protesting his innocence. I didn't believe him.

Then, to my surprise, Felix came to me with further evidence against Bonifacius. A seasoned adviser who had been close to Bonifacius reported that it had long been the general's design to usurp me, going all the way back to when he had cut off the grain supply to Rome in order to weaken Joannes and bring him down. Bonifacius had presumed I would be easier to overthrow than Joannes and had been biding his time until he got the right the opportunity. His only concern was Aetius. He feared Aetius would bring the Huns against him and had begun secretly negotiating with the Vandals to offset the possibility. This was worrisome indeed. If it were true, it meant Bonifacius was making common cause with the enemy against us.

Still, I was not convinced. The informer might easily have been planted by Aetius to mislead me. I made some discreet inquiries and found nothing to indicate that Bonifacius was in communication with the Vandals.

But Felix kept receiving new intelligence about how Bonifacius was plotting against me. He wanted to sack him. I thought this needlessly antagonistic. If I had learned anything over the years, it was not to alienate allies. To put Bonifacius on the defensive would run the risk of turning a friend into a foe and invite the very situation we were trying to avoid. Besides, I suspected Felix had his own reasons for wanting to get rid of Bonifacius. He suffered from the inferiority that comes from knowing your subordinates are more qualified than you. He feared Bonifacius would upstage him.

Two weeks later I received a letter from Aetius. Felix had written to him expressing his concerns and urging him to convince me of Bonifacius's treachery. However, Aetius did not agree with Felix. He believed Bonifacius was dangerously incompetent and should be relieved of his duties, but as to the charge that he had been working with the Vandals against us, he had heard nothing. He suspected, as I did, that Felix was exaggerating the situation to create an opportunity to remove a rival. Still, he thought I needed to be prudent. If Bonifacius revolted and it was later shown that I was aware of the threat and did nothing, I could lose the confidence of the military. Aetius suggested I summon Bonifacius to Ravenna to answer the allegations against him. If he were innocent, he would come at once. If not, he would hang back and resist. His reaction would tell me everything I needed to know.

In the event, there was no answer to my summons. I sent a second summons in case the first had gone astray, but again received no reply. I began to get suspicious. Could it be true? Was my most loyal general, my dearest friend, plotting against me? I dispatched a detachment of troops to Africa to bring him back. He fought them off.

I couldn't believe it. I sent a second detachment. They too were repelled.

That's when I overreacted. I could not let Africa fall into the hands of a rogue general. As the source of our grain supply it was simply too important.

I was going to need a capable general to lead the operation against Bonifacius. The obvious candidate was Aetius, but I couldn't trust him. It would do me no good to put down one usurper only to replace him with another. Likewise, Felix was not to be relied upon, not because he had designs on Africa, but because I feared he would be unequal to the task; he was simply not competent enough to get the job done. That's why I called upon two lower-ranking generals, Mavortius and Galbio.

I was warned – it was a bad idea. Both men were excessively ambitious with exaggerated opinions of themselves. Worse yet, they were fierce rivals known to resort to the most unscrupulous methods to get the advantage of one another. By asking them to share a position of such critical importance, I was flirting with disaster. But in the heat of the moment I felt I had to do something, and I overreacted. I didn't have to confront Bonifacius with such haste. I could have waited. A judicious pause would have saved a lot of trouble. But I panicked and it cost us all — dearly.

One of the most difficult things to do as a ruler is to keep your cool under pressure. It will be particularly challenging for you, my son. Your tendency to be impulsive is a character flaw you must work hard to overcome. You are not a child anymore. You are a grown man with awesome responsibilities. You can no longer afford to be juvenile and petulant. In the heat of the moment you must control your emotions and act like an adult. If you cannot, you should probably defer your decisions to others.

As predicted, Mavortius and Galbio squabbled. Their bickering divided the army and weakened its cohesion. By then Bonifacius had moved to strengthen his defenses. What might have been attainable a few weeks earlier was becoming increasingly difficult. Seeing the situation deteriorating, Mavortius pointed the finger at Galbio. Galbio vowed to get even. Mavortius had him murdered in his sleep. Almost immediately, those loyal to Galbio abandoned us and went over to Bonifacius. Suddenly we were on the back foot, and Bonifacius, astute general that he was, seized the opportunity to go on the offensive. Mavortius was routed. His army collapsed, and Bonifacius won a complete victory without the loss of a single man.

Then he did the one thing I feared most, the one thing I had been trying to avoid. In his desperation, knowing I would send Aetius to confront him, he reached out to the Vandals.

But Bonifacius had misjudged me. I had no intention of sending Aetius to Africa until I had exhausted all my other options. I asked around and learned there was a brilliant young general, a Goth by origin, who had assisted in several successful campaigns against the Franks. He was residing in Ravenna and acting as an adviser to Felix. His name was Sigisvultus[2] . I called him before me, and we spoke to each other in the Gothic tongue. He seemed intelligent and capable. I was entirely satisfied he could get the job done, so I dispatched him to Africa and left Aetius in Gaul.

Sigisvultus bided his time. He didn't confront Bonifacius at once but armed the garrisons at Carthago and Hippo, strengthening them against the possibility of a siege and using them as bases to marshal his forces. Only after he was fully outfitted and armed did he march.

By then Bonifacius was running low on provisions. He was no match for Sigisvultus. He went down in defeat, was taken prisoner, and held at Carthago. I sent strict orders that no harm was to come to him. I was going to needed him

---

2. Pronounced sig-ess-vul-tus

to renegotiate his arrangement with the Vandals, who had begun crossing over from Hispania with the object of coming to his defense.

Bonifacius was willing to cooperate. He wrote to me with the assurance that he would do everything in his power to set things right. He had already delayed the Vandals for weeks, miring them in complex negotiations while waiting to see if Aetius would be sent against him. When he received word that Aetius was in Gaul and would not be coming, he tried to cut off negotiations, but the Vandal king would hear nothing of it. He meant to accept Bonifacius's invitation whether he liked it or not.

Within a fortnight the Vandals came flooding across the narrow strait that separated Europe from Africa, overwhelming the defensive forces Sigisvultus sent to stop them. In hindsight, I should have dispatched Aetius from Gaul to fend them off and prevent them from getting a foothold in Africa, but by then I had discovered his part in the disaster and was determined not to reward him.

As it turned out, I had been right to be suspicious of Aetius. The letter intercepted by my spies, the letter from Bonifacius to his friends in Rome, had been entirely fabricated by Aetius. Bonifacius had never boasted of enjoying absolute sovereignty in Africa, and he had never bragged about his ability to seize power whenever he saw fit. Aetius had cooked the whole thing up to get Bonifacius removed from his post so he could replace him.

Then, when it became clear I had not fallen for his chicanery, Aetius went further and told Bonifacius I suspected him of treason and was getting ready to sack him and remove him from his position by force. Playing the concerned friend and colleague, he urged Bonifacius not to surrender, lest he be executed.

Heeding Aetius's warning, Bonifacius spurned my summons and resisted the troops I sent to bring him home. When I followed up by sending an even larger body of troops, Bonifacius took it as confirmation of the truth of what Aetius had told him and prepared for a long, drawn out fight. In order to offset the threat posed by Aetius's ability to call on the Huns, he reached out to the Vandals for help.

But it had all been a terrible misunderstanding. Bonifacius had never been anything but loyal to me until Aetius had put false ideas into his head. Such was Aetius's desire to take command in Africa that he had manipulated us into conflict with each another, hoping that I would remove Bonifacius and promote him in his stead. The result was a complete disaster.

After learning of Aetius's treachery, I had Bonifacius released from confinement and brought to me.

He knelt before me in shame, mortified at the irretrievable thing he had done.

"What did you promise them?" I asked.

"I told them they could have half of Africa."

I felt nauseous. Never before in my life had I received such devastating news. I asked a servant to bring me a chair. I sat for a while with my head in my hands. Tears fell from my eyes.

A top Roman general, a master of soldiers no less, had signed a treaty with a barbarian tribe that promised them half of our most vital province in exchange for – well – for very little as it turned out. Bonifacius had bargained poorly, and the Vandal king, a cold-blooded and ruthless negotiator, had extracted an enormous price.

From the Vandal's perspective, the fact that the troops were no longer needed did not absolve Rome of its part in the bargain. The Vandals fully expected half of Africa, and the troops they sent were but the vanguard of a much larger force already on their way from Hispania .

To buy them off, I sent Bonifacius back to Africa with a generous offer, six thousand pounds of gold, more than Honorius had offered Alaric to lift the siege of Rome, but King Genseric just laughed it off. His army had already marched halfway through Numidia[3] and were closing in on the metropolis of Hippo Regius[4] , the acquisition of which would more than compensate him for turning down my offer.

I sent an urgent message to Sigisvultus to remain where he was and prepare for an attack, but it was too late. He was already on his way back to Rome,

---

3. Modern day Algeria

4. Modern day Annaba, Algeria

following orders given to him by Felix to come back and assist Aetius in his fight against the Goths. It was the last straw when it came to Felix. Aetius had been right all along: Felix should never have been promoted to master of soldiers. He was a dangerous incompetent.

In the end, only the demoralized remnants of Bonifacius's tattered army stood between the Vandals and Hippo Regius. Nevertheless, that good and loyal general performed miracles in getting his troops organized and entrenched. As the Vandals came on, they engaged them with all the fervor of freshly minted troops, but it wasn't enough. Genseric and his Vandals struck them with overwhelming force and drove them back inside the city where they were besieged.

Perhaps it was his shame at what he had done. Perhaps it was always a part of him. But Bonifacius demonstrated extraordinary courage in rallying his troops to hold out. For fourteen months, the Vandals battered the walls of Hippo Regius, attacking it with withering intensity. Almost daily, they flung themselves against the walls with the fury of unhinged beasts. Still, Bonifacius and his men held out.

In the end, the Vandals ran short of ammunition and had to withdraw. The siege was lifted, and we were able to send in reinforcements. I can't tell you how relieved I was, but the fight for Africa was just beginning. Although the Vandals had withdrawn from Hippo, they still occupied a large portion of Numidia, and they were sending more troops every day from Hispania. I needed a way to counter them, but I refused to call on Aetius. I had to look elsewhere.

During this time, I contacted my darling Eustacia in Constantinople and enlisted her aid in persuading Theodosius to send troops to assist us. Our communications were secret, for if Pulcheria found out she would almost certainly try to prevent it. Such was her villainy that she would rather have seen the Western Empire lost to the barbarians than give me the satisfaction of a victory.

Theodosius sent our old friend Aspar along with ten thousand men. Together with Sigisvultus — who I wrested away from Felix — we were able to assemble an army large enough confront the Vandals in Numidia.

Notable by his exclusion from this operation was Aetius, who wrote to me wondering why he had been left out. I responded by saying I needed him in Gaul and praised him generously for his service there. He must have missed the irony because his next letter explained in great detail how it was possible for him to assist in Africa while still leaving enough troops behind in Gaul to keep it pacified. I answered his explanation with icy silence.

But Aetius persisted. He traveled to Ravenna to make his appeal in person. For three days, I refused to see him. Then I surprised him by calling him into my presence with great fanfare. I praised him for his victories against the Goths. I lauded him for his tenacity and cunning. The dignitaries who were there stood and applauded. Then, to his amazement, I rewarded him with the consulship and bequeathed to him the honorific of Flavius, making him one of the great men of Rome. He beamed like a happy child and gave long speeches and boasted of his achievements. All the while I was waiting to stick the knife in.

First, however, I had deal with my other liability. Felix was bungling and inept, which in a time of crisis is even more dangerous than a liar and a cheat. One is an emergency; the other is a slow, malignant disease. They both had to be addressed – the weakest one first.

Get rid of the incompetent and ineffectual before you do anything else, Placidius. You will want them out of the way, so you don't stumble over them when you go to take on your more formidable adversaries. For when it comes to fighting those who pose the worst threats to you, you can ill afford distractions.

Chapter Eighteen

Placidius looked at the sentence again. "A liar and a cheat." That was how his mother had described Aetius. That seemed about right.

Placidius couldn't help but smile. Now here was the woman he knew, prudent and self-possessed, yet lenient to the point where many thought her naïve. Her exoneration of Bonifacius after his rebellion struck some as completely mad, and her sudden, unexpected elevation of Aetius to the consulship made a lot of people think Aetius was pulling her strings. They whispered behind her back that her generals were manipulating her. They said it was because she was a woman. No woman had ever ruled Rome, and for good reason, they argued. Women were unfit to rule, and if you wanted to know the reason why, all you had to do was look at Galla Placidia.

Rome was not unacquainted with the phenomenon. They had seen it in other nations. A woman had ruled Egypt, and it had gone badly. Zenobia in Palmyra, Boudica in Britain – both disasters. The disease of female rule was a blight on the state. Rome's storied ancestors had known it and prohibited it. But now the Empire was crumbling on all sides because it was stuck with a weak and vacillating female at its head. How had it gotten itself into such a fix?

Placidius had heard the talk. At eleven years of age, he had been sentient enough to comprehend what was being said about his mother and sympathized with those who criticized her. If he had been in charge, he would not have let things get so out of hand. In his eleven-year-old mind, he was sure her could have done better.

Sadly, his attitude had not evolved much since then. Until he read the letter he was ignorant of the difficulties she'd faced. The situation was much more complex than he'd imagined. Now he saw her differently. She was not weak, she was canny. She was not timid, she was restrained. A wise emperor did not act impulsively, even if it made him look weak and tentative. A shrewd emperor took the time to weigh the situation carefully before acting. Yet once the decision was made a wise emperor acted swiftly and decisively, as his mother did.

The hard part was going to be the restraint. How had his mother put it? *God is testing you. Think of it as a chance to prove yourself.*

It was not going to be easy. Four people were dead, one of them as a result of his ineptitude, and Liberius had been silenced. It remained possible Arsenius had orchestrated the whole thing, but if so, he had neglected to include Otho in his plans. The big man's surprise at Liberius's death seemed genuine.

So, if not Arsenius, who?

He snapped his fingers. *Of course.* The person who had left the document in his tent in the first place. Candida! He needed to question her, and he would not put up with any of her antics.

The caravan had paused to allow the Emperor to promenade through the streets of a nearby town. It was an opportunity to give the citizenry a glimpse of his royal personage, which they were expected to cheer lustily. Placidius was less than enthusiastic. At other stops along the way, the populace had been less than welcoming. But this place promised to be different. This was Adrianopolis.

Adrianopolis held an important place in Roman history. It was here where the invading Goths routed a large Roman army led by the Emperor Valens, killed the Emperor, and then broke free into the countryside, raping and pillaging. All of Rome's troubles with the barbarians began here. As a result of their trauma, the people of Adrianopolis clung fiercely to their Roman identity. Here Placidius would encounter little of the smoldering resentment he had encountered at other places along the way. Here the people would be glad to see him and honored he had stopped to visit them.

And it was so. The people of Adrianopolis turned out in great numbers and showered him with praise. Placidius was delighted to be the recipient of such unbridled adulation and thrilled be treated like a real emperor for once. It gave him a taste of how he might be received if he could reverse the deteriorating state of affairs he had inherited from his mother and restore the Empire to its glorious past. Perhaps marrying his cousin could make that happen, inasmuch as it would give him access to the armies of the East, which could be used to expel the Vandals from Africa and suppress the Goths. His marriage was the key. He could see that now. His mother had been right.

But nothing of the sort could happen if the girl's family were set against him. Pulcheria was the problem. If she were behind all this, it was a good indication of how far she would go to prevent the marriage. Any notion he had of saving the Empire would be crushed. He needed to know the truth. He needed to get to the bottom of who had planted that confession of faith in his tent. He called for Candida.

It took a long time for her to answer his summons. Irritated, he called for her again. But she didn't come. Now he began to be concerned. Where was she? He was just about to go and get her when she showed up looking haggard and unkempt. She crossed the room like a ghost and sat down. She clutched her hands between her knees and straightened her arms. She stared straight ahead with a glazed expression. He saw the bruises on her arms.

"Are you all right?" he asked.

"I'm all right."

"What happened to your arms?"

She looked at the bruises in dull curiosity. "I don't know. I must have bumped into something."

They were silent for a moment.

He spoke up. "It's been a while since we talked. A lot has changed. Some disturbing information has come to light."

"Where's Stephanus?" she asked.

He didn't answer.

"Have you hurt him?"

"Stephanus was expelled."

She slumped forward like a puppet released from its strings. It would've been a surprisingly dramatic gesture from anyone else, but not from Candida, who was given to such theatrics.

Placidius went on, "He confessed everything. I must say I was horrified."

She looked up from under her lashes. "What are you talking about?"

"It's no use, Candida. He made a clean breast of it."

"And you didn't hurt him for it?"

"He was expelled."

"So he will meet the same fate as Isaac and Elpidia?"

"It's time you tell me the truth, Candida. Who's behind this? Is it Pulcheria?"

She wrinkled her brow. "Who?"

"Don't play dumb with me, Candida. Stephanus told me everything."

"I don't know what you're talking about."

"If you refuse to tell me, I have ways of making you talk."

She regarded him with the weary expression of someone who has been through a long ordeal and is being asked to go through more. "Oh, why don't you just arrest me and expel me? That way I can end up like the others."

"Listen to me, Candida. Someone is plotting against me. Stephanus was in on it. He implicated a lot of other people as well. My curator of correspondence Liberius, for one. I want to know who's behind it."

Candida sighed and shook her head. "Oh, Placidius. You're always so distrustful of everyone. It's really quite tiresome. Listen to me. There's no plot against you. No one is out to get you. It's all in your head."

"He told me."

"If he told you something, it must've been because he was afraid. He was telling you what you wanted to hear, so you wouldn't hurt him."

"He implicated Liberius. Then Liberius was murdered."

"Arsenius didn't like Liberius."

"Someone killed Liberius to silence him."

"Arsenius killed Liberius. If you must point the finger at someone, there's your answer — obviously."

Placidius felt his temper rising. He struggled to hold it back. He turned away, mastered it, then turned back. "I'm going to ask you again, Candida. Who's behind this?"

"I'm pregnant."

He took a step back. His hand went to his mouth.

"Of course you can kill me if you want to, but you'd be killing your own child too. Are you that much of a beast?"

"I don't believe it."

Candida looked down at her hands. "I've always wondered what you would do if it came to this, if you would be a man or a monster. I'm fairly certain what your mother would do."

"The child is not mine."

"Deny it all you want, but I'm pregnant. If it's a boy, it will be next in line for the throne."

Placidius waved this off. "You were sleeping with Stephanus too. It could be his."

To his surprise, she didn't deny it. She shrugged. "Maybe, but how can we know?"

His first impulse was to take her by the throat and choke the life out of her. If he killed her, no one would object. But then that was probably what his enemies wanted him to do. An unhinged emperor murdering his pregnant concubine would look bad; it would discredit him in the eyes of the Church and make him vulnerable to those who were trying to undermine him. He needed to think. What had his mother had said? Exercise restraint; don't overreact. Let them believe they have the advantage of you until you can discover their weaknesses and exploit them. But he wanted so much to make her pay for the spot she had put him in.

"Let me ask you something," he said. There was a tremor of anger in his voice.

"What?"

"If I wanted you to do something for me, for the good of the Empire, would you do it?"

Candida rolled her eyes. "Not this again."

"Just answer the question."

"It would depend on what it was."

"I want you to take your unborn child and go away from here. I don't ever want to see you again."

She looked as if she had been slapped. "You bastard! How dare you!"

"Drop it, Candida. Your little act doesn't affect me anymore. I'm sick of your histrionics. Don't push me. I warn you."

She made a strangled cry and was on him like a cat. He raised his hands to fend her off, but she penetrated his defenses and raked her nails across his face. He felt blood. He grabbed her around the waist, lifted her bodily, and threw her down. She writhed, kicked, and tried to squirm free. He pinned her down. She whipped her head from side to side and tried to bite him. He leaned into her wrists, straddled her, then pressed down with his hips and buttocks to make her stop. It was then he noticed what was happening to him. He was becoming aroused.

It had been weeks since they had made love, but the lack of sex by itself couldn't explain the powerful sensation coming over him. The exhilaration made him dizzy. In a matter of moments he was fully erect.

His erection didn't go unnoticed. Candida stopped struggling and looked down between his legs. A mischievous smile played around her lips. "My goodness, Placidius. Look at you. You are all grown up." He smile widened. "Take me," she hissed with feral sexuality.

He began to kiss her like a man devouring his last meal. He rubbed himself against her. He squeezed her breasts. He hiked up her stola and spread her legs.

She inhaled in expectation.

A drop of blood ran down his cheek and struck the ground. The sight of it made him stop. She had cut him deeply enough to draw blood, and she would hurt him again if he gave her the chance.

No more. No more, he thought. He pushed her away and stood up.

She gaped up at him in confusion. "What are you doing? Why did you stop?"

"I'm finished with you, Candida. It's time for you to go."

She got to her feet and pressed herself against him. She rubbed him through the fabric of his tunic. "We're not finished, Placidius. We're just getting started. Let's do it while we can."

He twisted free. "Go back to your tent and don't come near me again. You still have plenty to answer for, and I intend to get some answers. Arsenius will be sent to question you. Otho will be with him."

"But you can't do that. I'm the mother of your child! I'm the mother of the heir!"

"You're the mother of a child who shall have no father."

"Ah, so now we see the kind of monster you are —"

"The child is fatherless."

"Cruel, mean, and selfish—"

"The father is dead."

She started to protest, but then she read the look on his face, and her countenance melted.

"That's right. I killed him. I castrated Stephanus and killed him, if you must know."

Her face went white.

He called the guard to arrest her before she could come at him again. She was dragged away kicking and screaming.

But he didn't send Arsenius and Otho to question her. Instead, he held back. He decided to wait and see what his enemies would do. He had a plan in mind — the kind of plan his mother would approve of.

To use a man's weaknesses against him is the most effective way to lure him into a trap. Men in particular have a burning need to be recognized, to be praised and celebrated. Ironically, the impulse doesn't diminish with success. The more praised a man is, the more powerful is his need to be praised. Felix was no exception. During the formalities raising Aetius to the consulship, Felix stood in the background seething. It wouldn't be long before he made the critical error that would doom him.

While Aetius was in Ravenna receiving the honor, I met privately with him on the pretense of inviting him to visit our daughter. Justa was thirteen years old at the time and completely out of control, running away on a regular basis to live among the commoners and consorting with all sorts of low and unsavory people. I wanted Aetius to speak to her, to see if the affinity of their blood would permit him to get through to her where I had fallen short. But I cautioned him not to reveal that he was her father lest the shock of it cause her to become even more unmanageable.

The meeting didn't go well. She was uncooperative and sullen and barely looked at him when he spoke. He sought in vain to persuade her of the important role she had to play in the family. When he was done speaking, she looked at me with an aggrieved expression and asked if she could go. With a heavy sigh, I gave her leave. She got up and went out without saying good-bye to him.

"She's a stubborn one," he remarked.

"Reminds me of someone else I know."

"Maybe it could be an asset," he said. "Given the right opportunity."

I sniffed in contempt.

"I'm just saying, if something were to happen to Placidius, a disease or an accident, let's say, she could step in."

I looked at him to see if he was kidding. He wasn't.

"Are you mad? She would have the Empire in ruins inside of a week."

"I don't think you're giving her enough credit. Sometimes a certain wayward bent can be a sign of democratic sympathies, which can be helpful when you're trying to hold an empire together."

"You've given this a lot of thought, haven't you?"

He gave a little shrug. "I'm just saying. In case Placidius doesn't have any children."

"Well, Placidius is going to have children. He's betrothed to Licinia Eudocia in case you've forgotten."

"Yes. Yes. Still…"

"Let's move on to another topic," I suggested. "You'll be glad to know I've come around to your way of thinking on the matter of Flavius Felix."

"Praise be! At last!"

"I'm prepared to remove him and elevate someone else to his position, but I must go about it discreetly. Given all the unrest stirred up by the Pope, now is not the time to turn the aristocracy against me. I need an unassailable reason to demote him. That's where you come in, Aetius."

"I am always at your service, Augusta."

I gave him a dubious frown. "Felix has been watching your elevation to the consulship with envy. Although he has been honored with the consulship himself, he now feels he needs to distinguish himself to prove he's entitled to be your superior. He longs to fight, to lead troops in battle, but I've kept him near me in Ravenna. My plan is to lift the restriction and dispatch him to Gaul to review the troops under your command. Once he's there, he'll almost surely pull rank and demand to take over. I want you to let him."

Aetius watched me with the tickled expression of a man waiting for the punch-line of a joke. "Go on," he said. "What else?"

I turned up my hands. "That's it. Let him take charge. He can't make the blunders that would warrant my sacking him if he doesn't have a command."

Aetius shook his head in disbelief. "You can't be serious. I'm not going to lose all the progress I've made in Gaul by handing it over to him."

"I must have a reason to sack him. Surely you can see that."

Aetius put his finger to his brow and pretended to contemplate this. "Ah, I see," he said. "While Felix is in Gaul destroying my hard-earned efforts, I go to Africa and clean up the mess Bonifacius has made. Then, when I'm finished with that, I go back to Gaul and fix what Felix has broken. That way you can get rid of two incompetent generals and make me your new master of soldiers. That will work."

"No, Aetius. You misunderstand me. I don't want you to leave Gaul. I want you to stay there. That way when Felix makes a mess of things, you'll be nearby to fix them. Felix will be exposed as inept, and you will prove yourself worthy to be his successor."

"I don't go to Africa?"

"You don't go to Africa."

"You leave Bonifacius in charge there?"

"That's right."

"I remain in Gaul and become master of soldiers when Felix is dismissed."

"That's my idea."

"It seems to me that still leaves one incompetent general in charge."

"We mustn't get ahead of ourselves, Aetius. Once you become master of soldiers you can handle Bonifacius as you see fit."

He eyed me skeptically.

"First things first, Aetius."

"One problem," he said. "Felix will never let me stay there. He's dumb, but he's not that dumb. Once he assumes my command he'll send me back to Ravenna to safeguard the capital. I'll be too far away when things get out of hand."

"I've thought of that. I'm in possession of intelligence indicating the Juthungi are pressing Raetia again. They've already begun making forays across the border to test us. Yes, Felix will send you back, but I'll issue countervailing orders sending you north to deal with the Juthungi. You needn't go further than Valentia. When things go wrong in Gaul, you'll be close enough to turn back and set them right."

He tapped his finger on his lips. "This could actually work."

"Your star will only shine brighter because of it."

"And I will become master of soldiers at last."

"You will get what you deserve, Aetius."

He smiled mischievously. "You are a clever one, Galla Placidia."

"I do the best I can."

"One other thing," he said. "As long as we're about the business of trying to rectify past omissions, there's one thing past due."

"What's that?"

"Our marriage."

I had to laugh.

He looked hurt. "Don't be cruel. You know as well as I do that everything we've done has been calculated to culminate in our union. Surely, you recognize that."

"I recognize no such thing."

"But this is the realization of our childhood aspirations. This is what we dreamed of all those years ago."

"When I was a child, I spoke as a child, I understood as a child, I thought as a child, but when I became a woman, I put away childish things."

"Don't quote Paul to me, Galla. It doesn't suit you."

"I'm not going to marry you, Aetius."

He scoffed. "Do you know what your problem is? You fail to perceive our place in history. We are the agency by which the Empire will be revived. We are the freshening breeze. We are the wind in the embers."

"You are a grasping, vainglorious, overly ambitious man who will stop at nothing to force my hand."

"Everything I do is for the good of the Empire. In that we are alike, you and me. Marry me and together we can be greater than the sum of our parts."

"And that would satisfy you?"

"Of course."

"And you would not see me as your rival?"

"We would be equals."

"Be serious, Aetius. There's not a person alive who you consider your equal."

"You accuse me of vanity."

"*I have a vivid memory of a young man standing in a thunderstorm, railing at God, challenging Him to strike him down.*"

"*It was Jupiter, not God.*"

"*That's not how I remember it.*"

"*Oh, don't be such a pious old dogmatist, Galla. I liked it better before you became so devout.*"

"*Back before my vow of chastity?*"

"*Thank God you've put that behind you.*"

"*Have I?*"

He groaned. "*Not this again.*"

"*I'm afraid so, although it's more of a personal commitment than a political one these days.*"

"*So there's room to be flexible.*"

"If you marry me, it will be a dry time for you, Aetius, and if the stories I've heard are true, that may be a sentence you cannot endure."

"I require nothing so long as I have you, Galla."

"Pardon me if I fail to blush."

"Think about it, Galla. We should marry. The Empire would benefit."

"When Felix takes charge in Gaul, I want you to step aside. Can you do that for me — and for the Empire."

"I'm at your service, Galla. Always."

I had him where I wanted him. I had laid the trap and was ready to spring it.

When Felix sent Aetius back from Gaul, I would not issue the countervailing order sending him north to Raetia, so when Aetius took his army north instead of coming back to Ravenna, Felix would see it as an attempt to outflank him. Naturally, he would send troops to confront him, and, just as naturally, Aetius would resist. Under the circumstances, it would be easy to characterize Aetius's behavior as an out and out rebellion, and that's how I would frame it. But Felix would not be strong enough to defeat Aetius without help.

With Aspar and Sigisvultus on their way to reinforce Bonifacius in Africa, I figured I would have enough manpower there to pull Bonifacius away and send him north to reinforce Felix. As powerful as Aetius was, I was confident Felix and Bonifacius together could defeat him. When it was over, I would sack Felix and make Bonifacius the new master of soldiers. If it all went according to plan, I would finally be rid of both Felix and Aetius, and we could move on.

But it didn't work out that way.

You see, I was unable to pull Bonifacius away from Africa because the combined forces of Aspar, Sigisvultus, and Bonifacius were unable to keep the Vandals in check. They broke through our defenses and marched on Hippo Regius for a second time. After a brief, bloody siege, they took the city, before moving on to capture Neopolis, Hadrumentum, and the rest of Numidia.

As much as I hated to admit it, I was beginning to think I had made a dreadful mistake by refusing to send Aetius to Africa. Letting a personal grudge stand in the way of doing what was right for Rome was selfish and irresponsible.

As for the rest of my plan, Aetius foiled it before it got started. As soon as Felix arrived in Gaul, Aetius had him arrested him and tried for treason. The military tribunal assembled to hear the case found him guilty, and the next day Felix was executed.

It happened with the speed of lightning. By the time I got word of it, the entire senior military command was in disarray, and no one knew who was in charge.

I dashed off a letter to Aetius ordering him to appear before me without delay to answer for his insolence. Ten days later I got his reply. He told me he was heading north to Raetia to repel the Juthungi and could not answer my summons. He would be in touch when he got back. He concluded by saying that having some time apart would give us some perspective. What's more, he said, it would give me a chance to reconsider his proposal. Incredibly, he still wanted to marry me! I would rather have killed him instead.

No doubt his absence was calculated to benefit him in another way as well. With Africa reeling and the state of military affairs up in the air, it looked as if I had lost control of the situation, which brought me in for intense criticism from the Senate. The senators wanted answers, but I didn't have any. I was not about to promote Bonifacius to master of soldiers, not after he had been overrun by the Vandals and lost almost all of Africa, and I dared not make a move in that direction without consulting Aetius first, for I could ill afford a civil war with my rogue general. So, the best I could do was sit and wait until Aetius got back. The Senate waited as well. We all waited for Aetius. Aetius had the answers — which was just the way he wanted it.

Chapter Nineteen

Candida waited until after dark. She made her way along the picket line to a section of the cordon where the sentry was absent and decamped into the forest. Placidius followed her.

Magnified by the stillness, the crunch and snap of the underbrush alerted her that she was being followed. Placidius could hear her hastening away. He tried to keep up with her. Then he saw the firelight. Judging by the sound of her footsteps, she was heading straight for it. If he intended to carry out his plan, he needed to overtake her before she got there. Throwing caution to the wind, he plunged ahead and almost immediately slammed into a tree. Stunned, he reeled back. He took a moment to shake off the shock, and by the time he collected himself, she was gone. He listened hard but could not hear her. Then he headed toward the firelight.

When he got there, he could hardly believe his eyes. There, sitting before the fire, was Cyrus.

"Come along," Cyrus said. "I'm not a ghost. I won't hurt you."

Placidius stepped forward, looking warily around.

"Don't worry," Cyrus said. "We're alone."

"Where's Candida?"

"She's gone."

Placidius approached the fire.

Cyrus sat hunched over, prodding the fire with a stick. "Have you ever noticed?" he said. "A fire is a lot like a woman. If you poke it correctly, it blazes up, but if you poke it wrong, it goes out."

"What are you doing here?" Placidius asked.

"Tending a fire," Cyrus said.

Placidius was not amused.

"Sit down," Cyrus said. "Let's talk."

Placidius sat down across from him. The fire rippled and snapped. "Where is she? What's happened to her?"

Cyrus gave him an odd look.

"What have you done with her?" Placidius demanded.

"Less than you would have."

Placidius scowled.

"I'm sorry," Cyrus chuckled. "I didn't mean it that way. Candida and I barely know each other. I'm not her lover, if that's what you're worried about. I'm only here to protect her."

"From whom?"

"From you, Imperator."

"I'm not going to hurt her."

"You'll have to excuse me if I don't quite believe that. I heard what you did to Stephanus."

"That was an accident."

Cyrus gave him a skeptical look.

Placidius grew irritated. "Why am I talking to you?"

"I told you. I'm trying to protect Candida. She's innocent."

"She's as guilty as sin."

"All right," Cyrus said with a shrug. "Guilty of being unfaithful to you, perhaps. Guilty of trying to trick you into marrying her. But she's not guilty of planting the documents in your tent, not intentionally anyway."

"How do you know?"

"Because I know who is guilty."

"Liberius."

"Correct. But who was behind him?"

"I have my suspicions."

"I'm sure you do, but if you're wrong, more innocent people will die, so you'd better get it right this time."

Placidius fell silent.

Cyrus smirked. "Experience is a wonderful thing because it helps you to recognize when you make the same mistake again, but it's not the same thing as being correct. Repeated blunders don't make a person astute, just clumsy."

Placidius bridled. "You misrepresented yourself to me. You pretended to be my friend while all the time you were working behind my back to undermine me."

"Really? Tell me more."

"You packed my Candida's retinue with people who intended to harm me."

"Did Isaac tell you that?"

"More or less."

"Well, Isaac lied. He was working for Aetius. Isaac and Elpidia both were. They carried out the tasks assigned to them and were sent home."

"They were murdered to silence them."

"You're wrong about that, like you've been wrong about a lot of things."

"But I saw their bodies."

"Did you? You saw two bodies, but did you see their faces?"

Placidius tried to remember back. He couldn't remember actually seeing their faces. They had been dressed similarly — sandals unfastened at the ankles, a tunic with an untied sash, the rustic dress of a peasant woman. Placidius tried to change the subject. "Are you denying that you had a part in selecting Candida's retinue?"

"Candida's retinue was selected by the same person who intercepted your mother's letter and assigned us to modify it."

"Us?"

"Yes. The four of us. Isaac, Elpidia, Liberius, and me. We were tasked with making a few minor changes. We were hired by Aetius and overseen by Arsenius. It was our job to convince you."

"Convince me of what?"

"To cooperate."

"Cooperate with what?"

Cyrus looked at him in surprise, then his eyes registered comprehension. "Oh, I see. You haven't finished the letter yet. Well, once you finish the letter, you'll understand."

"You're lying," Placidius said. He didn't know why he said it. It just felt like the right thing to say. He needed to buy time until he could think through what Cyrus was telling him. "I could have you arrested," he said.

"You'll need help with that. Do you want to rely on Arsenius? Do you trust him to do what's best?"

Placidius's blood went cold. He felt cut off, boxed in.

"Don't take it so hard," Cyrus said. "I'll protect you."

"Oh, I see. You're my defender now. Is that it?"

Cyrus gave him a sad smile. "Make no mistake. It was absolutely my intention to betray you too. I was recruited by Aetius. I believed him when he told me you were unfit to rule. It was only after I got to know you that I began to have second thoughts."

Placidius didn't know whether to believe him or not.

"Aetius is a simple man. He thinks people are who they are. He thinks they're incapable of change. I don't agree. I've already seen how you've learned from your mistakes. I believe you'll be a good ruler. That's why I broke with the others. That's why I abandoned the project and ran away. And that's why I'm talking to you now. Go, read your mother's letter, and decide for yourself."

Placidius got to his feet. He slowly backed away, keeping his eyes on Cyrus until he reached the edge of the forest and the trees closed in around him. Then he hastened along, alert to every sound, cognizant of the fact that he could be being followed.

When he got back to the camp, the same incompetent sentry was missing from his post. Placidius returned to his tent, picked up his sword, and lay down on his back. He lay awake most of the night, gripping the sword, and trying to sort through his thoughts. Every little sound made him flinch.

At first light, he picked up his mother's letter and began to read it again, but the more he read, the more confused and frightened he got. The letter was a tapestry of truth and lies, but he lacked the capacity to distinguish which was which. He longed to make someone pay for his anxiety, but he feared taking another life. He longed for the freedom to react without thinking and resented the responsibility of having to consider others beyond himself. He was the emperor now. Shouldn't that make it easier?

Apparently not.

Anger and despair washed over him.

He continued reading.

In the course of my experience, I've learned a few things most women would never know. For example, during my time with the Goths, I became acquainted with the process of sword making. It really is quite fascinating. The metal is

heated to a malleable state and then hammered into shape. After it is formed, it is cooled and then heated again to build resistance. This heating and cooling goes on until the sword is ready. It's a rigorous process but in the end the blade is capable of cutting through sinew and flesh.

Despair not, Placidius. The challenges of being emperor will try you, but if you can stand up to the rigors, they will fortify you, and you will come to appreciate those who challenge you as your most generous benefactors.

When Aetius refused my summons to answer for the execution of Felix, I knew I had to do something to communicate my displeasure, so I recalled Bonifacius from Africa, leaving Aspar and Sigisvultus to keep guard, and told him to bring his army with him.

Bonifacius was worried that he was about to be sacked and thought again about resisting, as he had done before, but in the end he came. When he arrived, he was greeted by a full military procession and brought to the palace where he was given a warm reception and rewarded with the rank of patrician. That would have been enough for him, I'm sure, but to his surprise I went further, naming him master of soldiers, and giving him command of Felix's army. He fell to his knees and kissed my feet.

But the honors I bestowed upon him came with a price. The armies I had given him had a purpose. I wanted him as strong as possible for what would come next. I announced to the Senate that I was stripping Aetius of his command and sacking him for insubordination. A collective gasp went through the chamber. Not a man present missed the dire implications of my choice.

Aetius didn't immediately go on the attack but hastened back to Ravenna to plead his case, confident he could persuade me to change my mind. I was in a meeting with Bonifacius when he got there. Also present were Sebastianus, Bonifacius's son-in-law, and Pelagia, Bonifacius's comely young wife, who had accompanied her husband to the meeting for the honor of meeting me. We were all gathered together around a table when Aetius burst in, perspiring and out of breath, as if he had run all the way from Raetia.

Vexed at the intrusion, I ordered him removed, but the palace guard, who was still loyal to him for his brief tenure as governor of the palace, hesitated. Aetius marched forward and slammed his fist down on the table.

"Clear the room!" he shouted. "I demand to speak to the Augusta in private!"

I drew myself up in indignation. "Flavius Aetius! You go too far!"

Out of the corner of my eye, I saw Sebastianus go for his sword. Aetius saw it too and instantly changed his demeanor, dropping his chin on his chest like a chastened schoolboy and begging my pardon. His temper had run away with him, he said. He had ridden a great distance, burning with rage at the way he had been treated. When he had gotten to the palace and was told I was in a private meeting with the new master of soldiers, he had lost his mind. He regretted it now. He begged me to forgive him.

It was all an act; he regretted nothing, but he had sized up the situation and calculated that killing Bonifacius's son-in-law would not serve his purpose, so he assumed an attitude of contrition.

I was supposed to play along, but I didn't give him the satisfaction. "I have nothing to say to you," I said. "My decision is final."

He looked at me as though his feelings were hurt. He asked me what he had done to deserve such treatment. He thought he knew my answer. He thought I would reproach him for executing Felix without sanction. He was prepared to defend himself and make the argument that he lacked the time to consult with me, that Felix's treachery was too menacing to delay.

It was all nonsense, of course. We both knew Felix had to be eliminated. Aetius's only crime was doing it his way instead of mine, but he had put me in a difficult spot, and now I had to do something about it or lose credibility. I told him I knew all about his false letter to Bonifacius. I told him I was well aware of his cynical attempt to manipulate us. His meddling had destabilized the situation in Africa and brought about the Vandal invasion. I held him responsible.

To his credit he didn't try to deny it. His only defense was that he had done it for the good of the Empire. He was unapologetic in his insistence that he was the right man to protect Africa from the Vandals, and having failed to convince me of that, he had decided to take matters into his own hands.

But he had misjudged Bonifacius. He thought Bonifacius would crumble under the threat of official sanction and surrender his position without a fight. He never guessed Bonifacius would reject the will of the Augusta and fight back. Aetius gave Bonifacius an apologetic look, and then his eyes wandered to Bonifacius's comely young wife Pelagia. They lingered there for a moment before returning to mine.

Now Sebastianus spoke up. He addressed himself to Aetius. "So does this mean you are prepared to acknowledge Bonifacius as your superior?"

Sebastianus was a handsome, well-built young man, with self-confidence matching his good looks. Bonifacius had two children by a previous marriage, a boy and a girl. The son was a jokester and a rake, much given to drinking and gambling. He spent most of his time at the chariot races and showed no interest in military affairs. The daughter was a lovely girl, quiet and reserved. She had chosen a regimental staff officer with great promise as her husband - Sebastianus. As a surrogate for the profligate son, whose recklessness had compelled him to flee the city ahead of his creditors, Sebastianus was loyal and would defend his father-in-law to the last.

Again, Sebastianus asked the question, but this time with a measure of deference towards the man who would likely be his superior should he be granted the forgiveness he was seeking. "Will you acknowledge Bonifacius as your superior?"

Aetius looked at him like he was scum.

Sebastianus stiffened, squaring his shoulders.

Aetius glared.

An uneasy moment passed before Sebastianus dropped his eyes and resumed his seat.

Aetius turned to me. "Regardless of who's responsible for letting the Vandals into Africa — Bonifacius, who invited them to come, or me, who was a thousand miles away at the time — they are there now, and Bonifacius has failed to hold them back. He's proven himself incapable of doing the job you've asked of him. It's time to give somebody else a chance."

I gave him a patronizing smile. "Are you asking to be reinstated?"

I wanted him to swallow his pride and humble himself to me, but he simply said, "I have advised you on the best course of action."

"I don't like your attitude, Flavius Aetius," I snapped back. "You've committed capital crimes against the state, and I don't think you can be trusted."

It was a mistake. I had gone too far. We were within inches of a reconciliation, a reconciliation that would have seen him reinstated him on the spot and resulted in the combined armies of Aetius and Bonifacius marching on the Vandals en masse to drive them from Africa. But instead Aetius stormed out.

Before he went, however, he fixed me with a steely gaze and said, "You've convinced yourself that your interests and mine are at odds, but you've forgotten our pledge, and it makes me sad."

He was alluding to the conversation we had had many years before when we were children and our whole lives were in front of us, the conversation about love and fidelity and the bond between us. For a fleeting moment, I felt a dim echo of the affection I had felt for him as a girl, and my heart broke a little as he stormed out.

The guard looked to me to see if I wanted him arrested and brought back, but I let him go. I had it in mind that I would write to him privately later and offer to reinstate him as deputy general under Bonifacius's command. It would be enough to punish him for his wrongdoing, but not so much to insult him or push him away. After all, he was the best general we had, and I never had any intention of terminating him permanently.

Tragically, however, it did not end there. Aetius managed to get in one last parting shot, a final dig that pushed me over the brink. You see, he had not left the palace after the meeting as I thought, but lingered, doing God knows what, as he bided his time, not for the purpose of seeking amends, as might be expected, but to waylay Bonifacius's comely wife and try to seduce her. As I rounded the corner, I came upon them. He was leaning in close, pressing into her, whispering and stroking her hair. The poor thing was blushing and shrinking back.

Fortunately, Bonifacius and Sebastianus had exited by another route and had not seen them, or blood would have been shed. For my part, I was so affronted I lost control, swept up, and slapped him across the face.

He took a step back and put a hand to his reddening cheek. "Why, Galla," he said. "I suppose this means you don't want to marry me."

I flew at him. The guards had to pull me off.

He casually straightened himself out and dusted himself off.

The guards were still restraining me. My face was purple with rage. "Go!" I yelled. "Leave me! If you ever show your face around here again, I'll have you arrested for treason!"

Aetius made a slight bow, his face devoid of expression, and left.

I did not see him again for several months, not until after he had slain Bonifacius and brought the Huns to our doorstep. But that was not all my temper had cost us that day.

In between the moment Aetius had left the meeting and when he had been caught trying to seduce Bonifacius's wife, he had gone to Justa's apartments and told her the truth.

I only learned this later when I was forced to confine Justa to her rooms. She was furious with me, she spat in my face, and told me she despised me. She was incorrigible, her disobedience was intolerable, and I could bear no more of her. She was sixteen and out of control. She had slept with her servant and brought disgrace on all of us. The time had come to take more drastic action, so I reached out to Eustacia in Constantinople and asked if she could arrange to have her placed in a convent there. Eustacia, dear heart that she is, made the arrangements without hesitation.

You were fourteen at the time, so I'm quite sure you remember the day Justa was sent away, how she told us she was glad to be going, and how she insulted us and wished us ill. You'll probably remember how I showed her a stern countenance, but after she was gone, I wept.

It's a bitter thing to be at odds with your children, but everything gets easier with time. Obstacles, once surmounted, can never be so daunting again. Tests, successively endured, are more easily passed in the future. Trials are not a curse but a gift that fortifies us for the challenges ahead. Yet when we are young and inexperienced we naturally try to avoid them, thinking that the only way to get through them is to elude them. Nothing could be further from the truth. We must meet our difficulties head on, endure the pain and anxiety they cause us, and grow smarter and stronger by the experience. If we are not prepared to do that, we are ill suited to be rulers and must consider abdicating our responsibilities to those who know better.

After Justa was gone, I began to reflect on things, and I came to a startling realization. By strewing so many challenges in my path, Aetius had been testing me, slowly building my strength through trials, much in the way that steel is hardened through repeated heating and cooling until it is ready to be carried into the fight. Far from being my enemy, Aetius was my mentor and guide.

As for Justa, her time in Constantinople was a tonic for her. You saw the results yourself. When she got back, she was changed. No longer the spiteful, vindictive brat she had been on the day she left, she was courteous and kind, patient and forgiving. It was a remarkable transformation.

What you may not know is how it happened. It was not, as the public was led to believe because of prayer and penance. The truth is she remained at the convent less than a month. No, the change in her was almost entirely due to the influence of friends she met while residing at the palace in Constantinople, devout Christians who were calm and reserved, and wise beyond their years. They showed her the error of her ways and taught her how to be a better person.

Among Justa's new friends was a young man Eustacia found quite impressive. He combined a strong moral rectitude with a nimble wit. This remarkable fellow succeeded where others had failed. He penetrated Justa's sullen defenses and brought her out of herself. To him goes most of the credit for the improvement in her character. Eustacia told me his name, but I have since forgotten it. He was one of those angels in human form who show up every now and then to set things to right. He left Constantinople shortly thereafter, and Justa never saw him again.

Try as I might, I can't remember his name, but the result is the same. She is much more rational and amenable, which should come as a relief to both of us.

With all of the challenges ahead of us, at least we don't have to worry about Justa anymore.

"She's gone. The girl has fled."

Arsenius was standing in the doorway with two of Placidius's bodyguards. "We've dispatched a search party to look for her."

"Don't bother," Placidius said. "She's gone." He was reclining on his couch with the codex open before him. "She's been taken away by her friends."

"Friends? What friends?"

"The people who have been following us all along. The people you should've known about, if you'd been doing your job."

"I beg your pardon."

"Tell me something, Arsenius. Why are you here? Isn't it your job to protect me?"

Arsenius drew himself up. "I don't know what you mean. It seems to me I have protected you very well, Imperator. We are nearing Constantinople. Preparations are being made for your arrival. You are safe and unharmed."

"Did you find anyone else in the vicinity while you were searching for Candida?"

Arsenius was surprised. "Why, yes. We arrested a man this morning. We caught him trying to slip through the perimeter into the woods. We took him into custody. He was carrying these." Arsenius handed over a pair of documents, the confession of faith signed on the back with Placidius's name, and the scroll containing the transcript of a sermon by Nestorius.

Placidius stared down at them in amazement. "How did he get these?"

"One of two ways. Either he stole them, or you gave them to him."

Placidius bristled. "I would never give these to anyone. They could be used against me."

"Precisely, which is why I find it so astonishing that they ended up in his possession. I'm completely mystified, Imperator. Perhaps you can help me. Where were you last night when you were supposed to be in your tent?"

Placidius felt trapped. He averted his eyes and mumbled something incoherent.

Arsenius heaved a sigh like an exasperated parent. "Imperator, I *am* trying to protect you, but how can you expect me to do my job if you insist on trying to undermine me? It seems clear to me what happened. Somebody — perhaps the girl — lured you away, and while you were gone, the villain slipped into your tent and stole the incriminating documents. Why did you keep them anyway? Why didn't you give them to me as soon as you knew the danger they posed to you?"

Placidius had no answer.

"A signed document of faith alongside a sermon by Nestorius. Documents like that can be used to condemn you of heresy. I hope you can appreciate the weight of that. It would be enough to cancel your wedding."

"I know. I know," Placidius said.

Arsenius regarded him with the stern frowning face of a disapproving parent. He stuck out his hand. "Give them to me now. I'll destroy them."

Placidius started to hand them over but thought better of it. "I'm perfectly capable of destroying them myself."

Arsenius closed his eyes and pursed his lips. His nostrils flared. A moment later he opened his eyes again. They lighted on the codex lying on the couch. "Is that your mother's letter?"

"You know it is."

"I don't remember seeing it before."

"I don't know how you could've missed it. I've had it with me all along."

"It's quite thick, isn't it?"

"She had a lot to say. Plus, there were some last-minute addendums, as I understand it. She wanted to make it as current as possible."

"Your mother is quite thorough in that way. Are you almost finished with it?"

Placidius was instantly suspicious. "Why do you ask?"

"No reason."

Placidius narrowed his eyes at him.

Arsenius threw up his hands. "Oh, for God's sake, Imperator! Why can't you trust me? If you're upset about what happened to Stephanus, it's understandable, but I tried to warn you."

"I'm not upset about that."

"Then what? Has somebody been trying to turn you against me? At least let me know who it is so I can defend myself. Was it the girl? Did she say something against me? What was it? Tell me."

Placidius scoffed. "If you're quite finished, I think you should leave now."

"Just give me the documents. I'll destroy them."

"I told you, I'll destroy them myself."

"Fine. Then do it," he said, nodding at the brazier. "I'll stand here and watch."

Placidius took the documents over to a brazier. The previous night's fire had burned down to a few glowing embers in the basin. He hesitated. "Aren't you going to need them as evidence against the man you captured?"

"Don't be ridiculous. Burn them."

Placidius lay the documents on the embers. Then he blew on them until they caught fire. Arsenius and Placidius stood side by side and watched as they shriveled and blackened and turned to cinders.

Arsenius smiled his approval. "Good. That removes one threat. Now perhaps you can help me with another. The man we arrested, I want you to take a look at him and tell me if you recognize him."

Placidius was wary. "Why would I recognize him?"

"I don't know, but it can't hurt to take a look."

"I'm busy."

Arsenius pinched the bridge of his nose. He dragged in a long breath. "I'm trying to help you, Your Excellency. Please. Take a look."

Grumbling under his breath, Placidius went along.

When they got to the legionary tent where the fugitive was being held, the guard was not at his post. An eerie silence hung over the place.

Arsenius stood at the door of the tent, listening. "Stay here," he said and ducked inside. A moment later he emerged, ashen.

"What's wrong?"

Arsenius pulled back the flap, and Placidius looked inside.

A gruesome scene confronted him.

Otho lay on his back in a pool of blood, his eyes staring blankly at the ceiling. His throat had been slashed from ear to ear.

Placidius was shaken.

Arsenius stared off into the distance, tapping his lip in thought. "The man we apprehended wasn't alone. He had an accomplice, someone from inside the camp, maybe someone from the girl's entourage, one of the people I wasn't permitted to interrogate." He gave Placidius a scathing look.

Placidius started to object, but the words died on his lips.

"You left your tent last night," Arsenius said. "You sent your guard away and slipped out. Where did you go? Who did you meet with?"

Placidius refused to answer.

Arsenius seized him by the shoulders and shook him. "Tell me! Can't you see you're in danger?"

Placidius glimpsed a figure out of the corner of his eye, but before he could see it clearly, it slammed into Arsenius, driving him to the ground. The figure was not particularly large or heavy but seemed to have materialized out of nowhere and was attacking with the ferocity of a beast. Arsenius was overmatched. When the figure turned his head to one side, Placidius saw a knife clenched in his teeth.

"Do something!" Arsenius cried. "Help me!

Placidius looked around in confusion. There were no guards, no soldiers, nothing. Arsenius was appealing to him. He scanned the ground and caught sight of a misshapen chunk of granite about the size of a man's head. When he knelt down to pick it up, he glimpsed a second figure standing near the edge of the perimeter looking at him.

It was Cyrus.

Their eyes locked, and for a moment they observed each other with a strange, almost clinical detachment. Then Cyrus slowly shook his head.

Placidius set the rock back down.

Arsenius was stabbed. Placidius knew it by the sound, a ghastly punch-squish, repeated in rapid succession. Arsenius gasped, once, twice, then groaned and fell silent.

The shadowy figure of the killer rose and strode past him, the knife still in his hand. He was walking away toward the woods, his shoulders rising and falling with the exertion of his breath.

Placidius considered trying to stop him, but he was reminded of something his mother had said. *The measure of an effective ruler is restraint.* Placidius held back, not out of cowardice, but out of shrewdness — or at least that's what he told himself. He would learn more by waiting, by resisting the impulse to react, and he was almost instantly rewarded. The killer glanced back, and Placidius saw his face clearly for the first time.

His blood ran cold. His mother had warned him.

Beware the magician.

The interloper in the camp.

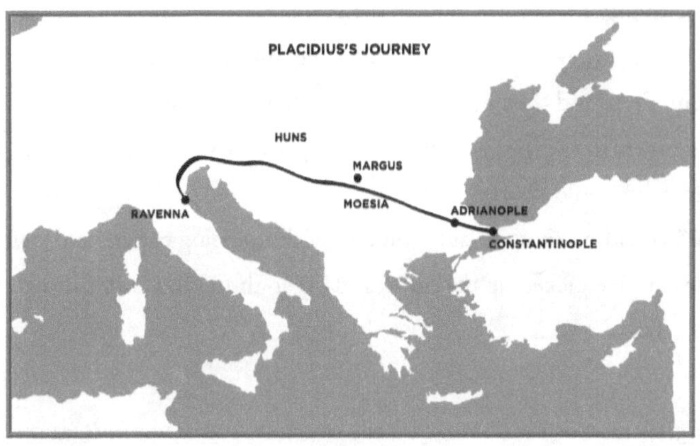

Chapter Twenty

The walls and towers of Constantinople stood out against the horizon, a jumble of planes and angles punctuated here and there with lofty columns. From this perspective, it hunkered low, hugging the earth, spreading its appendages in either direction like a mighty army cresting a ridge.

The murders of Otho and Arsenius gnawed at Placidius. He didn't know if their deaths removed the threat or heightened it. He felt more out of control than ever.

Immediately afterwards he called the guards together and reprimanded them for their gross dereliction of duty. The perpetrators had entered the camp unnoticed and gotten away unchallenged. Where had his guards been? He railed at them. They regarded him with sullen, resentful expressions.

He thought he should punish them, but he wasn't sure they would sit still for it. If they rose up against him, the rest of the troops might fall in behind them and then he could be overthrown — or worse. Maybe that's what his enemies expected him to do. Maybe they were counting on it. He decided he would disappoint them.

What had his mother said? Something about being patient and waiting them out. He picked up the codex and began thumbing back through the pages. There it was.

One of the most difficult things for any sovereign to do is to admit we are in the dark. This is especially true when we feel threatened. The tendency is to lash out, to act without thinking, which almost always makes things worse. We must resist the temptation to overreact. A good ruler, when faced with an inscrutable threat, acts with restraint and awaits his opportunity.

On the other hand, maybe the letter had been tampered with, maybe the advice was tainted. Nevertheless, under the circumstances, restraint seemed like the proper way to handle it. He decided to stick with his decision.

Curiously, both Arsenius and Cyrus had been anxious for him to finish the letter as if the answer to everything could be found there. Odder still, they could not both be exonerated by what it said. Could they?

He weighed the codex in his hands. He turned to the final pages and started reading again, determined to finish it before arriving in Constantinople.

Aetius revolted. I can't say I was surprised.

After our row at the palace, Aetius departed for Arelate and roused his troops to rebellion. I ordered Bonifacius to bring his troops from Africa in order to meet him. As Master of Soldiers, Bonifacius already had the army in the presence of the emperor under his command, but I feared it would take more than that to vanquish Aetius, so I made the regrettable decision to strip Africa of most of its troops in order to defend the capital. I left only a skeletal force behind to keep an eye on the Vandals.

From the beginning Aetius was at a disadvantage. Seeing he was outnumbered, he attempted to draw Bonifacius's armies westward toward the Apennines, and then veered south in an attempt to outflank him. But Bonifacius was not fooled. With his son-in-law Sebastianus leading the van, he attacked Aetius's forces outside of Araminum.[1]

The outcome was a foregone conclusion. Although Aetius fought hard, he could not overcome Bonifacius's superior numbers. But it had never been his intention to win. A victory would not have served him; it would only have alienated him from the army he hoped to command. No, his real purpose was much simpler: to kill Bonifacius. And in this he succeeded.

Aetius's army was already crumbling when a message arrived at Bonifacius's camp. It was from Aetius. It challenged Bonifacius to single combat. Boni-

---

1. Modern day Rimini, Italy

facius, a man of honor, could hardly refuse. Sebastianus tried to talk his father-in-law out of it, but Bonifacius was confident he could defeat Aetius in a fair fight. Unfortunately for him, it was not to be a fair fight.

As he prepared for combat, Aetius secretly modified his spear, making it longer. Before Bonifacius got within arm's length of him, Aetius stabbed him, mortally wounding him.

Bonifacius didn't immediately perish but grew weak from loss of blood and was carried to a nearby domus. There he lingered as his wound festered. Days turned into weeks. I traveled out from Ravenna to see him.

On his deathbed, Bonifacius warned me not to make an enemy of Aetius, not because he was invincible, but because he was the greatest commander of his time. Despite his unscrupulous methods, Aetius had a better grasp of battlefield tactics and diplomatic protocols than any man alive. I was astonished at the generosity of Bonifacius towards the lying cheat who had taken his life. It confirmed me in my high regard of Bonifacius. He died a week later. The next day Aetius withdrew.

Suddenly the Empire was without a master of soldiers to command its armies. Given the dangers surrounding us on every side, this could not stand. I went back to Ravenna and wrote to Aetius, offering him my forgiveness and asking him to come to Ravenna to discuss a way forward. It had been my intention to reach him at Arelate, but he had not gone back there. He had gone to Pannonia to seek the assistance of the Huns.

The Huns, under their king Rugila, had recently suffered a major setback to the Burgundians, and the king's brother and co-ruler Octar had been killed. The Huns are a vicious people, not unlike wolves, and they will turn on each other at the first opportunity. After his defeat at the hands of the Burgundians, Rugila's position was weakened. He was at risk of being overthrown if he didn't act at once to shore up his support. Aetius offered him a way to do so.

But Rugila was not as enamored of Aetius as his predecessor had been and wanted some surety that if he marched against Rome and lost, he would have something to show as proof of the good sense of his decision. Thus, in exchange for his Rugila's help, Aetius promised the Huns he would not challenge their dominion over a narrow stretch of territory nearly two hundred miles long along the Danube River in southern Pannonia. In effect, Aetius agreed to cede the territory to the Huns whether he succeeded or not. Rugila was no fool. He readily agreed.

The cruel irony is that I was already prepared to give Aetius what he wanted without being forced. The ceding of valuable territory to a wild and unruly band of barbarians was completely unnecessary. What's more, by granting them land along the Middle Danube in Pannonia, Aetius put them eyeball-to-eyeball with the peace loving Roman citizens living on the other side of the river, a fate they did not deserve.

If this were not already a tragic example of squandering our riches on swine, having exacted Aetius's promise, Rugila tried to cheat him. He would not grant Aetius the full might of the Hun army but only a small contingent, enough to frighten us into compliance. Aetius was furious but felt he needed the backing of the Huns to force my hand. Hence, Aetius took what troops Rugila was willing to spare and marched on Ravenna.

When news of their advance reached me, I proclaimed Sebastianus the new master of soldiers and ordered him to prepare a defense. Sebastianus was eager to meet Aetius in the field and avenge Bonifacius's death, but I ordered him to remain in the capital. If Aetius was advancing with the full strength of the Hun army, our forces, so recently depleted by civil war, would not be equal to the task. If the Huns defeated us in battle, they could break free and overrun Italia, destroying everything in their path. It would be a catastrophe of major proportions. Better to hole up behind the natural defenses of Ravenna's marshes and prepare for a long siege.

Then came the ultimatum. Aetius sent a message demanding to be named master of soldiers. In addition, he wanted to be granted the patricianship, the same honor I had given Bonifacius. If I agreed to his terms, he would send the Huns back to Pannonia and join me in the palace at Ravenna to reorganize the army and prepare to expel the Vandals from Africa.

It was really nothing more than I had been prepared to do anyway, so I met with Sebastianus and informed him of my decision.

Sebastianus was incredulous. He claimed to be in possession of intelligence that showed Aetius was bluffing. There was no Hun army, only a relatively small contingent of Hun forces, which could easily be defeated. Sebastianus was eager to win the day and take Aetius captive. He wanted to try Aetius for treason and execute him publicly as a warning to anyone else who might be thinking of testing me.

Sebastianus was my champion, but his loyalty was misguided. His allegiance should have been to Rome, not to me. Had it been, he would have seen, as Bonifacius did, that the best thing was to give Aetius what he wanted — what he had demanded all along — to be made master of soldiers and allowed to take the fight to the Vandals in Africa.

Aetius received my reply to his terms and asked for a meeting. I met him in the great hall surrounded by attendants and dignitaries. He requested a meeting in private; I granted his request. When we were alone he put his hands on my shoulders and looked me squarely in the eyes. Then he gathered me in his arms. We stood that way for a long time, knowing how close we had come to destroying everything.

Aetius sent the Huns back to Pannonia. Within weeks they overran the territory he had given them, expelling the inhabitants on both sides of the river. No attempt was made to retaliate.

As for Aetius, he was promoted to master of all soldiers, the highest rank in the Roman military, and honored with the patricianship, just as Bonifacius had been. Our years of antipathy were over; I was done trying to punish him. He was a formidable opponent, yes, but he was not my enemy. He never intended to usurp me. He always believed we were better together than apart. My failure to comprehend that earlier was the error that had cost us so much.

On the other hand, Aetius was never an easy man to deal with. Over the years, his arrogance and duplicity had caused me no end of misery. Even after he had gotten everything he wanted, he still tormented me.

To get even with me over the way I had treated him, he had Bonifacius posthumously declared a traitor, confiscated his properties, and detained his widow. That's right. Pelagia, the comely young woman he had cornered in the hallway with his wolfish advances, was taken prisoner and interrogated by him privately. The price for her freedom was her consent to marry him.

Of course I objected to this. It was needlessly cruel and provocative. But he would not be deterred. If I am to be honest, my feelings were hurt. I would have been uncomfortable with Aetius marrying anyone but me. But I was forty-five years old now and no longer an attractive young woman. What's more, Aetius was a celebrity, the talk of Rome. His admirers were many, and he could have had any young woman he wanted. In fact, he would bed many, after making Pelagia his wife.

It was petty and mean what he did, but I had to let it go. I could no longer let his personal peccadilloes be any part of my consideration. My primary focus had to be on the affairs of state and preparing a smooth transition to the principate for you. In this, Aetius proved to be a reliable partner.

Sebastianus would be less forgiving. Incensed at the way Aetius had denigrated the memory of his father-in-law, he challenged him to personal combat. Aetius laughed it off. When Sebastianus persisted, Aetius demanded his exile, which I granted. Sebastianus was appalled at his fate. He had never been disloyal. But he was standing in the way of the inevitable and had to be removed.

Later, we received reports that he had offered his services to the Eastern court at Constantinople. I'm certain the idea didn't originate with him. Pulcheria was behind it, as she is behind so many of our difficulties, which is one of the reasons I am writing to you now.

Beware of her. She is dangerous. She will seek out and recruit anyone with a grudge against us. She will pass up no opportunity to use our former enemies to undermine us. What's more, her insatiable thirst for revenge will persist beyond my stepping down, and it will fix on you. Unless you are able to render her ineffectual, she may destroy you.

Sebastianus made his way to Constantinople, and at the same time Justa made her way home to Ravenna. I'm informed they crossed paths in Servitium[2]. Justa reported that Sebastianus was remarkably gracious given the unfair way he had been treated by us. If he had not been married already, she might have agreed to see him again as he was a handsome young man from a good family and had a lot of promise. You can make of that what you will.

When Aetius got word that Justa was home, he wanted to see her, to apologize for whatever he had said to offend her. He was eager to get any hard feelings behind them. To his way of thinking, we were a family now and ought to come together. I could hardly deny him. We were partners, he and I, even if we weren't married. In a very real way we had become the parents of the Empire.

That's why when he asked me to name him your official "protector," I did. I have not told you this until now because I feared your reaction. But rest assured, having Aetius as your protector will reinforce your sovereignty. As

---

2. Modern day Gradiška, Bosnia-Herzegovina

your protector he will be unbound by law or edict to do whatever is necessary to protect you, like a father watching over a son.

You should accept this in the right spirit. Don't fight it. Aetius has never done anything to make you mistrust him. He has only ever worked to build the kind of strength and stability necessary to protect the Empire during the difficult transition of power from me to you. Without him at the head of our armies it would be an invitation for our enemies to strike. With him there, they wouldn't dare.

Aetius and I have had a long, difficult relationship. I won't pretend otherwise. I have laid it out for you here in all its sordid details so you will know I am not trying to minimize it. But just because something is forged in fire doesn't mean it isn't strong and reliable. Just the contrary, in fact. What Aetius and I have created out of our many struggles is something durable and dependable, something you can use to your advantage in the years ahead, if you act wisely.

Up until now you have misperceived me. You have thought me weak and tractable, which was by design. I have presented myself as cowed. I have shown myself to be entirely under the thumb of my Master of Soldiers, which is neither more nor less than my enemies want to believe. By this artifice, I am no longer threatened by would-be usurpers because Aetius presents a formidable challenge to anyone who might contemplate my overthrow. As a result, I have been able to rule unencumbered by many of the difficulties that plagued my predecessors. Now you can enjoy the same advantage.

If you learn anything from what I've been trying to tell you, learn this. It takes a strong person to be humble, and to the extent that I've been able to disregard others' opinions of me, I've grown stronger. For by doing so I've been able to take advantage of a common flaw afflicting many people, the desire to see the world not as it is, but as they want it to be.

Those who are misguided by their biases are made vulnerable by the very thing that appears to strengthen them. They imagine the world is predictable. They think people are fixed in their characters, and that these commonalities can be exploited. I disagree. The world is complex, and people are variable.

Perhaps for some this is of little consequence, this refusal to recognize the world as it is, but as rulers, it is incumbent on us, before we decide on great and momentous matters, to make a wise and judicious pause, and review, with honest scrutiny, those prejudices of the mind which may communicate an unfair bias and cause us to decide, not as things are, but as we wish them to be. Our ability to do so may mean the difference between success and failure.

And now, at the end of this long letter, having laid out the truth of my life and experiences, I urge you to take a clear-eyed view of things as you embark on your tenure as sole Augustus and Emperor of the Western Roman Empire. Look around around you; take note of the legacy I leave you.

In the past three years, unhindered by internal threats, Aetius and I have been able to drive the barbarians back and regain much of the territory lost. Aetius has thwarted the Burgundians in Belgica and repelled the Goths from the gates of Narbo. He has quelled the rebellion of the Bagaudae and fought the Suebi to a standstill in Gallaecia. All this time he has been carefully developing a plan to expel the Vandals from Africa. I am confident we can regain that precious territory before long, but we cannot do so without the cooperation of the East.

We must have access to their armies. Without the armies of the East to back us, we lack the overwhelming strength necessary to achieve our objectives.

But Theodosius and Pulcheria remain a problem. Should we have to rely on their fickle allegiance, even a complete triumph in Africa will be diluted by their demands to divide the spoils. We may end up taking Africa back from the Vandals only to find our grain supply impeded by Constantinople. It's unacceptable. We need a full victory without their interference.

So you see, your marriage to Licinia Eudocia is not merely a political convenience. It is absolutely essential to the survival of the West.

Your new father-in-law Theodosius is easily manipulated. Given enough time, you should be able to win him over. Show him the affection of a son-in-law. Flatter and cajole him. Relieve him of his burdens. Not only will it give us the manpower we need to win back Africa, but it will also remove the bone of contention that has troubled our relationship with the East for so long. I'm speaking, of course, of Illyricum. The East unlawfully retains it, even now, fifty-seven years after it was lent to them. It's time they returned it.

Of course, Pulcheria will try to stop you. She certainly realizes your marriage to Licinia Eudocia is a threat to her power, and Pulcheria is not someone who cedes power easily. This is a marriage she does not want. So beware of those around you. You have no idea what she's capable of. She may try to plant people near you with the intention of doing you harm. She may even try to mislead you.

Aetius and I are aware of the danger, which is why we've taken precautions to protect you. We've assigned a trusted surrogate as your chief of staff. Galerius Arsenius is a good man. He has served Aetius faithfully for years. You must trust him.

Having reached this point, you've probably guessed what we want from you. Knowing the background of these events and weighing the alternatives, you must see it's the only reasonable way forward.

Let me say this plainly, Placidius. You must remain in Constantinople. You must marry Licinia Eudocia and remain near Theodosius. By this method you can act as a counterweight to Pulcheria and help us achieve our objectives. Eustacia will help you. The three of you together should be enough to outweigh Pulcheria and convince Theodosius to save the West. But if you come back, Pulcheria will gain the upper hand and make our job immeasurably more difficult.

Please don't take my words as an attempt to force you to forego your birthright. You are still the Emperor of the West. For a short time you must restrain yourself, just until Africa is recovered, and Illyricum is returned to us. Once the tax revenues from those provinces are restored, the Empire will have the resources it needs to build a strong defense against the barbarians and forestall the kind of upheaval and chaos that has plagued it since my father passed away forty-two years ago.

I know this is asking a lot from you, but if you can find it in yourself to make a short-term sacrifice, you will go down in history as one of the greatest emperors

Rome has ever known. The name of Valentinian III will be entered in the Pantheon alongside the names of Hadrian, Trajan, and Augustus.

If an appeal to your vanity is not enough to sway you, then do it for the good of the Empire, and remember, sometimes we must sacrifice our allegiance to fulfill our duty. We are depending on you.

Now, after all, you see why I was so adamant about your marrying your Licinia Eudocia. These were not things I could explain to you in a brief and heated conversation. There was so much for you to learn, and you were in no mood to listen during the last hectic last days we were together before you left.

Fortunately, this letter, which I have been so long in preparing, and which I had feared lost forever, turned up again just before your departure. Still, I did not rush it out to you, but took the time to add some final reflections and bring it up to date, even past the point when you left for Constantinople. I will have to send it after you, carried by a trading party heading to Moesia.

I realize you may have some misgivings about its authorship. This is prudent. By no means should you allow yourself to be manipulated by someone pretending to be me. To ease your mind, I've arranged to provide you with proof of its authenticity. I've given Arsenius a token to pass on to you, something to prove beyond a doubt that I am the writer of these pages. Go to him. Tell him you've completed this letter. He will give it to you.

As I said in the beginning, I am not who you think I am. Perhaps you don't like the real Galla Placidia. Perhaps you think I'm too duplicitous and cunning, too cold-hearted and cruel. If so, it saddens me. I only did what I needed to do to ensure the Empire was still standing when it came time for you to inherit it. So, if my methods strike you as hard-hearted, forgive me. I did it for you. I am your mother, and I have only ever wanted what is best for you – and the Empire.

Placidius set the codex aside and touched his fingers to his lips.

After a moment's reflection, he ordered the caravan halted, his sedan chair lowered. He called for the wagon bearing Arsenius's belongings brought to him. When it arrived, he ordered it unloaded, its contents spread out on the ground.

Despite the objections of his deputies who were anxious to complete the journey, he began digging through the crates, overturning the barrels, and burrowing through the chests. It took a while, but he found it.

It was hidden under a glazed amphora and weighted down with bronze arrow heads. He knew what it was before he held it between his fingertips and lifted it up to the light. It was round and flat and outfitted with horse-hair strands, a curious amulet cast in lead, circular in shape, and showing a scene of Christ entering Jerusalem. At the bottom was an inscription: God be with you.

His heart sank.

Chapter Twenty-One

Nothing he had been told had prepared Placidius for the splendor of Constantinople. Its broad colonnaded thoroughfares, its lush gardens, its sparkling fountains. The majesty of its monuments, the arcades and stadia, the spacious plazas teeming with people. Its soaring columns of porphyry and marble. Its statues of gods and heroes. And its churches: the Church of the Holy Apostles, the Hagia Eirene, and the Magna Ecclesia. It was breathtaking. By comparison, Rome was old and dilapidated, and Ravenna a stinking backwater. He understood why someone would want to rule here, but he was disinclined to view his mother's admonition to remain here as some kind of wonderful gift.

An official reception committee headed by the High Chamberlain and a contingent of the Imperial Guard met him at the city gates and led his caravan down the main thoroughfare toward the Great Palace. The street was lined with cheering throngs, thrilled to be catching sight of the Emperor of the West, Valentinian III, the magnificent monarch who would soon wed their beloved princess, Licinia Eudocia. Placidius did not smile or wave but gazed straight ahead with an erect posture and a solemn expression. But deep down he was not feeling imperious.

Beneath the thin veneer of his excitement upon first seeing the city, he felt isolated and alone. Everyone who had been close to him upon setting out from Ravenna was gone, murdered, or fled. Truth be told, he had never enjoyed much intimacy with any of them, with the possible exception of Candida, but even that, impoverished as it was, had been taken away from him. Now he felt bereft, troubled by the notion that he was the sort of person others disdained, valued only in so far as he could be of use to them. It was depressing to think he was as disrespected as he was unloved and that the only warmth and understanding he got came from the pages of a letter telling him to stay away and not return the place he called home. It made his sad, then angry.

Near the center of the city, beside a magnificent statue depicting a gathering of Emperor Constantine's three sons, a reception committee awaited the entourage. The plaza was called the Philadelphion in honor of the statue, "the plaza of brotherly love." It mattered little that Constantine's three sons had loathed and tried to kill each other. The plaza represented an ideal, a concept of familial affection among the members of the ruling class that many preferred to believe, rather than the brutal reality.

With the reception committee acting as their guide, the Emperor's caravan left the plaza and headed south in the direction of the Sea of Marmara. The Chamberlain rode alongside Placidius's sedan chair and explained their destination, a pleasant seaside parade ground called the Hebdomon at the end of which stood the Palace of the Great Hall. There they would be greeted by the imperial family, and Placidius would meet his new bride. The prospect made him nervous. He felt ill prepared and out of sorts. The stress of the last few weeks combined with the demoralizing way things had turned out had given him a splitting headache. He wished he could put this off. But it was not to be.

Entering the parade ground, he was borne along past ranks of assembled legionaries standing at full attention, the plumes of their helmets stirring in the sea breeze. Presently, he came to the Palace of the Great Hall. The assemblage entered its environs through a vast courtyard where rows of solemn dignitaries formed a corridor down which he passed.

At the foot of the steps leading up to the colonnaded portico, the bearers lowered Placidius's sedan chair. He stepped out and waited for his personal attendants to gather up the long train of his ceremonial gown before he proceeded up the steps.

He walked through the portico and into the cavernous hall. At the far end on a raised dais sat Emperor Theodosius II on his golden throne. Beside him sat his wife, Aelia Eudocia, who went by the name of Eustacia, Galla's particular friend. On the opposite side sat his daughter, Licinia Eudocia. From a distance she seemed quite appealing. Conspicuous by her absence was the fearsome Pulcheria.

As Placidius proceeded down the aisle, the details of his betrothed's appearance came into focus. Licinia Eudocia had inherited much of her mother's beauty. She was dark haired with soulful eyes and full, shapely lips. As he got closer, her brows lifted, and she smiled a bright, vivacious smile. It was really quite disarming.

She likes what she sees, Placidius thought. *She's relieved as well.* His headache began to dissipate.

The Chamberlain made the formal introductions. Placidius climbed the steps to the dais where he halted one step below the top to acknowledge his position as the junior of the two Augusti. Theodosius stood up and extended his hands. Placidius grasped them. They bowed slightly to each other. The Great Hall erupted in applause.

At the conclusion of the formalities, they dined together in the Great Palace. Like the city itself, the imperial palace of Constantinople put the palace in Ravenna to shame. It was not a single structure, but a complex of handsome pavilions surrounding a central courtyard and bordered by a promenade overlooking the sea. The family's private triclinium was richly adorned and surprisingly intimate, much as one would find in a modest villa, not like the large, sterile dining hall in the palace at Ravenna.

They ate reclining on couches and arranged in accordance with protocol. As the guest of honor Placidius was seated in the center with Theodosius and Licinia to his left. Eustacia sat to his right. As before, Pulcheria was absent.

They inquired about the comfort of his journey. Placidius assured them it had been ideal in every way. He studied their reactions, suspecting they already knew every detail of what had happened.

Theodosius was particularly effusive about how much Placidius had changed since they had last met. "You were only this tall!" he said, indicating the distance with his hand. "You used to ride on my back like a soldier on a pony. You used to laugh and laugh. Oh, you were a happy child! Do you remember that?"

Placidius did not remember it, but he pretended he did, which pleased Theodosius.

Eustacia inquired after Galla's well-being. Placidius assured her she was well. They talked a bit about the weather. They exchanged opinions about the upcoming harvest. The sheer volume of what they were *not* discussing outweighed the commonplaces they were engaged in, but those were matters best discussed in a more official setting. Placidius, who might have been inclined to breach protocol in the past, minded his manners. There was one question, however, he could not resist asking.

"Where is the Augusta Pulcheria?"

She was not feeling well was the explanation. She regretted her absence but was recuperating now so she could be in good health for the wedding. On the other hand, she had arranged an entertainment as a gesture of her hospitality, a play, a comedy to be exact, which they would all enjoy after dinner.

They dined on eggs and oysters and drank honeyed wine. Theodosius toasted the upcoming nuptials. With a wry smile he asked Placidius what he thought of his bride-to-be. Licinia blushed, and her father grinned. Placidius replied in all sincerity that he thought her quite lovely. Licinia dropped her eyes bashfully, which Placidius found charming.

After the main course of peacock and suckling pig, they repaired to the reception hall to watch the play. Placidius sat next to Licinia while Theodosius and Eustacia sat on the other side of the stage. As the play was about to begin, Placidius asked Licinia if this was something they did often.

"Never," she said. "Usually my aunt frowns on this sort of thing. She's quite religious, you know. Frankly, I'm surprised she chose a play to welcome you to Constantinople. She must be softening in her old age." She smiled at Placidius, and Placidius smiled back.

The play was a traditional Greek comedy based on stock characters. The main character was an *adulescens,* a rich, spoiled teenager who bemoan his lot in life. Although he pretends to be brave, he is really a coward and needs a loyal servant to get him out of the trouble he keeps getting himself into.

The antagonist of the play is the *senex,* the boy's father. The *senex* wants to help, but the boy fears his father and doesn't trust him. The action of the play is complicated by the introduction of a girl, a prostitute with whom the boy falls madly in love. The girl is beneath him and unsuitable, but the boy, comically smitten, is unable to control his passions. When the father tries to intervene, the boy overreacts, and hilarity ensues.

The play was a rare treat. As the plot unfolded on the stage before them, the family laughed and applauded. Placidius pretended amusement but had a tight grin frozen on his face the entire time. When it was over, he excused himself, saying he was tired from his journey.

It was after nightfall by the time he arrived at his lodgings. Situated on a hillside, the palace rose above him in a series of terraced arcades. As he waited for the servant to admit him to his apartments, he chanced to glance up and saw a lone figure standing well back in an arcade, holding a candle. She wore a dark palla and a scarf drawn tightly around her chin. She was watching him.

Once settled into his room, he tried to sleep but couldn't. He got up and went to the window to take a breath of fresh air. Below him, on a strip of lawn bordering the sea, he saw the same woman gazing up at him. Behind her, a shimmering ribbon of moonlight stretched across the water. A shudder passed through his body.

The next morning Placidius woke early and went to the place where the woman had stood the night before. He looked up at his window. When someone came up behind him, he whipped around. It was Eustacia. She apologized for startling him.

They walked along the promenade and chatted. Before long, their conversation came around to the topic of Galla Placidia. Eustacia confirmed what his mother had written in the letter, that she and Eustacia had been the best of friends when Galla had been in exile in Constantinople.

"On the night of my wedding, she happened upon me burning a lock of my hair as an offering to the goddess Athena," Eustacia said. "Had Theodosius and Pulcheria found out, they would have called off the wedding. But your mother kept my secret, and I was grateful to her ever after."

Placidius watched her face. In it resided a deep sadness, something cherished and forsaken. Her beauty was now faded, and with it much of her power.

"Your mother and I shared a common goal," she told him. "We longed for the day our children would wed. Now our wish has come true."

"You sacrificed a great deal to arrange our betrothal. I thank you for that, and I promise I will be as good a husband to Licinia as I can be."

Something about the way he said it made Eustacia stop and turn to him. "Sacrificed? What do you mean?"

Placidius smiled. "I'm aware of your rivalry with Pulcheria. I know what she put you through. I know what it cost you."

Eustacia evinced surprised. "Did your mother tell you that?"

"She did, in the pages of the letter."

"The letter?"

"My mother wrote me a long letter as a way to advise me. Very revealing. In it she recounted the story of her life."

Eustacia looked perplexed. "But I thought she had lost that letter."

"She had, but she recovered it just before my departure."

Suddenly Eustacia was wary. She invited Placidius to sit down beside her. She paused for a moment, gathering her thoughts. Then she spoke, "Your sister was here with us for a while. She is not easy to get along with. But I'm not telling you anything you don't already know."

"She's horrible," Placidius said. "I'm sorry my mother felt the need to foist her on you."

"I was warned," Eustacia said. "Nevertheless, she surprised me."

"Quarrelsome and disagreeable," Placidius said.

"To say the least," Eustacia agreed.

"She was sent here to be confined to a convent," Placidius said. "It was to be her punishment for sleeping with her manservant. Did she ever go there."

"Yes, she went," Eustacia said, "kicking and screaming like a two-year-old child, but she went. That wasn't what surprised me."

Placidia was curious. "What did?"

"The way she behaved when she came out. She had changed completely. She was a different person."

"I've seen the new and improved Justa," Placidius remarked. "I'm not convinced."

"Pulcheria called it an act of God. It was remarkable the change that came over Justa. She was polite and friendly, warm and engaging. I would even go so far as to say she was winning. Everyone commented on it."

"She was acting," Placidius said.

"The funny this is she didn't credit the convent with the change in her character, despite how Pulcheria tried to spin it. She credited it all to a young man she had met, an amiable young fellow named Cyrus."

Placidius's breath caught in his throat.

"According to Justa, Cyrus was like a mentor to her. He took her under his wing and taught her everything she needed to know to become a better person. She spent days with him, and we all saw the results. After that, she lived here in the palace with us for the rest of the summer and got along well with everybody. But I have to tell you, there was something that didn't sit right with me."

"Go on," Placidius said.

"Her close relationship with Pulcheria. It didn't add up."

"Justa and Pulcheria were close?"

"As thick as thieves."

Placidius was speechless.

"What bothered me was the double standard. When your mother came here after the scandal involving her brother, Pulcheria was bitter and judgmental. Even when Galla told her the whole thing was a lie invented by her enemies to discredit her, Pulcheria refused to believe her. But when Justa came, it was completely different. Despite the fact that she had also been driven here by a sexual scandal, Pulcheria welcomed her with open arms. It was as if she had some special stake in your sister, as if she were anxious to get close to her, to enlist her in some scheme. At first I couldn't discern what it was, but now I think I understand."

"She wanted her to get hold of my mother's letter."

Eustacia nodded.

Placidius swallowed hard. "So the letter was never lost. Justa took it. She held on to it for a long time. It was missing for months. Do you think it's possible she sent it here so Pulcheria could make changes to it?"

Eustacia sighed. "I do."

"Then the letter I've been reading was not written by my mother."

"Probably not – or at least not entirely."

"Then I've been misled."

"Almost undoubtedly," Eustacia said, "but to what end?"

"I don't know," Placidius said through clenched teeth, "but I intend to find out."

Every morning at dawn Pulcheria prayed in the Chapel of St. Stephen, a squat octagonal building on the palace grounds built to house the relics of St. Stephen, who had been martyred by the Jews for calling into question their obedience to God. This morning Placidius waited for her. In one hand he held a dagger. In the other he held the amulet his mother had given him as proof of her identity.

It was a gray rainy day. As the sun came up, the chapel remained bathed in shadows. The walls of the nave were decorated with mosaics depicting the life of St. Stephen. The dome was inlaid with colored pieces of stone and glass to depict the corona of a blazing sun. But the pallid light from the arched windows was not enough to make it shine. On this day, the chapel was a dank and dreary dungeon.

Placidius weighed the dagger in his hand. People had died as a result of his suspicion and distrust. The gruesome death of Stephanus had been particularly upsetting and would remain with him forever. But none of it was his fault. He had been lured into it by the machinations of others, and they would have to answer for it. He slipped the dagger into the top of his boot where it was concealed beneath his dalmatic. Then he raised the amulet and examined it more closely. In the dim light the image on its surface nevertheless seemed to stand out: Christ entering Jerusalem. He read the three-line inscription and felt nothing.

He heard her footsteps coming from a long way off. When at last she appeared, she stood in the doorway and sniffed the air like a small feral animal suspicious of its surroundings. She was a tiny woman of delicate build. Her vestments were damp from the rain. There was nothing about her to suggest the lethal adversary he had been warned about. But even small animals can transmit deadly diseases.

Then she saw him and went stock still. It was eerie how motionless she became, as if she had turned to stone. He watched her, and she regarded him evenly, betraying no emotions. Then she stepped through the doorway and moved past him to the altar where she knelt and prayed.

When she was finished, she stood up and moved to the back of the chancel where she sat down on a plain wooden bench and faced him. Beside her, on the altar, rested a silver reliquary inlaid with jewels. She said, "Herein lies the right arm of St. Stephen, brought here from Jerusalem to sanctify our chapel. It is one of our greatest treasures."

The high register of her voice surprised him. It was the voice of a child. She beckoned him to come forward and look more closely at the box containing the relics.

He stood and went towards her. She moved aside, gesturing for him to sit down. He did so.

She watched him dispassionately. Her eyes were faintly slanted. She had a funny little twist about the mouth.

Something behind him made a sound. He swung around. It was apparently nothing, just the sound of the rain streaming off the roof. His nerves were on edge. When he turned back, he found her kneeling before him, kissing the hem of his garment. She was within inches of the knife in his boot. He pushed her gently away and asked her to stand up.

She did so, then bowed her head in humility.

"I know what you did," he said.

"Do you?" she asked. She sat down beside him again.

"You tried to discredit me as a heretic, to keep me from marrying Licinia, but it all went wrong. Innocent people lost their lives."

She chewed her lip and nodded in appreciation. "Did you figure that out all by yourself?"

"I'm not stupid."

"No," she said. "No one has ever accused you of being stupid. Impetuous, perhaps. Prone to act rashly. But not stupid. Tell me, what did you make of the letter?"

"You wrote it, with the help of Justa, to manipulate me."

"Hmm," she said. "Interesting. But not entirely true. The part you found the most threatening, the threat to your sovereignty, was not written by us. You can credit your mother for that."

"Are you trying to tell me my mother wrote the letter?"

"Most of it. Justa and I only added a few embellishments here and there to suit our purposes. Oh, and Elpidia gave it one last going over before it was handed over to you. But your mother and Aetius did most of the work. Our only objective was to dissuade you from marrying Licinia. The others had their own agendas."

"The others?"

"Your mother has a lot of enemies."

Placidius fought the urge to speak up, to demand an explanation. He remembered this line from the letter: *One of the most difficult things for any sovereign to do is to admit we are in the dark. This is especially true when we feel threatened. The tendency is to lash out, to act without thinking, which almost always makes things worse. We must resist the temptation to overreact. A good ruler, when faced with an inscrutable threat, acts with restraint and awaits his opportunity.*

Placidius waited. Outside, the rain drummed down on the roof of the chapel. In the distance was the low rumble of thunder. In due course Pulcheria went on.

"Elpidia. You remember Elpidia. She was the unlucky servant who lost her tongue for slander. Liberius. He was the loyal clerk of Pope Celestine."

"And Isaac?" Placidius asked.

"Him? That Jew? He was an impediment, a liability. We should never have allowed him to come along. When Elpidia was recruited, she asked that her husband be permitted to join her. Foolishly, her request was granted.

It was him and his stupid Saturday sabbath that caused the whole thing to unravel."

"And what about Stephanus?"

"Another case of misguided advocacy. Liberius saw how you were warming to Stephanus, so he decided to recruit him to convince you that Arsenius was the real threat. It worked as far as it went, but Zacharias was never comfortable with it. When he learned you were interrogating Stephanus, he warned Liberius that if he revealed anything of our plans, he would pay for it with his life. Liberius did, and Zacharias made good on his threat. He stuck a knife in his back."

"Zacharias. I'm assuming Zacharias was the magician."

Pulcheria gave him a cool smile. "My goodness, what penetration. Yes, of course, the son of Quirinus, the vile sorcerer your mother had executed in her bungled attempt to divorce your father."

"You deem Quirinus vile, but is not Zacharias vile as well? After all, you recruited him to mislead me. I, who never did him any harm."

Pulcheria shrugged. "Men are who they are. Only God can change them. If we make use of them before divine justice is served, it's all to our advantage. Your mother knows that."

Again the thunder rumbled. The heavens opened up and the rain came down in buckets.

"So am I to presume divine justice has been served on Zacharias?"

"If I can trust the word of my most loyal servant, he has been dealt with."

"You speak of Cyrus."

"My shining star. He played his part flawlessly. He recruited Justa, won your friendship, selected our agents, and put the whole plan together. And the plan would have gone swimmingly had it not been for Isaac and that annoying thorn in our side, Arsenius."

Placidius's heart sank. "So Arsenius was on my side all along."

"In spite of our best efforts to convince you otherwise."

Disheartened, Placidius turned his eyes to the mosaic. It depicted St. Stephen reaching his arms up to heaven and pleading with God to forgive his enemies, even as he was being stoned to death. At that moment, lightning flashed, bringing the colors to vivid life; a sharp crack of thunder made Placidius wince inadvertently. In the next instant, the room was bathed in shadows again.

Pulcheria was calm and rational. She seemed perfectly content to explain everything. "From the start, Arsenius sensed something wasn't right. Had it not been for you getting in his way, he would have discovered the truth and ruined everything. Cyrus could see Arsenius was getting close, so he slipped away."

"But he didn't go far. He was trailing us the whole time."

"Keeping tabs on you, receiving reports from the inside, monitoring things."

"He had friends on the inside," Placidius surmised.

"Cyrus never had any trouble making friends. Keeping them was his problem, which is why he fled from Ravenna and ended up in Constantinople."

"Fled from Ravenna?"

"He had a little problem paying his debts. He had a weakness for gambling. Chariot racing was his Achilles' heel. It probably would have ended badly for him if his brother-in-law hadn't stepped in to help him."

"His brother-in-law?"

"Sebastianus, of course. Cyrus has a winning way about him to be sure, but that wouldn't have been enough to ensure the cooperation of your guards. It took Sebastianus, their beloved former master of soldiers, to do that. You cannot imagine the level of devotion they felt toward Sebastianus and the enmity they felt toward your mother for sacking him without cause. They welcomed the opportunity to even the score against her."

"By furthering Cyrus's plot."

"Yes, and by helping poor Cyrus avenge his father's death by striking a blow on his behalf. You see, Cyrus and Bonifacius had a falling out. When Cyrus fled Ravenna, he hoped he would have a chance to return someday and make amends with his father, but Aetius put an end to that. He killed Bonifacius and removed any chance of rapprochement between father and son. When Cyrus got the news, he vowed to get even. He reached out to his brother-in-law Sebastianus and asked for the contacts he would need to accomplish his vengeance. Sebastianus, who by that time had suffered his own humiliation at the hands of Galla, was only too happy to oblige."

"And their main point of contact was you."

"Me and Justa, yes. It was the perfect convergence of all Galla's enemies. I couldn't have asked for more. It was the answer to my prayers."

"You prayed for vengeance against my mother?"

"Many times. You know the kind of person she is. You read the letter."

The lightning flashed and the thunder roared.

"And what about Candida?" Placidius asked. "What was her role in all of this?"

"Candida was too vain and self-absorbed to be a part of our well calibrated plan, which is not to say she was not of use to us. Her childish behavior came in handy in keeping you off balance. Still, it would have been a shame if you had killed her. It would have been like murdering an idiot."

Placidius's old impulse to defend Candida flickered briefly to life, then died out. The rain hammered on the roof.

"I'm surprised," Pulcheria said. "In all the advice your mother gave you, she never pointed out that some people are so shallow and predictable you can bend them to your will. It seems like she should have instructed you on that. It might have saved you a lot of trouble."

Placidius knew Pulcheria was trying to get under his skin. Nothing would suit her purposes better than to have the newly minted Augustus of the West attack the Augusta of the East on the eve of his wedding to the Emperor's daughter, so he held himself back, which only seemed to irritate her. For the first time her well-studied aplomb crumbled and her eyes flared with anger.

"There's one fundamental difference between your mother and me," she said. "Your mother thinks people can change. She thinks it's a matter of human will. She's like a Pelagian in that. But I believe in grace. People can only change by the will of God. Had you been my son, I would never have written a letter to advise you. I would have told you to go down on your knees and pray to God. As it is, you are an apostate and have no chance of ever being anything other than what you are, a reckless, impetuous young man driven by your impulses."

Placidius felt his temper rising, but he beat it back.

She watched him, waiting. The reflection of the rainwater running down the windows made shadows like grotesque runnels on her face. Seeing he was not going to take the bait, she added, "I forbid you to marry my niece, so why don't you pack up your things and go home. See to those two usurpers who are sitting on your throne. They are smug in the assurance that they've gotten rid of you. Your real enemies are there, not here."

Placidius reached down and took the dagger from his boot. She flinched, but she did not step back. He held it out in his hand. She stared at it, nostrils flaring. He took a step toward her. She stiffened. He took another step. She glared twin beams of contempt into his face. He turned the blade around in his hand and held it out to her, handle first. She looked at it, mystified.

"Take it," he said. "You're going to need it for what comes next."

She took it from him without a moment's hesitation.

"If I walk out of here alive, I'm going to marry your niece," he said. "And that's not all. After our wedding, we're going to spend some time honeymooning in Thessaloniki[1] . Do you know why we're going to go there?"

She squinted, holding the knife awkwardly in front of her like someone preparing to punch a hole in a wall.

"Because Thessaloniki is in Illyricum," he said, "and it will be the last time I'll be permitted to travel freely there without your permission."

She could not conceal her surprise.

He went on. "After I become full Augustus, one of my first acts will be to cede the province of Illyricum permanently to the Eastern Roman Empire. For sixty long years, it has been a bone of contention, opening a dangerous rift between us. This cannot go on."

She remained in the same posture. The befuddled look on her face seemed frozen there. The rain began to slacken.

"Here's what else," he said. "After our honeymoon, we are going to return to Ravenna, not because I'm afraid of you, and not because I'm hoping to get revenge on Aetius and my mother for their appalling lack of confidence in me, but because the West is rightfully mine and there are many trials ahead for me and Licinia. But know this. I will not contest either Theodosius's power in the East, or your right to rule after he dies. But if you both should die without producing a male heir, I will help Licinia

---

1. Modern day Thessalonica, Greece

claim her birthright here, and together we will reunite the Empire under a single ruler. Make no mistake. If that should come to pass, you will be stripped of your power and made to answer for your crimes."

She did not move. She stared at him with contempt.

"The two halves of the Empire have been at cross purposes for too long," he said. "It is my intention to correct that. I will not carry my mother's grudges into the future. I intend to start out fresh, with Licinia beside me."

The thunder moved into the distance. The rainfall diminished.

"I'm going to walk out now," Placidius said firmly. "If what I've offered you is not enough, you'll have to stop me. You have the weapon. I'm unarmed."

He turned his back on her and began to walk away up the aisle. As he did so, he reached down into his tunic, pulled up the amulet, and let it rest outside his clothes.

Then he heard the scrape of the bench, the rapid approach of her footsteps. He whipped around. She was coming at him with the knife, her eyes burning with hatred. Then — she stopped. Her eyes were riveted to the amulet. Her mouth fell open. Then she dropped her arm, and the knife clattered to the floor.

Outside, the rain abruptly stopped, and a ray of sunshine pierced the clouds illuminating the mosaics all around them. Placidius lifted his eyes and took in the image of St. Stephen cowering beneath a hail of stones.

"So, you're not willing to make me a martyr," he said. "You're not willing to kill me while I wear this talisman of the Lord. My mother is convinced it holds some divine power. Honestly, I'm not convinced. But it seems to work on you."

The color drained from her face.

"Too bad," he said. "It would've been easier for you if you had gotten rid of me when you had the chance, but you overestimated your gifts and underestimated mine. You thought you could get me to destroy myself. I must say, the arrogance of that is quite staggering. And you made another mistake. You let me read my mother's letter in its entirety, both the real stuff and the stuff you made up. It would've been better if you had fabricated the whole thing, but you let me read the words she wrote, and I have profited by them. Without them, I might not have been able to foil your plot."

"Don't flatter yourself," she snarled. "This is not over."

Placidius held the amulet up to her face.

She shrank back.

"God be with you," he said. Then he let the amulet fall back against his chest and walked out of the chapel into the clear morning air.

Afterword

I feel fortunate. Seldom does an author uncover a colorful historical figure like Galla Placidia who has not already been thoroughly covered by other novelists. To my knowledge, only two other writers have attempted to write a fictionalized account of this extraordinary woman. Neither of those efforts received much attention. Consequently, in endeavoring to take her on, I was keenly aware of sailing into uncharted territory. Nevertheless, I found the story remarkably easy to compose, owing to the fact that what is known historically about Galla is so compelling.

Given the fragmentary nature of the sources, much had to be filled in by inference and conjecture. For dramatic purposes I projected motives onto the characters that may not have existed. Yet the astonishing parts of Galla's story are not the parts I invented, but those attested to by history.

For example, Galla Placidia *was* in Rome during the Gothic invasion of 410. During the siege, she played a part in the killing of her guardian, Serena. She was kidnapped by the Goths, and she married the Gothic king Ataulf. They had a son named Theodosius, who died in infancy. Upon returning to Ravenna in 417, Galla was forced into marriage with the popular general Constantius. In 421, she was proclaimed Augusta for the first time.

At this point, there already existed enough juicy historical material to make for a thrilling novel, but the treasure trove continued to yield its jewels. The scandalous rumors of incest that stripped Galla of her title and drove her from Ravenna are a matter of historical record. Her arrival in Constantinople, children in tow, during the marriage of Theodosius and Aelia Eudocia (Eustacia), is also true. Her thorny relationship with

Pulcheria and Theodosius is evidenced by their foot dragging when it came to proclaiming her four-year-old son, Placidius, immediately upon the death of his uncle, a hesitancy that emboldened Castinus and Joannes to seize power.

Galla and her children accompanied Aspar on the campaign to win back the Western Roman Empire from the usurpers, and she was present in Ravenna when the usurpers fell. Her reign as Regent, which effectively made her sole ruler of the Western Roman Empire for twelve years – an event unprecedented in Roman history – is also an historical fact. Sources attest to the complex and difficult relationship she had with her generals.

What is not so clear is her relationship with Aetius. Contemporaries in age and social status, it seems likely they met before their encounter at Ravenna after the downfall of Joannes in 425, although there is no evidence to validate the assumption. That Aetius had some sort of hold over Galla seems obvious given the facts. However, their romantic involvement is pure speculation. Perhaps Aetius was so dangerous and fickle that Galla deemed it better to appease him than to oppose him.

The military exploits of Aetius as detailed in the novel are true. Among scholars, Aetius is considered one of the greatest generals in Roman history. His long tenure as a hostage among the Goths and Huns and the favorable way the barbarians regarded him are a matter of record. His depiction as an arrogant rogue, cunning and devious comes solely from the author's imagination. Details about his character are a matter of interpretation, but we know Aetius wrote misleading letters to Galla and Bonifacius in an attempt to open a rift between them, a dangerous gambit that led to the loss of Africa to the Vandals.

Pulcheria was a formidable figure at the Eastern court and highly in-fluential. She was intensely devout, a great patron of the Nicene Church, and deeply involved in the controversies that rent the Church in the early fifth century. Her rivalry with Eustacia is a matter of historical record, but the bitter enmity between her and Galla Placidia is largely fictitious. The elaborate plot to subvert the marriage of Placidius and Licinia Eudoxia is also an invention, although the marriage itself is not.

Basically, all the action that occurs in the caravan and most of the characters found there are fictional. Arsenius, Candida, Cyrus, Stephanus, and Liberius are inventions. But the enemies of Galla are real. Sebastianus the general, the magician Quirinus, and even Elpidia, the servant who betrayed her, are based on historical figures.

The historical authenticity of the popes and bishops depicted here is unassailable. However, I took a good deal of liberty with Pope Celestine, whose intolerance against the Nestorians and Pelagians is well documented. Still, as far as anyone knows, he did not confront Galla Placidia over it, nor was he involved in a conspiracy to shift papal authority from Rome to Alexandria in an effort to excommunicate Nestorius.

Pope Sixtus was a closet Pelagian, but his close relationship with Galla was entirely fabricated. They may have been friends, but there is no discussion of their relationship in the historical record.

The power of the African Fathers, the proliferation of schisms and heresies, and the Nicene Church's aggressive intolerance toward anything that challenged its primacy are all matters of historical record. Pulcheria could have tried to discredit Placidius by painting him as a Nestorian, although there is no evidence she did so.

Galla's children come off rather poorly in the estimation of history. Justa was reportedly as selfish and incorrigible as she is depicted here. Her effort to reach out to Attila the Hun later in life over petty resentments she felt toward her family is often cited as the spark that ignited the Hunnic invasion of Gaul.

As for Placidius, little is known of his life before his ascension, but afterward his legacy is marred by his inability to get along with Aetius, the one person able to forestall the deterioration of the Empire, which continued throughout Placidius's life. When Aetius died, the Western Roman Empire was all but doomed.

But the fate of Aetius and Placidius is a story for another day. This book has taken as its focus the remarkable woman who touched both their lives, Galla Placidia. Few women in history led a more colorful life or influenced events in more profound ways. I count myself fortunate to introduce her to a good many modern readers, and I hope you have found her story as compelling as I have.

Malcolm David Logan

Acknowledgements

I would like to acknowledge the help of several people without whom this book would not have been possible. Thanks to my editor Art Fogartie. This novel would not exist in its present form without his insights and suggestions. Thanks to Helen Hurwitz whose thorough first reading of the manuscript was indispensable. Thanks also to my my cover artist Rebekah Haskell and my cover designer Nick Paredes. Finally, thanks to my devoted wife, Marianne Grisdale, whose faith and perseverance made the realization of this ambition possible.

About the author

Malcolm David Logan is a writer, teacher, blogger, amateur historian, and entrepreneur. He is the writer and editor of *My American Odyssey.com*, a popular travel blog about unusual places to visit in the U.S. He lives in Chicago.

Want to learn more about the books in the Amulet Series?

Go to www.malcolmdavidlogan.com.

If you enjoyed *The Wind in the Embers*, please leave a review at Amazon—reviews are critical in helping a book to succeed, especially the first book in a new series. Please let other readers know what they can expect from Galla's story

Thank you